I0760969

HERS TO HOLD

QUINTESSENCE

SERENA AKEROYD

HERS TO HOLD

Triggers:

- General violence,
- Miscarriage,
- Torture,
- Kidnapping,
- Gun violence

PART 1

ONE

"I'M STILL NOT sure why it matters."

While the room, as a whole, appeared to grit their teeth, Sascha Dubois was left sighing. Reaching up, she rubbed her temple and murmured, "Devon, you know full well the rest of the world doesn't function the way we do."

Stubbornly, he grumbled, "And it is inefficient. Things would be a lot more practical if they did."

She sighed again—it was one of those days. You either sobbed or you sighed. "Well, inefficient or not, it is how it is. We're the odd ducks, and we just have to face the fact that people aren't going to understand what we have." At her words, Sawyer grabbed her hand and squeezed her fingers. She shot him a look and was surprised to note he appeared a little paler than usual. "Are you okay?" she blurted out.

He blinked at her. "Of course. Just worried like the rest of you."

She was tempted to test his temperature with the back of her hand—just didn't want to look like a nag. They'd been stuck in that graveyard for ages the other day when they attended Kurt's mother's funeral, and she'd been feeling a little under the weather herself, but before she could worry further, Andrei muttered, "I don't think we have much choice but to ride this out." Though his words were clinical, he appeared physically pained by the prospect. She couldn't exactly blame him, not when their very private lives had just gone public.

They were all, she realized, quite secretive by nature, so this level of notoriety was intense. And when she said notoriety, she meant it. It was turning into infamy, for God's sake.

Her face and theirs were splashed all over the papers—all over the world. They were on TV, and reporters had turned up at their hotel, most of them sticking to the outside, waiting on them to leave, but one had infiltrated the kitchen staff this morning—only chance had security realizing their room service was being delivered by someone who was not actually a hotel employee! God only knew what other levels the jackals would be willing to resort to in an effort to get their picture, to feed the hunger for their story.

It was, in a word, batshit.

And she'd thought she knew what batshit was, but she didn't. She hadn't really known the definition until that damn article outed them.

"And how do we do this?" Kurt demanded, breaking into her glum thoughts with a stress-filled English accent that sounded more German than she'd ever heard him. "We're already notorious—" there was that word again, "—for that psycho who attached herself to you, and now this? Riding out—"

Sascha raised a hand the second she saw Andrei's eyes spark with anger. "There's no point in worrying about that. What's done is done."

It wasn't okay, would *never* be okay that a child serial killer had been in their household for as long as she had, but—and it was a huge but—said psycho was where she needed to be, a thousand miles away from their son, Tin. As well as locked up behind at least, she hoped, fifty bars.

Though her words had the brows of her five lovers arching, almost like a Mexican wave of eyebrows, she muttered, "We have other things to think about, and Jane is firmly in the past, thank God."

"We're going to be in Veronia for the foreseeable future," Sean stated, and as he spoke, his fingers rubbed the button that was upholstered into the dense leather hide of the armchair he was seated on.

It was surprisingly difficult not to be turned on by that incessant *rubbing,* even if, when he got her into bed, she might just fall asleep—although a nap *and* an orgasm would probably do her mood the world of good right about now.

She licked her lips and forced her focus upward, and when she saw his smirk, she narrowed her eyes at him. Temptation struck, though, when that smirk deepened, and his own gaze grew heated so, she smiled, reached up, and began circling her nipple through her shirt.

There couldn't have been a more inappropriate time for such a move, but they were already being condemned in the press. If they were on their way to hell, she intended to go out in style. And it took two to tango, didn't it?

"Sascha, lass, are ye trying to kill us?"

She cut Sawyer a look, enjoying the fact his brogue was as dense as the fog over the moors by his parents' house in Glasgow. "No. Just stopping Sean from copulating with the furniture."

Sawyer snickered, then leaned over and shoved Sean's shoulder. "Stop it. We have to concentrate."

"I was fidgeting," Sean said dryly. "I can assure you, any dirtiness to the act was purely in Sascha's imagination."

Sascha grinned at him, surprising herself with how easy it was to smile.

She was stressed, overwhelmed, in need of a nap and a burger in that order, and beyond concerned about the article that had declared to the public that she was in a relationship with five different men, but somehow, it wasn't the end of the world.

She'd already endured a gamut of experiences with these men at her side, and they were more important than anything a shitty rag had to say.

In her time with her men, she'd almost been mowed down by a car, had learned of a grand murder plot to push her off this mortal coil in an attempt to keep her past buried, inherited billions, had been stalked by a reporter, lost her beloved child in a traumatic stillbirth, and had lived with a serial killer roaming the walls of her house.

Throw in the fact her lover's grandfather, who was Russian mafia, had kidnapped the reporter who'd stalked her, as well as the fact she'd recently met and befriended Veronian royalty all while learning that the queen of that country was also shared by three men—the king included—well, it was safe to say that it took a *lot* to surprise her now.

The world knowing about her sex life wasn't ideal, but things could be worse, couldn't they?

Almost as though she'd triggered the apocalypse with the thought alone, her cell rang. She peered down at the name, saw her father's on the caller ID, and cringed.

Andrei, ever insightful, winced with her. "Henry?"

She cleared her throat. "Yeah."

"Best to get it over with, lass. Pull off the plaster in one go, you know?"

"My sex life is not a Band-Aid," she grumbled at Sawyer. "And talking about said sex life is not something I want to do with my dad." Adopted or not, Henry was the only father she'd ever known, and though their relationship had been strained ever since he'd gotten back with his ex-wife, Loathsome Linda, Sascha would prefer for Sean to whip her a thousand times than to speak with Henry on this matter.

Shit, she couldn't manage five lashes with a flogger, never mind a thousand strokes of the whip, although, granted, Sean had never whipped her so an accurate guestimation wasn't—

Fuck!

Why was she thinking about stupid shit like this?

As her phone died off thanks to her not answering, she didn't even have the chance to release a relieved sigh when it began buzzing again.

"He won't stop," Andrei cautioned. "He can be surprisingly persistent when he so chooses."

As had been the way with his ex-wife. He'd grown tired of being lonely and had gone back to her, worn her down until she'd taken him back.

More's the pity.

Sascha didn't want her father to be alone, but neither did she want him to be tied to an old hag of a wife simply because he couldn't deal with living on his own unless he was drunk. Linda was why she barely spoke to Henry. Why he hadn't visited in years too.

Bitch.

What kind of weirdo was jealous of a father-daughter relationship?

Because he was right, however, she didn't hurl her irritation at Andrei and, instead, connected the call. "Dad," she greeted, her voice huskier than she'd have liked as she stared straight ahead at the baby grand piano that was in the salon of the hotel suite they were currently staying in.

The story had broken while they were in Germany, after having visited the country to attend the funeral of Kurt's mother. Due to return in two days time, it was looking like they were going to be heading back to Veronia ahead of schedule to avoid the press.

Veronia, thank the Lord, had a strict media policy. Gags could be bought at will, and Sascha felt no compunction in getting an injunction on this storyline that would save them from being hounded by reporters during their time there.

Of course, that was only putting off the inevitable.

When they returned to London, it wouldn't protect them in the city, but hopefully a Kardashian would have done something life altering and interest in Sascha's unusual household would have waned by that point.

Christ, a woman could only hope.

"The story's everywhere. You didn't think to warn me?"

You didn't think to warn me?

Six words that might have damned her, but they didn't.

She could have prevaricated. Could have tried to ease the situation, *appease* him, but she didn't feel like it. So, bluntly, she told him, "No."

"I'm annoyed, Sascha."

Her brow puckered. "So am I, Dad. This isn't exactly ideal for any of us."

"No, you misunderstand me. I'm pissed this is the first I'm hearing about it from you. Couldn't you have warned me this news was about to hit the press?"

Her eyes narrowed on Devon's shoelaces of all things. As she glared at the precisely tied knot, wondering which mathematical principle he'd followed to create it—if that was even possible... of course, Devon often made the impossible possible—she murmured, "Communication works both ways."

"Is that all you have to say?"

She stuck her tongue in her cheek, needing to bite back the irritated response that was forming. It would do neither of them any good if she got snippy, and that was definitely on the cards. Hell, it was more than on the cards. She could feel her agitation levels soaring with each second she remained on the phone with her dad.

Truth was, she was surprised Henry even cared. It wasn't like they talked that much anymore, and visits? Nope. Why did it matter what happened in her life if he wasn't interested enough to be a part of it?

Because she was pissed at how her privacy had been invaded, and because she was pissed at Henry's tone and the way he'd allowed himself to be cut from her life and Tin's, she retorted, "Yeah. That's pretty much all I have to say, Dad."

Silence fell at her words, and all around her, her men began shuffling in their seats. Whether they agreed with her or not was neither here nor there. This was *her* father, and this was a conversation about the sad state of that relationship. There was only so much someone could try to rectify things, and when that was all one-sided, she knew she wasn't in the wrong here. She'd tried, she really had. Sure, she didn't make it back to America as often as she'd like, but even if she did, she wasn't welcome at Linda's home. Her stepmother had made that clear one too many times, and Henry had never corrected his wife.

Back in those early days when she'd first learned of her pregnancy, and Henry had visited, she'd had real hope that things were going to change. Henry had stopped drinking, and during his holiday to London, he'd seemed to be almost rejuvenated. It was like he'd had a new lease on life.

They talked every couple of days at first, and she learned how he was doing, how he'd started dating again. Then the calls had begun to wane, not only in quantity but in length. When he'd begun ignoring her calls, what could she do? Nothing. Then she learned why.

Linda.

And she wasn't just blaming the wicked stepmother. This was as much on Henry as it was on Linda, more so even on her father. It was his duty to make sure that nothing interfered with his relationship with Sascha. More than that, Tin. He had a grandson now, had had a granddaughter too, but that hadn't seemed to matter to him, so why should his snit perturb her now?

"Why didn't you think to warn me?"

Her brow puckered. He sounded aggrieved when he had no right to be. Hell, he had no right at all. "It's not like we're close. It's not like I tell you the ins and outs of my everyday life. I mean, Christ, you never even made it back here for Camilla's funeral—"

"For God's sake, Sascha, I had to work! It wasn't like she—"

Her tone was icy as she bit off, "Be very careful of your next words, Dad. If you ever want to hear from me again, then don't finish that sentence."

From his armchair, Devon straightened up. The creak of the leather dragged her attention his way, and when she saw the fire in his eyes, the fury etched into his features, she felt justified. Christ, she felt more than that—she felt vindicated.

Camilla's death would always be a raw wound. It would never heal. It might close over temporarily, but it was like a scab. One wrong move, and it could be torn off.

Sascha knew her father was old school. He came from a different time, a different generation. A shittier time, a shittier generation. One that didn't seem to understand just how devastating the loss of a baby could be. Never mind the trauma of what she'd been through, and the reasons behind it were just as devastating. Of course, he didn't know that. Wasn't aware that she'd been the target of a zealous journalist, but he *shouldn't* need to know that. What had happened to her, the hows and the whys, shouldn't make her grief more or less important to him.

She hurt. That was what should have mattered to Henry.

"Look, I'm going to go. I didn't mean to start a war."

"You started nothing, Dad. As per damn usual. You call to preach at me. And yeah, it's shitty of me that you found this out in the news rather than from me. But to be completely honest, in the aftermath of what's just happened, you were the last person on my mind." At his indrawn hiss, she carried on, "And that's your fault. That's not on me. I've tried so many times to get close to you. You're the one who lets me down all the time. So no, you're not my priority." Then, before he could splutter or snap, snarl, or sneer, she cut the call.

As she stared down at the cell phone, her jaw worked as she processed what she'd just done. Harsh? Perhaps. But the second he'd been dismissive about Camilla, that was when any sympathy or softness had left the building.

When one of her guys cleared their throat, she ceased glaring at the cell she'd dropped in her lap and looked up. Seeing the five of them staring at her in concern, she shook her head. "I'm okay."

"Didn't sound like you're okay," Devon muttered, making her roll her eyes. "Sounded the exact opposite actually."

"Well, I'm not a hundred percent tickety boo, Devon, no. But fuck, I've dealt with worse, and I'll deal with worse in the future. My dad is—"

"A pain in the arse?"

She cut Sawyer a look, but hiding her smile was impossible. Tipping her chin, she agreed, "He is that."

"And more," Andrei inserted ruefully. "But he's family. Things will turn around, *katyonok*. They always do. I'm sorry though. I'm sorry if he hurt your feelings."

With a sigh, she pushed herself off the sofa she'd slumped in earlier. Heading over to him, and smiling when he opened his arms, she sank into his lap and let him hold her in a tight embrace.

As the connection between them blossomed to life, she murmured, "I don't care what he thinks. I really don't. I don't care if he's mad at me for not warning him, and I don't care if he approves or not. But I won't let him make me feel bad about Camilla."

In contrast to her fervent tone, his was soft, soothing. "Nor should he even try. You suffered a great trauma, and if he doesn't understand that, that's on him. Not you. Losing Camilla was one of the worst days of my life. I've never been so scared. Not just for her, but for you. And ever since, though I know we haven't been losing you, it's been hard. Hard because I love you, because you're my world, and there's been nothing I can do to make it better. To make you feel better."

"There was nothing you could do," she replied huskily. "I hate to say it, but I just needed time. I love you for giving that to me. I love you for not judging me, for just giving me what I needed from you." She sighed as his hand, warm and strong, moved between her shoulder blades. It was a grounding touch, one that made her feel their connection all the more. "But my dad is nothing in the scheme of things. The rest of the world knows about us now and we need to figure out how we're going to handle that."

"I don't think we should worry about it."

She didn't have to look at Sawyer to see he was rolling his eyes again. "No, Devon, we all ken what ye think. But let's thank God that the rest of the world doesnae think like ye do, eh?"

"If people did, things would be a lot more rational," was Devon's pious retort.

Rational? Sascha didn't know about that. For somebody who was so rational, Devon was incredibly irrational at times. But that was one of the unique things about him that she loved. Well, when she didn't want to smack him.

Wrapped up in Andrei's embrace, she felt safe and protected, and amid the circle of her men, she felt that even more so. This was what counted, this was all that mattered. But did she care if some bored housewife wanted to judge her? Nope. It didn't bother her if some random guy thought she was a slut. Mostly, she was worried about their careers and Tin's future. That was what bothered her the most.

As she gnawed on her bottom lip, Sean declared, "I don't think there's much point in fretting over this—Sascha's right. It will die down, interest will diminish. Yes, it's big news now. Especially with Kurt being in the limelight with his movie. And after the situation with Jane, as well as what Andrei, Devon, and Sawyer are doing in Veronia...It's no wonder we're of interest to the public. But infamy never lasts long, especially without fodder. We just need to keep on doing what we are doing. Leading quiet lives—"

"I don't want to go back to London," she blurted out, interrupting his statement with a rush of words.

All around her, the men shifted, shuffling in their seats in surprise at her outburst. Not that she blamed them. It wasn't the first time she'd mentioned this, but it was the first time since before Christmas.

"What do you mean? You don't want to return with us?" Even from across the room, she could sense Devon's panic at the question, and understood instantly *why*.

She hurried to say, "No! No, I didn't mean that. God, Devon! How could you even think that? Of course, I want to return with you, just not to London." Flustered, the words carried on spilling from her lips as she attempted to calm him down. "Can't we go somewhere else? Somewhere that isn't there? Hell, England is a big place. There's my estate in Surrey. We could try it there. Tin would love the countryside—"

"You've mentioned that before, Sascha. Are you sure that's what you really want?" Kurt asked softly, but she saw his tension as he'd gone from sitting slouched in his armchair to leaning forward with his elbows on his knees.

Somehow, she sensed they weren't understanding her. They were taking her desire to move away from the capital as a desire to be away from them. But why?

Her brow puckered as she stared at them, not understanding how they could even think something so stupid.

She tilted her head so she could stare at Andrei's features, and when his tension transmitted itself to her as well? God, how could she be surrounded by five of the smartest men she knew, and how could they all be so crazy?

"What have I done to make you doubt me?"

Andrei stiffened. "What do you mean?"

"We don't doubt you," Kurt replied immediately.

She shook her head. "You do. Or you wouldn't think what you're thinking."

Sean raised a hand. "Let's calm down. You have to understand, Sascha—"

"No, Sean, I don't have to do dick." She narrowed her eyes at him for a second then, flashing each of them a glare, scrambled off her delicious, *stupid* Russian's lap and got to her feet. "You're stuck with me. Whether you like it or not, that's how it is. Wherever I am, you are. Wherever you are, I am. Misunderstand me again and I won't be the one being spanked," she warned, angry enough that there was a definite bite to her tone. "While we're at it, *don't* doubt me again. Sure, you've been bitten by other women, and badly, but fuck, how many years do we have to be together for you to realize I'm not them? In fact, that you can even think to compare me is a gross insult—"

She gritted her teeth. When Sean made to speak again, she held up a hand and lifted her chin at his narrowed eyes because she recognized that look. Knew what it meant, was aware that it had repercussions, but she didn't care. She was angry. And that was the truth of it.

Before she could get into an argument that she really didn't want or need after the day she'd had, she turned on her heel and left the room. Her aim was Tin's bedroom, and when she'd ascended the fancy marble staircase within the hotel suite, she peered around the open doorway and found him on the floor with one of his jigsaws out on display as he puzzled over it.

Taking in the picture of her son on his belly, his eyes drifting over the image as though she weren't there at all, she murmured, "Baby, aren't you supposed to be asleep?" There was no point in getting mad. She'd learned that a few months ago when Tin had learned to talk—being diplomatically herded into a corner by a toddler was not one of the high points of her life.

Tin pouted, but he didn't look up from his puzzle as he groused, "Daddy Devon no sleep."

She released a tired sigh—this was just what she needed. A toddler with a teenager's attitude and a penchant for mimicking his insomniac father.

Great.

Lifting a hand, Sascha began to rub her eyes, well aware this evening had just lengthened exponentially. Knowing that somebody had to be the adult here, she began to walk into the room, intent on talking Tin back into bed, but a hand grabbed her by the shoulder and stopped her. She allowed herself to be drawn into his chest, knowing from his scent that it was Devon. And God, what a scent. He smelled like man, soap, a hint of cologne, and fuck, *hers*.

She sighed, wanting to stay mad at him, but when he smelled like that, how could she ignore the way his arms circled her? How could she refrain from tucking herself into him?

Sometimes, where Devon was concerned, it was easy to forget just how much of a man he was. There were so many aspects to his character, of his personality, so many traits and quirks to his genius, that it was easy to believe he was just a label. But Devon had no label. Nothing could describe him. He was impossible to explain, and truth be told, anyone who asked her to didn't deserve the explanation.

His chin settled on her shoulder, and as he tilted his head, she expected the warm brush of his mouth against her cheek, but it still sent a shiver down her spine as his soft lips caressed the sensitive flesh. "I'm sorry."

Her nostrils flared in irritation, because his apology was as sincere as it was ardent, and she wasn't ready for that. She wanted to hold onto her anger a little longer, because hell, they'd hurt her feelings. By making out she was like one of the other bitches they'd dealt with in the past diminished her importance in their lives. At least, that was her initial reaction. And yeah, it might have been a hair-trigger response to the press' word vomit, but Christ, it wasn't every day that something like this happened, was it?

Because she was uncertain how to respond to him, she mumbled, "What are you sorry for? That our son is an insomniac like you or the fact that you just accused me of—"

He hushed her. "Don't say it out loud. It isn't worthy of you, nor was it right of us to even infer it."

Blowing out a breath, she relaxed deeper into his hold, loving how he pulled her even tighter into him, how he pushed his face deeper into her throat so she could feel the tickle of his breath. "Thank you."

"You don't need to thank me for the truth." She sensed his hesitation, let him process his thoughts in silence as she watched her baby boy complete a puzzle that a six-year-old would struggle with. She knew Devon would speak eventually, and given time and patience, he'd be able to convey exactly what he needed her to know. "I panicked."

Well, that wasn't as eloquent as she'd have appreciated, but this was Devon. Such a declaration was actually pretty big news. Where his emotions were concerned, Devon could be as frustrating as Tin come bath time.

"I noticed." She kept her answer terse, not because she was still mad, simply because where he was concerned, she didn't want to confuse him more.

For someone so intelligent, so special, he could be remarkably simple sometimes. Emotions, of course, were the least simple things out there, so maybe it made sense.

In fact, to him, she knew he'd prefer to dive headfirst into pure math than deal with the aftermath of a single argument.

Because of that, she retained her patience, appreciating the fact he'd come to her when this was his idea of wandering into a minefield.

"I can't be without you."

Her eyes flared at that and then she sighed, because he meant it. Literally meant it. Word for word. It wasn't a metaphor or an analogy or a euphemism or anything like that. It was real and it was heartbreaking.

"Of course, you can." It was silly to say that, silly because he never said anything he didn't mean, but she didn't want to think of him like that. Think of him having to *be* without her.

"I can't."

She released a hissed breath, unsure what to say, unsure what to do. His statement touched her so intrinsically that it resonated in her very soul. She knew she was loved, knew it because they showed her every day in so many ways that they were impossible to number. In that regard, she was living a dream. A perfect happily ever after. She was adored by five guys, each of them unique, each of them special. And yet, this was no fairy tale. This was reality. And reality? Sucked. What she'd gone through these past twelve months was something she wouldn't wish on her worst enemy. The only bearable aspect of it was being with her men.

But life happened.

Illnesses happened. Accidents happened.

She might...

Releasing a sigh, she raised a hand and pinched the bridge of her nose. She could have died when she had miscarried Camilla. That could have so easily been worse than it already was. She'd lost so much blood, had endured something that was completely annihilating, and all for a newspaper story. But that didn't take away from the fact that Devon might have lost her. That he might have to be, at some point in his life, without her.

Was it worth talking about now? Worth discussing something that would only distress him even more when it wasn't necessary?

She was young, relatively healthy. As far as she was aware, her father had lived to a grand old age, her biological father, of course, and had only died because of a money obsessed daughter-in-law. If there were any genetic illnesses in her past, she wasn't aware of them. Maybe she should look into her mother's line to find out if there was something there to be concerned about... But then, even as the thought crossed her mind, she was aware that she was borrowing trouble, and in her world, she had enough on her plate.

Releasing a sigh, she whispered, "You don't have to be without me." It wasn't a promise she could keep. Not really. But it was one she intended to sustain, however life, as she'd said already, sucked. She hoped, no, fuck, she prayed, this was never an issue.

"Devon, will you promise me something?"

His answer was immediate. "Of course."

God, she had to word this so carefully. If she didn't, it could derail him, and that was the last thing any of them needed. In a few days, they'd be on their way back to Veronia to solve the nation's economic woes while dealing with the gossip train and Kurt's schedule for his new movie. None of that permitted a mental breakdown just because his wording bothered her on a base level.

"You will always protect Tin, won't you?"

He stiffened behind her. "Of course." It was amazing how those two words could mean something so different because of his tone. One so easy yet passionate, the other ferocious.

But it was the ferocity that calmed her, that enabled her to sink a little easier into him. If anything did happen to her…she knew he'd protect their son which, she hoped, in turn, would protect him. "Good. Let's put him to bed."

"But he has to finish the puzzle," Devon argued, and she had to shake her head at him.

"You know we're the parents, right? He needs sleep more than he needs to finish the puzzle," she muttered, but she was amused. Devon, as always, managed to put a smile on her face even after a serious conversation like the one they'd just had. Even if Devon had been an unknowing participant in it.

"Well, we can be parents, but let him finish the damn puzzle," he groused with a huff.

She blew out a breath. "When he has a tantrum tomorrow on the plane, you can deal with him. How about that?"

She felt rather than saw his smile. "Deal."

"You like it on here, don't you?"

Devon peered around the cabin of the private jet and took in the home comforts on board. He couldn't deny that this was a delightful way to travel.

With wooden paneling and low lights that gave the main room a cozy charm, there were sofas and armchairs that created a feeling of home rather than the cold sterility he was accustomed to while on a plane.

Sascha was on a sofa. Her shoes were on the thick blue carpet since she had her feet tucked under her. She was leaning against the side of the deep bucket seat of the settee and was using the armrest to prop up her phone. At her side, Sawyer was splayed out, legs crossed at the ankle as he slouched down, his focus on the report in his hand.

Opposite him, Andrei and Kurt shared a matching sofa, while Devon and Sean were on the armchairs that sat at the top and bottom end. Between them was a coffee table loaded down with a bowl of fruit and a tray of cold brew coffee, which Devon wasn't allowed to drink because it exacerbated his insomnia.

Behind them were the seats they had to take off and land in, and Tin was nestled in there with one of those cute little sweater-blankets Sascha had bought him. The thing was about four times too big and made him look like he was about to climb Everest, but he looked cute as hell in it.

He took it all in before replying to Sascha, then he muttered, "I'd prefer to be on the ground."

"If it was down to him, we'd be traveling via train," Kurt retorted, his focus on his laptop.

Sawyer's brogue was particularly thick this morning thanks to a cold he was blaming on Germany—*like a country could pass on a virus*, Devon thought with an inner sniff—as he rumbled, "The Orient Express would probably suit. He'd want the whole damn train to hisself though."

"Hisself isn't a word," Devon retorted.

"It is where I'm from," Sawyer countered. "And you're only picking because you ken I'm right."

"I like trains."

"Trains crash more than planes," Andrei pointed out.

Devon narrowed his eyes. "You can't blind me with science."

"I'm not trying to," Andrei said around a laugh as he pulled off his glasses and began nibbling on the tip of the arm.

"You are. Trains crash more than planes, but more people die on a plane." Devon huffed. "Those aren't the kind of statistics I appreciate."

"And yet you know them anyway," Sean remarked. "Why am I not surprised?"

"Ignorance isn't bliss."

"It would be for us. Might shut you up from time to time," Sawyer grumbled.

"Especially around our very young son, who understands more than you think," Sascha chirped brightly, but her eyes were narrowed. "Why do normal conversations always end in statistics with you?"

Devon shrugged. "Statistics are important."

"Be grateful he doesn't know what dying is yet," she said on a hiss, as a rather loud squeal came from the tablet Tin was watching on his lap. There were all kinds of godawful noises from a show with a pig as the central character.

There were many things Devon was sure of in this world, but he wasn't sure if he wanted a pig being his son's primary teaching influence.

Why Tin couldn't watch documentaries, Devon didn't know. But Sascha said he needed at least one thing that was normal.

Apparently talking and walking pigs were normal, but as far as Devon was concerned, they were the antithesis of that. He'd never seen a talking pig, and if he ever came across one, he'd have no problem with checking himself into the local mental health facility, that was for damn sure.

"I hate that pig," Kurt grumbled.

"Me, too."

"Ach, it's only a little show. Let the kid have something kiddy for once," Sawyer stated, punching Andrei in the arm for complaining.

Sean hummed. "I agree. He does many things that are above his age bracket. Considering Tin's current goal is to emulate Devon in every which way, the last thing we need is for our boy to turn out like him."

Devon scowled. "There's an insult in there."

"There are several," Sean rejoined, finally looking up at him just so he could see his grin.

Was that supposed to lessen the sting?

Huffing, he replied, "I'm not that bad."

Sascha snorted. "Darling, I love you, but we really don't need two of you roaming around the place. One is quite enough."

He squinted at her. "Another insult." At least this one was fancied up with love words. As she stood to get another coffee, he intercepted her path and hauled her down onto his lap.

She laughed as she fell, and cocking a brow at him, asked, "You got a problem, bud?"

"I've got ninety-nine of them."

"Devon! Did you just quote Jay-Z? Oh my God, I'm so proud of you!"

He tilted his head to the side, surprised by her glee. "Who's Jay-Z?"

Her face fell and guilt hit him as she answered, "Beyonce's husband."

"Who's that?"

She frowned. "Are you joking?"

"Ask a silly question, Sascha," Sawyer rumbled around a laugh. "Of course, he doesnae know."

"Then how did he know the quote?"

"What quote?" Devon's brow puckered.

"Ninety-nine problems of course!"

"I'm confused."

"I am, too," Sascha retorted, laughing as she shook her head. "Never mind. What are these ninety-nine problems then?"

"My major problem is Veronia."

"What about it?"

"It smells."

She blinked. "The country as a whole?"

Sawyer chuckled. "He isn't wrong. It does whiff."

Sean's lips twitched. "The entire country can *not* smell."

"It does. And you know it," Devon argued. "It must be the flora. Some kind of weird flower that—"

"Smells of shit?" Sascha inserted dryly.

"Not shit." Devon pondered what it actually did smell of. "Just earthy. A bit like pee."

Her nose crinkled. "Pee? Veronia does *not* smell like pee."

Sean snickered. "You know jasmine? When you get the fake stuff, it can smell a bit like a urinal."

She gaped at him. "What kind of noses do you guys have?"

"Functioning ones." He rubbed his jaw. "That thing with all the reeds in the hall smells a bit like that."

"That reed 'thing' cost over three hundred pounds!" she spluttered.

"Should have just asked us all to take a piss on the welcome mat," Sawyer muttered, ducking his head when she glared at him.

"Women have a better sense of smell than men." She looked at him pointedly. "If I can't smell it, then it's phantom."

"How can a few of us all smell the same phantom thing?"

"Because he planted it in your mind that there's a weird odor, and now you can all smell it. That's how suggestible you are," she countered with a sniff.

"No need to look so smug, lass." Sawyer chuckled.

"There's every need when I'm right and you're wrong."

"When you get off the plane, you'll smell it," Devon stated swiftly. "Just see if you don't."

"I refuse to try and smell for the scent of pee," she grumbled. "I had enough of that after dealing with Tin's diapers."

Devon was in full agreement with that. Of course, Camilla would have required nappies too, but he'd have changed those even if they did contain Satan's slurry.

He shuddered at the memory of the bombs Tin had been hiding away in those reusable cloths Sascha had insisted on using.

The memory was enough to make him gip.

Tightening his arms around Sascha's waist, he pressed his face into her throat and took a deep breath. "I wish I could smell you all the time."

"Maybe Veronia would smell nice if you could," she said wryly. "You could carry me around like one of those Victorian vinaigrettes. Sniff me whenever there's a stench."

Kurt cleared his throat. "Vinaigrettes? Like the salad dressing?"

Sascha laughed. "No. But I think it's the same spelling. One's the salad dressing, but the other were these little silver flasks that had perforated lids. Women used to put smelling salts or little lavender buds inside and they'd sniff them whenever they walked close to something gross. They had open sewers back then, and hell, no deodorant." She shuddered. "Smelling salts were probably pleasant in comparison to stinky men."

"Women stink too. We all have sweat glands, Sascha."

"If you think my stink is the same as yours, you're crazy. I love you, Dev, but when you've worked out, you reek."

He blinked. "Why do you keep saying you love me then passing around an insult or two?"

"Because she's a woman," Andrei commented.

"I know she's a woman. I'm well aware of that, Andrei," he scoffed, and just to remind himself, he reached around and tweaked both her breasts. She squealed then grabbed his wrists but, he noticed smugly, she didn't pull his hands away.

"They like to tell you something nice before destroying it." Andrei rolled his eyes, but his focus turned to Sascha's tits—how could it not? They were perfection. "It's how they work, and if you haven't noticed that before reaching your advanced age, then I despair of you."

"We all despair of you," Sawyer grumbled.

"I *do* love you," Sascha said with a pout. "That means something."

"That means everything."

She tilted her head at him and reached up to cup his chin. "I know it does." When she pressed a kiss to his lips, he sighed.

"I forgive you for all the insults."

Her grin felt like it could warm him up from the inside out. "Thank you. But you still reek when you workout."

Sawyer snickered. "And you don't?"

Andrei grumbled, "How did our conversation devolve to this extent? Weird smells, body odor, and train crashes."

"Do you think Vasily would be able to hook us up with a train? I mean, he hooked us up with this jet, why not a train?"

Andrei blinked at Devon. "You honestly mean that, don't you? My grandfather might be a Czar of crime, but he isn't the Czar of Russia. They stopped traveling in private trains when the Romanovs died out."

"Inaccurate. I bet Stalin had a train. Bet Putin has one too."

"That's not something you think you'll hear often," Sawyer mumbled.

"What? He existed, and I bet he had a train. Maybe we could buy that."

"Buy a train?" Sascha sputtered. "Why?"

"Because you want to travel more, and I don't like traveling." He shrugged. "I like trains though."

"*Mein Gott*, I swear, talking to you, Devon, is a bit like talking to a wall."

"Walls don't talk back, Kurt. I'm surprised you don't know that already."

He grunted. "Walls have switches. Can I switch you off?"

"No. You can't. I can afford a train, can't I, Sawyer?"

"Don't get me involved."

"Why not? You know how much money we have. Sascha has a couple of billion, doesn't she?"

"You only want me for my money," she wailed, but her arms squeezed his neck before she started laughing.

"I want you for many things, but the money would be nice if I can get a train."

"Goddammit, can we stop talking about trains?" Andrei burst out. "I'm trying to work here!"

Sascha snickered. "Now you've done it. You've made Mr. Calm blow his top."

He scanned his friend and decided Andrei was the exact opposite of calm. "What is it, Andrei? It isn't like you to get angry."

"I'm not angry. I'm just irritated." He glowered at Dev.

"Synonyms."

"Hardly."

"I'd know. I'm the English one here."

Sascha inserted, "Andrei speaks English better than us."

Andrei flipped Devon the bird. "See? Irritated and angry are *not* synonyms. They're similar—"

"Which is what a synonym is." Devon grunted. "I might buy you a dictionary for your birthday."

"Do. I'll throw it at you when you piss me off."

Devon discarded that notion and tilted his head to the side as he stared at the man who was closer than a brother to him. "Something's wrong. What is it? You've been acting oddly since we boarded."

They'd managed to avoid most of the press after they'd left their hotel, but a few straggling journalists had been waiting at the airport.

"It's nothing." Andrei caught Devon's eye. "Leave it."

But if Devon had noticed something was wrong, then something was *truly* wrong. Well aware that he was often blind to people's moods, that he wasn't in this instance was telling.

Sean shuffled around in his seat. "He's right. You are on edge. What did they say to you?"

Andrei pinched the bridge of his nose. "Just...can you believe the audacity? They bought seats on flights they had no intention of taking just so they could get some access to us."

"We know the lengths they'll go to," Devon replied, his tone somber, "and they're far worse than that."

Andrei's jaw worked. "I know. It just got to me today."

The nerve of some reporters was getting beyond a joke, Devon agreed. They'd been bombarded by the press ever since they'd made it out of the hotel, and when they'd thought they'd escaped them in the terminal—they hadn't. They'd been waiting. Like lions readying themselves to attack weak prey.

"It will get to you worse on some days more than others," Sascha soothed softly. "When we get to Veronia, it will be better."

"Will it?" He shook his head. "I don't think so."

"We can get injunctions, and..." She winced. "I spoke with Perry."

"You did?" Sean's brow furrowed.

"I asked her for her help. Figured there has to be an advantage to having friends in high places. They already heard about the scandal because, hell, they have news channels. She got the palace's lawyers on it for us.

"If they can arrange it so we're not bothered—"

"How can they do that? Sure, people can't write about us *there,* but it won't stop them from hounding us to get a story they can write elsewhere," Devon pointed out.

That had her grimacing. "Stop being logical."

He stared at her. Then stared at her some more.

A breath gusted from her lips. "Okay, I know that's like telling the Tin Man to stop being made from tin, but you know what I'm saying."

Actually, he didn't, but he decided she looked frazzled enough as it was, so he began to pat her on the arm.

She watched his hand, followed the movements for a few seconds, then cocked a brow at him. "Are you stroking me?"

"Is it working?"

"What was the intention behind it?"

"To soothe you." He shrugged. "Is it working?"

Her lips twitched. "Yes, baby, it is."

So, he carried on stroking her as Peppa Pig squealed and chatted in the background, and the conversation drifted onto work for Andrei and Sawyer, while Sean and Kurt focused on their respective laptops.

As always, there was an ease in being around his family. A simplicity that the rest of the world lacked. But he could feel the tension among them. It simmered beneath everything, each touch and each spoken word.

He wished he could heal that breach, but only time would do that, and the one comfort he had?

Sascha was going nowhere.

She was here come what may, and as long as he had her with them, then he could deal with anything.

Even hordes of hungry journalists who wanted a story. Except, this time, he wouldn't beat any of them up for getting too close. No matter how tempted he was, he'd refrain, because that was what being a dad meant.

He was no longer just a mad genius, responsible for no one, a wild card able to do as he willed.

He was Tin's dad, and father was the only adjective he was willing to label himself with. In the haze of Sascha's grief, of their loss, he'd been blinded. Hell, he'd been a fool. But he'd never jeopardize his family again. If he did, he was the one who deserved to rot in jail for the rest of his life.

And in jail he'd have to wear shoes. Wouldn't be able to hug Sascha or Tin every day and, when he couldn't sleep, he couldn't sneak into the kitchen for cocoa or cookies...

A fate worse than death, that was for sure.

TWO

AS HE SETTLED back into the desk chair, he sighed in relief. The leather seat was padded just so, the wide, antique desk was surprisingly suitable for a modern office worker with its squishy leather surface, and the room, though not his study back at home, was certainly comfortable.

In fact, it was like working in Sean's office.

There were books lining the walls, an expansive fireplace in the center of the left wall, and two chunky sofas that were set beside that.

From his position at the desk, he couldn't see out into the gardens, which was why he'd chosen this room for his own. He preferred to stare inward rather than outward—too many distractions that way. However, the painting of the dog above the fireplace *did* hold his attention more than it should.

As he gazed at the beast that had to stand at around four or maybe even five feet high, the door opened without a knock. Only his brothers or Sascha would do that, so he didn't bother shifting his attention.

"What are you looking at?"

"The dog." He shot Sascha a look. "I think we should get one."

"What dog?" She peered around the room. "The one on the mantel?" A groan escaped her. "I'm not against getting a dog, but hell, Dev, you want us to get an Irish Wolfhound? Do you know how much they'll crap?"

He blinked. "I don't know the quantity." Shuddering, he mumbled, "Not in grams anyway."

"I don't want pound weight, Devon. Jesus wept."

"I wonder if it will be on Google," he mused.

Her scowl deepened. "Just trust me when I say it'll be a lot. Huge piles of poop." She grimaced. "I'm not going to be the one who picks that up."

"All dogs poo," he pointed out.

"How many times? *Poop*. That's one British word I refuse to use." She folded her arms across her chest. "Some *poop* more than others. If we're going to get one, I want one that barely poops at all."

Tapping his fingers on the edge of his desk, he considered her demands. "That's an odd requirement."

She hitched a shoulder. "I like dogs."

"I didn't know that."

"You don't know everything."

"True." He pursed his lips. "I know a lot."

"You do," she agreed with a smile, but insisted, "Just not everything."

Unsure if he liked that, especially where she was concerned, he tilted his head to the side and contemplated her.

"What kind of dogs do you like?" he inquired, rocking back in his seat as he watched her slink over to the desk.

After she moved around so she was beside him, she leaned back and pressed her hands to the leather-padded surface. The move did marvelous things to her breasts, and his glance flickered over them before she cleared her throat, drawing his gaze to her eyes. Unashamed, he stared at her, seeing the amused twitch of her lips and knowing she wasn't mad.

"I like Yorkshire Terriers," she stated. "They're cute. Poodles are sweet too. Not the big ones. I was bitten by a poodle once," she mused. "But the teacup ones are definitely cute."

He pulled a face. "If that means they can fit in a teacup—"

"It does," she interjected, her lips curving wider.

"—then I don't want one," he finished. "I'd be frightened of falling over it."

"You could fall over any dog. Whatever their size."

"You couldn't fall over that one," he argued, pointing to the dog in the painting.

"No, it would fall over you," she teased. "Or, shit, it might even be able to push you over. Tin would be trampled—"

"He could just move out of the way," was his diplomatic answer.

"No. Too big. He'd never fit in the house either."

"Thought we were moving to the estate?" he countered. "That place is big enough for thirty dogs." When she stared at him, lips parted, he tilted his head to the side. "What is it?"

"You said that so easily. Like we'll be moving the instant we get back to England."

He frowned. "Won't we?"

"N-No. At least, I didn't think we would." Her brow puckered. "I don't think Sean wants to move. Or Andrei."

He pondered that. "I think they'd be the most inconvenienced, but Sean will retire soon—"

"What?" She straightened. "How do you know that? Has he said something?"

"No, of course not, but he didn't have to, did he?"

"Well, apparently so, because I didn't pick up on anything like him retiring."

"He doesn't think he is, but he will."

"Why?" She winced and her shoulders drooped. "Because of the bad press?"

"No, because the stress is getting to him. Badly." He shrugged. "He's burnt out. He'll realize that soon, and after what happened with the last case...well, it's obvious. Change is coming in more ways than one."

When she gnawed on her bottom lip, it didn't take a genius to figure out she wanted that change. As for him, once upon a time, the prospect would have terrified him. Now, he could handle it because of her. If change made her happy, then he'd just deal with it. Her happiness meant more to him than anything.

As she stared down at her brown, suede leather loafers that hid her cute hot pink lacquered nails from his gaze, she muttered, "I can't see him retiring."

"I can," Devon said quietly, reaching over and resting his hand on her knee. Not to tease, just to comfort. This last year had been hard on them all, but Sascha? He knew it had been a thousand times worse than 'turbulent.' "He's not about to turn into a pensioner, Sascha. I can't see him playing bowls on a Wednesday afternoon. He might return to private practice or something. Do counseling maybe, but the criminology and profiling is too much for him."

She frowned. "How do you know this? Most of that is reading between the lines stuff, Dev. Things even I didn't pick up on." Sascha reached up and began plucking at her bottom lip this time. "He hasn't talked to me about anything like that. That can't be good."

"Sean doesn't share. It's not in his nature. But I've known him a long time. Did you know he only started profiling by accident? He was friends with a policeman who asked him to look over this cold case. His insight cracked things wide open, and slowly but surely a career was formed." When he saw her deeply puckered brow, he sat up a little. "Sascha? What is it?"

"I'm upset, Dev."

"Why?" If he sounded bewildered, that was because he was.

"Because I don't like that Sean is so closed to me. I-I didn't know that."

"He's a closed book to everyone. You have to know which signs to read." He thought about how he could explain that better then realized he couldn't.

Years of living with Sean, of being around him, just sitting with him and working in his office in silence had taught him a lot. No, Devon *wasn't* good at reading between the lines, but that didn't mean he couldn't pick things up by osmosis.

Even a moron learned something when listening in on phone calls and conversations. Because Devon was *always* there, almost like a piece of furniture, Sean forgot about him hanging around. That meant he learned more than the rest of the household about their brother. Hell, about all of them.

Her cheek was tugged inward, concaving before she mumbled, "Don't worry, Devon. It's all good."

It was the opposite of 'all good,' but he sensed she didn't want him to point that out.

Wanting to help but unsure how to—where the hell was Sawyer?—

and just knowing that he couldn't let her go when she seemed so upset, he squeezed her knee again. "Did you come in for a reason?"

"Do I have to have a reason to come see you?"

Relieved to hear the playful note return to her voice, he sighed. "It depends."

She laughed. "On what?"

"No, you don't have to have a reason, but you usually do, therefore there has to be one." He smiled at her. "However, if you want to come and sit with me for no reason whatsoever, I'd be amenable to that."

"You would, would you?" she teased.

"Yes. I would. I just said that."

"Like me to come and sit on your lap while you're working, huh? Administer succor when you're stressed?"

His lips twitched. "I'd be acquiescent to something being sucked when I'm stressed."

Her eyes flashed before she snickered. "I fell right into that one." She winked. "Good one. Word play never was your forte."

Yet another flaw of his. He huffed. "I can be funny."

She smiled. "Yes. You can." Leaning over, she cupped his chin, her thumb swiping over the stubble gathered there for a second before she murmured, "You're right, by the way."

"About what?"

"I did come in for a reason."

"Oh?"

"I just can't remember it." When he chuckled, she pulled back and shoved his arm. "It's your fault. Talking about dogs that shit more than they weigh—"

"*Poop*. No curse words in the vicinity of Tin," he pointed out, mostly because she always did.

She scowled. "He's napping upstairs."

"He's napping? Why? He napped a bunch on the plane. Is he okay?" Devon straightened in his seat, concern filling him at her news. If Sawyer could come down with a cold, then what was stopping their son from catching one too?

"Hey," she soothed. "Tin's fine. You know he likes flying, but it just knocks him out."

"I-I guess." He rocked back in his seat, her pacifying having worked. "Think he'll sleep the night through?"

Snorting, she grumbled, "I wish, but I doubt it—"

The door creaked open and Kurt popped his head around it to peer in. "Doubt what?"

"That Tin will sleep the night through."

Kurt laughed. "He's already awake."

"He is?" She groaned and made to stand, but Kurt shook his head.

"Stay. He's currently riding Andrei's shoulders."

Her eyes widened. "That's a really weird way of phrasing it."

"It is?" He grunted. "Well, you know what I mean."

"I do." She bit her lip again. "I hate it when you guys do that. What if he falls?"

"He won't."

Devon cleared his throat. "Want me to work out the probability—"

"No!" Kurt barked, shooting Dev a glower. "Tin likes it and we're careful."

Sascha sighed. "I guess." Still twisted around to face Kurt, she asked, "Everything okay?"

"Came to see how you're doing." He stepped over to the desk, and the second he was there, slipped an arm around her shoulders.

Watching him, Devon wondered if he should have done that. Was touching her knee too sexual a response to her distress? And how had Kurt seen, just from the doorway, that something was wrong with their woman?

He didn't mind when he didn't understand the minutiae of a conversation. Sometimes, the varying nuances were more difficult than higher order math to him, and everyone had their strengths and weaknesses, but feeling like he was failing Sascha was his biggest fear. God, it was more than that. It was his idea of a nightmare.

As he watched Sascha curl into Kurt's embrace, he realized he *had* let her down. Sure, it had been unintentional, but Sascha deserved more than that from him.

He sat up straighter as she murmured, "Do you think Sean will retire?"

Kurt cut him a questioning glance over the top of her head to which he shrugged. "I do."

"Has he said something about that to you as well?"

"There's no 'as well,'" Devon corrected. "Sean hasn't talked about this to me. But even I can see he's fatigued."

"This press situation won't help. Living under the radar hasn't always been easy for him," Kurt reasoned, "but we've always, by the skin of our teeth, managed to keep things quiet. Now?" He shrugged. "That's all up shit creek."

She blew out a breath. "Lots is up shit creek."

"Everything is," Kurt replied, his voice somber. "But we'll get through it, Sascha."

"We have no choice," Devon retorted staunchly.

Sascha, frowning, shot him a look. "What do you mean?"

Ignoring Kurt's glower, he answered, "We have no choice but to get through it."

She heaved a sigh. "I knew what you were saying, Devon, just not what you meant."

He shrugged. "You're ours and we're yours. That's not going to change, is it?"

Before panic could flare at the possibility that it *could* change, Sascha snorted. "Nope."

The word, so simple, was imbued with a hard, indefatigable, undeniable truth.

She felt just as strongly as he did.

Even though this past year *had* been a nightmare for her, she wasn't going anywhere. He hadn't thought she would, to be honest, but he'd slipped that kernel of doubt into his own brain...

Not for the first time in these past few days either.

Paranoid fool.

She grabbed the hand he'd left resting on her knee and, after squeezing it, assured him, "I'm going nowhere, Devon. You have nothing to fear on that score."

"What if I—"

"What if you what?" she interrupted. "What's the worst you can do? Beat someone up? Nope, did that already. How about you—"

Kurt cleared his throat. "Sascha."

The warning note in his voice had Devon tipping his head to the side. "What?"

She'd tensed in Kurt's arms, but at Kurt's cautionary tone in a statement that, in Dev's eyes at least, required no caution at all, she fell silent.

"Never mind," she mumbled. "Just don't kill anyone. That's a hard limit. Even for me."

With that, she pulled out of Kurt's embrace, and before either of them could say another word, stalked out of the office, leaving Devon staring puzzled at her back.

"What was that about?" he demanded, looking at his brother.

"Nothing."

"Don't lie, Kurt. What was that?"

"Don't worry about it. I want to talk to you about something."

He blinked. "About what?"

"Sawyer."

Devon stilled. "What about him?"

Kurt sighed. "Have you seen him lately?"

"Yes. Fifty minutes ago. You did too. On the plane."

"Don't be pedantic, Devon. I mean in general. He's working out too much. Pushing things too hard."

"He's always been big." Devon shrugged. "You know he works out his stress in the gym."

"Yes. I do know that, and I think he's taking it to the nth degree. What with Sascha dropping all that weight because she won't eat and now Sawyer working himself into an early grave in the gym—" Kurt's jaw tensed. "God only knows what's going to come of Sean after the exposé. You know he takes stress the worst out of all of us."

Devon thought about that for a second and had to agree. "You're just as front line as him and Andrei."

Kurt snorted. "I can be notorious. I'm an author. I don't have a serious job. Not in the eyes of the world."

Devon laughed. "Remember when you tried to get that mortgage—?"

Kurt rolled his eyes. "Thank you for finding my financial woes amusing."

"Your own fault for asking," Dev pointed out. "Why go to a bank when your family is mega rich?"

Kurt scowled. "I'd never go to my family."

He tutted. "I don't mean your parents. I meant us. Or is our money not as good as the bank's?"

"I couldn't ask that of you." Kurt flushed.

"Why not?" Dev's lips pursed. "Far as I know, my cock has pretty much touched yours at some point when we've been fucking Sascha, we have a child together, lost a child together, have been outed to the world together—"

Kurt raised a hand. "I get the picture. A man has his pride, Dev."

"Well, that's just stupid."

"Maybe it is," Kurt retorted, stubborn as ever. "But that's how I want to play it. And anyway, it doesn't even matter. I only wanted a mortgage when I was with the witch!"

He shuddered. "Katrina."

"*Ja*. Her. I don't need a mortgage now, do I?"

"True." He pondered Kurt's words for a second then murmured, "Do you truly think Sawyer is hurting himself?"

When he thought about his brother, he only saw a strong man. Someone who worked out a lot, to be sure, but he was health conscious to the max. Not just with himself but with Dev too. Gone were the days when he was a sugar Nazi with Dev's diet, but he was still always making him eat superfoods and trying to sabotage Sascha's meals with them too.

His nose wrinkled when he thought about the salads he kept sprinkling spirulina into. No matter how many times Sawyer told him it was rich in B vitamins and helped lower cholesterol, that didn't make the damn stuff taste any less like the sea *weed*.

"I think he's allaying the pressure we're all under in the gym. We've barely arrived and the first thing he's done is go for a jog."

Devon thought about that too. "What pressure?" he asked carefully, and wasn't surprised when Kurt pinched the bridge of his nose.

"Dev, I wish I had your brain," was all he said, and somehow, that was worse than being called an idiot.

Stomach churning, Dev questioned, "What should I be feeling, Kurt?"

His brother sighed as he got to his feet. "Nothing, Dev. Don't worry about it."

Feeling like he'd been slapped, he watched as Kurt walked off, his shoulders hunched.

What had just happened?

Twice?

His mouth worked for a few seconds, his brain processing things at too fast a rate for him to comprehend what was occurring. Then, when his computer made a beeping noise, he clutched at that with both hands. Instantly, he forgot about Kurt and forgot about Sawyer, because work was safe.

Numbers were safer still.

❖

THE DINNER TABLE was quiet the following evening, so quiet that Sascha wondered what was wrong. She fussed around Tin for a few moments, mostly just trying to make sure he had whatever Dev had to hand because he'd pull a tantrum if he couldn't eat the same meal. She didn't care if it was enabling or not, she was hungry today and totally didn't intend on having to convince Tin to eat before she could.

As she plowed through her own meal—a really delicious Beef Wellington with tiny new potatoes braised in browned butter—she kept shooting glances at her guys.

Quiet was odd.

It wasn't something you grew used to after living with five men and one son. If anything, it was the exact opposite of what she was used to, and though it weirded her out, she was too hungry to care.

"You cleaned your plate."

The statement came after she scraped her knife over the dish to make sure she didn't miss a damn bite. "It was good," she said with a shrug, casting a smile at Dev. There were shadows in his eyes, and she knew from that alone whose bed she'd be sleeping in tonight.

"Yes, it is good," he replied, his tone a little wooden as he stared down at his three-quarters full plate. "It's just unlike you. You haven't been eating."

Her lips twitched. "Nope, but I'm hungry today."

His chin tipped to the side at that. "Why?"

She shrugged. "I don't know." Well, she did know. At least, she had an idea *why*. Hungry? Sore boobs? Super sniffer? Yeah, she had an idea why, just needed to get a test to confirm her suspicions.

Eying the rest of her men, it was clear to see she was the only one with an appetite... She knew it was weird to say she felt relieved, so that wasn't the correct choice of word. But like a weight had been lifted off her shoulders. Maybe.

Sure, she had become more infamous than ever, seemingly overnight, but she'd had one foot in that particular door since the news surrounding her inheritance had spread to the papers. It wasn't the notoriety that bothered her, more that she cared about how it affected her family, but the truth was, if Sean was going to quit soon, and people wanted to take full advantage of Andrei's, Sawyer's, and Devon's smarts, then they weren't going to stop, not when they made money in their sleep. As for Kurt? Infamy always sold well.

Time would tell how Tin would be affected, but for the moment he was protected, and that was all that mattered. So, knowing that she didn't have to hide anymore, knowing that she was notorious, Sascha figured she could own it, or she could cower under the weight of the revelations that had been so outrageously thrown into the public's reach.

Sascha didn't cower.

Not anymore.

Not when she'd endured what she'd suffered and had come out stronger than ever.

And that was why she had two servings of the Baked Alaska a footman served up next. Hell, she'd have eaten more if the guys hadn't been watching her. She wouldn't have minded if it was with sex in mind, but it was more like they'd picked up on what Dev had said and were wondering at her change in appetite too.

From losing a shit ton of weight and being spanked because you weren't eating to suddenly wanting three portions of Baked Alaska? She knew they thought it was shady, but fuck it.

Their life had been one whole host of shady until the news had broken. With it out in the open she could own it , and she'd come to that decision today when she'd seen two maids giggling over Sawyer when he went running in the grounds. They'd been eying him like he was cherry pie, then they'd seen her.

And they'd blanched.

They knew he belonged to her, and that was the most delicious of realizations.

The whole world knew who these men belonged to now. She had a claim, at long last, and that meant notoriety suited her down to the damn ground.

With a huff at their continued stares, she demanded, "What's wrong with everyone tonight? I haven't seen such miserable faces since the last time the S&P 500 dropped ten points."

Andrei's lips twitched. "Do you even know what that is?"

She squinted at him as she wagged a finger his way. "It's a stock market. I know stuff."

"Yeah? What kind of stuff, lass?" Sawyer teased, his brogue making a delicious appearance.

"Heaps of stuff. I'm a veritable fountain of information on the stock exchange. In fact, I bet I could turn a profit if I tried to play the markets."

Sean slouched back in his seat. He'd taken the head of the table as was his wont, opposite her—even when they weren't in their own residence—and the dining room was a grand affair with a polished walnut veneer and matching carver chairs. He looked like a king sitting the way he was, relaxed in body and position if not in mind. His brow was still loaded with the tension from whatever was eating at them all, but his lips had begun to twitch at her declaration.

"I sense a wager, gentlemen," he intoned, and her eyes sparkled.

Her lips pursed. "A wager? For what? Money's boring." Only the elite could say that, and until them, she'd never been one of those. Still, her life had changed, and money wasn't as important as it had once been. When it flowed in abundance, so much so she offset millions a year to hundreds of charities around the world, winning it in a bet held no temptation.

Kurt rapped his fingers against the table and questioned, "What are you willing to lose?"

"I won't lose," she retorted, confident now. After all, she'd been around these five for a helluva long time. There was plenty of shit she'd picked up on and, call her a cheat, she knew Dev would help her if she asked the right questions. He wouldn't even know she was cheating.

Yes, yes, yes, that was taking advantage of him, but fuck it. If it turned their frowns upside down, she'd wager her—

In fact.

Why not?

Her lips twitched. "I won't wear panties for a year if I lose."

Dev straightened. "Not specific enough."

She rolled her eyes. For the vaguest of her men, trust him to realize there were specifics where that item of clothing was concerned. "No panties, briefs, thongs, or G-strings," she recounted on her fingers.

He pulled a face. "Unless we want you in them?"

Laughing, she nodded. "Unless you specifically want me in them."

Dev tugged at his bottom lip. "I do like your arse in boy shorts, Sascha."

"Arse, arse, arse," Tin cackled, clutching onto the one word in Dev's comment that he didn't really need to know.

Of course.

Shooting her son a look and seeing his childish mirth—how had he even known that was a curse word?—she didn't tell him off. She was way past that point.

Safe to say, her son had her around his pinkie finger because sometimes, it was just too fucking difficult to say no. That probably made her sound like a terrible mother, but Tin wasn't an ordinary child. His stubbornness knew no bounds, and she fully admitted that his strength of purpose outweighed hers—meaning she knew when to bow out of a fight.

It surprised her when Sean frowned and chided, "Tin." His tone wasn't hard, nor was it loud, but it was unusual enough for Tin to pause in his incantation of 'arses' to stare at his father with rounded eyes.

Sean wasn't a distant dad. He took part, played, hugged him, and kissed him before bed, but he was a busy man. His focus wasn't always one hundred percent. That was the joy of having five equally busy men for fathers though. When one was busy, another would always have the time.

But Tin wasn't used to Sean being anything other than a kisser and cuddler, and it showed in his slack mouth and big, diamond blue eyes that made newly minted pennies look dull.

"No swearing at the table," Sean carried on silkily, with too much nuance for a child Tin's age to really pick up on, but Tin was no ordinary kid.

He dipped his head and began fidgeting with the dish in front of him. "Sorry, Daddy," he muttered, making Sascha's lips curve at how pitiful he'd sounded.

It was a testament, really, to how little he was ever chastised. A thought that had her questioning if she wasn't telling him off enough.

Sheesh, this parenting shit was hard.

"Good boy," Sean stated, his tone kinder now, and Tin, upon hearing it, beamed at him and instantly started wiggling in his seat, as though his joy at being forgiven was too much for him to contain.

Her smile was fully formed by this point, but Devon had a one-track mind that had just been knocked off course by his recalcitrant offspring. "Boy shorts, Sascha," he prompted eagerly, like he was asking her to wear sexy lingerie and not comfortable underwear.

She shrugged. "I won't wear them unless you ask me to."

His eyes sparkled with a fire that belied his baby blues. "I like this bet."

Sascha would have to be *very* careful how she phrased anything she asked of him. Not that she minded losing, not when it had him looking like that, but a girl had to give it her all, didn't she?

Andrei murmured, "What do you want from us if you win?"

As she thought about it, thought about something utterly ridiculous that she wanted, something popped into her head.

Something she couldn't avoid.

"I want a long vacation with each of you. Minimal work—enough for you not to go insane—but I want us to go somewhere warm, not wear many clothes, and to relax."

Sean frowned. "Individually?"

She smirked at him. "That would be so much easier for you, wouldn't it? But nope. All of you. Tin can't be without you for the length of time I'd want us to be away."

Sawyer frowned. "How long are you thinking, lass?"

"At least two months."

His eyes flared wide. "We can't be away for two months."

"Sure, you can. The wonders of the World Wide Web, no?" Her lips curved as she rubbed her hands together. "Eight weeks of us just relaxing...even if it kills *you*."

They laughed, as she'd known they would, and she smirked to herself as she spooned some of the Baked Alaska between her lips.

Okay, so she may have made sure the spoon was super clean after, but that was her prerogative, wasn't it?

When she was sure their focus was on her mouth, she stated, "I'll start with a thousand dollars. If I double the money, then I win?"

Andrei narrowed his eyes. "That's too little a profit. You could do that by chance."

She squinted at him. "Is that confidence I hear in your voice?"

He shrugged. "We'd be foolish to forget how smart you are."

Because she liked that, Sascha purred, "Okay. Triple it?"

Andrei hummed. "Make it five thousand. But you have three months to do it."

"Deal," she murmured. "So, let's have less of the long faces."

"I've never heard you sound more British," Kurt commented wryly.

She laughed. "It did *rather*, didn't it? What can I say? You rub up against so many Brits for so long, you pick up some things."

"Be grateful it isn't Chlamydia."

Whatever she'd expected as a reply, that wasn't it. "Even after all this time, Devon, you can still surprise me. What the hell does the Clap have to do with anything?"

"Isn't the Clap Gonorrhea?" Andrei asked, but Devon ignored him.

"It's the most common STD in the UK." He shrugged. Like that made perfect sense.

Sawyer snorted. "Yer a fucking lunatic, Devon."

That had him scowling. "I'm clinically *sane*."

"Yeah, you keep on saying that, but I'm starting to doubt it. Our girl gives us the eye and you start talking aboot STDs?"

"It seemed pertinent."

"I'm glad I'm not in yer head."

Sascha cleared her throat to hide a laugh, just because Devon looked offended and Sawyer disgusted. What amused her the most was how the others just accepted it all. Kurt and Andrei had carried on eating their own desserts and Sean was still looking at her as though she was a hotdog he wanted to swallow whole.

"Okay, well, I don't have the Clap. Or VD."

"Never thought you did," Devon retorted, confused now. "I was just making a statement."

"Well, keep yer mouth shut if yer cannae say anything decent. Talking aboot—"

"Stop swearing. He's already saying too many bad words," Sascha inserted swiftly.

Sawyer shrugged. "It's bound to happen. Especially the more Devon starts pissing me off."

Devon huffed at that. "That's not fair."

"Life ain't fair, bud." Sawyer grunted. "Anyway, before things derailed, what were you going to say?"

"I was saying I'm tired of seeing you all look grumpy. We're together, we love each other, Tin's happy, you're saving Veronia's economy, what more do we need?"

Sean laughed, but there was a tinge of bitterness to it. "How about we turn back the clock a year and start it again?"

She pursed her lips. "If that was possible, then I'd definitely try to, but also..." Sucking in a breath, she decided to be honest. "I'm not sad that everyone knows the truth about us now."

Okay, so that had all their attention.

Even Tin was gaping at her like he knew what she was saying. Mostly, of course, he was just mimicking Devon.

"Maybe that makes me nuts, but I'm tired of hiding what you mean to me." She fidgeted with her teaspoon and rubbed it around the edge of the glass dish that held her dessert. When the crystal sang, she muttered, "Don't look at me like *I'm* the crazy one. Let's all gape at Devon again."

Sawyer shook his head. "I cannae believe you just said that."

"Why?" she countered stubbornly. "Why would it be so hard for you to believe that it wasn't hard for me keeping things quiet? It wasn't planned, and it was out of our hands, so I think we should just embrace the fact that we've been outed."

"That we've been outed, as you say, has great repercussions—"

"Like what?" she retorted. "The more time passes, the more I appreciate it. Your careers aren't going anywhere, are they? You're all rich enough and influential enough to do whatever the hell you want with your lives. Plus, like I already said, when was the last time any of you had a holiday?"

She was on the receiving end of a lot of sheepish looks.

"Exactly," she continued. "You live on your nerves, all of you. I swear. You never have time off. Even when we go somewhere different, it's for work. There's always work at the heart of everything you do.

"Not only is that not healthy, but is that how you want the rest of your lives to be? Just one more round of work after work? No play?"

"Work is fun though," Devon muttered, sounding like Tin did when he demanded the same drink as Devon for his meal.

"You're different, Dev. I know you find order in your work, but the rest of you aren't the same. You can find joy in other things."

"I like origami," he muttered mulishly.

She pinched the bridge of her nose. "You like origami when you can't solve a puzzle you're working on. Devon, math is your lifeblood. I get that. But I'm just saying that Andrei, Sean, Sawyer, and Kurt aren't the same as you. They're similar, sure, but not the same."

"That's right, Dev, you're unique," Andrei teased, earning himself a glower.

Sascha sighed. "Look, I wasn't insulting anyone, I was just saying that I think we should take this as an opportunity to look at our lives and figure out what we do and don't like about them.

"I know I, for one, am sick of getting funny looks from people when I take you guys someplace with Tin, and then when I take another one of you to that same place the next week...They either think I have some dirty uncles, am a sugar baby, or...well, I don't know what they think. I'm also sick of women coming on to you and me not having the right to bitch slap them."

"I'd like to see you in a cat fight, Sascha," Devon murmured. "A topless one."

"Preferably in mud too, eh?" Kurt inserted wryly.

"Yes, that would definitely be your thing, wouldn't it, Kurt?" she said snootily. "I don't intend on getting into any fights, but the fact that I can stake a claim is something I'm going to enjoy.

"When I was at the ball, knowing that other women were looking at you, Kurt, like you were an eligible bachelor..." She shook her head. "Don't you think that hurt me? Seeing them eying you up like you were prime marriage material?"

His eyes widened. "I didn't think about it. Not really. You know I'm yours."

"Of course, I do. I wasn't jealous. Not like that. But I was just..." She sighed again. "Look, I'm explaining this badly."

"No, you're not. We're just being awkward." Sean's eyes narrowed on her. "It's a learning curve. Yet another for us all. But we're relatively intelligent human beings and we're going to adapt to the new status quo, aren't we?" He said the words like an edict, one that was his 'head of the household' voice.

It always amazed her when the others fell in line when he spoke that way, each of them nodding or grunting in agreement.

Because that was exactly what she wanted to hear, she merely dipped her chin and murmured, "Good."

THREE

WATCHING as Sean stuck a vibrator in Sascha's ass, he tipped his chin to the side and stated, "I have a penis."

"Yes, Dev, I'm well aware of that," Sean replied dryly.

"Then why not use me instead of that?" He eyed the plastic with disdain. "I don't vibrate, but Sascha usually climaxes. Don't you, Sascha?"

"Y-Yes, Devon," she whispered around a low moan that sounded borderline painful. "A-Always."

"I'm working here, Devon. You're not supposed to interrupt."

Devon grunted at that, but he tilted his head to the side and watched as her belly quivered from the deep vibrations pulsing through her.

"I don't need vibrations to make her come," he muttered under his breath.

"Devon, do you want me to flog you too?" Sean hissed, shooting him a glower over his shoulder.

Though he rolled his eyes, he also raised his hands in apology. Moving around the bed, he came and sat on the edge so he could see Sascha's face. She was always so expressive during sex, and even though Devon admitted he wasn't the best at reading expressions, it was so much simpler during intercourse. Pleasure and revulsion were easy to discern between.

Even though Sean kept sticking things into Sascha or whipping her with something, she never showed revulsion which, he had to accept, meant she enjoyed the random things he did to her.

A light swooshing sound had him peering over at Sean. Unsurprisingly, in the background, Kurt was jacking off as he watched Sean work Sascha over with a flogger. He did this odd thing with the piece of equipment, swirling it in a constant circle that connected lightly with her behind. Up and down, he moved the flogger, letting it dance along her spine before moving along her legs, down her thighs to her calves. The only time she flinched was when it hit her feet—Sean liked touching her there, Devon had noticed.

"Do you have a foot fetish?" he queried quietly.

"Devon, shut up," Sascha gasped, her back arching as Sean sent the flogger along her other leg. When it moved between her thighs, she face-planted the bed, smooshing into the soft covers as he carried on hitting the vibrator that was protruding from her arsehole.

When another flogger appeared, Devon wondered if Sean was some kind of damn magician. Where he kept all this stuff had him wanting to explore his brother's bedroom the next time he knew Sean was elsewhere.

The two leather wheels ran along Sascha's creamy flesh, leaving a light pink wherever they touched.

"C-Can I come?" Sascha groaned, startling Devon because as far as he could see, there was no real reason why she should be near climax.

"No," Sean told her, his tone absentminded.

It was then Devon realized Sean was doing something. Well, that was inaccurate. Of course, he was doing *something*, but there was a method to his madness. All along her back, the pink that was starting to blossom from a blush into a hazy line was showing crisscrosses all from where he'd touched.

The pattern, now that it was revealed to him, had him licking his lips as he eyed the different angles Sean had created.

For a second, he was lost in them, eying the forms and shapes Sean had crafted, and then he registered what Sean had said.

She couldn't climax?

What was the point in sex if you couldn't come?

A little confused, he tumbled into the world of angles. His brain twining sex and math for the first time in his life as he watched the pattern form.

When the whooshing sound came to a halt, Devon noticed Sean had dropped the floggers to the floor before he reached for one of Sascha's feet. His fingers began to ply along its dainty length until he dug his thumb into her instep.

Sascha gasped as though he'd sucked on her clit!

Amazed and aghast, Devon watched as Sean massaged her foot, first the left, and then the right, until her toes were curling. When he dragged his nails down her sole, she moaned once more.

"P-Please! Please, Sean!" she implored; her face still burrowed into the sheets. She pushed her forehead deeper against the mattress, using it as a fulcrum to pivot from one side to the other.

Unappreciative of his inability to see her face, Devon reached forward and made to move the sheets out of the way. Sean got there first, however. He grabbed her hair in a ponytail and tugged her head up. Wincing at the sight, as well as Sascha's yelp, Devon had to fight the urge to slap the shit out of Sean, and only didn't because Sascha looked...

He swallowed.

Incandescent.

She loved this.

She truly did.

He didn't know how, didn't know why, but she did, and he loved her so he had to let her have this even if it scared him. Even if the sight of Sean doing these things to her was something that was hard to behold.

His father had often grabbed his mother's hair, using it to make her do something. Dev could easily remember the last time he'd ever seen the bastard do that.

They'd been eating dinner. Quietly, calmly. Nothing was amiss. Then he'd gotten to his feet, grabbed her by the hair, and dragged her off her seat before hauling her into the kitchen.

Devon couldn't say what had even triggered the event, just knew it had been followed by his mother's sobs and a great feeling of futility.

He'd been skinny back then. Skinny and weak. He'd stayed there, listening to his mother being beaten for a good three minutes and twenty-one seconds before rage had overtaken his good sense.

For the first time in his life, he'd hit his father, and once he'd started, he hadn't been able to stop. Of course, he'd earned himself a black eye for his pains, but that was better than listening to his mother being beaten.

Sascha screamed at that exact moment, dragging him from the past and into the present. She climaxed as Sean thrust the vibrator in and out of her ass, even as he tightened his fist around her hair, tugging it harder, rounding her back so her belly was pushing into the mattress, her body in a wheel-like position.

Devon bit down on his bottom lip, unsure what he was seeing, unsure if he could correlate the past and the present, but when her eyes opened wide, she stared at him. Looked at him so directly that he couldn't evade what he was seeing.

She needed this.

Loved it.

Loved that he was watching. That Kurt was too.

Loved that Sean was in control of her pleasure, that they were satellites to that pleasure as well.

Her mouth worked for a second before her eyes shuttered closed, and he watched her orgasm and orgasm. It seemed to last for a lifetime, her body strung taut, each muscle tensing with the pleasure Sean had wrung from her.

He sensed the exact moment the pleasure became painful, and a second later, she began to sob and shudder. He reached out, unable to stop himself, and cupped her chin.

Hushing her, he rubbed his thumb along the line of her jaw, then he smoothed it along her bottom lip. When her tongue flickered out, lashing it, his cock instantly hardened. Throughout all that, he hadn't even had a semi, but the second she touched him? Fuck. Every ounce of arousal that had been put in cold storage thanks to his memory bank breaking open burst forth like an overflowing spring ruptured a dam.

His cock went to full mast, and he had no choice but to shove his thumb into her mouth, had no alternative but to watch her suck it like she would his cock.

"I think she should beg to suck your dick, Devon."

Sean's words had him blinking, taken aback at the request. "Beg?" he croaked out. "Shouldn't I beg *her*?"

Sean's lips twitched, and over the length of Sascha's body, he watched Sean's fingers run over the curve of her butt before they whispered between her legs. It was only then he realized he'd switched off the vibrator, but a keening cry escaped her when Sean evidently began playing with her clit.

"Why shouldn't she beg for your cock? She's the one who needs filling, aren't you, Sascha?"

"Filling?" he whispered, the word felt alien to him.

"I'm empty," she moaned.

"She has a dildo in her ass," he pointed out. Hell, he could even see the dark onyx tip peeping out from between her cheeks.

"That's cold, though, isn't it, Sascha?" Sean prompted, like he knew exactly what she was thinking, *feeling*.

But, how could he?

How did he know any of that? Understand what she was going through?

As Devon ran his eyes over Sean, who was dressed in the same outfit as he'd been wearing at dinner—a shirt with his sleeves rolled up to his forearms, and a pair of pants that matched a suit jacket—it was difficult to believe he was in the middle of sex play.

If anything, he could have put on his sports coat and gone out for a meeting. Well, save for the fact he was barefoot.

Whereas Sascha?

She looked wrecked.

But in a good way.

She wasn't crying tears of pain, of misery. She was crying tears of release. And yes, there was a difference.

A difference that he was only just beginning to learn.

"Y-Yes," she moaned. "So cold."

"Don't you want to be filled, Sascha?" he replied, teasing her with his words.

Devon studied him, wondering what he was playing at.

"More than anything," she whispered.

"Ask him for it then. Dev isn't comfortable here, Sascha. You know that as well as I do. So, I think you should do something to make him comfortable. Don't you?"

She licked her lips. "Y-Yes, sir. I do."

The second she said that, his erection wavered. He fought the memories, fought the times he'd had to call his father that, the times he'd even heard his mother say it, then when Sascha licked her lips, he was reminded, once more, that Sascha was not his mother.

Sean was not his father.

And Devon was no longer helpless.

Four times a week, Sawyer and he worked to ensure he'd never be helpless ever again.

Because he wanted to own this moment, because he wanted to be a part of something his love enjoyed, something he might never be able to do again, he stood up. Temptation struck him, something that urged him to head on out, to leave them to this.

Sean loved it, that was clear to see. If Sascha was incandescent, so was he. In his element, he controlled everything, and for a man like Sean, Devon knew how much that meant to him. It was, Dev realized, a wonder that he'd gone this long without this side of his nature bursting free.

Kurt also enjoyed watching. Why that was, Devon couldn't say. He was too used to Kurt enjoying being in the background for it to bother him, but that he liked seeing their woman pushed to the outer edges of her limits told Devon that this wasn't as foreign as it seemed.

There was no violence here.

This wasn't like what he'd seen as a boy.

His mother had been cowed, browbeaten, *scared*.

Sascha wasn't scared. She was just alive and loving every second of that.

So, instead of heading to the doorway, instead of escaping to his office and diving into his work where he'd find the kind of freedom only math offered him, he sucked in a breath and reached for the buckle on his belt.

Catching Sean's eye with his, he swallowed, showing his nerves. No, this wasn't the first time he'd been a part of this play, but it wasn't getting easier. Each time broke open a memory he'd long since hidden, and for a reason, but there was no denying that he was hard.

There was also no denying the way Sascha was watching his hands. She looked starved. Like she'd die without his cock.

The thought fed him, urged him on, and he stopped messing with his belt buckle, concentrated instead on unzipping the fly and pulling his cock out from between the tines.

"Show Devon your appreciation, Sascha," Sean intoned, folding his arms across his chest. His forearms bulged as he did so, and there was faint amusement on his face, etched in his eyes as he watched her scrabble across the bed to do something Sawyer had told Devon a lot of women didn't even like.

Sascha liked it. That was quite clear to see.

He'd never know why he did it, maybe would never understand it, but when she was in front of him, kneeling at the side of the bed, her hands on her legs, her thighs spread wide so he could see the puffy, wet lips there, when she leaned down to taste him, he didn't let her.

Instead, he tapped her bottom lip with his cock, letting the pre-cum gathering there moisten her mouth. He rimmed her lips with his dick, using his own arousal as a kind of paint, and a part of him thrilled when she moaned as he muttered, "Taste me, Sascha."

Her tongue circled every inch of her lips, taking him at his word and savoring every drop.

"Do you like that?" he whispered, tapping her again. When she popped her mouth open, ready to suck in the tip of his shaft, he pulled back. "Do you like that, Sascha?" he repeated.

Her eyes were dazed, hazy with something he could only class as arousal. "I need more, Devon."

"You want my cum?" he retorted.

"I-I do."

"Open your mouth then." She instantly obeyed in a way that was totally *not* Sascha. He was used to her being bolshy, butting heads with him over things, arguing with the others. She wasn't one to hold her tongue if a situation bothered her, and yet, here she was, obeying.

To him, it was a paradox, but she was so far into this she might as well have been sucking his cock down like it was a lollipop.

He inserted the tip between her lips and murmured, "Don't close your mouth."

Her eyes flared wide, then they shuttered and she moaned as he rocked his hips back and forth, letting his cock come into contact with her tongue, but fucking her mouth in a way that he'd never wanted to do before.

"Play with your tits, Sascha," he ordered, watching as she cupped them then ran her fingers over her nipples—the second she did, she half-squeaked, then shivered, the buds puckering something fierce under her touch. "Do you want to pinch them?" he questioned absently, watching her squeeze down on them a lot harder than he would have. Another nod. "Do it then." And as she did, she shuddered, and that prompted him to drop the hold he had on his dick, thrust into her mouth, and grasp her head, holding her there.

A throaty moan vibrated around his cock, and the sound had him jerking back. Letting go of her.

He stared at his hands, where they'd been on her head, and he thought about what he'd just done.

"Dev? Please! Don't tease!"

Her plea stunned him. Bewildered him. Why wasn't she screaming at him? Demanding he apologize?

"She likes it, Devon." Sean's words were reassuring, but when he shot him a look, Devon saw an understanding written onto his face that put him on edge. "She wants it. Just like you wanted to do that, she wanted you to do it."

"But why?" he whispered, almost swallowing the words in his haste to understand.

"Why must there be an answer to that? You like your cock being sucked, don't you?"

"Of course."

"Well, it's as simple as that. Need and desire. That's all that matters here. Give her your cock, Dev. She's been a good girl."

Sascha moaned at that, twisting around to look at Sean as his words hit home.

Sean's smile was soft, tender. *Loving.*

The exact opposite of the angry scowl Devon's father had shot his mother when he'd been done with her. Throwing her down on the ground like she was trash...

Devon gulped, and reaching forward, grabbed her chin. "You want my cock?"

"You know I do."

The coyness was new, but it was a shade of Sascha he knew and understood. So, he took a deep breath, and gave her exactly what she'd asked for.

Him.

To say that Sascha ached the next day was an understatement.

She wasn't complaining, however, but taking three hard fucks? Yeah, that made for a very sore pussy.

She fidgeted in her armchair as she thought about what had gone down the previous evening, and had to smile when she felt her body heat up some.

How Sean, Devon, and Kurt hadn't wrung every ounce of pleasure out of her, she'd never know. Why it kept reappearing, as though it had never been sated, she wasn't sure.

Sascha could only liken her arousal to a beast that was constantly hungry, and it was a beast that had been borne from grief and loss and anger. It was amazing how good it felt when she confronted those emotions each and every time one of her men took her control from her grasp, and yet there was no evading the truth of that either.

"Sascha?"

She blinked, surprised to hear her name being spoken when she knew all her men were busy...but then, she realized it was a female voice.

Twisting in her seat, she saw it was Perry. The Queen of Veronia stood in the doorway in a pair of jeans that had seen better days, a thick Arran sweater that was bulky around the waist, and a pair of riding boots that appeared like they were semi-caked in mud.

Despite herself, Sascha had to smile.

The queen definitely didn't stand on ceremony.

Something she appreciated, because she didn't either. Still, she wasn't a queen and Perry was.

Unsure of what to say, she just smiled. "Hi." When Perry hovered in the doorway, she cocked a brow at her. "You going to come in or just let all the heat out?"

Perry snorted. "Well, I just wasn't sure if you wanted to talk to me."

"Why wouldn't I?" she queried, her brow puckering. "We spoke on the phone the other day."

"It's been a tough couple of days. I-I know that when I get vilified in the press, it's always easier to ignore everyone and everything."

"Does that happen often?" Sascha inquired, getting to her feet and walking over to Veronian royalty, of whom she proceeded to treat like she was a bag of laundry when she dragged her out of the doorway and deeper into the sitting room that she'd claimed as her own.

It was a large space that looked onto the lake in the distance, and she liked how it was on the second floor. It meant she could stay away from her men who'd all taken offices on the ground.

Just because she loved them didn't mean she wanted to be in their pockets all the time, and as much as at the start of their relationship their talking work got her hot, now? She just preferred to enjoy the silence while she had it.

"Does what happen often?" Perry asked, as Sascha practically shoved her in the armchair opposite the sofa she'd just taken as her own.

That was another reason why she'd claimed this room. Not only was there a log fire that she didn't have to clean out herself—an actual footman did the chore for her—but the sofa wasn't a Chesterfield like all the ones downstairs. It was filled with feathers and felt like heaven to sit on.

"You getting vilified in the press."

She waved a hand at that. "Only if I do something they don't like." Her lips curved. "Which is quite often."

Because Perry slipped out of her boots and stuck her sock-covered feet in front of the fire, Sascha decided to chill out too and scooped her feet under her butt.

"What don't they like you to do?"

"It's mostly petty stuff. They didn't like what I wore, or they didn't like something I said." She shrugged. "Edward says not to let it get to me, *or* if I do let it get to me, then to wear what they'll appreciate and to say only what they want me to say."

Well, that was *charming*, wasn't it? If one of her guys had told her that, she'd probably have shoved him then made him pay in other, devious ways.

"Who's they? The public or your...I guess you have a staff who tell you whom to visit and things? Like with the British royal family?" She winced. "I have to admit, I know more about them."

"Well, you would, wouldn't you? You live there." Perry's lips curved. "I'm sure Megan and Kate suffer just as much as I do. We're always told what to wear and where to go."

"So, did Edward's advice help?" Sascha wasn't sure if it would help her or not.

Conform or do whatever you want.

"Wasn't much of an option, was it?"

She smiled. "He knows me too well for my own good," she admitted wryly. "He knows I can't conform. I don't have it in me."

"So you carry on doing what you want regardless of what anyone has to say?"

"Yes." She grimaced. "But if it blows back in my face then I don't seek comfort from him."

"Who's the comfort giver?" she asked softly, unsure if Perry would answer.

"George. I knew him first. We were in college together. He's used to my ways. But he's a bit too much like Edward sometimes, so usually it's George, but in that situation, it's more often Xavier than not." She tipped back into the seat, let her head rest against the wing tip of the chair, and murmured, "Who's the comfort giver in your group?"

Sascha blew out a breath as she thought about that and realized how damn nice it was to talk about her men as though it was a normal relationship.

Maybe discussing this stuff with Perry before Germany had made her appreciate the truth being revealed to the world. It was nice being normal after so much time being weird. She knew, of course, that was too facile. To some people, her life was one bucketful of sin in a hand basket.

"I know what you mean about going to Xavier over George, circumstances depending." She plucked at her bottom lip. "Sean is who I go to when I need a strong shoulder to cry on. I feel like he can take on the world, but he can't. I've seen him break, Perry, and it isn't pretty."

"We all have a melting point," the queen replied, her voice soothing, low. It felt right, oddly enough, to talk to her about this. This woman who she barely knew, and yet, by shared circumstance, who she knew too well.

"We do. Devon melts faster, I suppose, but in his own way, he's the simplest. He never understands *why* I'm upset, and can freak out if I am, but there's comfort in knowing that whether the situation is dire or minor, his response will always be the same." Her lips curved. "Then there's Kurt. He *always* has time for me. Doesn't matter if he's writing or not. I try not to interrupt because his work is important, you know?"

"I do. Edward's like that. Always working. I wish he didn't work so hard, but what can he do? It isn't like he can stop and quit, is it?"

"We've picked difficult men, haven't we?" Sascha mused dryly.

"That we have. Xavier started working with the government more after we all got together, but it burns him out. He's been working here more."

"I barely see him." Sascha's brow rose. "Where does he work?"

"In the greenhouse. He's a sneak." She pursed her lips. "I'm worried about him, truth be told."

"Is there something I can do to help?"

Perry laughed. "Get your men to ease Veronia's woes?"

She winced. "They'll do their best, and knowing just how damn mulish and obstinate they are, I wouldn't fret. They're good at what they do, Perry. The best."

"You never mentioned the others. Andrei and Sawyer, right?"

Sascha laughed. "Sawyer isn't very restful, but he's never scared if I cry, and when I *am* scared, Andrei's always there to hold me." Her laughter turned into a gentle smile. "I never thought I could love a single man this much, and yet, I love five of them."

"Isn't life strange?" Perry mused. "Although, how you deal with five, I don't know. Three wear me out."

Sascha whistled under her breath. "Tell me about it."

"Busy night, hmm?" the other woman said with a laugh so bawdy that Sascha had no alternative but to join in.

"Yes. Very busy." She winked at her, feeling strangely comfortable as she maneuvered into the queen's true reason for visiting. "Is everything okay, Perry? You were kind of off at the start."

"No, I just...I wanted to reach out to you before, but wasn't really sure what to say. We didn't speak that much on the phone when you called last..." She pulled a face. "I didn't want to make things awkward."

"Things aren't awkward," Sascha told her wryly. "Maybe for my men, but not for me."

"No?" She tipped her head to the side. "Why not?"

"Because I'm glad the news is out."

Her blunt remark was met with silence, then Perry got to her feet and headed over to the fireplace. "I think we need coffee and cake, don't you?"

Unable to stop herself, Sascha laughed. "Please."

She pulled the long swathe of fabric that hung from the ceiling twice, and thanks to the antiquated *Downton Abbey*-esque way of summoning servants, she meandered back to the armchair and plunked herself down into its soft embrace.

"This is nice, isn't it?" she murmured, staring into the fire.

"Talking about things we can't talk about with anyone else?" Sascha queried softly. "Yeah, it's nice."

Perry cut her a look. "Are you really okay with the world knowing?"

"Oddly enough, yes. It's strange, but all the stuff that used to piss me off doesn't have to anymore. Sure, people will call me a slut, think I'm worse than scum, but do I give a fuck?"

Perry laughed. "Zero fucks to give, huh?"

"Exactly."

When a knock sounded at the door, Perry called out, "Come in." Seeing the maid, she smiled, "Hi, Heather. Are you well?"

"Yes, ma'am." Heather didn't even bat an eyelash at the queen's sudden appearance in Sascha's sitting room. That told Sascha how used they were to her just coming and visiting Xavier.

Even as she wondered if the staff knew of what their royals were doing, Perry ordered afternoon tea. When the door was firmly closed behind the maid, she asked, "Where's Tin?"

"With his fathers. Thank God," she grumbled, then yawned because she was seriously tired. "I didn't have the energy today, so Sean took him. Sean spends the least time with him. I want to change that.

"Normally he's all kisses and hugs before bedtime, and they never really do anything that fun together, so I'd like to work on rectifying that."

Perry pulled a face. "God, Sean reminds me so much of Edward. He's so focused on the wrong things that sometimes, I just want to head-butt him."

Sascha snickered. "All that would do is give you a headache."

"True." She hummed. "Might shake some sense into him. Alice is a good girl, you know? Edward is just grouchy after a long day of work."

"I understand, Perry." Giving her a gentle smile, she murmured, "I wasn't judging."

The other woman winced, then shook her head. "I know you weren't. My mom was bitching at me over this the other day. She visited recently, and ever since, whenever we Skype, she checks in to make sure I'm badgering Edward about how he treats Alice.

"I mean, God, you'd think he was terrible the way she goes on but—"

"She's probably picking up on your feelings about the situation too."

"Probably." Perry pinched the bridge of her nose. "I should have brought her. She liked Tin. She doesn't like many people," she tacked on drolly. "She wasn't happy when I'd told her you had to go away."

"Bring her tomorrow if you want."

"I'm busy. I'm only here because I snuck out. One of Edward's cousins is going to have to open a new hospital because I couldn't."

"Why?" From what Sascha had read about Perry in the papers, and from what she'd seen of the woman in the flesh, she knew she wasn't the kind of person to be lax in her duties.

Sascha knew she'd been a scientist, and they were always dedicated to whatever their cause was.

Perry muttered, "Edward and I argued."

"Over Alice?" Sascha pressed gently, knowing that was the source of the problem.

She sucked her lips between her teeth and began nibbling on them. "He was talking about sending her off to boarding school, Sascha. Boarding school!"

Eyes wide, Sascha shot up in her seat. "She's only a baby."

"Well, he doesn't want to send her now, just enroll her." She shook her head. "But I can't allow him to do that. Can I? It's the start of the slippery slope. Next thing I know I'll be buying her a goddamn uniform."

"No, you damn well can't allow him to do that!"

"Exactly." Perry straightened up too, taking comfort in Sascha's umbrage. "George and Xavier just said that's what they did—"

"And if they'd jumped off a bridge, would they expect that of her too?"

"If it was royal protocol, then probably." The knock sounded at the door again, and Perry barked, "Come in."

With a quick curtsey, Heather left a tray of cakes, sandwiches without the crust on, and a pot of steaming coffee on the coffee table before departing with another curtsey.

Even as she eyed the gesture, shaking her head over just how many times the woman had bobbed and genuflected, Sascha sat up the second the door was closed once more and began pouring their drinks.

"I don't want her to go to boarding school."

"Then don't let her go. Simple."

"Nothing's simple. It's how they do it over here. It's what they expect of their royals."

"Screw that," she muttered.

Perry winced. "It's not as easy as that. Even though," she groused, lifting her hands in surrender, "I know it should be. But everything works a certain way and I'm just..."

"Just what?" Sascha prompted softly. "What is it, Perry?" Eying the queen, seeing how upset she was, how close to tears she had become, Sascha couldn't stop herself from shifting over to the other armchair so she could grab her hand. Squeezing it between her own, she repeated, "What is it?"

"Do you ever feel like you're losing yourself?"

Sascha blinked at that, not having expected that response. "I-I guess. It's easy to get lost in your day. We have so many men pulling us one way, then we have kids, and then we have other responsibilities. I mean, Christ, my duties aren't like yours. I just have a lot of money and have one of the guys slough it off to charities. That's it. You have queen stuff to do."

Perry's smile was miserable. "Yeah, 'queen stuff.' Back when Edward proposed, I was kind of swept away by everything. Not the royal crap, if anything that turned me off. But them? All three of them?" She whistled under her breath. "They packed a mean punch, and I was just knocked out by them all. I figured I'd bring an American's viewpoint to royalty.

Calm things down, you know? But there's no calming them down. They're like battering rams.

"I never imagined the day when I thought I was helpless to stop my child from attending a school, but here I am wondering if, in a few years, I'll watch Alice get taller or if, one day, she'll just return home from school a foot taller and I'll never have had the opportunity to mark her growth spurt on a goddamn door in our suite."

With her free hand, she rubbed at her eyes and Sascha, bracing herself for tears, wasn't surprised when Perry turned to her and buried her face in her shoulder.

It was easy for Sascha to say it was simple, to tell Perry she should have a say in something as important as this, but she knew how it went when you felt like you were being swept along in a tide you had no control over.

She knew that, and her advice couldn't help.

Back when she'd learned the truth of her parentage, when she'd learned that her heritage made it worth someone's while to kill her to gain access to the estate that was her inheritance from parents she didn't know about, she'd felt like she was drowning. Sascha could easily remember finding comfort in sweets and candy, in holing up in one of the living rooms, and just not wanting to talk for days on end.

Sometimes, the shit life threw at you was bigger than you and totally out of your control.

When they'd lost Camilla, that feeling of drowning had been even worse. When Devon might have gone to court, to jail, she'd felt like she was suffocating without even being swept up in the tide.

Blowing out a breath as she squeezed Perry in her embrace, she whispered, "I understand, Perry. My life is different than yours, but everyone knows what it feels like to have to deal with something that's beyond our control. In this, I get it. I do, but I think if you don't talk to your men about it, if you don't stop things in their tracks and make a stand, you never will and you'll never stop regretting it."

Perry tensed, then whispered, "I know you're right."

"Are you scared of them or something?" Sascha questioned hesitantly. She didn't get that vibe, but something was going on here.

A watery chuckle escaped the queen. "No, not at all. But they're as much a product of their environment as I am. Just as I feel like I'm fighting for our daughter's future, they are too, and it's three against one. How am I going to win? Especially when it's expected of Alice to attend this godawful school in Alsine. The privy council, even the damn government expects it.

"She's the heir to the throne," Perry whispered, "and I knew there were always going to be some hoops we'd have to jump through, but—this? I just didn't think they'd want her to go away so young."

Sascha thought about that. "So, you'd be okay with her attending a boarding school when she was older?"

Perry pulled back to stare at her. After she'd gnawed on her bottom lip, she whispered, "Like when she was sixteen or something."

Unable to help it, Sascha snorted. "So, pretty much when she was an adult?"

"Yeah." Perry giggled. "Eighteen would be much better."

Sascha laughed. "I'll bet." Then, releasing a sigh, she admitted, "I don't think you have any choice, Perry. You're going to have to butt heads with your guys over this. Doesn't matter if you're breaking with protocol or tradition, it all boils down to this—when you're looking back over Alice's childhood, do you want all of those memories to have taken place during holidays? Do you want to miss out on the everyday stuff that we had with our parents? Do you want to be a parent in absentia all because a privy council thinks that's how you should raise a future queen?"

FOUR

"I DON'T THINK you have any right to—"

"George?" Perry spun around in her seat and faced the only one of her men that Sascha hadn't actually met.

Well, *officially*, she hadn't met any of them.

She figured meeting the king and his cousin in their private rooms after a quickie wasn't considered an official meet and greet.

But she knew George from the news.

Hell, *everyone* knew George. He was one of the most eligible bachelors in the entirety of Europe, and Sascha knew how that had to feel for Perry.

It sucked when the world wanted your man and you couldn't put a claim on him.

Still, the charming George who was present in the media who, along with his brother and sister-in-law, was changing the face of royalty in this part of the world was definitely *not* present at that precise moment.

If anything, Sascha was on the receiving end of a glower that, back in the day, would have probably led her to being executed or some shit like that. Unfortunately for George, she had a toddler and five men to contend with, so she was no pushover.

Cocking a brow at him as he continued scowling at her, she murmured, "I assume you're George."

"I think Perry's greeting was a big enough clue," he retorted succinctly. His accent could cut glass—enough to slice through anyone's ego.

"George, what are you doing here?" Perry inquired, but she didn't get up to go and greet him. Didn't move toward him for a welcome kiss.

Sascha gave the other woman a look and saw that, if anything, Perry had hunched in on herself, and she also noticed that *George* saw that too.

His glower morphed into a pained frown, but to Sascha, he murmured, "Perry assures us that you know of our situation and mean us no harm." He cleared his throat. "Considering your own personal arrangement..."

She raised a hand. "I already told Perry I wouldn't say anything. My 'personal arrangement' is a lot different than yours because, you know, I'm not a queen."

"Lucky you," Perry muttered under her breath, reaching forward to grab a piece of cake and shoving it in her mouth.

"Perry," George said on a sigh, as he stepped farther into the room.

Her eyes tracked his movement, and Sascha felt Perry tense up when he came and perched his butt on the coffee table. Uncertain if she should stay or not, she moved forward, only for Perry to grab a firm hold of her hand and squeeze her fingers.

Wanting to support her new friend, but wary of the awkward situation, she just hovered there, uncertain to the last.

"You're getting in the way of the cake," Perry scolded when George settled himself.

At that, he grunted, twisted around, and raised the platter onto his knee. She eyed the new display with a grumpy grunt, then reached for a sandwich which she began to tear into two parts before shoving half in her mouth and, almost defiantly, chomping down on the snack.

He rolled his eyes. "I've seen you dancing with ten tequila shots in your belly and picking out baby vomit from your hair, Perry. Takes a lot more than bad eating habits to slow me down."

She narrowed her eyes at him, then took another defiant chomp.

"Have you been crying?" he questioned quietly, then his gaze cut to Sascha who merely grimaced.

"No. I don't cry. There's no point in crying," she muttered.

"What's that supposed to mean?" His bewilderment was evident.

"It means there's no point," she snapped back. "How much did you overhear?"

"Enough to discern that you're upset. That's why I followed you here. I knew you weren't happy about what we were discussing this morning."

"Can you blame me?" she demanded, her voice low and hoarse, and in her eyes, Sascha saw a welter of misery that she, one mother to another, totally comprehended.

"It's how it's always been," George mumbled uneasily, and Sascha wasn't surprised when he reached up and tugged at his collar. "I'm fine, aren't I? I went when I was six."

"Six?" Sascha whistled under her breath. "You were at boarding school from that young of an age?"

"It's standard," he stated woodenly.

"Didn't you hate that? Didn't you wish you were home instead?"

"Of course, I did, but I got used to it."

Perry jerked back, and Sascha got the vibe that that was pretty much the worst thing he could have said. "You got used to being away from home? You *got used* to feeling like you'd been dumped in a school away from your family and everyone you knew?"

"It's different for us! You know we weren't raised like you, Perry!"

"Fuck that," she spat. "I'm raising my daughter the way I was raised because, apparently, that's the one dose of normalcy she's ever going to have in her life.

"Soon, she'll have no choice about the lessons she has to learn and the way her days will be formed and ruled as though she has no say in any of it, but I'm not sending her away too. Everything you learned at boarding school she can learn by attending a day school." She raised her hand and, brandishing her finger as though it were a weapon, she jabbed it forward into his chest. "Don't you wish that your mother had been like me? Fighting for you to stay home?" When he opened his mouth, his intent to argue, she snapped, "And don't answer that as George the man. Think about George the little boy, who was dumped somewhere away from everything he knew and loved."

"Edward was there," he muttered. "Xavier, too."

"And that's supposed to make me feel better?" she shrieked. "Edward was all alone. He experienced that on his own. Xavier had him, you had them both, but what about Alice? She won't be like Edward."

"It's good for a child's character. She needs to become independent fast, Perry."

"Fuck that and fuck you," she screamed, jerking up into a standing position and stunning the hell out of both Sascha and George by shoving her hands against his shoulders and pushing him backwards.

The movement, because it came as a surprise, had him jolting and the tray of afternoon tea in his lap went sliding onto the floor, creating a cacophony of crashes, as Perry spat, "My daughter will not be attending any boarding school, George. I don't give a shit if it means I leave you and go and live in a house near the fucking school. She will not board. I won't have it, do you hear me?"

George, his butt in a pool of spilled coffee, his boots slowly being dampened by more of the brew, and his lap full of cake, just gaped at her. Then, to Sascha, he requested calmly, "Please, leave us."

Sascha stiffened. "I'm not leaving her—"

He glowered at her. "Leave us." The two words were imbued with a royal command, but Sascha didn't give a shit. When she made no move to do as ordered, his nostrils flared and he got to his feet. When he took a step closer to Perry, she didn't retreat, just stood her ground, her hands balled into fists at her sides, every inch of her daring him to defy her, to argue with what she'd said.

Maybe Sascha shouldn't have been surprised when he grabbed her cheeks in his hands and hauled her into him. As he kissed her, Sascha watched Perry tense up then melt as George took all distance away, removed anything and everything that parted them.

It wasn't a dominant kiss—Sascha would know. George didn't tip her chin up, didn't force her back against the wall, didn't even bend her over slightly so he carried her weight. If anything, it was a worshipful kiss, and Sascha, though she shouldn't have been looking, felt her eyes watering because she knew exactly what it was.

The little boy in George was thanking Perry for doing what his own mother hadn't for him.

Being a tigress defending her young.

When Perry moaned, she pulled a face then carefully got to her feet. Making sure she made no noise, she slipped out of the room without a backward's glance, leaving them to their kiss. When Heather bustled along, a dustpan in her hand—how the hell had she heard that crash?—Sascha stopped her.

"Please inform the staff that no one is to go in there until the queen leaves."

Heather blinked, but dipped into a curtsey. In any other world, they'd have strode down the corridor together, but the staff always froze in place, waiting for the guest to make a move first.

A few seconds after she reached the top of the stairs, she heard Heather shuffle along behind her and shook her head at the oddity of having a team of servants who acted as though they didn't all put on their shoes the same way.

As she skipped down the steps toward the front hall, she aimed herself at Andrei's office. Talking about him with Perry made her want to see him. Was she testing him? Testing to see if he'd still drop everything if she wandered in?

Maybe.

And he passed with flying colors, because the second she tapped on the open door, he hollered, "Come in." She saw that he was on the phone, but when she meandered inside, his eyes lit up—literally lit up like Tin's did when she gave him some cake—and he muttered, "I'll call you back later on." Then he scowled. "When? I don't know exactly. I'll just call later on."

Her lips curved as he disconnected the call, and she murmured, "You could have finished talking with him." Though every inch of her was loaded down with satisfaction at the fact he'd done exactly as he had—that she couldn't deny.

"Why would I talk to him when I can talk to you?" he demanded, sounding so perplexed that she had to laugh. Sometimes he really was like Devon. Everything was so cut and dry.

She figured most people knew the world came in black, white, and gray. Devon saw only black and white, as did Andrei, but he was aware of the gray and, she thought, dismissed it as useless territory. It was why they were similar but different too. Andrei was more worldly. He could survive out there without his brothers. Devon? Nope. And now that they had Tin? Definitely not.

If she'd learned anything this year, it was that. Devon, without them, would subsist. That, in her opinion, was not living.

Shucking off the thought because it was gloomy and, to be honest, she'd spent so fucking long being gloomy and grief-stricken that she couldn't abide a moment more of it, she turned to peer around Andrei's office.

His was set up differently than the ones the others had picked. They'd all settled into rooms with a desk that sat by a window, which overlooked the lake, while a fire burned behind a seating area. Andrei's was in a library with no windows. Surrounded by books on all sides, except for where a hearth puttered merrily away, he was cloistered in.

"It's a bit airless in here, isn't it?" she muttered, gazing around her and tugging at her shirt collar. "Hot, too."

He shot her a swarthy grin as he rocked back in his seat, then making a bridge with his hands, he settled them on top of his belly—his flat, corrugated belly. Yum. "Feel free to take some clothes off," he encouraged.

Laughing, she did as bid, stripping off the thin cardigan she wore that staved off the faint chill in all the rooms here. When she tossed it in the direction of a high-backed armchair, he pouted.

"I meant more interesting clothing."

"You should have been more specific," she told him promptly. "You know I like direction."

He narrowed his eyes at her, then rocked forward and challenged, "How about you set your panties on my desk so I can see them all day?"

She snorted, then murmured, "I'll give you the panties on the proviso that that's all you want."

His pout deepened. "Sore, are you?" Then his eyes started twinkling. "I had a full accounting this morning from Devon. It was like a book report. I've never been more fascinated. If only school had been—"

"Oh boy, I'm glad I wasn't around for that conversation," she butted in dryly, and as was their habit, she rounded the desk as he pushed back, creating a small sliver of space for her to settle between his legs. Then, she pulled a face, and asked, "Exactly how detailed?"

His grin was so dirty that if they hadn't put her through her paces as much as they had, she'd have blushed. As it was, it was difficult to blush around guys who'd seen you at the worst and the best moments of your life.

"*Detailed.*" He rested a hand on the side of her hip, and his handspan was so big that when his thumb dug into her inner thigh, she bit her lip. Fuck, with just a touch he had her thinking things her body was soooo not ready to deal with. "Enough to understand why you're sore."

She wrinkled her nose. "Since when is Devon an over-sharer?"

"Apparently Sean's bringing out a side in both of you that's new to us all."

Laughing, she replied, "Well, if that isn't a terrifying prospect, I don't know what is."

His eyes were twinkling again, and in contrast to when she'd walked in and how he was scowling and growling at the person on the other end of the line, she figured she'd cheered him up by that alone.

Unable to help herself, she leaned forward and cupped his chin. "How are you doing?" she inquired, her voice turning soft but serious.

She knew she'd surprised him, because he bounced a little in his seat. His hand grabbed her wrist, and he twisted it around so the veins were facing him, then after he pressed a kiss to her pulse point—swoon—he rocked back in his chair. With his head tilted to the side, she could see he was considering her, wondering why she was asking that.

But this wasn't about her.

This was about him.

"I'm okay," he told her. "I'm always okay."

Her brow puckered the teensiest bit at that. "You sure?"

"Positive."

"You were growly before."

He shrugged. "That's because Dyrk on the other end of the line wasn't listening." His phone began buzzing, and even Sascha had to admit how perfect that timing was, especially when he glowered at the screen as he tilted his cell so he could see the ID. "See? Doesn't listen. Didn't I tell him I'd call him back later?"

"Is there a language barrier?"

"He's American," Andrei responded dryly. "Do you understand me? Or have I suddenly developed a Russian accent?"

Her lips twitched. "No, you haven't, but I wouldn't be averse to you developing one."

A snicker escaped him, and his accent, usually so subtle to the point where he sounded more like a Brit than a Russian, became more accentuated. "You like it when I talk like my grandfather, *mahyah dahrahgahyah.*"

Sascha's brows lifted at that. "Wow. That's a new one."

He smirked at her. "I have plenty of words to throw at you if you want me to talk dirty to you?"

She laughed, then leaned forward again to buss him on the head. "I'll remind you of that. When I'm not out of order." Then, with a twinkle of her own in her eye, she reached down and rubbed his cock. "Of course, other parts are fully functional."

His phone began buzzing again, and this time, his Russian came so fast and thick that there wasn't a damn thing she could make out.

Snickering, even if she was a little disappointed at not being able to suck him off, she winked and slipped away from the desk. "You're busy."

"Later," he grated out, his need in both the word and his eyes.

"Promises, promises," she teased, before she pretty much danced out of the room.

Okay, so he hadn't answered her question, but she had to believe that he'd have told her if things weren't good with him, right?

Andrei, in truth, was actually the least temperamental of all her men and probably the one who was most adept at handling his emotions. She figured that had to do with his Russian heritage. Very few guys that she knew were okay with their grandfather kissing them right on the lips when they were as old as Andrei. But a big smacking kiss, complete with cheek pull, before his head was tilted this way and that for Vasili to study every inch of his face, was their standard greeting.

She also knew that when Andrei was mad at his grandfather, or vice versa, they yelled something fierce at one another. So, yeah, she had to believe that if Andrei had a problem, he'd tell her about it.

When she was back in the hall, she hovered, uncertain if she should return to her sitting room which might contain a fornicating queen and prince, or whether just to go for broke and find one of her men who *wasn't* busy, and who would like to take her out into the city.

Deciding that that sounded more fun, especially if Tin had woken up from his nap and could visit with them, she began the short walk to Kurt's room, because he usually had more time on his hands than anyone else. Especially if he had writer's block.

Before she made it there, she heard a soft, intimate chuckle, and turned and saw Perry, with George's arm around her shoulders, walking down the stairs.

She definitely looked brighter, and Sascha was glad for that. No kid deserved to be shoved in a boarding school before they were old enough to tie their shoelaces, and Perry's distress and her evident fear at how helpless she was to stop things in their tracks had truly touched Sascha.

Clearing her throat when they made it to the ground step, the board of which was shiny in the center after centuries of being trod upon, she asked, "Everything okay?"

Perry's eyes caught hers. "Things are better."

George dipped his chin at her. There was a brusqueness about the gesture, but she sensed some gratitude to it, even if it was quite clear he wasn't about to out-and-out thank her for her interference.

"I'm glad," she replied, meaning it.

With a short sigh, George muttered, "I heard about the bet."

Sascha's eyes rounded. "Excuse me?"

It was his turn to clear his throat. "Devon, your man. He was discussing it this morning and I happened to walk in on the meeting."

Okay, so maybe she hadn't outgrown the ability to blush.

Had George heard about last night's escapades?

Or solely the fact that her ability to wear underwear for a year was under threat?

"What about it?" she questioned gruffly, dipping her chin to avoid his gaze.

"I can help you decide on which stocks to share. In thanks for your aid. What hurts Perry, hurts me."

With wide eyes, Sascha mumbled, "I'd really appreciate that."

Perry, her gaze darting between them, murmured, "I'd like to know what can make a mother of a toddler, one who has five men for lovers, and who's just been outed by the press, blush like that."

George laughed. "Nosiness is not a seemly quality in a queen."

She snorted. "Good thing that this queen makes her own rules. Right, Sascha?"

"Right!"

❖

"On a scale of one to ten, how busy are you?"

When Kurt looked up from his desk, Sawyer did as well. He was sitting in the armchair in front of Kurt's desk, evidently working on something that also had him scowling at whatever he was doing.

Seriously, her men scowled way too much.

The sight of Sawyer in this office didn't altogether surprise her. In their own way, her men liked to be among their pack. It was something she'd noticed right from the start, and something, truth be told, that, to this day, still had the ability to charm her.

They weren't just living together to help maintain Devon's sanity—although that was definitely a huge part of it—but because they loved one another. Maybe only in a fraternal way, but that love was true nonetheless.

Unless it was for work, most of their social time was spent with either her or one of the others, and the tight-knit nature of her household was something she'd never complain about because she loved it too.

Tin was making her need to spread her own network a little, because he needed to know how to make friends, but she'd always keep things close to home. She wasn't like the other mothers who were worried about regular life issues. Sure, Sascha had them, but money eased so many troubles and there was no hiding from that fact.

Still, being sociable was important for Tin's sake.

Didn't mean she was happy about that, however.

Sascha was more than content with staying close to home, being antisocial, and always living in yoga pants. Unfortunately for her, her son was a mime. That meant whatever they did, he'd follow, and she didn't want that for him. She needed him to be who *he* wanted to be, and for that, he had to develop in ways that necessitated her putting on a bra sometimes.

Sigh.

Sawyer's chin jerked up. "Yer asking me, or boy wonder over there?"

Her lips quirked up in a grin. "What makes you boy wonder, Kurt?"

He winked at her. "Oh, nothing."

"False modesty will get you nowhere," she teased back.

"Just did a phone interview with a film magazine about *Black Blood.* It went well."

Sawyer snorted. "You shoulda heard the lass fawning all over him like he shat gold."

She blinked at that. "Why have you gone all Scottish on me?" What with him and Andrei, sheesh, what a time for her bits to need a rest.

He pshawed. "I'm Scottish. A hundred percent Scottish stud."

"Prime beef?" she mocked, but she couldn't stop the laughter from escaping her as she moved over to him and plunked herself in his lap. He gripped her tightly, and she reached up to press a kiss to his throat.

"Well, I'm sure as feck not secondary beef," he retorted, making her snicker. He definitely wasn't *secondary* anything, although he was still a bit pale. She definitely needed to win that wager. He needed some color in his cheeks, some sun on his skin—a break would do them all a world of good.

Kurt snorted. "She's right, though, Sawyer. You *are* talking more Scottish today."

He winced. "Ma called. What was I supposed to do? Not answer?"

"Not complaining, just pointing out that you sound very broad today. Is she okay?" Sascha murmured, "I should call Jacinta myself. It's been a while."

"Dad's got a cold, and she's driving him insane bleaching everything around him."

"Did she talk to Tin?"

"Of course." He sniffed. "More interested in the lad than in me."

"That's because you're a big lad and he's a wee lad," she teased, knowing he was joking.

"I'll show yer big—"

"Wait! No!" she wailed. "No 'big' references and no sex. I'm literally relieved I can walk today."

Sawyer snorted. "I heard over breakfast."

She scowled. "I'm not sure I like Devon talking about—"

"Wasnae just Devon. Boy wonder was talking about it too."

Whipping her head around to glower at Kurt, she noticed his ears were burning. "You encouraged Devon? My God, we'll never get him to stop talking about it if you embolden him!"

Kurt's shoulders bunched up around his ears. "It wasn't like that, *meine Liebchen*—"

"Don't '*meine Liebchen*' me, dammit." She pouted. "I'm not sure I want to go out with you now."

"What? You're breaking up with him?" Sawyer joked. "And before prom too."

"Like you even know what prom is," she retorted.

"I've seen movies," he countered.

"Well, I'm not breaking up with him before prom, but I'm sure as hell not taking him out!" She huffed. "And I wanted us to all have a nice day together too."

Curling his arm about her waist, Sawyer chivvied, "We all know this stuff anyway, love. It's only Devon who's just noticed it."

"Noticed what?" she grumbled.

"The noises you make and the way your expression changes when you come." He shrugged. "Nothing to be embarrassed about, but you know what he's like. He'll probably know the exact angle of your nose, but won't know how it crinkles, right here" —he brushed the bridge— "when you get over-excited."

Said nose crinkled again. "Okay. I forgive you."

"And you say I'm not charming," Sawyer scoffed, but he winked at her. "Come on then, where are you taking us? Are you buying?"

Kurt grunted. "You Scots. Always so damn tight."

"She's richer than me," Sawyer countered primly. "And I'm all about equality in this day and age."

"You're all heart," she mocked back, laughing at him. "And I don't know really. I just fancied getting out. I feel like we've been stuck inside for a hell of a long time. Even back in London I wasn't going out, and I spent most of the time in Moscow rattling around Vasily's house."

Sawyer grabbed her chin. "You want to go shopping, don't you?"

With a laugh, she nodded. "I do."

"Fucking hell," he grumbled. "Okay, I'll go. On one condition."

"Name it."

"I get to see you trying on some clothes."

"That can be arranged," she purred. "I'll grab Tin and get us ready for the weather. It looks freezing." He slapped her on the ass, hard enough to make her yelp and giggle at the same time. As she darted toward the door, she jerked to a halt in surprise. "Dev! What are you doing there?"

Sitting on the floor, between a grandfather clock and the wall, he had a cushion at his back, one leg crossed at the knee, and a tablet in his hand.

"Dev's here?" Kurt's surprise was as strong as Sascha's, but Sawyer just grunted.

"He's my ghost at the minute. More than usual."

Because Devon hadn't replied and appeared to be engrossed in whatever the hell he was reading, Sascha returned to Sawyer's side.

"Why?"

The simple question had him fidgeting. "No reason, or one I can't figure out. Nearly scared the shite out of me this morning though."

Feeling like she was a broken record, Sascha inquired, "Why?" She'd gone for a patient tone, but Devon's behavior was only unusual if something was going down with him. The sooner she figured out what that was, the better.

Plus, now that she thought about it, Devon hadn't been there when she'd woken up. When they had sex, normally he *slept,* and that meant he'd be conked out in the bed beside her until either Tin clambered in and woke them up *or* if she disturbed him by going to the bathroom first.

"When I went to take a slash this morning, he was in the bathroom, snoring."

Unable to help it, Sascha's lips twitched. Sure, this was a serious conversation, because all conversations were serious when it came down to talk of her partner's mental health, but she'd have fucking *paid* to see Sawyer scared shitless.

Which, okay, sounded cruel...

Didn't stop her snickering.

"Shut yer gob, yoo," came the densely Glaswegian retort. Peering over his shoulder, he scowled at the man who'd been lying in a bathtub like a weirdo rather than sleeping in comfort with her. "What's goin' on with ye anyway?"

Devon hummed. "Nothing."

"Nothing? The next time I find you in the bathroom at four in the morning, I'll—"

"You'll what?" Sascha prompted, eyes flashing as she tried not to laugh.

"I dinnae know," Sawyer said gruffly. "It was pitch-black, all was still and silent, then the fecker starts snoring like a train's going through my room. Pissed all over the floor and everything."

She pulled a face. "Ew."

"Aye, exactly. Ew," Sawyer retorted with a grunt.

"So, technically, I scared the piss out of you. Not the shite," Devon murmured, his tone disinterested and his focus evidently still on his work.

For a second, Sascha's eyes could only widen, then she began to hoot. "Oh my God, Dev! You did it! Another joke!" Jesus, she was so proud she could burst.

Sawyer grunted, but Devon countered, "Hardly, Sascha. I was there. Nothing funny about it."

Her lips quivered. "Why not?"

"I had to watch him clean it up."

She snickered, but her hand came to rest on Sawyer's shoulder and she squeezed. "You went to bed in the raw?"

"O' course," he scoffed. "When don't I?"

True. And a naked Sawyer was her favorite kind. Yum.

"He flashed me. He's the one going on about being traumatized. What about me?"

"Yer no' the one with a problem seeing my ballsack," Sawyer rumbled.

"Not from that angle," Dev argued.

Sascha pushed her hand against her belly. "Oh, God, stop!" Then, she couldn't help it, she keeled over, propped herself on her knees and laughed. Then laughed. Then laughed some more.

"What's wrong with her?" Sascha heard Devon mutter, but not even the sound of his concern could stop her from giggling as she thought about Sawyer peeing in the dark, then pissing all over the floor when Devon started snoring. Then Devon getting a flash of Sawyer's ass when he cleaned it up.

"Think she's laughing at our expense," Sawyer groused, but she heard the amusement in his tone.

"Mommy laugh!"

Tin's sweet voice penetrated her laughing fit, but she couldn't even stop then.

"What's she laughing at?" Sean asked, and she knew he was close to laughing too just because she heard the smile in his voice.

"Never ye mind," Sawyer muttered. "Dinnae be saying a word, Kurt, Devon."

Kurt snorted. "I have more important secrets to keep."

"Tough shite. Yer keeping this one. Andrei'll never let me live it down. He's already told me to lock my doors against Devon."

"Seriously?" Sean questioned, and his surprise had her laughter morphing into hiccuping.

Because she was interested too, and a little pissed at Andrei, she gulped down her amusement.

Sawyer wafted a hand when he saw he had both their focus—even if she was busy wiping her tear-soaked eyes. "He keeps doing weird shite."

"Like what?"

He winced. "Woke up with his hand on my pulse the other day. Then he put a thermometer in my mouth—" He gusted out a breath. "Only, I moved in my sleep, so it ended up in my nose. Would have feckin' brained me if I hadnae woken up in time."

Though her nostrils flared with the need to laugh some more, she croaked out, "It's because you look peaky." She pointed to Kurt. "He saw it too. You're working out like mad. Don't you think you should cut yourself some slack? You must have caught a cold when we were at the graveyard. Or maybe when you went running? It's freezing out there and you're in a pair of damn shorts."

Sawyer frowned, then shot a glower at Kurt. "I dinnae have a cold. I'm not sniffling, am I?"

"No," she agreed, "but something's going on. You're pale as milk."

"It's winter!" he retorted. "What would yer like me to be? Brown as a hazelnut?"

"Hazelnuts have more color than you," she muttered, shoving his arm. "You need to see a doctor if you're not feeling well."

His eyes flared. "Who said I wasn't feeling well? I just said that Devon keeps doing weird stuff!"

"That's because he usually sees things we don't," she argued, and ignoring his eye roll, continued, "Promise that if you start to feel worse, you'll go."

"I hate the doctor."

"You don't know a doctor here," Devon pointed out, making Sawyer twist around to glower at him.

"I'm all right!" he boomed. "If I'm sick, I'll tell ye. Damn, a man can be tired ye ken without there being something wrong wi' him."

"So you *are* feeling under the weather?"

He scowled. "Stop putting words in my mouth. I said I'm tired. It doesnae help when Dick over there keeps waking me up in the middle of the night—"

"My name's Devon, not Dick," Dev grouched.

"Plus, we're busy! We've plenty going on, and things aren't going to slow with this situation here, are they?"

She blew out a breath. "No, I guess not. If you're tired, I can sleep with you some. Devon usually finds his way to me anyway. You might get more rest."

At that, his scowl disappeared. "I wouldnae be averse to that."

A snort escaped her. "I'm out of action tonight, remember?"

"I can handle that." Then, he shot a scowl at Sean. "Don't break her next time."

"I wasn't the only one behind the breaking," came Sean's smooth response.

Her cheeks flushed. "I really need us to not be talking about this right now."

The guys laughed, and she shot each of them a glare. Well, not Devon. He was selectively listening again.

With a grunt, she strolled over to Sean and hauled Tin out of his arms and into hers. "You want to go shopping with Mommy, baby boy?"

"Noooo," he howled, like she'd tried to make him eat a vat of cauliflower—his least favorite veggie, not even dousing it in mint sauce like she did for Devon worked on his mini me.

She snickered. "Well, that's that plan scuppered. Feel like playing in the yard?" He always had some energy in need of burning.

"I'll join you," Sean volunteered, grabbing her hand and slipping his fingers into hers.

Never opposed to spending some one-on-one time with her man, she beamed a smile at him. "That would be brilliant."

"Go get wrapped up," he ordered, just putting a teeny-weeny bit of dominance into it, making it more of a command than an order.

Dealing with a shiver she was in no way ready to handle, she muttered, "Yes, sir," before she hauled ass and rushed up the stairs to the bedroom she'd claimed as hers. Dragging out a long, thick coat and switching her loafers for leather boots, she grabbed one of Tin's sweaters, a down plushy jacket, and some Wellington boots for him too.

Once she was dressed, she retreated to the hall and found Sean standing there. She'd barely been a couple of minutes, but he was already wearing a coat and, somehow, had managed to get Tin into some outdoor gear also.

Her eyes widened at the sight—Tin had arms made of Jell-O. "How did you change him so fast? And where did you get those clothes from?"

"We grabbed some stuff from the cloakroom." Sean shrugged. "There's some of our things in there."

"Huh. I didn't know that." She went to the cupboard he'd pointed at, which was just off the foyer, and saw he was right. Hell, there was even a coat of hers in there that she hadn't noticed was missing and a heavy pair of UGGs.

"When they did our unpacking, they must have put some of our things in here," Sean explained as, bored with her confusion, he grabbed her and tugged her toward the stained-glass door.

Once they were outside, the crisp notes in the air hit her and she frowned. "It doesn't smell of pee here."

He laughed, but didn't reply as he hauled Tin onto his shoulders. She hid a wince because she knew the guys would hurt themselves before they ever let Tin come to harm, but it always put her on edge when they did this. Still, Tin loved it and it would keep him occupied for the chat she wanted to have.

With both of his hands on Tin's little legs, she couldn't link up with him, so she shoved her fingers down his butt pocket.

"You thinking of retribution?" he teased.

"Wouldn't get me anywhere, would it?" she retorted dryly.

"No." His eyes gleamed and she sighed as she took in the sight of him. Damn, he was beautiful. Sure, he'd aged a little—hadn't they all? A little more gray here and there in his hair, and a few more wrinkles on his brow and around his eyes. Better still, he had more laugh lines. She felt like they were *her* badges of honor. She'd done that, she knew. She brought light to their days, and sure, that sounded bigheaded, but she knew it was true. Even in the recent past, when things had been darker, when she'd been grieving, she'd brought something they'd been missing.

A sigh escaped her as she stared at him before she admitted, "Just looking at you still makes me hot."

His eyes gleamed some more. "Don't give me ammunition, Sascha," he rasped, and from that note in his voice alone, she knew he'd be sporting a semi. Ever since the kinks had come out to party between them, she'd started to recognize when he was most affected.

That would be now.

"I'm not teasing," she whined. "Just being honest. Thought that was a rule now."

"True." He pursed his lips, wincing when Tin tugged at his hair. Only then did she realize they'd both stopped walking.

Laughing at the kid equivalent of 'giddy up,' they carried on down a path that would, in summer, be lined with lovely bushes that probably flowered in technicolor. Now? It was a little dark, a lot gray, but the path led to the lake. It wasn't something she'd managed to do yet, but she'd like to get to the shore, look at it closer. She was a homebody, but this was a nice excuse for Sean and her to spend some one-on-one time without sex getting into it.

That, she knew, was her fault.

She hadn't been lying. Just looking at him did get her hot—what was a girl to do? Complain about that?

She squeezed his butt cheek as much as she could within the confines of his pocket, then murmured, "I wanted to ask you something."

He arched a brow at her. "Ask away."

"Devon said something to me the day we arrived here."

"What?" Sean scowled when she hesitated. "Did he upset you?"

"No, well, a little. He said you were burned out."

"He shouldn't have," was his firm response, but she didn't think it boded well that he was looking toward the lake and not at her when he said that. Nor did it bode well that he neither confirmed nor denied the statement.

"No, maybe he shouldn't have, but it made me think that he saw something I hadn't. I know he's dense where some things are concerned, but he does pick up on some stuff. And that stuff tends to be pretty on the ball."

He sighed. "It doesn't take a rocket scientist to figure I'm tired, love."

"No, it doesn't." She hesitated. "Tired enough to retire?"

His answer was a shrug.

"It's never too late to change things up."

"Because I'm ancient?" He grinned at her.

She snorted. "You're as old as the woman you feel."

"True." And while that gleam made a short-lived reappearance in his eyes, he pursed his lips. "I don't really know what I'd do if I didn't—"

"That's no excuse to stick to doing the same old thing," she inserted quickly.

Maybe too quickly.

"Why?"

"Why what?"

"Why are you asking this now?" He winced. "Stupid question considering everything that's happened."

"Maybe to some, but no. Not really." She blew out a breath. "I-I, well, I just, this situation, it's made me question some things. Made me think about what I want to do with my life. How I want things to be. Not only do I not want to live in London anymore, but I'd like to be out of the city, somewhere quiet. Deep in the country." She peered around her. "Somewhere like this. Where Tin has room to grow, and I don't have to worry about him running into the road, you know?"

"I get that. We've been discussing it."

"You have?" She frowned at the ground where a slushy pile of mud and snow was scuffing up her boots. "What do you think?"

"The consensus is that we'll do it, but there might be some issues with Andrei."

"What kind of issues?"

Sean shrugged. "You know he needs to be in the city a lot."

"Too much," she grumbled. "You guys work too hard."

"It's not work for us," he said softly. "You know that."

"I do, but still, it's good to have a break. I don't think we've ever been away as a family, have we? Devon and another one of you are always working." She blew out her cheeks. "Look, if you want to stay doing what you're doing, that's fine, but I think when you're in your position, and you want a change, you should really think about what you want to do with your life. That's all."

"You want me to stop."

Did she?

Sascha pulled a face. "I genuinely don't mind. Mostly, I want you to be happy. Then, after that, I want you to be able to spend more time with Tin. I don't want you to be the distant dad, Sean."

"I spend time with him," he argued.

"Yeah, you do, but not enough. All of you could take a page out of Devon's book. You all do a lot, don't get me wrong, but is that enough for our boy?" She shot Tin a look, and was well aware that just like Perry, she'd be a tigress for him. Hell, she'd even maul her mates on his behalf. "I want him to know all of you well. I want you to have a solid relationship, not like the ones we have with our families."

"Your dad really hurt you the other day, didn't he?" Sean asked, voice whisper soft.

She shrugged. "Yeah."

"He pissed me off." Sean visibly gritted his teeth. "The last time Henry visited, I liked him. Now? Not so much."

"Exactly. That's not what I want for our family. This past year has shown me how much crap life can throw at us, and we have to stick together against the world because the world *will* let us down."

He moved closer to her. "For the moment, I want things to remain how they are. My caseload has diminished ever since..." It was no surprise that he let his words wane.

"Yeah, I know since when," she replied dryly.

"I'm sorry, love."

"No, don't be. You don't need to be. We've already gone through that, and look, this isn't about *that*. Mostly it's about Tin. Mostly it's about the future." She hitched her shoulder. "I guess what I'm trying to say is that I want us to focus more on being happy."

"Happy?"

When he blinked, she muttered, "You say that like it's a foreign word."

"Maybe it is." His brow puckered. "My life is split into two parts, Sascha. Home and work. At home, I'm happy. At work, I'm not."

Surprised by his blunt response, she didn't say anything, just hoped he was piecing things together in his head.

"I don't think I can be. It isn't a job where you *can* be happy, is it? I mean, I catch killers. Get into their brains and try to figure out the reasons behind the weird stuff they do. It isn't like the others. Kurt gets to create worlds, and Devon, Sawyer, and Andrei are in their own universe, making more money and solving problems that will change how society works. Me? I'm dealing with destruction."

She gnawed on her lip, wondering if she should prod or let him carry on thinking, but she couldn't stop herself from whispering, "I want more for you."

His lips twitched. "You do?"

"I do." She slipped her hand out of his jeans pocket then moved it around his waist.

"Mommy!" Tin squealed, bowing over to smack a kiss on her head.

She laughed. "Hey, baby." When he chortled and clapped his hands, she knew his attention had moved on, especially when the cry of a bird had him peering skyward. "I want everything for you, Sean."

"Everything's a bit much," he teased, "but thank you, love." Those words were less amused and more genuine. "I appreciate that. I guess I need to think about the upcoming months."

"You do." She shot him a smile. "And hey, I'm going to be helping Kurt with his screenplays, aren't I? Maybe you can help too? I'm sure he'd love you to—"

Sean laughed. "Don't tell Kurt you said that. He'll snatch them out of your hands."

"Why?"

"We used to read his books before...then we'd argue over little points and he'd sulk." His nose crinkled. "I'm pretty sure that's how he ended up married to Katrina."

Her mouth dropped open. "Huh?"

Sean shrugged, which jostled Tin who shrieked with glee. "Sawyer pointed something out in one of his books...I forget which one exactly. Kurt got offended, decided he just *had* to visit his parents, and then, a year later, he was married."

"A year? That's hardly cause and effect."

"You know Kurt. For him, that's faster than lightning."

Her lips twitched. "True. Okay, so that was a bad idea, but maybe we can do something together," she suggested brightly.

"Like what?"

She knew she had his interest, so she blurted out the first thing that came to mind. "Well, you know how I donate to charities? I was thinking of setting up my own foundation."

His eyes flared wider with interest. "What kind of foundation?"

But even though she'd made it up off the cuff, it flowed out of her mouth when she said, "Women's shelters, so no kid has to go through what Andrei and Devon did."

Sean's gaze softened. "That sounds like a marvelous idea."

She gave him a smile. "Yeah, it does, doesn't it?"

FIVE

SMIRKING AT THE COMPUTER, Devon eyed the formulations he'd been crafting for no less than six weeks and studied their perfection.

The days had been long, the nights had been longer, and his frustration was evident in the room around him. If he'd bothered to look, he'd have seen over a hundred paper cranes that he'd folded into existence over the tedious hours of thinking and crafting and perfecting, but they were beyond his awareness.

Beyond his interest even.

All he saw was the perfect formulae, and Devon wasn't sure whether to laugh with joy, weep with relief, or go get Sascha riled up to deal with both bewildering emotions.

What he was looking at wouldn't make Veronia rich, but it was an algorithm that would explain *why* the country was poor when it should have been wealthy. It pinpointed exactly where money was going.

As a nation, they had ample mineral reserves, and even had enough gas to have Russia eying them with respect. Their amber deposits outmatched Poland's desirous cache, and on the whole, though the financial tsunami hit everyone from time to time, there was no reason for their sudden plunge in the indexes.

Well, that was yesterday.

Yesterday, there'd been no reason for the money that was leaving Veronia like rats abandoning a sinking ship.

Now?

Well, now was a different matter.

"Devon? Where the hell are you?" Sascha muttered from somewhere within the room.

Only she and Tin ever truly made him curious enough to glance away from his work, and when he heard Tin gurgling too, Devon looked over and saw her peering at his desk and empty chair.

"Cwane, cwane."

"Cruh-ane," Sascha corrected tiredly. "Tin, you can speak Russian. There's no reason you can't pronounce the letter 'R' all of a sudden."

Devon watched as Sascha moved behind his desk and peeked under there, evidently on the hunt for something. Most likely *him*.

"Why would I be under the desk?" he inquired, ever curious about the way her mind worked. Or, that's to say, how her mind worked where he was concerned.

She released a sharp shriek, jumping enough for Tin to go airborne for a few seconds before she grabbed him and hauled him close to her chest. "Devon!" she bit off, her eyes on fire as she stalked over to him, then, when she saw where he was sitting, she rolled her eyes. "You've been there all night, haven't you? That's why I couldn't find you."

"I didn't hear you," he replied instead. "When did you try to find me?"

"Twice last night," she answered dryly and, dumping Tin on his lap —his computer be damned—crouched beside him. "There a reason you've found a den here?"

He shrugged, watching as Tin reached for one of his last creations and began to pluck the crane apart. "It's warm here."

His office had a large fireplace that was sheltered by a fireguard. Next to it was a grandfather clock, but the floor had a fitted carpet, and he'd found himself a comfortable nook between both. Evidently, the fireguard hid him from the rest of the room, especially, he thought as he scanned the other pieces of furniture, with the sofa and armchairs positioned in that specific way.

Making a mental note, because it was always good to hide out from Sawyer if he was on the warpath, he reached for Tin's fingers and began to fold the crane back together again with his son's digits doing most of the work.

Sascha, shaking her head at the sight, released a 'whoofing' sound as she plunked down on her behind then scooted over so she was next to him.

"Care to explain why there are hundreds of cranes everywhere?" She peered around him. "I mean, there has to be a tree here, Dev."

He shrugged. "I'll unfold them and use them in the printer."

Her lips twitched. "As pleased as I am to know your eco consciousness is still running, mostly I'm just wondering why so many?"

"Because they're easy to make and don't take much thinking."

"And that was what you needed last night?" she queried, humming when he nodded. After studying him for a second, she tilted her head to the side then stared at his computer. "Bad news?" she questioned warily, cutting him a look.

It surprised him that she couldn't read him, but maybe it made sense considering he couldn't read himself. The desire to kiss her senseless warred with the urge to laugh with joy at having figured out a puzzle that had been irritating him for over a month.

Math didn't make him happy. Sascha and Tin did that. Math brought him relief. Where there was order, there was calm, *peace*. Since Sascha had come into his life, there was less peace than ever, and while that didn't bother him, sometimes, it just meant the math had to work harder to calm him down.

"No, good news." He hauled Tin back up to his chest when his son began scrambling down his knees, hunting for more cranes and uncaring that Dev's laptop was resting precariously on his lap.

"Why are you hiding then?"

"I wasn't. I wanted to sit on the floor," he replied.

She frowned. "Okay, so why are you being weird?"

"Am I?" His lips twitched. "I didn't know."

"Weirder than usual," she amended with a laugh, leaning into him and pressing a kiss to his cheek, even as she snuggled into his side.

"Glad to know I offer variety."

"Anything I can do?"

He shook his head. "No. Nothing's wrong. It just took longer than I expected to figure everything out, so it's nice to know it's resolved."

"Will it help the country?"

"Without a doubt. They're hemorrhaging cash for a reason."

Her brow cocked up at that. "They are? Why?"

"Because someone's stealing it from them."

Her mouth dropped open at that, then she blinked, processed the repercussions, and murmured, "Oh, boy. Like embezzlement?"

He scoffed, "Like fraud, embezzlement, theft...it's been going on for a while too. Since the previous king's reign. Over six billion dollars have been laundered out of the country."

"Six billion?" She gasped. "That's insane."

"Then it truly must be, because you're a billionaire. You have billions."

Laughing a little, she muttered, "True, but I didn't steal it. Well, my family might think otherwise, but I didn't, did I?"

"No, you didn't." He pursed his lips. "The systematic shedding of cash like this...it's unusual. I've only ever heard of anything like it in Malaysia."

"Oh, that whole 1MDB thing?"

"Yeah, that *thing*," he retorted dryly. "I'm surprised you know about that."

She sniffed. "I watch the news as well, you know."

"Do you?" He frowned, thinking about all the times he'd seen Sascha watching TV. "I don't think I've seen you watch it once."

She blinked. "You're not with me twenty-four seven."

He blinked back. "No. True. But..."

"But what?" she countered with a huff. "Tin, tell Daddy Devon that he's being a pain in Mommy's butt."

Tin wrinkled his nose. "Daddy Devon, Mommy is being a pain in the butt."

Sascha's mouth rounded into a startled 'O.' "So that's how it is, huh, monster?" She laughed. "I'm the bad guy."

Devon grinned, even though he chucked his son under the chin and informed him, "Life lesson, son. Mommy is always right."

Sascha beamed at him, and Devon felt his heart expand at the sight. The way her smile made him feel was a thousand times better than foiling the plot against the Veronian royal family and the nation's economy.

Yeah, that was how much making Sascha happy meant to him.

She dipped her chin and made to kiss him, but as her lips brushed his, a sudden thunking sound made itself known to him.

Sascha too.

She stilled, her lips a few centimeters away from his—more's the pity—before she twisted her head to the side.

"What was that?"

Devon shrugged. "I don't—"

"Sawyer!"

The panic in Kurt's voice hit Devon hard, but Sascha? She scrambled to her feet, hauled Tin into her arms, and in less than a millisecond was running out of the office and into the hall.

"Kurt? Where are you?" she screamed, and though the sound filled Devon with terror, it also made him begin to freeze with what that could potentially mean.

Sawyer was...

He was heavy.

Heavy enough to make that thunking sound somewhere nearby if he fell.

Sawyer couldn't have hurt himself.

Devon wouldn't allow it.

Sucking in a careful breath, he placed his laptop on the floor beside him. With each move measured, he neatly got to his feet, not scampering the way his woman had, and instead of running like Sascha—because that would only induce panic—he, with more care than usual, wandered out into the hall.

He was just in time to see her running, Tin flailing in her arms as she moved down the corridor to Kurt's office.

Sawyer wasn't supposed to be in there. He was supposed to be with Andrei, wasn't he?

Devon remembered their schedule, because he'd memorized it earlier this week. Sawyer and Andrei were discussing ways to counter the income loss and drive investors back into the nation.

That was what they were discussing.

In Andrei's office.

Not Kurt's.

He inhaled another careful breath, closing his ears to the sound of the house starting to stir.

Knowing they were all inside, knowing they were in the estate, calmed him. Whatever was wrong, Kurt had only shouted Sawyer's name.

He only had to fret about one brother.

Emotions clogged his throat, making him feel like he was going to puke, and even as he wanted to vomit, he could feel the sides of his eyes starting to turn black, and his sight was suddenly limited to a very narrow stream.

That was, of course, when he realized he hadn't taken a breath since that calming inhalation back in his office.

So he breathed a little more and hurried his pace. Just as he did that, Sean and Andrei came winging their way on either side of him. He didn't hear their footsteps, all he could hear was his heart beating, pounding in his ears. Making his body throb with the power of his pulse.

When he made it to the doorway of Kurt's study, he paused there and quickly scanned the room, hoping he'd see Sawyer and Kurt arguing over something.

Instead, he saw his family on the floor. Tin was sobbing. Sascha was too. Sean had rolled Sawyer onto his side so his back was to the door, and he was doing something.

Something Devon didn't quite comprehend.

Because he didn't comprehend, *couldn't*, he twisted on his heel and hurried back to where he'd come from.

He slammed himself on the ground, grabbed his laptop, and focused on the math.

The math never hurt him.

Never let him down.

Never collapsed.

So the math claimed him, and the panic?

It took a hold of him between clawed fingers and fanged teeth and embraced him like a fly in a sticky spider's web.

SIX

TWO MONTHS later

"HE HASN'T BEEN the same since—" She closed her eyes. None of them had been the same since Sawyer had collapsed that day.

Perry squeezed Sascha's shoulder. "It's okay."

"It's the opposite of okay," Sascha rasped, staring at Devon.

He wasn't eating, he wasn't sleeping, and getting him to drink some days was a chore that made getting Tin into a pair of pants look simple.

Devon wasn't her son. Tin was. And yet, her lover required more care than her toddler.

Sucking in a breath, Sascha turned to her friend and muttered, "You didn't have to come here."

"Of course I did. The second you said Tin was bored, I knew Alice would cheer him up. Plus, you know, what with everything going down, it's kind of you to offer us sanctuary."

"Don't be silly," Sascha replied, and she meant it. Perry was helping her get through this crazy time in her life, because, yeah, shit was crazier than ever before, and in a way she couldn't handle. "It's been wonderful having you near. I'm sure you've kept me sane."

Perry sighed and hugged her, and though Sascha wanted to tense up because if she didn't, she'd start weeping, she couldn't reject Perry's affection, not when it was so well meant. So, to stop herself from crying, she focused on three of the loves of her life—two of whom were the reason for her terror...just for different reasons.

Tin was on the floor, cackling as he and Alice built something with blocks before they knocked it down. It was quite cute actually—their small heads almost touched as they made their plans, plotting the best way to make taller towers they could knock over.

Devon was on his laptop, as he always was at the moment. She hadn't even realized something was wrong with him until a few days after—

No. She couldn't think of that now. If she did, the last two months would cascade in her memory, and that was a nightmare waiting to happen.

Hospitals, doctors, surgery, test results, waiting rooms... No. Just no.

She had to believe that things were getting better.

Had to.

Or she'd lose it, and no one needed to see that.

Fuck, being strong sucked.

Perry squeezed her once more. "I met your father a little while ago."

Bitterness filled her. "Took him long enough to get here."

"You can't be mad at him."

"Can't I?" She sniffed. "I think I can. He took his sweet time about it." She pursed her lips. "Sean says he's left Linda—*again*. That's probably bullshit he spouted to get Sean to let him through the front gates."

"We do the craziest things when we're lonely."

Sascha's brow puckered. "I know." She bit her lip. "I miss him, Perry."

Her friend pressed her head to Sascha's shoulder as she slipped an arm around her waist. "He'll be back."

"He doesn't even realize what's happened. Not really. I think Tin has a deeper understanding of what's gone on."

"He's protecting himself."

"I know he is, but things are different now."

"How so?"

"We have a son." She patted her belly. "Only God knows what are in here." Her eyes fluttered shut. "This is so stressful, Perry. I never imagined things could get worse after these past twelve months, but I was wrong. I feel like I tempted fate or something. Did I ask for this—"

"Don't be stupid," Perry scolded sharply, making Sascha jerk in response to the hard tone. "How could you ask for this?"

"You haven't seen the letters," Sascha whispered, and even though she'd vowed to not let the vitriol get to her, her eyes stung with tears. "I don't even know how they get to us, but they do. How can our love cause so much hatred—"

Hatred was an understatement.

Polyamory wasn't a crime, so why was she left feeling like scum when she faced the public's wrath?

"People don't understand what we have. That's okay. They don't have to understand. Just ignore them." Perry blew out a breath. "Love, I'm the queen, and I get shitty letters. I don't have to read them. But I still get them. Haters gonna hate."

"Don't think you can get away with quoting Taylor Swift at me."

Perry sniffed. "I'm not. I'm speaking the truth and you know it. No matter what you do, there's always someone who's not going to like you or what you're doing or the choices you've made. In this instance, you're doing nothing wrong. You're in love. That's it. How can that be wrong?"

But it was easy for Perry to say that. Her secret remained in the shadows. Sascha was glad for her friend, but after two months of dealing with an aftermath that sucked balls, quite frankly, she was starting to regret ever being okay with their secret being out.

As a result, heads were rolling at several newspapers. At her instigation, Andrei had undertaken a hostile takeover that meant three tabloids were now under her estate's control. She could do with them as she wished, and that was a level of power that pleased her because, to be blunt, that was the only thing she could control at the moment—her money, her estate, and through them, she could wreak havoc on those who had wished her harm.

For too long she'd stayed in the shadows, content with being a homemaker, content with staying behind the scenes.

Now?

She refused.

And that was why she was getting the hate mail.

Biting her lip, she turned to Tin, saw he was okay, then turned to Devon, and saw he wasn't. Next, she turned to her biggest concern.

Sawyer.

God, he was so thin at the moment. So fucking thin. Her heart clenched every time she looked at him, and she just wanted to wrap him up, hold him tight. Cling to him and have him cling to her.

Her eyes watered before she rubbed them, and Perry, seeing that, patted her hand. "I'll look after the children."

"Thank you, love," she whispered, drifting off. Devon, at the moment, was a lost cause to her. She could do nothing to ease his pain, his distress.

Sawyer's?

She could make him feel better. Even if, sometimes, she just wanted to cry.

"Ach, nae more tears, lass," he rumbled, sounding grumpy but playful at the same time, yet he surprised her because she thought he'd been napping. He did that a lot now. And when he slept, occasionally, he was so still that she thought...

God, she couldn't think about what she thought.

She squinted at him as she moved toward him, coming to the sofa he'd claimed as his own in the library at the Surrey estate. The second they'd been able to stabilize Sawyer, they'd flown him out of Madela and back to the UK. Instead of returning to the townhouse, however, they'd gone straight to her estate in the country. She'd gotten her wish on that score, but out of the worst possible scenario.

Fuck, she'd live in London forever if it meant erasing Sawyer's pain.

Plunking herself at his side, she watched as Perry gathered Alice and Tin, leaving her with Devon and Sawyer who, now that they were alone, raised his arm with a wince, and tucked it around her shoulder.

"It's all right, lass."

She firmed her mouth because she refused to start sobbing. She was sick of being told it was 'okay' or 'all right' when it was the opposite.

"It is," he chided, pressing a kiss to her temple, rubbing his nose against her hairline, like he was trying to inhale her scent.

God, maybe he was.

Maybe...

"I love you," she whispered.

"God, lass, I love ye. You'll get me through it. Ye know that, don't ye?"

She tugged her top lip down, drawing it into her mouth. The pinching sensation didn't stop her jaw from rattling as she withheld the flood that was threatening to overtake her, threatening to lay claim to her.

"You don't want me there," she whispered.

"Nae, I dinnae."

With a huff, she raised her legs and tucked them to her chest. "Why not?"

"Because I'd prefer to think of you here, with the people I love the most, keeping them comfortable."

Her throat felt thick again and she reached for his hand, sucked in a breath, and whispered, "It'll be okay, won't it?"

"It's got nae choice, lass." He raised their joined hands and pressed his mouth to her knuckles. As she looked into his eyes, saw the love in that gaze that reminded her of a sunny Scottish day on the moors, she tried to ignore the ravages of his illness. An illness none of them had even known about until he'd been rushed to the hospital.

She pushed her forehead against his, missing the sensation of his silky locks rubbing against her skin—that had gone with the chemo.

"I love you," she repeated.

"I know you do."

"I will kill you if you die tomorrow, and don't think I won't make good on that threat. Even if it's impossible. For you, I'll make the impossible happen."

His lips curved. "I know if anyone can do that, then it's you." The smile he gave her about broke her, and she didn't understand why he was being like this.

Her man was a braw bastard. A man who never sat down in the face of a fight. And while he hadn't in this, while he *was* fighting, he was calm. Too calm.

Like he was accepting that he was going to die or something.

Like he was making peace with his fate.

She closed her eyes again as her entire being rebelled at the prospect.

"Anyway, I need to know who's the daddy of these two, don't I?" he teased, making her open her eyes.

She squeezed his fingers until her knuckles ached. "Don't you dare forget that."

A part of her had known that was one reason he was hanging on and that was why she was refusing to go to her sonogram. Irresponsible, maybe, but if she knew, she fretted that Sawyer would have less to hold on for.

And that hurt.

There was her, Tin, and God, Devon. Devon who was taking this even harder than any of them could have ever imagined.

She was losing him to the math, losing him to the chaos that was overtaking him, and she didn't know what to do.

On tomorrow's operating table it wasn't just Sawyer's life on the line, but Devon's too.

"You ken I have to go soon. If Sean clears his throat outside the library any more than he already has, I'm going to be thinking he's coming down with a fucking cold or something."

"Don't joke about that. I don't want your immune system compromised."

He sighed, chucked her under the chin. "Always the worrier."

"Only where my family is concerned."

"You going to let up on your da?"

The question came out of nowhere, and she didn't appreciate it. Then, of course, it resonated.

"You asked him to come, didn't you?"

He dipped his chin. "Wanted you with your family if—"

"Don't you fucking say it," she rasped, pressing the palm of her hand to his mouth. "Don't finish that goddamn sentence or I'll—"

"What?" His lips twisted under her palm. "What will you do, sweetheart?" He sighed. "I love ye."

"I love you." She repeated the words once more, making them a vow, one that he'd have to listen to. One that he couldn't ignore. Licking her lips, she whispered, "After, when you're home, and when you're well..."

He arched a brow. "Aye?"

There was a look in his eye that said that wasn't how it was going to be.

The words nearly choked her, but she managed to get them out. "Will you marry me?"

His head jerked back at that, and he stared at her, mouth agape, as he whispered, "Me? You want to marry me?"

"I could think of no honor deeper than being your wife." She bit her upper lip again. "What do you say? Will you?"

"*You'd* be honored? Lass, I'd lay down my life for yers—"

"No. I don't want you to do that. I want you to fucking live, Sawyer. Do you hear me, goddammit?" The emotion clogging her seemed to disappear as the desire to shake him hit her, and she snapped, "You're going to go into that surgery, and I don't care that the anesthesia might be too much strain for your heart, that fucking heart is mine. *Mine*, goddammit. I'm telling it what to do. It's going to beat. And it's going to carry on goddamn beating throughout the surgery.

"Then, when you're out of there, and they've taken that bastard out, you're going to come home to me, and you're going to get better so we can get married. Do you hear me?"

A smile lit his eyes, and it felt like the first genuine one she'd seen in a while. "I hear ye."

She pressed her hand to his chest. "I'm warning you, Sawyer."

"I can sense the threat from o'er here, lass. I'm listening." He grinned. "I like the idea of this. Shotgun wedding where the bride's holding the groom hostage. That sounds like my style."

"Yeah, it does." She pressed a kiss to his lips. "So, now that you have the invitation, you can make sure you turn up on the day, can't you?"

His top lip quirked up in a smirk that was more like the man she loved. The sight buoyed her, and she knew, over the next thirty-six hours, it would be what gave her the strength to believe that everything *would* turn out okay. Even if that was her least favorite word right now.

Her tongue delved between his lips, flickering there, fluttering. Wanting to taste him, savor him. Not because this was their last kiss, but because ever since the diagnosis, he'd been distant in this way. She wanted to reconnect. Needed to.

She sighed into the kiss, breathing him in, exhaling her love for him. And he did the same. His tongue tangled with hers, he gave her his air, he showed her his love.

She pulled back when Sean cleared his throat one more time and nipped his bottom lip. The kiss hadn't been passionate. It hadn't been about desire. It had been about need and love. Her need for him, her love for him. His need for her, his love for her.

It had been poignant and desperate and, fuck, she...

Pressing her forehead against his again, she whispered, "Don't let me down."

"I've got a wedding to plan," he retorted, making her smile.

"That you do, lad. Because you know I'm shit at organizing stuff," she joked.

He smirked. "Yeah, we had a really shitty housekeeper a while back. Never could organize for toffee. Couldn't have arranged a piss up in a brewery."

She quirked a brow at him. "That so?" A laugh escaped her, one that was genuine this time. "Come on, love. Let's get you to the car before Sean ruptures his throat or something."

He laughed again and the sound made her heart flare with happiness, and to that beautiful sound she clambered off the seat, bent over, and reached for his arm.

He stared straight down her blouse, right at her cleavage, and muttered, "Now that's a sight to come home for."

A laugh escaped her and she cupped her tits, jiggled them, and murmured, "Do what you will with them. You can have them to yourself."

"Until the bairns come," he countered, grinning.

"Until the babies come, that's true. Then I'll have enough mouths gnawing at them without you latching on too."

Another snort, and this time, he accepted her hand when she held it out and she levered him up. Even though he'd lost a lot of weight in such a short span of time, he was still heavy. Still bulky.

It boggled her mind that her health nut could have cancer.

Where, in the rules, did that happen?

He ate healthily, worked out twice a day some days...what more did his body need not to sabotage him?

She gritted her teeth because she didn't want to cry again, not when she seemed to have jerked him from the weird stupor he was in.

Every man and woman faced the end in different ways. Sawyer had been quite zen about it. Almost relaxed. Well, she wasn't about to accept that.

With him on his feet, she helped him over to the other side of the room, and when she opened the door, Sean was there, waiting. He was leaning against a console table in the hall, and his focus was on his phone. The second he heard their steps, his head popped up and he blinked at them.

"Ready to go?"

"Ready as I'll ever be," Sawyer said gruffly.

"Hey, you have something to be excited about now," she chided. "We want tomorrow over with so we can plan."

Sean tilted his head to the side in question. "What's going on?"

"She's going to make an honest man out of me."

Though Sean's brows rose, he just commented, "About time, Sascha. We've been dithering like wallflowers, wondering who you'll make an honest man out of."

She snorted. "I'll bet." She squeezed Sawyer's hand even as she tucked herself into his side for support.

With Sean at his left, they shuffled through the house to the foyer. The library was their favorite room, Devon's too, and unfortunately it was at the other side of the house.

Sawyer, being an asshole, refused to have a wheelchair, so he tended to stay put for hours on end.

The walk took ages at the pace they were going, and when they reached the doorway and she saw their family gathered there?

Her eyes burned with tears once more.

The grand hall looked like it belonged in some kind of historical drama with its glass dome that let in a bunch of light, and a massive table that had been loaded down with family photographs right in the center. The ones of the bitch who'd killed Sascha's parents had been tossed out, replaced with pictures she'd taken over the years, and all around that table were the people who mattered most to her.

Kurt, Andrei, Tin with Alice, and Perry waited off to the side. Her dad was there, as were Hamish and Jacinta. Nobody else mattered except for Devon, and he was in La La Land at the moment. Somewhere she feared he'd be staying if tomorrow didn't go well.

Releasing her hold on Sawyer was hard, but she had to. He was hugged by his family, and his mom fussed over him as she bitched about his dictate that nobody be at the hospital but Sean.

It was a ridiculous rule, one she loathed, but when he'd made the request, tears had been in his eyes, and she'd had to obey.

Even though it killed her to think he'd be going through the pre-surgery checks without her. She'd been through every step with him up to now, and it hurt her something fierce that he didn't want her at his side over the next few days. But it was his request, and what was she supposed to do? Ignore it? Ignore it when the prospect of her seeing him like that had made him fucking cry?

When it was time for them to go for real, she helped him down the steps that were guarded by two grand lions and onto the gravel where the car was waiting.

He grunted in pain as he sank into the passenger seat, then sighed when she leaned in, and muttered, "I have to get better, Sascha. Those tits o' yours are enough to keep a man going."

Her lips curved as she realized where his gaze was directly trained *again*, and she murmured, "I told you. They're yours."

He grunted. "Fucking body. All those years of being damn healthy and for what? Sabotage, that's what it is. My woman's got the best tits when she's got a bun in the oven—"

"Two buns," Sean pointed out when he ducked into the back of the car to drop a bag behind Sawyer's seat.

"Aye, two buns make them even bigger, and I cannae do a feckin' thing aboot it." He smacked his lips, then tipped his head back to look her in the eye. "Love you, lass."

She bit down hard on her lip as she desperately sought composure. It wasn't life-threatening surgery he was going in for, but there could be complications—more so than with a regular patient who was going in to get their spleen removed.

Such a simple operation, but for Sawyer it could be deadly. That spleen was riddled with cancer, and that cancer, if they didn't act fast, could spread. Lord, it might have already spread. They'd be finding that out tomorrow.

"I love you, too, darling," she whispered, which she kept on telling him just as much as he told her. It was like if they kept on saying it, the words would be imprinted on their damn souls. "So very much. More than I know what to do with."

His eyes sparkled, not with tears though. "Fancy a wedding in Gretna Green?"

"On your home turf? Why not?"

He reached for her hand. "Look after him. He doesn't get it."

She tensed. It didn't take a genius to know whom he was talking about.

"I know he doesn't," she muttered. 'Doesn't get it' was an understatement for what Devon was going through.

"Watch him."

"I am. I've been doing nothing but. I watch him more than I watch Tin!" She reached up and pinched the bridge of her nose. "I love him, Sawyer."

"I know you do. And he loves you. He's just panicking, and panic for a man like him isn't something he can just process. So he works. And works. And works."

"I know. I'll try to be more patient."

He reached for her hand and tilted her knuckles just so. When he pressed a kiss there, her heart fucking melted. "Thank ye, lass."

"You don't have to thank me," she retorted, her voice raspy. "He's as much mine as he's yours."

His lips twisted. "I ken that. Now, one last kiss to see me through?"

She pressed closer, not stopping until their mouths were connected. It wasn't what either of them needed—a heart-stopping kiss that would make them burn in the heat of their passion—it was only a peck. A simple, soft kiss that reflected their feelings for one another, but not how magnificent their love was.

But love came in different shapes and sizes, didn't it?

Her love for him wasn't just a grand passion. It was enduring. It was soul deep.

As she pulled back, she pushed her forehead against his and muttered, "Remember my threat?"

"About you killing me if I die? Aye. A man cannae forget fighting talk like that."

"Feel free to flog me into shape when you're home," she countered, some sass in her voice as she pulled back.

"More fighting talk?" He whistled between his teeth. "Now you're talking."

She smiled at him even as she closed the passenger door. When she saw Sean there, waiting on her, she hurled herself into his arms, loving just how tightly he held her.

Fuck.

She needed her quintet of lovers to get her through. How was she going to cope with two of them being AWOL in London and Devon in another world?

Kurt and Andrei were going to have to pick up the slack, and what a slack.

She blew out a breath as she hugged him tight. "Text me every half hour and call me every two."

He snorted at her command. "Bossy boots."

"Get used to it, mister," she growled. "In the bedroom, you can do whatever you want with me. But here? No way."

He pulled back to look at her while keeping a tight hold on her waist so he could stare into her eyes. "You're more fiery than usual."

"Got a lot of feelings I'm dealing with."

"Or not dealing with, as the case may be." He hummed under his breath and loosened his hold on her, letting one hand come up to pinch her chin. "I want to walk you down the aisle."

She smiled. "Gladly."

"We could do a handfasting ceremony afterward," he rasped. "You're the wife of my heart, love, but it would be nice to formalize it. Even if it's only spiritually."

Her eyes flared wide. "I'd love that."

"You would?"

"I would," she confirmed.

"Why did you never mention it before?"

"Because how would I decide whom to marry? This situation has changed things." She blew out a breath. "Sawyer...it felt like he was giving up. I couldn't have that. Where would we be without him?"

Sean sighed, but in his eyes, she saw fear, and if that didn't fuck with her head, she wasn't sure what could. "I know, love. We'll get him there."

"Damn straight we will," she muttered.

"I think he's been in more pain than he's let on."

"More pain?" She pulled a face at him. "He was hiding from the symptoms for months, Sean." Sascha shook her head. "How can someone so health focused be so fucking useless at spotting the signs that something wasn't right?"

He tapped her chin with his pointer finger. "We were busy, lots going on. Sometimes we don't have time to be ill, then, when it's too late—"

"It will never be too late for him," she ground out.

And it wouldn't.

Not if she had to spend every single dollar in her bank account.

She'd dragged surgeons and specialists and doctors—the best in the world—all to England. All to ensure that Sawyer got the best treatment possible.

Sean bowed his head and kissed her, a simple kiss, somewhat like what she'd just shared with Sawyer. "Thank you for fighting for us."

"I will always fight for you," she vowed. "I don't need your ring on my finger for that to be the case."

He smiled, then with one last squeeze, told her, "A text every half hour, a call every two. I have my orders."

"No salute?" she complained when he pulled back.

His lips twisted. "Now you're just pushing your luck."

A laugh escaped her. "But I do it with style."

"That you do."

He rounded the car, his feet crunching on the gravel. When he made it to the driver's door, he paused and looked at her, and she blew him a kiss. He smiled a little, reached up, and caught it. The faint act of whimsy was nothing like her Sean, but they were all reacting to Sawyer's health scare differently.

Most of them, except for Devon, in good ways.

Sean was lightening up—although pulling back from his practice had helped achieve that—and he smiled more, seemed to worry less. It was like the weight of the world had been lifted from his shoulders and he could finally see the woods for the trees. Even if the woods were definitely overshadowed with Sawyer's health scare.

Andrei and Kurt, both of whom spent most of their time alone in their offices, had taken to working in the family room.

She wasn't sure how Kurt managed to get anything done when he needed the quiet to write, but he was managing. He'd pulled back on meetings regarding the film production that needed him to be in the city, and had started holding video conferences in his office. But he refused to leave the estate, and she got it. Both of them wanted to be near her, near Tin, near Sawyer.

As a family, they were pulling closer together. Only Devon was out in the cold, and that not only terrified the shit out of her, it made her feel like she was breaking a silent promise to him.

After Sean blew her a kiss back then ducked into the car, she bit her lip once more and took a step away so she wouldn't be in the path of the vehicle.

When she collided with someone, it didn't surprise her when Andrei murmured, "All will be well."

He didn't know that.

None of them did.

But she replied, "He has no choice in the matter. He will get better."

A faint laugh escaped him as he brushed a kiss to her cheek and wrapped his arms around her waist, pulling her so that she was tighter against him.

The car's engine purred to life, and she watched as the Jag pulled out then started down the long drive that would take them to the road.

She raised a hand and started waving, and didn't stop until the rolling curves of the drive took the sight of the car away from her.

The instant it was no longer visible, she sagged. Kurt was there in a heartbeat, at her front. Between him and Andrei, they propped her up. She shoved her arms around Kurt's waist and pushed herself against him, letting him take her weight, even as she sobbed against his chest.

Her world was mad.

For so long, they'd had peace. Their unit tying neatly together while she was pregnant and for Tin's first eighteen months, then it had just been hit after hit after hit.

The tears burned as they escaped her, tears she hadn't let herself shed when Sawyer was around because he always knew when she was upset, so she let them fall and prayed they'd be cleansing.

Not surprisingly, they weren't.

❖

A COUPLE OF HOURS LATER, feeling a little better for having received a text from Sean that they'd made it to the hospital with no issues, chatting with him after seeing she'd missed his call, and after a small nap that Kurt and Andrei had forced her to take—literally by dragging her to the bed and sleeping with her—she returned to the library.

Devon was still there, in the same position.

She knew he had to use the bathroom at some point, but he never seemed to move. Never seemed to alter his location.

He was always in here, but then, physical location and mental/psychological were two separate entities.

He was here in body, but not in spirit.

She stared at him from the doorway, just as she had earlier, but this time she knew she had to do something.

He was getting worse.

He wasn't the sick one. But somehow, he looked just as bad as Sawyer whose anemia, chemo treatments, and meds made him look like walking death sometimes.

Devon's hair was still shiny, still thick, but it was long and shaggy, falling to his chin in a mass of tumbling waves that hadn't seen a brush or shampoo in—God, was it weeks?

He didn't stink, though, so that meant he had to be showering, but if he ate, she didn't know when.

It was like living with a ghost. Or a mouse. Maybe a mouse because mice ate things in cupboards without telling anyone.

She'd never anticipated that her move to the family estate would be in the shadow of Sawyer's illness and their subsequent retreat from London.

With the news of their unusual household still fodder for the gossip upon their return home, it had been impossible to stay at the townhouse. Here, there was space for the security they suddenly required, and here they could protect their family with cameras and alarms and men patrolling the land. There were walls and gates and long driveways that kept them apart from the public.

Even today, though she hadn't seen them, she knew at the gatehouse, a little building just off the gate that was the demarcation line of her property, that a car would have followed Sawyer and Sean as they surged onto the public road.

It was crazy to think they needed so much security, but they did. And as a result, they were here. In the home she'd been pinning her hopes of a fresh start, a new leaf, on.

She'd gotten her wish, but it hadn't taken a shape of anything she'd wished for.

The day of Sawyer's collapse, they'd learned a few things back-to-back.

One, a severe case of anemia had caused his blood pressure to drop to the extent that it triggered a heart attack.

Her rough, braw Scotsman, who was strong and healthy, muscular from working out so much, had been hiding the signs from them for months. Hell, maybe Sean was right, maybe he'd been hiding from himself too. He'd been doping himself with caffeine tablets because he'd been fatigued, and he'd been pushing himself to work out because he'd thought—

Fuck, a man's pride and ego were as much of a deadly killer as cancer.

He'd been too tired to workout. Too exhausted to train.

And he'd thought it was because he was getting old.

It wasn't.

It was a sign of his sickness.

And only when he'd been hospitalized, after weeks of different treatments, had they learned what was really happening.

He had cancer of the spleen.

They'd been blasting it with chemo ever since, but it hadn't worked. They were removing it tomorrow, and that was only because he was strong enough to survive the surgery. It had been touch-and-go for the past three weeks.

But, for all her man was suffering, Devon was too.

Cancer wasn't eating into him, but his mental suffering might as well be.

She'd always known he was different, delicate in a way and so strong in others, but this? This was proof of just how mentally fragile he could be.

It made her wonder what he'd been like before the guys had met him and they had lived together in their unit of five. Had he been like this then? Maybe he had. None of her guys seemed to find his behavior surprising, which had to mean this wasn't the first time he'd been like this.

Was there a comfort to be found in that? Or not?

Pushing into the room, she stepped toward him. Previously, he'd have watched her, and when she approached, he'd have pressed his hands to her hips, held her close before hauling her onto his lap.

Now?

His focus didn't leave his laptop.

She wasn't sure whether to be offended or not.

Approaching him didn't break his focus, not by one whit, so when she neared the seating area he'd claimed as his upon their move to the house—something that probably hadn't helped his state of mind if she was being honest. Devon liked change less than Tin did, and that was saying something—she plunked herself down on his sofa, grimacing as her back instantly started to ache, and the babies in her belly seemed to grumble with the new position. Getting comfortable with this huge ass stomach was an exercise in torture, her rainbow babies certainly knew how to make Mommy feel good.

Not.

The jolting of the cushions had his attention shifting.

Slightly.

His gaze darted over to her.

Then immediately returned to the screen.

She tugged at the inside of her cheek with her teeth, seeking patience and knowing she was going to have to call on reserves that hadn't been tested in years.

Only with Linda did she have to make sure she didn't lose patience, because if she did, she'd have decked the bitch. Her stepmom was the most irritating person on God's green earth—she made Katrina, Kurt's bitch ex-wife look like a fucking saint, and that really was saying something.

This was going to take levels of calm she wasn't sure she even possessed.

So she pulled out her phone and wriggled around, not stopping until she was comfortable and had stacked three cushions behind her back. Once she made sure her arm brushed his, she settled and opened her Kindle app.

Devon didn't make a mutter at her position, didn't stir, so neither did she. She pressed her sock-clad feet to the coffee table where his laptop was, settled them right next to the machine so that the fan heated her feet too, and began reading a book she'd started a few days ago but hadn't had time to complete.

Every now and then, she'd check to see if he realized she was present, but mostly she stayed absorbed in the book.

With Sawyer so ill, she'd spent most of her time running around after him, then Tin, and then the rest of her men, all while taking more naps, and trying not to puke up everything she ate—not easy when her nose had become so incredibly sensitive that she could have picked out each of her men from a line-up blindfolded.

Life, it was safe to say, had been busy.

In truth, this was probably the first bit of quiet she'd had in months.

Knowing Perry had Tin and Alice, that Sean and Sawyer were at the hospital, and that Kurt and Andrei were still in bed where she'd left them dozing—they needed the Zs as much as she did—had peace settling inside her.

As well as some guilt.

She'd had no time for Devon, and that was the truth of it.

Had no time to just sit here and let him feel her presence.

Well, now she had some.

Not much, but some.

Even if he didn't register her existence, she *was* here, and he needed to know that.

So, she sat there for a good ninety minutes, and only started to move when the daring duo inside her began dancing on her bladder.

Only trouble was, she'd gotten really comfortable. *Really* comfortable. As in, she was amid the cushions and tucked deep inside the cocoon of her own making.

Wiggling off the sofa was a bit of a nightmare with her belly as big as it was, and she had to almost snake her way toward the edge of the seat.

Not once did he move to help her, which was indicative of where he was—deep in the math—until she used her leverage on the table where her feet were pressed to the rim, and her sock-clad foot slipped, kicking his laptop. It jerked to the side and Devon jolted like he'd been shot.

His gaze darted to the computer, then her foot, then he twisted to face her.

She eyed him guiltily. "Sorry."

He blinked. "What are you doing?"

His voice was raw, a rasp. Like he hadn't used it in—

God, maybe he hadn't.

She'd thought he was talking to Sawyer, but maybe he hadn't been.

Maybe no one had heard his beautiful voice since the day of Sawyer's heart attack?

"I need to pee."

Devon frowned. "Why don't you then?"

"I can't get up." She huffed. She knew he was in La La Land, but couldn't he see her stomach?

She'd even told him she was pregnant—

"Why can't you?" But she sensed she was losing his interest since his gaze was starting to drift from her and back to his laptop. Only, when he skimmed a look over her, one that drifted down her body with as much interest as if she were an amoeba and not a woman who could drive him wild, he suddenly froze.

Her belly had gotten in the way of his perusal.

"I can't move with as much agility as I could before," she grumbled. "Being pregnant does that to you," she tacked on, hoping to take advantage of his surprise to keep him engaged.

"You're pregnant?"

God, he really hadn't processed anything they'd told him, had they?

Her brow puckered. "I haven't just gained thirty pounds and all on my stomach, Dev." A huff escaped her.

Damn cheek.

"Pregnant?" he rasped, his eyes wide, and when she looked into them, she forgave him for thinking she was an elephant.

Terror.

There was a yawning pool of terror buried within his blue, blue eyes.

She got it.

For the first time in weeks, she understood him.

She hadn't been able to comprehend how he could shut down when Sawyer needed him, when *she* and Tin needed him. In a way, and maybe it was horrible of her, but she felt like he'd let her down. Let them all down.

But as she stared into those gorgeous baby blues, she understood.

His fear was so strong, it was paralyzing.

And she was bringing another life into the mix.

God help her, he didn't know there were two inside her belly.

Because she wanted to kiss him and make it all better, she knew neither option was the best foot forward. She needed to take this calmly, rationally, and not be stupid about it.

The guys didn't crowd him, and they'd been the ones who'd kept him sane long before she'd come along. So, instead, she reached for his hand and tugged it.

"Help me up. I need to pee."

His brow puckered.

"Am I speaking French?" she muttered. "Or maybe Veronian?"

This time he jerked to his feet and, within a second, she was standing there too. Her bladder instantly protested the new movement and she winced, because being desperate a second ago was nothing to what she felt now.

What these kids could do to her bladder made Tin's antics small fry. She'd felt like a trampoline when she was carrying him. These two? She was sure her organs were a diving board.

Blowing out a breath, she started to hustle toward the door, hobbling with need.

Yeah, sexy.

She hadn't felt sexy in quite a while, not since she'd fainted—

Fuck, these past two months had been such a pain in the ass.

Waiting on news of the test results from Sawyer's initial blood transfusion, which had gone down once they'd learned he was suffering with hemolytic anemia, which was the reason behind his heart attack, she'd leaped to her feet the second the doctor had come into his private room, only to come crashing down to the ground seconds later.

That she was three and a half months pregnant, with twins, had come as a big surprise. That she would be lucky to carry them to term? Another surprise.

Which meant, very likely, within the next twelve or so weeks, she'd be in labor.

Fun.

A hand appeared around her waist, making her jump, and she twisted to look at who the hand belonged to—even if she knew. It just came as a surprise. She'd half expected him to get back to work.

He frowned at her, then looked around the hall. "Where are we?" he muttered. "This isn't the townhouse."

He was only just figuring that out?

What the fuck was it with his brain?

In a hundred years, if he donated his brain to science, they'd still be marveling over it. Not just because of what it could achieve, but that level of self-isolation? Surely it was unusual?

Blowing out a breath, she muttered, "We need to go down there, then take the second left." She pointed straight ahead. "We're in Surrey. The estate. You know, the one that's my birthright?"

Sure, she was being sarcastic, but she needed to piss.

Badly.

"Surrey?" he mumbled like she was still speaking another language, but thankfully, he'd started moving.

As he propped her up, they hobbled down the hall together. He helped her get there faster though, and when she wandered into the first toilet she'd had redecorated since her return, she shut the door in his face and headed off to do her business.

This room had been converted into a full bath instead of just a lavatory. It connected with the bedroom they'd renovated for Sawyer, keeping it on the ground floor so he didn't have to waste his energy going up the stairs—he'd refused to let her install an elevator.

Stubborn man.

So, this bathroom had a little wall made of glass wavy bricks that separated her from the shower, which was then separate from the vanity.

It was all whites and blues and greens, because she'd tried to keep things super masculine for Sawyer. There were expensive fittings here and there, handrails that had cost a fortune because she wanted them to help him without making him feel like he was still in the hospital.

Sawyer and hospitals weren't the best of friends on any given day, but after he'd been locked up in one for weeks after his initial diagnosis?

He'd been going stir crazy, so they'd figured out a compromise.

He could come here where it was quiet and peaceful and be surrounded by his family.

But he'd have to be prepared to transfer to London for any major surgery.

And, in the interim, they had two nurses on staff and a private doctor who tended to him and consulted with the team who was treating him.

Yeah, she was blowing cash like it had gone out of fashion, but what did money matter if it wasn't there to improve the lives of those she loved?

She didn't give a fuck about designer purses and shoes, but Sawyer's comfort? Hell yeah.

Devon, even though he was so dense he hadn't realized they'd moved to another goddamn county in England, who'd been here as long as she had without knowing they were in a different house—how that was possible, she really didn't fucking know—finally showed some ingenuity.

As she finished up, the door opened, and he was there. Helping her roll up her leggings, assisting her to her feet, and lowering the toilet lid before flushing it.

"Having kids isn't sexy, is it?" she muttered, thinking about what he'd just done and how, before Tin, she'd never have imagined letting a dude help her stand up from the toilet.

"I should have realized sooner," he stated grimly, and she cast him a look, saw the tension about his mouth, and knew it was self-deprecating.

"Yes, you should have," she told him softly, not giving him any quarter. "But you realize what's happening now. That's something."

His lashes fluttered and he tipped his head to the side, like he was trying to look away from her and couldn't.

It felt like...

She pulled in a breath.

It was like the chaos of life was pushing him toward the math, but the fact that she was pregnant was somehow a lodestone.

Then, she remembered how he'd been during her pregnancy with Tin.

Like a magnet, always at her side, never too far from her so that he could help.

It was one of the reasons why this pregnancy had been so hard without him. Not only because she was worried about him, but because pregnancy with Tin had been easy because Devon had always been there.

It was weird, she knew, but Devon didn't react like the others. She wanted to be sexy for them, wanted them to still think she was hot, but Devon? It didn't matter. So long as she wasn't covered in baby poop or vomit, he thought she was hot.

He could crouch in front of the toilet, help her up to her feet, eye the stretch marks on her overloaded stomach, and not see them somehow.

He saw her.

Sascha.

The ethereal creature.

Like...almost...he could see her soul and that was what he found sexy and what he loved.

It was remarkably freeing.

She knew her other men adored her, and that even if she felt like a frump, they found her sexy as hell—just look at Sawyer in the car with her tits! Sean, Kurt, and Andrei were just as bad. As they'd fallen asleep, Sascha sandwiched between Andrei and Kurt, their boners had been digging into her side. They always wanted her—not in a way that made her feel pressured. Their attraction for her just *was*.

Even if she didn't get it.

But with Devon? She did get it. He liked her body, whether she was too thin or too fat. He didn't see it somehow.

And maybe that was how his brain worked, compartmentalizing in a way that she couldn't understand, but had to be thankful for.

"I love you," she said softly, twisting away from him so she could wash her hands.

"I-I love you, too." His voice quavered, and she could hear the confusion in it.

What could she do to keep him locked to her?

Her brain tugged and pulled at her memory banks, trying to find a way to hold him at her side.

The only thing she could think of was not to mention Sawyer. He needed to think Sawyer was on the mend. That was where his sanity pivoted.

Yeah, his goddamn *sanity*.

She closed her eyes at the thought, terrified even more that something would happen to Sawyer—

No.

NO!

She couldn't go there.

Keep to the here and now, Sascha, she told herself. There was no point in thinking about the variables. Sawyer's blood tests had come back strong enough for Dr. Davidson to approve surgery. She had to have faith in the millions she was blowing on a medical team that was fit for a league of princes.

When she twisted back around, she saw that haze around his eyes once more, like he was thinking of math again, but math couldn't have him anymore. So she grabbed his hand and plopped it on her stomach.

To tell him there were twins in there or not?

That was the question.

His hand spread out, his fingers seeking the ripe curve of her belly the second his touch connected with her midriff.

Of course, that wasn't enough for him. He tugged at the waistband he'd just helped pull up, shoved it down under her stomach and stared at it.

There were train track stretch marks. Deep and red. No amount of shea butter had done shit for them, and every night she applied it. Wanting to cry when she remembered how Devon had put it on for her before...

He softly touched her, seeming to remember how to massage her here and there. The skin was itchy and tight. She wasn't approaching the explosion scene in *Alien*, but she felt like she was getting there. His caresses helped ease that infernal itch, and she arched her back, loving the feel of him against her.

It made her feel bad when she recognized how she cut off her other guys from seeing this side of her. She handled everything on her own even though she knew they'd drop anything they were doing to help her, but she didn't want them to see her like this.

Devon?

She needed him to see her.

This was as real and as raw as it got between them.

That freaky ass fucker of a brain was what allowed her to let him in.

It was the key to the door she kept closed when she was embarrassed about her body, uncomfortable in her skin. With that door open, she didn't want to have to close it again.

Her bond with each man was unique to them. Each of them gave her something she needed. Be it stalwart strength with Sean, a soothing calm that never failed to bring her peace with Kurt, or logic and rationale from Andrei, and Sawyer, whose catalytic personality prompted her to act. For Devon, it was this. He was a brilliant father, and the only time he'd let her down was these past two months.

"Your back must be hurting," he muttered.

"Like a bitch," she whispered, groaning when he slipped his hands around her waist, and began to rub her there.

She tipped forward, letting herself rest against him as he plied her skin.

When his hands came down to grab her butt, he mumbled, "Do we have any cream? I can't do it right like this."

Ah, her perfectionist.

Her smile was faint. "In the cabinet. Baby oil."

He squeezed her slightly, then reached to open the medicine cabinet. When he'd grabbed what he needed, he also tucked a few towels on the side under his arm and admitted, "I-I don't know where we are."

The shaky note to his voice concerned her. Was she pushing too hard? Or was this the right direction to take?

Something had to give here...just not his sanity.

"Sawyer's room is just off this bathroom," she informed him carefully.

His immediate tension let her know where his mind wandered. He knew. He knew Sawyer was ill and couldn't deal with it.

Inwardly, she raged. He needed to deal with reality, needed to be there for Sawyer...but there was no point in raging.

Raging would only make him seek solace in math once more, and now that she'd chipped away at the ice around him, she needed to carry on with the thaw.

It was a falsehood, but she moaned. It wasn't a pleased moan. It was a pained one.

He was back with her in an instant.

Like she'd known he'd be.

"What is it?" he barked, sounding sharper than she'd ever expected.

"My back twinged," she lied, glad when he hustled her toward another door in the bathroom which led into Sawyer's temporary bedroom—she refused to think he'd be down here much longer.

There was a bunch of medical kits, lots of drawers that were loaded with things the purpose of which she had no desire to understand. Sharps containers, monitors, the whole kit and kaboodle. All of it for her man.

All of it to keep him at ease, comfortable.

With the spleen gone, and another blast of chemo and radiation therapy, the doctors were hoping that would be enough to contain the threat of cancer.

So long as the tumors hadn't metastasized elsewhere, there would be no reason why, with care and time, he wouldn't go into remission.

And he *would* go into remission. Even if she had to bribe God himself, she'd make sure Sawyer didn't leave them.

The thought made her heart pound with resolve. It took away the defeat that had been riding her hard, the fear, the worry. Instead, she was angry. Angry and determined.

Once this was done with Devon, when she helped him open up a little more, she was going to London.

Fuck Sawyer's edicts.

He didn't want her at his side while he recuperated?

Tough shit.

He didn't want her to help him?

Tough shit.

And, she recognized, she was being unfair to all her guys.

Maybe that was why Sawyer didn't want her to see him so weak, because she always did her best to look as presentable as she could.

She could count on two hands when she'd let herself go. In the immediate aftermath of Camilla's death, and back when she'd learned about the truth of her past.

That was it.

You didn't keep a man by looking like shit and never putting out.

And she had five men. *Five* to love. Five to keep, to cherish, to hold.

That came with pressure.

Pressure that, in her own way, she loved, but pressure nonetheless.

If she needed help going for a piss, she really shouldn't just be relying on Devon to help her there.

If she needed her back rubbed, she shouldn't be fretting about Kurt seeing her stretch marks. Or worrying that Andrei thought her ass was fleshy. She shouldn't care if Sawyer wondered if her tits were saggy or if Sean didn't find her as sexy as he used to.

No.

No more.

The doors were going to open wide, and she was going to be the one to blast through them.

Starting with Sawyer.

She would be there when he woke up. His pride and ego be damned.

Just like she'd have to damn hers to hell too.

That revelation took place as Devon helped her onto the crisp, navy linen comforter and shucked her loose gypsy top over her shoulders so he could get to work.

When he started to rub the second she was on her side, she released a breath.

The day had been full of revelations and spur of the moment decisions...why not go for broke?

"I'm having twins."

His hands froze, just as she'd thought they would.

"I understand the math helps you. I get that it keeps you from going crazy, but you're going to be a daddy again. Devon, I need you. We need you. Use the math, let it be your crutch, but don't let it overtake you again. Not like it has been doing."

His hands didn't falter after her initial words, and she wasn't sure if he was going to reply or not.

Then, he rasped, "I don't want it to."

Her brow puckered. "You don't?"

She'd thought, kind of like a diving board, he'd thrust himself into it.

"No. It overtakes *me*." He sighed, and his breath gusted over her spine, making the tiny hairs quiver and stand. But he sounded weary. Exhausted. And she understood that because he looked ill. Ill from no sleep and probably little food.

She closed her eyes and rocked her face into the sheets. The bed smelled of Sawyer, even if there was a faint tinge of medical equipment and disinfectant in the air, and Devon was at her back. She wasn't as happy as a pig in shit, but Sawyer's scent and Devon's touch certainly made her a lot happier than she'd been all afternoon. She rubbed her face into the comforter, taking a deeper pull of Sawyer-fragranced linens, and muttered, "What can I do to stop it? I need you with me, Devon. Please, don't leave me again."

"I don't know what to say, Sascha," he whispered after a while. "I don't know how to let you help me."

"Will the babies do that?"

Tin hadn't worked a miracle, and he was the one who suffered more than her.

He was Devon's mini me. Only the fact that Alice and Perry had been staying with them for the past six weeks had stopped Tin from going ape over his father's state—he was absent but present all at the same time. Tin wasn't used to that. He was used to his father's full attention whenever he wanted it.

They'd had to deal with tantrums galore, and Perry's and Alice's presence had been a Godsend even if it was rotten too.

Edward, George, and Xavier had sent them here with more security to drift around the estate like armed specters in the aftermath of what Devon had discovered.

It had taken her two weeks—with Devon in mental lockdown, and Sawyer under treatment but as okay as he could be in the circumstances —to remember that Devon said he'd found out how the Veronian economy was crumbling.

The news had Andrei spinning into high gear, and ever since there'd been more madness.

A bomb in Madela and an assassination attempt on two Veronian government ministers had been all it took for a state of emergency to be called in Veronia.

Perry was shipped to them a week after they'd returned to the estate. Maybe it wasn't the most sensible place to store a wife who was a queen consort and a daughter who was the future queen, but Sascha was damn glad about it.

Even if, she figured, Perry had twisted Edward's arm hard enough to break to get her way.

If only Sascha could get her own way, could get Devon back onto the road to normalcy. Surely there was something she could do, something she could say—

A kiss was pressed to her side, where her belly was at its most rotund, and she sighed, loving the caress. She arched slightly, letting her arm come around so she could burrow her fingers in Devon's hair. It was thicker than she was used to because it was just one big mass of waves. She wasn't sure she'd ever seen him with hair this long, and she preferred it short on him, especially when it was mostly knotted.

Devon hadn't been taking care of himself, that was for sure.

And the damn thing was, she couldn't take care of him either. He wouldn't let her. You couldn't take care of a ghost, could you?

She'd thought the math was an escape, a pressure valve almost, that he could let out when things were taking over him, rupturing his control.

But the way he made it sound, it was almost like it was a prison or something, and that upset her. That upset her something fierce.

It was all well and good to do something because you loved it and found solace in it, but if it was a trap, a pretty one formed in integers and equations, then it was a cage.

Which meant Devon wasn't free.

The notion had her closing her eyes even as she whispered, "Come back to me, love. Please?"

She didn't want to add to the pressure he was under, didn't want to say anything that would nudge him toward that prison that was his own mind's construct, but she had to say something.

Had to do something.

"You're not a single man anymore, love," she murmured, keeping her voice gentle. She didn't want to cause him stress, didn't want to pile on his responsibilities, just wanted to remind him that there was more to his life than numbers. "You've got Tin, and he misses his daddy so much. You've got me, and you've got these babies, and then there's Sawyer, never mind the rest." She released a shaky breath. "Without you, we're not complete, darling. Can't you see that?"

He pressed his forehead against her oily belly, whispering, "I-I don't know what—"

"You don't have to say anything. Don't even have to do anything. Just try. Try to fight its pull." To her, it sounded like it was like an addiction of some kind. A weird one, to be sure, but that was Devon, wasn't it? Weird.

She blew out a breath. "If you want to go back to the library, I'll show you how. I'm going out in a little while. I won't be home for a few days."

Maybe even a week, or longer. Depending on the results of the surgery.

"W-What?" he rasped, stiffening and surging into an upright position.

"I'm going to London."

"I'll come with you."

Though her heart leaped at his fervent tone, she shook her head, peering at him over her shoulder, stating, "No. You're better off here. I'm going to the hospital."

His eyes flickered. "For Sawyer?"

"Yes." Her hand grabbed his and as they bridged fingers, she let them rest on her belly. "Not for the babies. I've had no complications."

"There are two. Surely—"

"The risks are always higher, Devon."

His eyes clenched closed at that, so fiercely that the muscles tinged white. She almost regretted saying that, fearing that it would push him over the deep end, then he sighed. "You won't leave me, Sascha."

"I haven't gone anywhere, love," she reminded him gently. "You're the one who left me."

He froze, this time with a ferocity that made his stillness from before seem like he'd been fidgeting. Hell, she'd seen statues with more life than he had.

"I'll never leave you."

"You already did," she whispered. "I've been doing this all alone,

Dev. Where were you when I needed help getting dressed? When I was getting ready to speak with the OB-GYN? When I had to—"

"I'm sorry. I'm so sorry," he rasped, leaning over and caging her when his forearms came down to rest on either side of her head so she was locked into him. Unable to see anything that wasn't him.

He brushed her lips with his, even as he rested their foreheads together again.

"I need you, Sascha."

"And I need you, Dev," she whispered. "Always and forever."

He gulped. "I let you down."

"Yes."

"I-I can't promise I won't do it again—"

"I know." And she did. It was distressing to think he could check out on her again, even as soon as in the next hour, but what could she do? She loved him. Flaws and all. Just as he loved her. Flaws and all. If anything, he loved the flaws in her more than the parts of her that were flaw*less*.

It was unfair if she couldn't reciprocate that. But God help her, she needed him with her, at her side, at her back, just as she needed Kurt, Andrei, Sean, and Sawyer.

Without her dream team, she was walking wreckage.

The only person who got it was Perry. Sascha felt more normal recognizing that Perry was just as lost without her men who were still in Veronia, still trying to sort out the fuck up that was going down over there.

Even as she felt for her, Sascha was relieved to note that instead of being more independent when you had multiple men in a relationship with you, if anything, the level of interdependence grew tenfold.

"I don't expect you to come with me to visit Sawyer," she told him, keeping her eyes closed just in case she saw that blankness overtake his gaze like he was checking out on her again. "But I don't want to bring Tin with me, and he needs his daddy," she whispered, because she knew, point blank, Andrei and Kurt wouldn't let her travel without them. "Can you be there for him for me?"

A sigh gusted over her lips. "I have to try, don't I?"

"That's all any of us can do," she concurred. "Just remember him. Focus on him. Not on me, not on any of the others. Just him. He needs you more than any of us. Remember your promise? Back when we were in Germany? You have to be there for him."

This time, she opened her eyes and dared to look at him. He appeared a little pale, a lot shaken, but that was only natural, she figured.

"Love you," he muttered.

"Love you more," she replied, smiling when he got a mulish expression on his face that reminded her of Tin when he was refusing to eat Weetabix for breakfast.

A breath gusted from him.

"You look at me like I can give you the world, Sascha, but I know I can't—"

"You give me your world, Devon," she corrected. "I never asked for the universe. Never asked for the moon and the stars. Just you. With your flaws, with your nuttiness." She shrugged. "So don't deny me you, yeah?"

He bit his lip and nodded, and somehow that felt like the grandest victory of them all.

SEVEN

SHE WAS THERE when Sawyer woke up, and she was there to see his first scowl. It had taken a crazy amount of arguing with Kurt and Andrei to get them to agree to it, especially when they'd been grouchy from waking up without her. As she'd argued with them, she resented being pregnant at that moment, because had she just been herself, regular old one-unit Sascha and not sharing her body with two of their spawn, she'd have just hightailed it to fucking London, damn their opinions.

But, and it was a big ole but, they were in uber protective mode, and she liked that they gave a damn.

She couldn't give Devon grief over his checking out on her then bitch at the men who were there for her through it all.

Still, she won, and, as expected, they were here too. Which meant the room was crowded when Sawyer had insisted it be empty.

He was pale and wan, the exact opposite of the man she was used to seeing who had always appeared stalwart and strong.

This past year, she'd learned a lot about her men and their breaking points, a lot about them that she hadn't come to know in the years they'd been together.

They were her knights in shining armor, but even knights creaked from time to time, didn't they? And she knew she wanted their relationship to be more open. For them all to be able to open up to her, to reveal their weaknesses as well as their strengths.

That was what happened in long-term relationships, wasn't it? The good came out along with the bad.

"Yer nae supposed to be here," he slurred, managing to look pissed off even though he was still doped up.

She beamed at him. "Since when do I listen?"

"You were gonnae. I ken that much."

"You're right, I was going to listen. Then I realized it was a damn fool request you made. Why would you want to wake up without me here?"

He pulled a face. "Damn sight prettier than waking up to his ugly mug, I s'pose," he garbled, then glowered at Sean. "You could have locked her out."

Sean snorted, but he didn't look up from his book. "Yeah, it would have been easier getting Boadicea to back down."

Sascha shrugged. "I'll go to war for any of you."

Sawyer huffed. "I ken that." His hand grabbed hers, and she was careful not to nudge any of the lines coming out of the IV on the back of his hand. "I've watched you go to war these past two months. Should have known you wouldn't let me get my own way."

"Yes, you should have." She sniffed. "Now, the doctor said the surgery went well. It hadn't metastasized, and without that motherfucker they can start a different treatment plan."

He released a shaky breath. "Wasn't sure I'd be waking up today, lass."

"I know. And I also know that's why you didn't want me here. But, you *are* here. You survived, so I won't have to kill you now."

Kurt snorted. "And they say romance is dead."

"It is in our house. At least for the moment." She arched a brow at him. "Now that we're here, I want to talk to all of you. Sawyer, you can zone out, but the rest of you, I want you to listen. If you ever have any symptoms of *anything*, even if it's a fucking cold, I want to know about it. Yeah, you're older than me, and yeah, that means things are going to happen that probably wouldn't happen if I was dating someone my age, but fuck, cancer has no age group. I could be the one in that bed.

"So we need to stop with the bullshit. You don't have to keep up with me, and you certainly don't have to fight your body to make it do things just to prove to yourselves that you can keep up with a younger woman, because the joys of being tied to a younger woman is that she can kick your ass if so required." She glared at them all. "Capiche?"

She got a lot of eye rolls for her pains, but Kurt looked at her, nodded, and murmured, "You're right. Pride and ego and vanity get in the way sometimes, *Liebchen*."

"I know it does," she muttered. "But let your vanity be soothed by the fact that you have a hot piece of tail on your arms. The rest? Just go to the fucking doctor. This sexy piece of ass will kick yours if you don't look after yourselves." Her voice broke, then, after being so strident, she added, "You can leave me. You can walk out of the fucking door, but you cannot die on me. Do you understand?"

Andrei clucked his tongue, and though he'd rolled his eyes at her before, so he definitely deserved a sucker punch, she forgave him when he got to his feet and strolled over to her.

When he crouched before her, his hands came to her belly, and he murmured, "We have plenty to live for. There has been too much death for all of us, *katyonok*. We need to live."

"Yes, we do. Once Sawyer's out of here, when he's in remission because I won't take no for an answer, we will get things back on track."

"Aye aye," Sean mocked, but his eyes twinkled when she turned to glare at him.

"And you, you're just as bad." She pointed her finger at him and stabbed the air with it. "Things are better now that you've quit working with the police force, but I'm here, do you get that? You talk to me. You don't let things boil down to the point where you *break down*."

He nodded, his expression cast into serious lines that made her realize her words had resonated. "It's time for a change for all of us. Surrey will be good for us." He looked around the ward. "I almost forgot how cloying London can be."

She tipped her head to the side, smiling when Andrei rocked forward and pressed his head to her lap. She knew he was tired. He'd been working hard with the Veronian government to help kickstart the economy and fuel a lot of drives that would safeguard it in future, while also creating resources that funded the police force and the army to help them fight the UnReals—a body of rebels who were little better than terrorists.

She ran her fingers through his hair, petting him almost, as Sean muttered, "I like the estate. I didn't think I would. I thought I'd miss how the city is always open, but I don't. I like that there are no sounds outside the house at night. I like that we're mostly alone, our own little world inside the grounds." He shrugged. "I'm surprised by how much better it makes me feel."

No more surprised than she was.

She knew that, originally, her suggestion to move there hadn't been a popular one, but they'd started to come around before Sawyer had fallen ill. Then, when Sawyer needed room as well as peace and quiet, it had been an obvious solution to keep him at home rather than locked in a hospital.

"I'm not itching to stay in London either," Andrei murmured, the words muffled half in her lap.

She snorted. "You can't say that. You're always here and there."

He shrugged. "You can't buy me a helicopter and then not expect me to use it. That would be such a waste."

A laugh escaped her. "True. I just didn't want you to feel trapped." She shrugged. "The money is there to be used. So long as you keep on making me more of it, I figure Tin and these babies will be set for life."

Kurt snorted. "More like four lifetimes. Their great grandchildren couldn't run through all the money in your bank account, love."

"Accurate." She smiled at him. "I'm glad. I don't want them to ever have to worry—"

Sawyer snorted, prompting her to realize he hadn't drifted to sleep. "We need to teach them the value of coin, lass. Otherwise we'll have a bunch of precocious hell spawn wandering around. I cannae be doin' with that. Spoiled heathens." He huffed. "Dinnae worry, I'll keep them on the right track."

That had her sniffing, but she didn't argue. That he was thinking of the future made her entire body feel energized.

"I'll leave you in charge of that," she mock-groused, "but I won't have you complaining if I buy them stuff."

"Ye've gone all these years without spending anything. What's gone wrong, lass?"

"I bought things," she argued, but she knew what he meant.

The money had mostly been sitting around in bank accounts. Sure, if she wanted a new dress or whatever, she bought it, no questions asked, but she hadn't really felt comfortable using it.

Here? Now? She used it. And she used its might like it was a goddamn sword.

She was sick of being told what to do, sick of *reacting* instead of just acting. Now? People danced to her tune or they'd feel her wrath.

Just like those bastard journalists on the papers she now owned.

They'd never write shit about any of her men or her family ever again.

The very thought made her blood boil so she fell quiet, unaware that she looked like she was heading into war and that none of her men wanted to prick her temper. A temper that had become more volatile than ever with the double surge in hormones.

Andrei pressed a kiss to her knee as he rocked back on his heels, and when he looked into her eyes, she blinked, realizing she'd wandered down a mental path she really hadn't meant to revisit.

The past few months had been beyond hard. The last year had been impossible. But, out of that madness, she had her men around her, Tin at home, two babies in her belly, Sawyer, if not *right*, on his way to being so—at least if she had her way—and the entire world knew she was theirs and they were hers.

Hers to goddamn hold. Forever.

❖

"THOSE GLASSES SUIT YOU."

Devon raised his hand to his face and held onto the frames. "They're mine."

Henry frowned at him. "I know. They're on your face." He heaved a sigh. "I don't want them, son."

Devon squinted at him, then turned to his computer. "I'm not your son." Just as he'd started going through the spreadsheet he'd been working on, Tin squealed, and though the spreadsheet interested him, Devon forced himself to look at what was happening.

Despite himself, despite the clouds in his mind he wanted to hide behind, the clouds that protected him from the chaos that wanted to suffocate him, he had to smile when he saw Jacinta was blowing raspberries on his belly.

The disconnect was large, the vast chasm between reality and math was absorbing, but he'd been fighting it. Or trying to.

Working harder, faster, longer hours, all in the vain attempt at liberating himself.

Maybe when he stopped his work on the Hodge Conjecture, maybe when it was complete, it would relinquish its hold on him.

Thus far, it hadn't worked, and only when he'd seen the size of Sascha's belly had he recognized what was happening.

There was a yawning darkness in Devon's mind. Sascha was his only guiding light sometimes. His brothers were, but as Sascha had become his partner, *their* partner, she'd taken over that role. Becoming pivotal.

And he was letting her down.

Not even the math could fight that. Not even the math could shield him from the reality that his Sascha was carrying two babies.

Two more vulnerable creatures who could be injured. Who were being brought into this strange, cruel world where people hurt each other on purpose, where—

No.

He sucked in a breath.

He couldn't think that way.

He stared at Tin, saw his little boy's smile, and let it penetrate the gloom. Tin was another flashlight. Another connection to this world.

He deserved Devon to be present.

Active.

Truth was, it hurt that Tin hadn't already run up to him. Hadn't clambered onto his knee, hadn't done the myriad things that were his usual routine when he was copying Devon's every move.

That told him Tin had grown used to being ignored, and that? Well, it broke his heart.

He was surrounded by people who loved him—well, maybe not Henry. Henry didn't love him, but he didn't loathe him—and that he'd been pushing them away agitated him more than the catalyst for all this.

The prospect of losing Sawyer.

If Sascha and Tin were lights in the dark, Sawyer was the ground beneath him.

Devon didn't think he could live in a world without him, but he couldn't think that way.

Couldn't. Or the numbers would drown him again.

"You all right, son?"

Hamish's question had him blinking as he twisted his focus from Tin and Jacinta to Sawyer's father. Hamish could call him that. He was a son to Hamish. He just wished they'd been his birth parents.

"I've been better," he rasped, honest to the last.

"You look a wee bit better than ye did yesterday," Jacinta replied, candid as ever, her eyes shrewd as they took him in, absorbing every inch. "Ye need to wash yer hair though. Maybe shear it off. Looks like ye may have a rat living in it."

Devon's eyes widened and he reached up, patted his head, and released a relieved breath. "There's no rat in there."

Jacinta snorted. "Glad to hear it. If there was, I'd be shooing you outside and washing you down with the hose."

"I should be grateful for small mercies, then, shouldn't I?"

She laughed. "You've got some sass back. Good to see. Been like a walking shadow since we got here."

Hamish nodded. "Not seen you that way for a long time, lad. Let's keep yer with the land of the living, eh?"

His mouth worked, but no words came out. He wasn't sure what he wanted to ask, didn't know how to verbalize—

But Jacinta knew him well. "He's on the mend, lad. My boy is far tae Scottish to let that bastard disease grind him down."

Devon thought about that. "Scottish people die."

"Sawyer's *tae* Scottish to die just yet. He's got our genes in him," Jacinta said with a sniff. "My grandda dinnae die until he was a hundred and eight! And dinnae get me started on my great great grandma." She whistled, and the sound had Tin giggling and spluttering everywhere as he tried to recreate the sound.

"My parents and grandparents lived for a long time tae—"

Devon's brow puckered. "But..." Then he shut his mouth.

Sheila.

She'd died of cancer.

They didn't need the reminder. They knew they'd lost a daughter, and Devon, even though he was still shaken, knew they couldn't lose a son without it killing something inside them too.

God, they weren't the only ones who'd be unable to deal with losing their son as well as their daughter.

Losing Sheila had nearly killed him. Sawyer?

He blew out a breath.

No, he'd made Sascha a promise even if she hadn't asked it of him. He'd made himself vow that he'd try. That he wouldn't check out on her or Tin, and he couldn't let her down.

Henry was eying him like he'd grown another head which wasn't altogether unusual. Devon shot him the stink eye. "What's prompted your arrival?"

Jacinta snorted, but Hamish shook his head and warned, "Nae in front of the lad, Devon."

Devon hunched his shoulders. "You never came before. Why now?"

It irritated him that Henry was here, to be honest. The last time he and Sascha had spoken, there'd been some kind of inference that Camilla meant less, like she was *nothing* because she hadn't been born.

Like their child didn't matter because they hadn't known her.

Just thinking that made him want to ram his fist into Henry's throat.

But Sascha had told him the only thing she wouldn't forgive him for was killing someone. A throat punch, if maneuvered effectively, could kill someone. And while she and her father had a love-hate relationship, he doubted she'd forgive him for accidentally killing Henry.

"Sawyer called me," Henry muttered, nestling into his armchair and crossing his feet at the ankle. "Said Sascha needed me. So I'm here."

"You haven't been here before," he pointed out.

"I made a lot of mistakes," Henry muttered.

"Damn right you have," Devon retorted. "You're lucky she let you in the door."

His lips twisted. "I don't think she wanted to."

"Sean and I let him in," Hamish mumbled. "Couldnae see him out on the doorstep. We all make mistakes—"

"Aye, ye'd be aware of that more than me," Jacinta sniped. "There's been many a time I'da liked to kick you out onto the doorstep—"

"But you dinnae, did ye?" Hamish chivvied.

"That's because you're good at apologizing."

Devon wasn't sure he wanted to see the gleam in Jacinta's eyes at *that* particular statement. But hell, there was a reason why Hamish was perpetually cheerful, wasn't there?

Clearing his throat, he grumbled, "As long as you don't upset her, you can stay."

"By the looks of things, I haven't been the one upsetting her," Henry countered. "Where's your head been at?"

"Henry!" Jacinta barked, making Tin jerk. He'd stopped fussing with some toys he had in front of him and stared up at Jacinta like he was frozen. "Don't ye dare make comments like that about my boy."

Warmth filled him, as it always did when Jacinta and Hamish claimed him.

Henry frowned. "I didn't say a word against Sawyer."

"Devon's our lad too," was Hamish's gruff retort, and Devon saw that even cheerful Hamish looked annoyed.

That made Devon smile to himself, even though Henry was right. "I've let her down," he admitted.

"It wasnae like you could help it—"

Devon raised a hand at Jacinta's staunch defense. "I'm a dad, Jacinta. I can't be held to the same standards as before."

"Dinnae think I've ever been prouder of ye," Hamish murmured, his eyes wide.

"You can't be proud of me," he reasoned. "I did let Sascha and Tin and Sawyer and all of you down."

"Aye, but yer aware of it. Ye wouldnae have been like that afore."

Jacinta's words had him frowning. "Wouldn't I?"

"Nae. You'd just...I dinnae know..." She pulled a face. "Carried on being a ghost until you weren't anymore."

Hamish nodded. "Ye've come on leaps and bounds, lad."

It felt weird to be congratulated for being a fuck up, but Devon wasn't going to be so easy on himself.

He'd seen the size of Sascha's belly the other day. He'd cupped the curve, held the weight in his hands, and knew how much extra she was carrying. Her feet were swollen, her legs too, and when she stood, she did this odd stretch that made him think her back ached.

On top of that, when he looked at her, he saw little shadows under her eyes, and deep within those beautiful orbs, worse still, he'd seen sadness.

And fear.

She'd been dealing with Sawyer, worrying over him. He was ashamed of himself that she'd had to worry over Dev too, but, and it was a large but, he hadn't done it on purpose. He hadn't actively gone out to hurt anyone. He'd just done what he always had—turtled up when times got hard.

Like a pussy.

But always wasn't *now*. He couldn't continuously do the same things he had before because he was no longer young, free, and single. He was a father. He was a husband. He had responsibilities. And he'd let them all down.

The thought made his throat thick with worry—what if Sascha didn't really forgive him? What if she wouldn't let the babies near him because she didn't think she could trust him?

As his heart pounded, he knew he had no choice. Jerking up into a standing position, he hustled out of the room without another word and retreated to the library where he usually sat.

It was strange to recognize where he usually moved around this estate but, as for the rest of the place, to feel like he'd never been here before. He wasn't sure how his mind had compartmentalized things to that extent, and to him, he didn't think it was an improvement! But it meant he knew his way for once—Jacinta had been showing him around the estate every couple of hours since Sascha had gone to London to be with Sawyer, Kurt, and Andrei on either side of her like scowling bookends.

Together, he and his mother had gone through the different wings and the many rooms, but there were so many parts that it was taking a while, and Jacinta wasn't as young on her feet anymore so she needed a break.

Still, the library didn't require a guide, so he hustled in there and found what he was looking for.

The landline.

He picked it up and dialed Sascha's number—the only number he remembered. When it rang and she didn't pick up, his heart pounded some more, then, the call connected and he heard a chirpy, "Jacinta? Is everything okay?"

Instantly, his pulse settled. "Sascha, I'm sorry."

"Devon?"

"Yes. I'm sorry for being useless."

A sigh gusted down the line. "You're not useless. You're *never* useless, do you hear me?" Now she sounded cross. "In fact, you take that back, Devon."

"Take what back? It's the truth."

"No, it isn't. You're wonderful and you're mine. Do you hear me?"

"I hear you." He gulped and, reaching up, he ran a shaky hand over his face. "Please don't take the babies away from me."

A shocked gasp escaped her. "Devon, what on earth makes you think I'd do something like that?"

"Because I showed you that you can't trust me."

Silence fell at his words, and that compounded his fear that he was right. Then he heard a door close, and some humming in the background made an appearance.

"I didn't want to talk in front of the others, Devon, because if I get mad, they'll tell me to calm down, but I don't want to calm down."

Warily, he straightened his shoulders. "Okay."

"Yeah, not okay, buddy," she growled, and he could hear her feet slapping against the floor like her pace had increased. "Devon Jerome, where do you get these crazy fool ideas, huh? What made you think I'd keep these babies from you?"

"I don't deserve them. Or Tin, or you," he whispered, his tone miserable.

"You made a mistake. A *long* one, granted, and I will pull your hair if you do it again, or if you decide to start being weird on me again, *but* don't for one second think that—" A sigh slipped from her. "I missed you. That's what happened. I missed *you*. It hurt that you were gone, there but not. I missed you so damn badly it made me ache. I wanted to tell you things, wanted to ask you for help, but you were gone.

"I'm not mad that you shut down to protect yourself. I'm not even mad that you did it for two damn months. It hurt me. But I don't think you're crazy, and I don't think you're undependable. These were extenuating circumstances, baby. Sawyer is your lifeline, I know that."

His mouth trembled. "Life happens."

"It does," she agreed softly. "And health scares are a part of life, aren't they? You can't be going into your shell every time something bad happens." She groaned. "I was lucky you didn't really react so badly when Camilla passed, but this was different. I know. Accidents and their aftermath are different than chronic illness, but, Devon, Sawyer's better, except he's going to be having treatment for a long time to come. You know that, don't you?"

"No, I didn't," he admitted. "I guess, if I thought about it, he would."

"Well, okay, now you know. We need to figure out a way to keep you with us, to keep you present."

His throat grew thick with emotions again, and he wasn't sure if he was going to cry or laugh.

That she wanted him present at all made him a lucky bastard. He wasn't sure any other woman would put up with this, put up with *him*, when he was like that.

"I-I'm trying. Tin hasn't been running to me—"

"Baby, he will. He just adapted, that's all. He'll be your little shadow soon enough."

"I don't want to lose that. I don't want to lose you," he rasped miserably.

"And you won't. Even if you turtle up to protect yourself, you won't lose us."

"How can you say that? You don't need—" He blew out a breath. "You don't need another child, Sascha. You have one already, and two on the way."

"You're not a child. You're just you. You do things your way. You do things that are unique to you, and those are things that made me miss you so damn hard I wanted to cry every morning when you weren't there to be with me."

"What things?" he whispered, needing to hear that he wasn't use*less* but useful.

A shaky breath escaped her. "I missed you putting on my shoes for me, and I missed me squeezing your butt when you stood back up again. I missed us having brunch together—remember? You made it a thing because I kept getting shaky at ten when I was carrying Tin. Not that I am this time, but still, I missed it. We had this whole routine down, and I missed that."

He gnawed on his bottom lip. "There's still time."

"There is." She sounded a little brighter at that.

"When will you be home?"

"Probably two days' time. He's doing well, Dev. The surgery went well, and after a little while, maybe two weeks, he'll have his follow up treatment."

Devon gulped. "Will he be okay?"

"We'll make him okay. Devon, you know he needs you just as much as you need him, don't you?"

"Sawyer doesn't need anyone," Devon denied. "He's the strongest man I know."

"He might be," she whispered softly, "but he isn't impervious to illness, is he? He isn't resistant to being lonely or scared. You two are like these twins in my belly. Sure, you might not have popped out together at the same time, but you're connected in ways that few will ever understand.

"If you're reeling from this, how do you think he feels?"

Devon thought about that, then he closed his eyes and asked, "How do I make it up to him?"

"You don't have to. He understands you better than you understand yourself. Just, when he's home, be there again. Tease him and drive him crazy by being you. Drive us all crazy by being you. Please?"

"O-Okay. I p-promise." He couldn't even promise to try. This needed more than just trying. He needed to *act*.

"Thank you. Now, no more silly talk, yeah? No way in hell are these babies not knowing you, do you hear me? You're one of the best fathers I've ever met. Your patience knows no bounds, you're gentle and kind and strong and good-hearted. You made a mistake, Devon, and you're sorry for it—that makes you a good man. Stop beating yourself up over it, and just try to make sure it doesn't happen again."

"That's just it, Sascha," he mumbled. "I-I want to tell you that I won't do it again, that it will *never* happen again, but I can't. I don't know how to stop it."

"Then we need to figure out what to do, don't we?"

"What if there's no solution?"

"There's always a solution, isn't there? Didn't you teach me that?"

"In math, sure, but this is life—"

"No," she interjected. "Life is just one big problem, and my Devon is the best problem solver in the land. We'll figure it out, baby, we'll figure it out together." She grunted. "Shit."

"What? What is it?" he blurted out, surprised by her cursing.

"The daddy patrol has come to keep me in line," she muttered glumly.

"Who?" He stared down at the receiver with bewilderment.

"Kurt and Andrei are like my personal guards or something. If I'm on my feet too long, they start shoving chairs at me." She huffed. "Baby, I have to go, but you can call me any time, and we'll be back soon."

"Okay, Sascha. Be safe and—" He pulled in a breath. "Tell Sawyer I'm sorry and that I'll make it up to him."

He could hear the smile in her voice. "I will, love. Speak soon."

She cut the call first, but he heard her mutter, "Kurt, are you sure you weren't in the Stasi, because you're pretty damn good at—"

Then the line went dead.

He carefully replaced the receiver on the unit and sucked down a deep breath.

She didn't hate him. Well, he hadn't thought she did, to be honest, but he'd been worried something could have changed.

"I didn't mean to scare you."

Henry's voice had him twisting around to look at the doorway where his father-in-law was standing.

Scare him?

Was that what he'd done?

Swallowing, he muttered, "I just needed to make sure—"

Henry raised a hand. "I understand. I overheard. Sometimes, it's our mistakes that define us, Devon, because it's how we overcome them, and how we apologize that shows the type of men we are."

His eyes widened. "Do you really think that?"

"I do, and I pray that Sascha does too, because if anyone here has a lot to make up for, it's me. I've been absent a damn sight longer than two months and with no legitimate reason." His smile was tight. "Maybe we can work toward earning her forgiveness together?"

Devon blinked, took in his father-in-law's earnestness, and nodded. Then, he murmured, "I think I know of a way to make that first step."

Henry raised a brow. "You do?"

"Yes. Want to help me?"

Henry smiled. "I'd love to."

❖

WHEN WARM ARMS slipped around her waist, she sighed. "Didn't think you were coming to bed."

Kurt shrugged. "I got stuck in a scene. Had to finish it or it would have gnawed at me."

"I'll gnaw on something," Sascha teased, then she groaned when he reached down and rubbed her belly.

Fuck, could it really be that that felt better than him rubbing her clit?

A snort escaped him. "That was far too carnal a groan for my own good."

She laughed a little. "I was just thinking that." Sighing, she admitted, "You all must have blue balls."

"Hardly." Kurt grunted. "*Liebchen*, don't worry about things like that. We've been just as stressed as you have, and you're carrying our babies. It's not like—"

She twisted a little in his arms, careful not to jolt Andrei who was beside her. She was trying not to fret over her Russian because he'd come to bed with a migraine two nights in a row.

After Sawyer, she'd admit to being a bit neurotic. Andrei just said it was after a few days of dealing with the lights at the hospital, exacerbated by the night he'd spent there keeping Sawyer company, and she couldn't really blame him for that, could she? Her eyes were strained too.

Still, she'd babied him a little, made him come to bed early by pretending that *she* needed the sleep and couldn't without him.

Devon wasn't the only one she had to treat like a child occasionally.

The thought made her lips twitch.

Men. So impervious to their own weaknesses sometimes. Like purposely attaching yourself to a toddler, only you didn't know that until you were cleaved to one another. While hers didn't have that many brain farts, she still dealt with them from time to time.

"You doing okay?" Kurt questioned, his voice low as he tucked himself into her so that every inch of her back rested in the curve of his body—fuck, that was better than those pregnancy bolster cushions any damn day of the week.

"I am now that I know he's coming home tomorrow." And not to this townhouse either. It was weird being back. Weird because, this had been home for longer than the estate, and yet, she was happier in Surrey. She felt sure her men were too.

Kurt released a relieved breath. "We'll all be happy once the grumpy arse is home. Bet Sean will be too. I slept in that cot last night at the hospital—my back still aches."

She giggled. "Things aren't the same without Old Misery around, are they?"

He snorted. "Nope." His face burrowed into her neck. "This feels good."

"What? The calm before the storm?"

He laughed. "Two babies. I wonder whose fault that is."

She grinned into the darkness. "I wonder if they'll look like one of you."

"That would be cool. Then we'd know who to blame for being too efficient."

"Efficient? You call popping out two babies efficient?"

He shrugged. "One pregnancy, two babies. What do they call it in the shops? BOGO?"

Her eyes flared wide. "They do call it that. Since when do you know what the inside of a grocery store looks like?"

Sheepishly, he muttered, "I googled one."

"Why?"

"Well, I had a murder take place in there, of course."

"Of course." She rolled her eyes. Not that he saw in the darkness. "If it weren't for me, none of you would eat."

"You don't go into grocery stores either," Kurt retorted. "You deliver in."

"I used to. Now there's no point. It's easier to do it from home." She sniffed. "We weren't all born with a silver spoon in our mouths."

"That is very true," Andrei rumbled, making her wince.

"Sorry, love. Didn't mean to wake you."

"I wasn't sleeping. Just dozing."

"Your head still hurting?" Kurt queried.

"Yeah. Like a bitch. But it's better in the dark." He rolled over so she was sandwiched between them once more.

She liked this new habit of theirs. They often sandwiched her between them now. She guessed it was more doable since Devon had been sleeping where he worked, so they'd had more of a chance at being with her in bed. Not that they'd taken advantage of the situation or anything.

Sascha knew Kurt was right—as exhausted as she was, they were too. Dealing with everything had been tough, draining. Just getting through the days had been a slog.

Nestled between them, she sighed, then murmured, "It'll be better when we're back home."

"*Da*," Andrei rumbled. "I miss my home comforts."

"You're the one out of the house more than any of us," Kurt pointed out.

"Not for long."

She arched a brow. "Huh?"

"Not for long," he repeated. "I'm sticking close to home for the foreseeable future."

"Why?"

"Because you're going to pop soon. We'll have two babies to look after. Plus, the world is crazy. I'm tired of it. I want to just be with my family for a little while."

It didn't surprise her he felt that way, but she still had to ask, "You're not doing this for me, are you? I don't need you to stick to the estate if it will drive you crazy."

"There's plenty of work for me to do from home. I might have people come visit me instead of going to them," he admitted. "But I'm tired of traveling. I need a break. This situation with Veronia was more of a mess than I anticipated.

"The second Devon realized what was going on, who the source of the issues was..." He gently shook his head. "I don't want to go back there until things are sorted out, and that's the only place I need to be right now anyway."

"What about Vasily? He's too old to travel," Kurt reasoned. "He'll want to meet the babies."

"I figured that out."

"You have?" She placed a hand on his belly. "What's the plan?"

"I bought a boat."

Her eyes widened then she started snickering. "Are you being serious?"

"*Niet*. I also bought a train."

"Are you kidding me?" she blurted out at the same time Kurt muttered, "Well, Devon will be happy."

Andrei snorted. "I wanted to tie Vasily in knots."

"Why?" she queried. "I mean, he could just use the jet."

"He hates it worse than Devon now. It messes with his breathing. I figured with the train and then the boat across the English Channel, he might consider it an adventure. You know what he's like. If it interests him, then he'll do it."

"I can't believe you bought a train for him."

"For him and Devon, and us, because..."

"Because what?" she prompted, when he broke off.

"Although Veronia is off limits to us for the moment, I figure we'll be visiting a lot."

Her heart warmed at that. "Thank you."

He sighed. "I've seen how close you and Perry have grown over the past two months. And Tin and Alice? It would be cruel to deny them access to one another. This way, we can all travel together, privately, with no issues. Devon's precarious as it stands. I don't want to make things worse by forcing him to get into a plane."

Sascha grimaced—Andrei wasn't wrong. Even if it seemed a bit excessive to her to buy a fucking train, she kind of knew where he was coming from.

He'd definitely gotten better with planes, especially when he knew they were flying private, but to be honest, in this day and age, it was environmentally irresponsible to travel that way all the time.

"Is the train just going to hold your grandfather?" she asked.

He shook his head. "*Niet*."

"This isn't some shady Bratva deal, is it?" she grumbled.

He laughed. "No. I have ideas to use it for freight as well as passenger cabins, but it depends."

"On what?"

"Demand. I haven't looked into it yet."

"Wait, so you bought a train without figuring things out first?" That wasn't like him.

"I just happened to hear that the train was available."

Blinking at him in the dark, she was about to argue when Kurt yawned. "Leave him to it, Sascha. Andrei's so tied up in shady dealings sometimes that he can't see the woods for the trees."

Andrei blew him a raspberry. "It isn't illegal," he argued.

"Sounds weird as fuck to me."

Especially with his grandfather's ties.

"Anyway, even if it wasn't, you know damn good and well that Vasily will use it to transport only God knows what into whichever country he crosses through."

Andrei laughed, and that said it all. Then he confirmed her 'hunch.'

"Yes. I know."

"Incorrigible." She shook her head. "You amaze me sometimes. So moral in some ways, and so *not* in others."

"You wound me," he mocked, then he shrugged. "It is in my blood. One cannot avoid it all the time. I merely offset it with the good things I do."

"What good things?" she grumbled.

"The work we did for Veronia," he countered. "All *pro bono*."

That had her brow lifting. "Seriously?"

"Yes, seriously. I don't need to make money all the time." He hummed. "Speaking of, did you forget about our wager?"

Though she'd have liked to lie, she couldn't. "I didn't, but I haven't done anything for it. My head wasn't in the game."

Which sucked actually. She'd have liked to have a little break before the babies came. And she was still certain she could have made some money on the stock markets.

Andrei clucked his tongue. "I thought you might have, but you're right. We do work all the time."

Kurt hummed. "We do, and we need to change that for the children."

She warmed, deep inside, melting at their care and consideration. "I just want them to know you like I do. I love you so much, all of you, and if you're working all the time, how can they know the real you?"

Kurt squeezed her gently, evidently aware, though they were in the dark, that her eyes had grown weepy. These babies were making her soggy.

"They will know us," Andrei murmured, "but even though you haven't gone through with the wager, which we will hold you to later when you have more time—"

"Because time is what I'll have plenty of when I have two babies to cart around?"

He ignored her interruption, and told her, "So, Kurt and I decided to take things in hand."

"You did?" She frowned. "How?"

"We're going away."

"We are?" She started to get excited, then her shoulders slumped. "But we can't go far. We need to be at the house for Sawyer, plus, I can't fly—"

"We're going to the seaside."

Sascha's brows rose. "Which seaside?"

"Cornwall. Just for two weeks. Sawyer's healing. He can't have treatment just yet. I know it isn't the length of time you wanted, but it will be enough, won't it? Just to calm down and relax? It's near enough to drive, and the place...it's divine. You'll love it."

"You haven't bought a house there, have you?" she inquired warily, something in his voice making her question his too-good-to-be-true offer. Andrei had a habit of using a snake oil salesman's tone when he was pitching something at her, and it had a little bit more of his Russian accent in it because he knew she liked it when she heard his homeland in his words. If that voice came into play, she knew he'd bought something that he wanted her to like.

Like when he'd bought Tin, who'd been a baby at the time, a train set. Not one of the Fisher Price sets, nope, a train set that would easily have fit into their living room. It had been miniature but strangely life size, with bridges and little dolls that manned train stations. She didn't know where the hell he made these deals or where he found them—or why they tended to revolve around trains—but they were often irritating. So, wary? Yup.

He cleared his throat. "It was a very good deal." Ha. Theory confirmed right there.

She smacked his hip. "You're supposed to talk to me before you buy property. I might not like it!"

"It was a bargain, I couldn't resist! Anyway, if you don't like it, I'll sell it." He shrugged. "But it will be nice for a little holiday home. The house is large enough for all of us, it's right on the sea...you'll love it. I promise."

"Have you been?" she argued.

"Well, no. I saw pictures though."

Rolling her eyes again, she decided not to be too grouchy.

It wasn't every day a husband bought a house for a 'holiday home' just so they could stay there for two weeks.

Pressing her lips to his chest, she murmured, "Thank you."

A breath gusted from his lips. "Really?"

Kurt snorted. "I was sure you'd give him a much harder time, Sascha."

"You knew about it?" she groused.

"I know most things," he teased. "I listen."

"So do I, but I'm always in the dark," she complained.

"Never. You're always in the light, that's how you keep track of us."

Well, that was cute. "Charmer," she teased, pleased when he laughed.

"Only for you."

"That was an even better answer," she retorted, sliding her arm over the one he had surrounding her waist. "Guys?"

They both hummed.

"Sawyer will be okay, won't he?" she asked softly, feeling silly for needing the reassurance, but still needing to ask.

"*Da*, Sascha. He knows you won't let him be anything other than okay, and that's what will make him better."

"I'm good, but I'm not that good," she whispered. "I can't heal him."

"No, but you can give him something to strive for. We heard about the proposal by the way," he whispered. "That was a very good thing of you to do. It kept him going. Sean said he talked of nothing else all the way down to London."

Her eyes widened—she couldn't imagine Sawyer getting giddy at the prospect of a wedding. "Really?"

"Really," Kurt assured her.

"He wants to get married in Gretna Green," she whispered, charmed by the idea.

"Why don't we go there instead of down to Cornwall?" Kurt suggested. "Isn't the cottage in Penzance? Land's End?"

"Oh my God, it's a cottage?" she half-squealed, jerking up at the news. "Why didn't you say?"

Andrei laughed. "It was supposed to be a surprise."

"Oops," Kurt mumbled. "Sorry."

Andrei just snorted. "He's probably right, Sascha. Either way, you're talking five hours in a car."

She didn't have to worry over the idea for long. The sooner she could tie herself to Sawyer, the sooner she could threaten him with more bodily harm if he dared get sicker.

Feeling a tad bloodthirsty, she muttered, "Let's do it."

"Well, that sounds grim," Kurt teased, hugging her a little harder to him as he laughed. "What are you planning to do? Marry him or murder him?"

"Murder him if he gets sick again. As his wife, he'll have to listen to me."

Andrei laughed. "Aren't you the wife of all of us?"

That made her heart go boom. "True. I think, if any of you ever get sick, I'll have to get divorced each time just so I can marry you and threaten you with violence." She shuddered. "I know the whole sickness and in health thing is a part of life, but I'd really appreciate it if you all ate the sorcerer's stone."

"Aren't you supposed to touch it?" Kurt mused.

"Touch it, suck it, swallow it, I don't give a shit," she groused.

"Hey, it's the same for us with you, you know?" Andrei rasped, tucking himself tighter into her. "We're nothing without you, *katyonok*. Never forget that."

She pushed her face into his throat. "You never let me forget."

He pressed a kiss to her temple. "A man cherishes his most precious treasure."

And coming from a man with more treasure than King Solomon, that meant something.

She shivered and, in his ear, whispered, "*Ya lyublyu tebya.*" She felt his smile against her cheek as he tipped his head down so he could whisper the same back in her ear.

I love you.

Then, when Kurt sighed, and she knew he was drifting closer to sleep, she murmured, "*Ich liebe dich.*"

He rumbled, "*Ich liebe dich, sehr.*"

She smiled into the darkness, wrapped up in their love in more ways than one, and for the first time in a while, she was excited about what tomorrow, and the days after, would bring.

❖

"IS THIS REALLY WISE?"

Devon shrugged. "It's too late now, and I couldn't say no. How could I? Tin loved them."

Henry sighed. "She's going to give birth to two babies in a very short space of time, Devon. I'm not sure she's going to appreciate—"

"She said she wanted a dog too," Devon muttered. "She specifically said Yorkshire Terriers as well."

"She said too, but she meant 'also,' Devon. For God's sake. She didn't ask for four."

He wrinkled his nose. "How could I say no?"

"You keep saying that," Henry muttered.

"Because it's true. Those puppies fell in love with Tin and he fell in love with them. What was I supposed to do? Leave the other one? And their mother?"

Henry reached up and pinched the bridge of his nose. "She's going to lose her top."

"At some point, I'm sure she will."

"At some point? The second she sees the new additions to the family she will."

His brows lifted at that, but he wasn't averse to the idea. Still, he was surprised Henry was. "You think she'll take her top off in the middle of the drive?"

"Devon, now is not the time to be hyper-realistic. Please, listen to me. We have just enough time to take the dogs back."

Devon folded his arms across his chest. "Look at Tin, Henry. Look at him. The second Sascha does, she'll know I did the right thing."

"We should never have taken him with us."

"In hindsight, maybe not," was all Devon would agree with, but still, he was pretty pleased with their choice.

From one mother to another, Devon felt sure Sascha would understand.

And if she didn't, then Jacinta promised she'd take two if Sascha was too overwhelmed to deal with four.

The puppies' barks were high-pitched and noisy, but Tin squealed back, rolling around with them in a way Devon wasn't sure was hygienic, but he'd read an article about how animals improved children's immune systems.

He could see how.

Tin had been kissing the tiny dogs ever since they'd brought them home from the shelter, and even though Devon kept telling him to stop, Hamish too, Tin wouldn't, and Jacinta just snorted every time they tried.

Henry's reaction was a little disappointing. He'd been okay with the idea until Devon and Tin, walking along that depressing corridor of large, walk-in cages filled with animals craving a good home, had found a nursing mother. The puppies were nearly finished weaning, at just eight weeks old, but the sight of the tired mother, the pups so energetic, had stirred something in him.

She'd seemed so sad. A single mother? Who could blame her?

"We had to keep the family together," Devon muttered, then

shrugged when Henry lifted his arms, mumbled, "Why bother?" then strode off to another part of the estate.

"Devon, ye need to get the mop again."

His nose wrinkled.

This part of babies he definitely didn't appreciate.

With a huff, he strode out of the salon and toward the mudroom. They'd already dragged out different mops and buckets to prepare for the mess that was to come, but the mother, Ilsa, was a very good girl. Hadn't messed in the house once.

To be fair, she was probably relieved Tin had taken over parenting duties on her behalf. She'd been snoozing in the basket they'd bought her most of the past two days.

Grabbing the bucket, the disinfectant, and the mop, he went to fill up the bucket in the sink. It was where, historically, dirty boots would be cleaned, and it came in damn useful.

Only, over the sound of the water, he didn't hear the roar until he switched it off.

"Devon Jerome! Where the hell are you?"

Hunching his shoulders, he grabbed the cleaning materials and trudged out into the hall.

Of course Sascha had returned home when a puppy had messed in the room. And of course he'd missed her arrival. Talk about Murphy's law.

He found his family standing in the foyer, just outside the salon. To a one, they were all standing there gaping in—save for Sawyer, of course, who was in a wheelchair. But even he looked pretty taken aback.

Clearing his throat, he muttered, "You hollered?"

"Four?" Sascha blustered, turning her gaze on him.

"Four?" Sean repeated.

Devon shrugged. "Four."

"Four?" Andrei demanded.

"Do you have a problem with numbers?" Devon countered. "Yes, there are four. They're a family. The mother's in her bed. What could I do? Take a puppy away from her?"

"They're dogs, Devon," Andrei grumbled. "That's what happens."

"Not on my watch. Anyway, look at Tin."

"I am!" Sascha declared. "He's about to jump into a puddle of—"

"Tin!" Devon barked. "What did I tell you? That's not for playing with."

Jacinta bustled out of the doorway and grabbed the mop. "Don't worry, lass, we stopped him from peeing with them."

Sascha squeaked. "Peeing with them?"

"He thought it was a—" Devon winced. "A, well, solidarity thing."

"Four dogs, Devon, Jesus Christ." On her way into the room, Sawyer grabbed Jacinta's hand, and she bopped down to kiss him on the cheek. "Alright, Ma?"

"Alright, son. You okay?"

"Be better if there weren't four rats running around my room."

She snorted. "Don't be daft. Look at the bairn. He loves them. Can't get them to separate. He keeps trying to sleep with the dogs, and trust me, Sascha, I wouldnae discourage him. The second he's in that basket, he sleeps like a charm. I'm half-tempted to leave him there when I find him after he's sneaked in."

Another squeak escaped Sascha. "Dear Lord. My son prefers a dog's basket to his bed."

"Wouldnae you at his age?" Hamish queried, heading into the conversation so he could kiss Sascha's cheek. He leaned over the wheelchair and demanded, "Ye okay, lad?"

"Felt better, Da, but I'm on the mend."

"Good." Hamish beamed at him. "Now then, these dogs might be a wee bit inconvenient, but the laddie's cheered up something fierce."

Stomping sounds came from down the hall, and giggles soon followed as Perry helped Alice down the stairs where she was promptly abandoned as the little girl hurled herself toward Tin and the dogs.

"Take it that means Alice loves them too," was Sascha's glum retort.

"She loves whatever Tin loves," Perry said wryly. "You know that." She leaned into Sascha for a half hug and questioned, "You okay?"

Sascha's eyes widened. "Didn't you think to stop him?"

"Didn't know about it until he came back with them." She shrugged. "He was adamant that he couldn't tear up their home." In a soft voice, which Devon could still hear, she whispered, "I don't think he understands the difference between kids and dogs."

"Of course I do," Devon scoffed. "I'm not an idiot. But they're a family." He lifted his nose in the air. "I wasn't going to be a home-wrecker."

Sascha growled under her breath. "I'll wreck something. You expect me to have three puppies and a dog underfoot while I have two babies and a toddler to care for?"

Kurt cleared his throat. "You've five men to help, *Liebchen.* Plus Jacinta and Hamish aren't going anywhere, are they?"

"Nae without looking at the bairns," Jacinta called out.

"You can't be okay with this," Sascha sputtered.

Kurt shrugged. "Look at Tin."

Devon smiled when Kurt used the same argument he had with Henry. And when Sascha did as Kurt said, her shoulders slouched.

"Dammit," she whispered under her breath, then, shooting him a glare, she muttered, "At least you got Yorkies."

He hid a smile. "I also asked about how much they poop."

EIGHT

"WITH THIS RING, I thee wed. With my body, I thee worship..." With her eyes on Sawyer's, she spoke her vows, her love for him throbbing through each word in the tiny sanctuary that had been the haven for star-crossed lovers since the seventeen hundreds.

Back in the day when couples under the age of twenty-one couldn't marry without their parents' approval, they'd fled north of the border where the Scots hadn't given a damn about parental consent.

If someone wanted to be married, then be married they would.

The First Blacksmith's House was a small, low ceilinged building. It looked like what it was—ancient. And not necessarily in a good way. The walls were rough and tumble, none straight, but they were painted a bright white, and the outside was a little too commercialized for her taste, but even she couldn't deny it was romantic to be in a hearth, in a tiny room, standing in front of a blacksmith's anvil with her men at her back, her family at their sides, as she pledged her troth to the man she loved like millions of other women before her.

Though it was Sawyer's ring on her finger, she knew it wasn't. Each of them had gone out and picked the strange little confection two weeks ago, and she didn't even want to know what it had cost to get the jewelers to create it then and there, with such short notice.

Made up of five separate bands of gold, the bands were shaped like ropes, and each one, was a different color, and there was a tiny little knot, formed with a gemstone, penetrating the center.

The work and detailing were enough to take her breath away, and she loved how it took up such a large space on her finger. What she loved most of all was how she wasn't behind the idea of this design. It was, what the Victorians called, a regard ring. Each gemstone not only represented a feeling or sentiment, but also the initial stood for something. So, the first gem was Labradorite, the second, Onyx, the third, Verdite, the fourth, Emerald, and the final stone, Diamond.

L

O

V

E

D

This was a regard, wedding, engagement, and eternity ring combined. It was a declaration and a statement all in one.

She was, quite thoroughly, taken.

With their vows spoken, the registrar told them to place their hands on the anvil—the heavy metal block where a blacksmith hammered metal—and at the side, the man banged a hammer against the metal until it rang clear—twice.

The noise had, once upon a time, been loud enough to inform the nearby village that someone was wed.

Now, it made her smile as she turned to look at her family.

The ceiling was too low for all her men's good. They were all stooped as they witnessed her marriage to Sawyer. At their back was the wooden fireplace that had forged plenty of fires in its day, and she smiled at her loved ones, happy knowing that they were joyous for her. The only people missing were the dogs who'd been tacked onto the family—some of the guards were stuck making sure the puppies didn't destroy the house. They were a set of four girls, but for some reason, Tin had given the puppies all boys' names, and he refused to call them anything else—so they had a trio named Trever, Alan, and Derek. Guards' names, she'd come to learn. The ones who tended to be with her and Tin whenever they went into the nearby town. To be frank, she was past caring about the names and the dogs. Devon was right—they made Tin happy, and with two babies on the way, she was hoping the pups would make sure he didn't feel displaced.

Sawyer was still weak from his surgery, but he was strong enough to stand now, and strong enough to tuck her into his side and mutter, "There, now you're stuck with us."

Her lips twisted. "Don't you think you're the one who's stuck?"

His eyes gleamed. "You going tae turn into a harpy?"

"You sound like you're looking forward to it."

He grinned. "Looking forward to a future with you, lass. Harpy or no, long as you're there, I'll be having a blast."

With a sigh, she reached up on tiptoe and pressed her lips to his. "When I'm too much of a harpy, feel free to spank me into shape."

A laugh escaped him. "Why d'ye think I'm looking forrard tae it?" His grin was sneaky. "Feel free to boss me around, lassie. I know where my place is."

"Fucking me senseless?"

"You got that right."

The registrar, being a spoilsport, ruptured the moment by gently murmuring, "If you'd like to sign the certificate?"

Though she liked that Sawyer felt bright enough to start talking dirty to her, she knew that was down to the wedding. It really had brightened him up, she'd never have imagined it possible—men hated weddings, didn't they? Seemed like he didn't, and at the registrar's statement, Sawyer practically dragged her down the path the man guided them to. Where, in the corner of the room, there was a table and the document that made all this official.

Mrs. Sascha Bennett.

Her lips twitched as she signed her life into Sawyer's keeping, and Jacinta being Jacinta, took a few pictures of them—Sawyer at her back, Sascha with the pen in her hand. Then Sawyer, of course, kissing her.

The second they were done, she was pulled into hugs from Jacinta, then Hamish, and then her father.

"Congrats, darling," Henry told her, appearing genuine, and though she was still mad at him, he'd stuck around longer than she'd anticipated. Not just for the ceremony, but at the house too.

Warily, she eyed him. "Wasn't sure if you'd approve."

"What? Of them finalizing things? They should have done it from the start. It's clear to anyone with eyes how they feel about you."

She blinked. "Thank you."

"No need. I was never mad about the relationship you've got going on, Sascha," he chided. "Just that I wasn't in the loop. That's all. And yeah, that was my own doing, I know." He blew out a breath. "We're done for real this time, and I was wondering—"

Her brows rose—Sean had already told her Henry had claimed that, but this was the first she was hearing it straight from his mouth. "You broke up with Linda?"

"I did. I knew it wasn't right how every time I made plans to visit you, something urgent would crop up, but...sometimes the easiest path to tread down is one you've already walked." He scrubbed a hand over his face. "I've wasted a lot of time, love, and I don't want to waste anymore."

She stared at him, analyzing his expression, and seeing only sincerity. "Good," she replied briskly. She wasn't about to forgive him, not totally, especially for missing Camilla's funeral, but he was her dad. What was she supposed to do? Stay mad at him forever? "You're welcome to stay with us if you'd like."

"Really?"

He sounded surprised, enough for her to shrug. "In the main house or in one of the cottages. Whichever suits. I'd like my daddy around, especially when these babies get here."

"I'd like to know them," he admitted. "And Tin too."

Because she liked the idea of that too—and hoped Henry's attention would be something else that would keep Tin on the straight and narrow when two babies started taking all the attention off him—she reached for his hand and squeezed his fingers, but he didn't stop there. He lifted hers to his mouth and pressed a kiss to her knuckles.

"You go and enjoy yourselves. Jacinta, Hamish, and I are taking care of Tin."

Her mouth grew slack. "Are you sure?"

"Of course I am. Anyway, it's all arranged."

"I thought we were going to a pub or something?"

His eyes sparkled with the secret. "I don't think the guys have a pub in mind."

Curious, she beamed a smile at him, kissed him on the cheek, then found Tin who was in Jacinta's arms—this had definitely been planned.

She kissed his cheek which had jam on it—somehow, when he hadn't eaten any goddamn jam at all today—and murmured, "See you later, baby."

He kissed her, tugged at her hair, then giggled when Jacinta winked and began to walk out of the room.

When she was left alone with the registrar and her men, she just said, "We're unchaperoned for the rest of the evening. Who feels like rebelling?"

Sean snorted as he strode toward her, slipped his hand around her waist, then began to guide her out of the parlor with a wave of thanks to the registrar.

"Rebelling? Think you're too pregnant for that, love. But we've a nice picnic planned."

"A picnic?" Her eyes widened. "Where?"

"There's a river nearby."

"Please tell me Andrei found it?"

Sean cocked a brow at her. "Why would it be important that Andrei found it?"

She huffed. "Did he or not?"

"He did."

"Phew! Andrei is the most precise, practical, and discerning man I know."

"Thanks, I think," came his retort from somewhere behind her.

"What's that got tae do with rivers?"

"It means he'll have picked one that is perfect for the day." She smiled up at the sky and the sun that was gleaming hotly for them. "Shame we didn't want to get married outside. It's a perfect day for it."

"There'll be plenty of ceremonies in your future," Kurt commented glibly. So glibly that she froze.

"Huh?"

But he just winked at her, and when she got into the SUV that could seat them all *and* Tin, and were instantly followed by their guards, they wouldn't say a damn word about what Kurt had meant. Instead, they discussed some story they'd heard on the radio this morning.

Because it was about Perry and Veronia—her friend had returned two days ago to a country that was still being plagued with issues, but the UnReal threat was currently subdued, which was great for the nation but it would have rocked to have her best friend here today—she couldn't overly complain.

And, to be fair, she was kind of tired, so chatting wasn't that big a deal. It was warm enough to make her feel lethargic, and the passenger seat supported her back just so, especially if she lifted her leg and rested it on the slight ledge that peeped out from the glovebox.

So she was content to let the conversation flow around her as she half-dozed, and when they drove into the countryside, going only God knew where, she enjoyed the sights, satisfied, once more, to just relax as the calm of the moment filled her. After months of stress, it was nice to just be, and the ring on her finger, growing warm from contact with her, felt like a solid weight on her hand. Justification, proof, fact. Three things no one could deny.

She enjoyed the sight of the buildings that morphed into rolling hills, appreciated the heather that flossed the sides of the roads, and the deep green grass that was so bright it hurt the eye. She relished in the daffodils which still bloomed, and cherished the dotting on the field ahead that spoke of cows and sheep in the distance.

When they approached a riverbank, her eyes lit up when she saw a scene straight from a movie. There was a—

She blinked. "How long have you been planning this?" she queried, surprised, because she thought it had all been spur of the moment.

"A week."

The gazebo looked like it was made of wood...and it was large. Large enough to have a kind of sunken seating area in the middle of it. Cushions were piled high, the delicious fabrics the color of jewels, and the food on the table at the very center of that seating area?

She could smell it the second they pulled up and she'd opened the door.

She didn't wait for help in getting out of the car, just unfastened herself, heaved off the seat, and used it as momentum to head over to the gazebo.

It was so much more than she'd expected, especially considering the capriciousness of the weather here.

"You really did put an order in with the weather gods, didn't you?"

she murmured, but she didn't turn back to look at them, instead, she wandered to the gazebo and immediately slipped out of her sandals.

She wore nothing that befit a bride, not really. A pair of white leggings that stretched over her belly and a pretty midi dress that rivaled the cushions for their explosion of colors. She'd covered her hair with a white silk shawl for a mock veil, but that was it. Her men all wore linen pants and shirts with loafers in varying colors—and the theme of their day was that they were relaxed. They didn't need the formality, but it was nice to know the claim was staked.

For everyone.

She hadn't needed the big dress or the huge reception. This, alone, was enough for her.

"Won't people be able to see us as they drive down the road?" Not only because of the road being nearby, but she had to think about crap like that now. People were still interested in her unusual relationship—she didn't want to know how Andrei, Sean, and the guards had made sure no one intruded on their special day. Except the parking lot outside the wedding venue had been empty, and she got the feeling that rarely happened, so she definitely saw their hand at play there.

Sawyer cleared his throat. "I own this land."

Her eyes flashed. "You bought it just for today?"

"Nae, I bought it a long while ago fer a friend I knew from school."

Andrei sniffed. "After you asked me if the land was—"

Sawyer glowered at him. "Aye, I asked yer advice on whether it was a good place, but it's nae my problem. My pal's a dairy farmer. This is all his land, but he let me have my way on this as a favor returned."

"What favor did you give him?" she queried, curious.

"There were a couple of times when things weren't looking tae good for the dairy industry. I just floated him through those tough times."

She smiled, expecting that response, and murmured, "Well, it's beautiful."

"I'm glad you like it," Kurt replied, coming up behind her and lifting her belly in his hands as he pressed a kiss to her shoulder. "Are you ready for surprise number two?"

She laughed but kind of wanted to groan in delight at his taking some of the belly weight off her back. Fuck, that felt good. "Of course. If it's as nice as this one."

Andrei murmured, "I hope so," and before she could say another word, he was down on the ground, on his knees, and in his hand, he held a box.

Startled, she froze in Kurt's arms as she stared at, not only her man, but the velvet box in his hand. It was too big to house a ring, but he opened it and she didn't have to wonder for long as he held it up in offering. Her eyes danced along the pretty chain, which was designed in the same rope style that matched her ring.

"Sascha, you are the love of my life, wife in everything but name. You make me happy by breathing and fill me with joy thanks to the light you've brought to our lives. Will you do me the greatest honor of marrying me?"

Her cheeks turned pink. "Of course I will! But, I mean, I really don't want to go to prison. Orange isn't my color, and I'm a married woman now." She had the papers to prove it tucked in her purse.

"There are many different ceremonies that celebrate a union such as ours," he rasped, his eyes earnest as he stared at her, still on his knees. "It would be my honor that we plan a service for our union."

"I'd love to," she whispered. "When I'm not carrying two kids?" Even now, as charming as this was, she knew she was going to have to pee soon.

Devon, goddamn him, seemed to read her mind. "The farmhouse is just down the way, Sascha. When you need the bathroom, we can take you."

"You did not just ruin my proposal," she groused.

Devon blinked. "You pulled the same face Tin does when he needs to go potty."

Her eyes widened. "I did not!"

"Did too," was his mulish retort.

She huffed, but Kurt squeezed her. "Calm down. He's only thinking of you."

"Yeah, but..." She wrinkled her nose. "Can we get handfasted on the beach?"

Andrei grinned. "If you want."

Then, she blinked. "No." Her mind whirled. "We'll get married in Russia. So Vasily can attend."

His smile widened, deepened, turned warm and wicked and loving. "Thank you, *katyonok*."

She smiled back. "I love him. You know that. He's my family too."

His hand reached for hers and he squeezed it as he got to his feet. When he was at her side, she glanced around and saw that Devon had slouched down on the low sofas, as had Sean and Sawyer.

She tilted her head to the side and inquired, "Are you going to ask me to marry you too? All of you?"

"When you least expect it," Kurt murmured in her ear.

And that had her eyes flashing as she thought about what he meant and, reading between the lines, questioned, "Three more proposals and four more ceremonies?" She laughed. "I think that will make pretty damn certain that everyone the world over knows whom you belong to."

Andrei growled as he loomed over her. "More importantly, *milaya moya*, they'll know whom *you* belong to."

And like she didn't already know the answer to that question, coyly, she queried, "Who?"

As one, like they'd rehearsed it, they murmured, "Us," and Sascha? Well, she couldn't disagree with that, now could she?

And now, darling reader, I welcome you to the future...

PART 2

TIN & ALICE

NINE

TIN

SOME PEOPLE WERE BORN to be regular.

Alice DeSauvier wasn't one of them.

It just wasn't something she was capable of. She tried, I knew, but it just wasn't doable. Everything about her was royal. From her haircut—a cascade of waves that were trimmed to hang just below her shoulders—to her clothes...

Even now, though she was heading into class, a class where other attending students wore slouchy jeans and tees, Alice wore a pencil skirt with a blouse tucked in at the waist. There was no denying that the navy pinstripe did things for her olive skin tone, and the crisp white shirt showcased her figure to perfection beneath a swinging peacoat that gave her a jaunty flair, but she looked like she was about to open a hospital.

No fucking joke.

Especially when I took in the high heels that no woman would wear for class—not unless she was trying to flirt with her professor, at any rate. While that might have been a possibility, I knew her schedule. Her next class, Art History, was taught by a woman, and Alice did *not* bat for the other team.

Not unless things had changed in the last two years anyway...

And I highly doubted that was the case.

Not because I had a big head which, admittedly, I did—literally—

but because of the kind of connection we had. It didn't go away. It couldn't. And I'd tried. Many times. To no avail. But there was just no getting rid of the ties that bound us together. So no matter how much I'd angered her, upset her, or irritated the living shit out of her, I didn't think I'd turned her gay.

As I studied her ass, which swayed thanks to her heels and tight skirt, I whistled under my breath, fully appreciating the sight and, slouching back in my seat, reached for my cell.

As I connected the call, I watched the outer doors to one of Madela's most prestigious colleges swing to a close and settled in for a long conversation, as well as a long wait for Alice's final class of the semester to end.

"Are you there?" My father's face appeared on the screen. Ever serious, his brow was puckered as he stared at me. Dogs barked in the background, like usual, and they made me smile. Mum had a thing for Yorkies and, ever since I was a kid, we'd had a little pack wandering the grounds like they ruled the roost—which they totally did.

"No greeting for the prodigal son?"

"You have to return home to be the prodigal son." My mother's wry voice echoed in the background. "Far as I'm aware, you're not here. If you were then I'm pretty sure the laundry would be overflowing, and the fridge would be empty."

Within seconds, she was there, her warm eyes twinkling as she smiled at me. Sean moved his hand to cover hers which she rested on his shoulder, and the sight, as always, settled something inside me.

Five dads, one mum. Some kids might say two parents were too many to handle, never mind six, but for me? It was perfect, and the love between them all was just a life goal in the making.

"What can I say? I'm a growing boy."

A snort sounded in the background. "Shouldn't you have stopped growing by now?"

"What does laundry have to do with the fridge?"

Sawyer, ignoring Devon and Andrei's remarks, muttered, "What mischief are you up to, lad?"

The gruff Scot's voice had my lips twitching even as I snarked, "It's rude not to be on the screen when you talk to someone."

A sniffing sound was all I heard before Sean grunted, peered over his glasses, and started tapping the screen.

I wasn't surprised when the call disconnected, I just rolled my eyes and waited for him to call me back.

After two minutes of staring at the craggy walls of Casterby College, wondering if Alice was as bored in Art History as I'd been when I'd taken the class, I accepted the call when my phone rang, and found myself staring at the breakfast table as a whole, which meant I'd been put on the big screen, with all of my fathers and my mother in attendance.

Not that it came as a shock.

Breakfast was a big deal in my house. And ever since Mum had made my fathers slow down after Kurt's second heart attack scare last year, breakfast could last upward of three hours.

They all stayed around the dining table, reading papers, grazing on the superfoods Mum shoved down their gullets, drinking tea and coffee. In fact, it was getting to be a ritual, one even I appreciated when I was back home and taking part in the process with them.

Mum said the forced meal had made my most *temperamental* father calm down, but as I stared at Devon, I recognized the familiar exhaustion that was etched into his face.

I didn't suffer with insomnia as badly as he did, but I definitely had trouble sleeping, so I knew how he felt. Our demons were in no way similar. I'd had an idyllic childhood whereas he'd been raised under a storm cloud thanks to an abusive father.

I wasn't necessarily violent by nature, but I truly wished my grandfather hadn't died while in service to the queen just so I could beat the shit out of him. Make him pay for just how badly my father had suffered.

Undoubtedly, Devon would have always had his quirks. But his past, I was sure, had exacerbated them to the point where he'd always be a bit otherworldly.

My mum called him ET, and I could genuinely see that. He was innocent in a way that invited protection, all while being one of the smartest men I'd ever known. I'd been schooled with smart guys, but none compared to my fathers.

They said that children were supposed to be better than their parents. The sum of their strengths and their weaknesses. For me? I highly doubted I'd ever achieve anything like they had.

My mother was an ambassador for several charities, and had dedicated herself to not only international aid groups, but also to opening dozens of shelters around the U.K. All because Devon's and Andrei's mothers had both died in violence wrought from their partners' hands.

Andrei was an oligarch. Perhaps that wasn't his official title, but we all knew that was true. He had power at home and back in Russia. My great grandfather might have died when I was eleven, and his reign might have passed on to someone else, but Andrei still got calls. I'd been there when he'd received some of them.

My naturally calm father had grown angry, which had been like flashing a neon sign over his head and, as such, I always knew when someone from the organization had been in touch. My father handled the stock exchange like it was a finely tuned car. He'd made billions gambling and should have been able to retire in his twenties...he even dealt with Devon every day and all without losing his cool. But the Bratva? That got to him. As well it should, considering it was an illegal brotherhood of criminals.

Sawyer and Devon were Nobel prize laureates, had crafted algorithms which had been fundamental in producing software that reduced cybercrime and, on the regular, came up with bits of math that changed the way mathematicians saw the subject itself.

Then there was Sean. Over a dozen murderers were behind bars because of him, and he and my mum worked together on women's charities, dedicating countless hours to bettering the lives of many.

And last, but by no means least, there was Kurt. The winner of a Pulitzer prize and two Academy Awards...

I didn't have much to live up to, did I? The only thing my family hadn't achieved was world peace—not without trying—oh, and none of them had traveled into space. So, yeah, by comparison, I was hopeless.

I'd long since stopped any attempts at trying to match their brilliance and had decided that being me was all they could hope for. Luckily, my parents didn't give a shit about me being ambitious or making a gazillion on the Exchange. They just wanted me to be happy, which, regardless of all the opportunities I'd had as their child, I actually wasn't.

Oh, sure, I was pleased with what I'd done for the past few years. But happy?

Nope.

It was sickening that the only person who could make me happy was the one who'd made me question *everything*. That person, of course, was the one who'd just sashayed into Casterby College...

"For God's sake, Sascha, don't mother the lad." Sawyer's bark made me realize I'd zoned out. I did that a lot. Especially when I dealt with my parents en masse. Having a conversation between seven people took work. And when my brother and twin sisters were involved, sweet Jesus, getting a word in edgewise was like going for gold at the Olympics.

"She can mother me," I slotted into the conversation, just to watch Sawyer scowl at me.

I smirked at him as he narrowed his eyes even more. The shock of red hair atop his head hadn't faded, and he wore it long, usually in a stubby ponytail, mostly to piss off Sean. Time hadn't been as kind to my other father's hair. Sean still had a lot of it, but no one had a mane like Sawyer's. Even though cancer had kneed him in the balls twice, and he'd lost his hair twice, it still grew back like his feet were in fertilizer.

"What are you smirking at?" he groused.

"I'm the one who gets care packages if she mothers me." I shrugged. "I'm not about to turn those down, am I?"

"Care packages?" Sawyer grumbled some more. "The lad's on the continent, for God's sake. He's not in the Middle East."

My lips twitched. "I was two weeks ago."

My mother's eyes widened. "You'd better be joking, Valentin."

The full name. Ouch.

"I can't say. It's classified."

Devon's head tilted to the side while his eyes remained on the tablet in front of him—the only indication he was interested. "What clearance level?"

A laugh escaped me. "You can know."

Devon hummed. "I'll tell you later, love."

I rolled my eyes, but I wasn't too mad. You couldn't really get mad at Devon. Sure, you could get exasperated, but he'd just look at you like you were from another country and he didn't understand your language, then he'd proceed to ignore you and return to whatever he was doing which, of course, was far more interesting. Still, even though I wasn't mad, I had to chide him. "What's the point of clearance levels if you're going to tell people who'd be better off in the dark?"

"You know how your mother worries, son."

"Don't make out like I'm a nag," came her waspish retort. "My child goes off to only God knows where at the drop of a hat and on the government's tab...you can't expect me not to worry."

Though her concern made me wince, I muttered truthfully, "Don't worry, Mum. That's all over with now."

That caught everyone's attention. Even Devon gave me his focus, going so far as to switch off his tablet to peer at me.

"How is it all over with?" she inquired carefully, and I got the impression she was trying not to get her hopes up, which I understood.

The second I'd told her who'd headhunted me from Cambridge, I knew she'd been terrified. It wasn't like I'd gone on any 'missions,' and it sure as hell wasn't like I was James fucking Bond or something, but I'd definitely traveled on His Majesty's budget.

And what a budget.

If I'd traveled like Bond, I'd have been happy. It had been Ryanair all the way.

Tight arses.

"I mean I have one more mission."

Devon frowned. "Why one more?"

"Because I'm where I should be."

Mum frowned. "But you're in Madela. Why would the Foreign Office send you there?"

Another lie. I hadn't worked for the Foreign Office, but MI6.

Sean sniffed. "I told you he had feelings for Alice."

She shoved him in the side. "Don't start Mr. 'I Know Everything.'"

My lips twitched. "Dad's right."

Andrei cleared his throat. "When Edward pops his clogs, son, she'll be queen."

"The boy's a genius. I think he worked that out for himself," Kurt said dryly.

He wasn't wrong. I *was* a genius. Went through college at fourteen and, at eighteen, after I scored my Master's in Criminology, I'd been hand selected by MI6 where I liaised with the Foreign Office on the regular—see, the best lies were couched in the truth too.

It had helped that my father broke code for them from time to time. Nepotism was definitely at play, but whether or not they'd done Devon a favor, I'd given them their money's worth. And more.

"She's mine," I told them simply. Because it *was* simple. As simple as their relationship. No matter the complications life threw underfoot. "Enough to overlook the fact I'd be a consort to the crown."

Mum pulled a face. "Don't make me the grandmother of the heir to the Veronian throne, Tin. Please."

I sniggered. "But you'd pull it off so well," I remarked dryly, and though I was definitely teasing, I meant it.

My mother had an elegance about her that was undeniable, but more than that, she had the best heart. If anyone could deal with the scrutiny that was about to fall on our family, it was Sascha Bennett.

"You mean it, don't you?" she whispered, her eyes widening.

"I've loved her since we were twelve." The admission came freely now. Freely when I'd been fighting it for so fucking long.

I couldn't even say what I'd been fighting. The future? The past? Overlooking her position had been impossible, and for a kid like me, who'd been raised the way I had?

Living in the fishbowl of the Madelan royal court had felt insurmountable. But after a few years of doing random shit for the government, of working on jobs that had opened my eyes? Yeah, I'd woken up and smelled the roses. Enough that I knew what I wanted. More, I knew to take what I wanted with both hands before it was taken from me.

Grateful that the wounds on my torso, the bulky bandages, were covered by a thick flannel shirt and down coat—it was cold as hell in Veronia's capital today—I focused on my mother's pursed lips. Did she disapprove? Really?

I'd be surprised if she did. Our families were close, had been ever since Devon, Andrei, and Sawyer had worked hard to kickstart the Veronian economy in the wake of a rebellion that had managed to destabilize the country itself.

The DeSauviers' situation was not unlike my own family's. Though everyone knew about my parents' lifestyle, thanks to a news report that had made it public knowledge, which had subsequently gone viral, back when I was a baby, the fact that the Queen of Veronia was shared by the king, his brother the prince, and their cousin, the Duke of Ansian and Lorrena, was still a secret with only a few people in the know. Our family was one of the few groups who knew that truth, and while we were close because of it, that friendship had further been forged over twenty years of trips and shared vacations. We had a holiday home in Madela, built on the Duchy of Ansian and Lorrena's land, for God's sake. Alice and I had known each other since we were toddlers and while, for a time, our relationship had been almost fraternal, my feelings for her now were anything but brotherly.

I tuned into my mother's conversation when she snapped, "Tin, are you listening to me?"

Sawyer frowned. "Are you taking your meds?"

I rolled my eyes. "Of course I am." For once, I wasn't lying. My ADHD was under control for the most part, and though I had been known to skip them, after the 'incident,' I'd been religious in taking them.

Why?

Because I was more introspective of late, and focusing, which was never easy for me, was more difficult than usual.

"I said," Mum grated out, "have you realized what the repercussions are?"

"I repeat, the lad's a genius. Of course he knows." Sawyer's defense of me had me smiling faintly. It was usually the way with them. They all ganged up on her on my behalf.

"Did you know what the repercussions would be when you took on five men?" Her cheeks flushed, but Devon snorted even as the others shot her wry smiles.

"He has a point, Sascha," Andrei told her, his tone droll.

"I know he does, but for God's sake, he's talking about Alice here. You know what she's like."

Devon pulled a face. "What's wrong with her?"

My mother sighed. "She's difficult."

And that was why I fucking adored the shit out of her.

Alice was like no other woman I'd ever come across, and she'd been mine for a long time.

"Anyway, I called for a reason," I stated, interjecting an argument between Sean and Andrei over, what sounded like, this morning's edition of *The Times* and an article they'd just published on the DeSauviers.

"Not just to announce that you're intending on dating the future Queen of Veronia?" Kurt tacked on wryly.

I wasn't surprised at his chilled tone. Very little actually riled Kurt. It was why I found it so easy to talk to him.

He stared at me intently and, so softly that I knew no one else would notice, he dipped his chin in soft encouragement. *Because Kurt knew.*

He'd known for the past two years and, not once, had he urged me to share the truth with my other parents. He'd let me live my life. Had let me make bad decision after bad decision and all without judgment.

Knowing I always had him at my back, I whispered, "Do you remember my gap year?"

Sean blinked. "The year you spent in the U.S.? After you graduated Cambridge? What about it?"

I blew out a breath. "Alice visited the States when one of her friends was getting married. It was a bachelorette party."

Mother frowned, her stare taking in my intent as well as the seriousness of my tone. "So?"

"Well, we hung out for a while." The urge to pull at my collar was immense. But I wasn't wearing a suit, and my T-shirt was actually not restricting me at all. The reason I felt like I was choking was because I knew she was going to kill me.

It was why I'd waited until I was a few thousand miles away until I shared the truth.

"I repeat, Tin, so?" She huffed. "Although why you'd think it necessary to keep something from me—"

"Well, we met up, *hung out*," I interrupted meaningfully, then, when she stared at me some more, evidently refusing to get where I was coming from, I cleared my throat. "It was during that time when I was in Vegas."

"What are you trying to tell us, Tin?"

"We got really drunk one night and..."

"And what?" She laughed, but it sounded a little forced. "You got married in front of Elvis?" She laughed again, but her eyes were kind of wild, like she was just waiting on me to tell her she was talking crap.

But she wasn't.

I gulped. "Well...yeah."

TEN

ALICE

THE SECOND CLASS WAS OUT, I released a deep breath.

This course had been my dad's idea. An attempt to help me settle down but, in my opinion, twenty-three was way too young to settle. I didn't see why I should have to, period, but shit was different when you were the future queen of a country.

Shit was, in fact, *shit*.

There were more rules, more responsibilities. In fact, it never ended.

Ever.

Being at the university was making the dads, as I called them, cut me some slack, but I wished they'd cut me some more. As it was, in Madela, I was on their leash, and I hated it.

I hated Art History even more. Everything about the course, from the reading list to the professor, irritated the hell out of me.

Unfortunately with my education and crappy grades, it was the only course the prestigious college had been willing to accept me in. I was, in more ways than one, a complete failure in my parents' eyes, but they were stuck with me and I with them because I never did anything *bad* enough to be cut off.

Getting Cs and Ds in school, while bad for the family's rep, wasn't exactly execution worthy.

Neither was liking to go to one or two parties every once in a while.

I was rarely in the press, fulfilled every shitty engagement the privy council and my dads insisted upon, and pretty much did as I was told.

Save for my one rebellion. A rebellion no one even knew of. A secret I held to my chest because it was so delicious.

So naughty.

So perfect.

With winter break ahead of me, and Christmas with the folks in the near distance, I'd need to hold onto my secret with both arms. Not because I wanted to share the truth with my family, but because it would keep me sane.

Only knowing that in this, I couldn't be controlled, kept me going. When I thought about how often my father spoke of marital alliances, I relished the knowledge that I couldn't marry who they thought was best for me.

Nobody was best for me unless I picked them, but unfortunately because my choice had national, as well as international, implications, they thought they had a say. And when I said 'they,' I was including the government in the collective.

With a sigh, I packed my cell phone into my purse and grabbed the rest of my crap together. Everyone here was so earnest. All of them with their laptops on, everyone taking notes, everyone staring at the professor with an intent that was so engaged.

Me?

I took a few notes on my cellphone and that was it. I didn't want to be here. I was here under duress, and while I kind of tried, I also kind of didn't. Spoiled? Yeah. But it wasn't my choice to be here. I'd have far preferred to help my dad out in his greenhouse, except that wasn't allowed and this torment was.

As I headed out of the lecture hall, I froze when Professor Granger declared, "Alice DeSauvier, can you stay back, please? I need to speak with you."

Of course, because my name was Alice fucking DeSauvier, the entire student body had stilled. Each goddamn student sucked in a breath that culminated in a silence so shrill, they'd hear it in fucking America. When everyone turned to peer at me over their shoulders, I forced myself not to blush.

Compelling my face to behave was par for the course when you were queen-in-waiting. Sometimes, on occasions like today, I had to dig my nails into my palms, but that came with its own irritation—it stopped me from wanting to rake my nails down the bitch's face.

She couldn't have just said, 'Alice?' Could she? Oh, no. She had to use my full name. Draw attention to the fact she wanted to talk to me, undoubtedly, about my shitty paper on a shitty topic I didn't give a shit about.

Well, she could wait.

As my row emptied, I didn't make a goddamn move until most people had exited the hall. Not just because the nosy bastards would try to listen in, and even though everyone in my classes had been made to sign an NDA by the Guard Elect, our version of the Secret Service, something would always end up in the papers, but also because I could. She was my professor. I was her princess.

If she wanted me to be Alice DeSauvier, then I'd be her all the way to the fucking bank.

As I trudged down the few stairs to the podium and the desk where Granger was waiting on me, I rued the day my daddy, George, had dated the bitch. Mostly because he'd never called her again after the date, and even though in the eyes of the world, I was only his niece, Granger kept making me pay for my 'uncle's' mistake. Far as I could see, he'd been pretty damn smart to coyote ugly the bitch.

"Ms. DeSauvier, did you even read the course directive?" She waggled a printout that was titled, *Rembrandt—The Lost Years*.

"Yes, I did," I told her calmly.

"Well, I'd never have guessed." She pursed her lips. "I didn't ask for you to psychoanalyze Rembrandt, and poorly at that...I asked for you to—"

Before she could continue dissecting my work in a loud voice that had to carry to the few people still slowly exiting the hall so they could listen in on this conversation—seriously, koalas moved faster than some of the students—I raised a hand and stated, "Is there a point to this?" Her eyes flashed and her chin dropped in agitation. She hadn't expected me to bite back. I never had before, but today, I really fucking wanted to.

"Yes," she hissed, "there's a point. This, as it stands, is worth zero points because you didn't read the directive properly."

I shrugged. "Fine."

She pursed her lips again, looking ever more like the prune she was. "Your disinterest in this course shines through everything you do."

"Picked up on that, did you?" I asked dryly.

She ground her teeth—that wasn't the first, nor would it be the last time, that I inspired that particular reaction in someone, so I didn't take offense. "What's the point in your being here then? You're taking the place of someone who'd actually like to attend this class."

That someone might find her tedious lectures interesting, which were recounted in a dull as dishwater voice, seemed highly unlikely to me. But I decided it was prudent not to insult the woman further. She couldn't help being boring.

"Do you have a boss, Professor?" I inquired politely.

She scowled. "What does that—"

"Do you have a boss?" I repeated, interrupting her to enunciate the question clearly.

Her eyes glittered with irritation. "Yes. Of course I have a boss."

"Then consider yourself fortunate. Because you only answer to the Dean and perhaps a board of governors or something. Me?" I pointed to myself with a finger that was tipped with a pristinely manicured nail. "I answer to my father, who happens to be the king. I also answer to a government and a council of royal advisors.

"They insisted I take this course. I didn't want to, but when your boss tells you to do something, you do it, don't you?" At her tight nod, I shot her a tired smile. "Therefore, we have no choice but to make the best of things. Whether or not someone more worthy than myself merits my position in this class, it isn't by royal decree, whereas my being here *is*."

She shook her head. "That's ludicrous!"

"You're preaching to the choir, sister." I reached for the paper she'd been wafting around. "Now, would you like me to rework this or have you given up on me entirely?"

A few moments later, with the paper in my hand, and a weary rebuke to actually read the questions rather than go off on a tangent of my own making in my ears, I headed up the stairs to the exit which was empty save for Andrea, my guard—the only one I permitted to follow me.

Of course, there was a SWAT team in my vicinity—a veritable

battalion of bodyguards that my fathers insisted upon, and while I didn't blame them, equally, I wasn't about to have them in my face. Hovering around me every time I took a goddamn leak.

The second the doors to the lecture hall were closed behind me, I released a relieved breath.

The outer corridor, lined with artwork from the undergraduates' finals last year—anything from Buddhas fabricated out of paper mâché to classics that would give John Turner, Picasso, and Marcus Gregory a run for their money—was thankfully empty. Even though people undoubtedly enjoyed watching the black sheep of the royal family having her ass reamed, most of them didn't want to watch it enough to stick around when school was out. Thank God.

Something would, undoubtedly, appear on Twitter later on, but my secretary was used to that.

As I pondered whether it was wise to give Lucy a heads-up, I headed outside the second Andrea peered through the door, opened it up, then checked out the area. After she uttered something into her discreet earpiece, she nodded at me.

Andrea never smiled, and considering she looked like a stacked Angelina Jolie, I thought that was a damned shame. Her dark eyes were rich as chestnuts, but they were always cool. Always untouched. Even though she'd guarded me for close to five years, we weren't close. She never allowed it and, frankly, I'd stopped caring a long time ago if we couldn't be friends. As it stood, I knew as much about her as I could, because the prospect of being guarded by someone I didn't know was abhorrent to me.

I was in the know where all my personal security was concerned. I'd read all their background reports, and when they opened up, I listened. I knew Yann was having issues with his thirteen-year-old daughter because she wanted to start dating, and I knew Mika's Dad was ill enough to require a permanent move into a nursing home. Whatever I could learn, I remembered. I needed to.

These people were serving me, protecting me with their lives on the line. The least I could do was remember they were more than just guards—they were husbands and fathers, wives and daughters. They had families and friends, hopes and dreams. They were more to me than just a badge—even if Andrea, by being more close-mouthed than a mute, didn't help me out on that score.

My stance was a little unusual, but then, my position was too. My sisters dealt with the fawners and the guys who wanted them only for trophy fucks. Me? People tended to avoid me, and I wasn't about to complain about that. Not when I was only useful for tidbits of gossip people wanted to sell to the press. We were all commodities in our own way, but because I merited more security, I dealt with it less than most. I preferred to be close to my guards, whereas to my sisters, their security was a necessary nuisance.

At Andrea's direction, I stepped toward the glass doors. As I glanced outside, I frowned when I saw the man, his face half shielded by his upturned coat collar, standing on the top step just beyond the entryway to Casterby.

I knew he wasn't a threat because Andrea wouldn't have allowed me to leave the building, but his presence had red flags shooting up around me as I took him in. There was something about him I recognized—that solid jaw that was turned into his coat collar to evade the bitter cold outside, that silky skin that reminded me of fresh cream, and that shock of white blond hair which, in the bleak midwinter sun, couldn't decide whether to refract as silver or gold.

As I stepped through the doors, I called out, "Tin?" If I sounded wary, that was because I was.

Tin had been my best friend up until I'd shepherded him into doing something I shouldn't have done.

He hadn't forgiven me, not that I blamed him. He was my husband, but I'd forced him. And while our marriage had given me a freedom he'd never be able to understand, it had lost me the one friend I had who loved me for me. Who loved me despite the fact I was the Veronian royal family version of Calamity Jane.

His eyes sparkled a bright blue as he turned to face me, and the smile in them surprised me considering the last time we'd spoken, *truly* spoken, there'd been harsh words between us.

The smile made my heart skip a beat and my bones started to melt. He'd always been the epitome of masculine beauty to me, the man I measured against every other.

It had been five months since I'd last seen him at our family's regular get-together in August. We'd all traveled to the Laurela Summer Palace in Northern Veronia and spent twelve days doing whatever we wanted. It was the only time we were permitted a break, and Father never scheduled any engagements during that period.

Tin had shown up during the vacation, and had stayed for a weekend before pleading a work emergency and getting the hell out of Dodge.

He'd barely looked at me in that short time and didn't speak to me once. And God, that had fucking hurt. Just having him close enough to talk to, but so distant he might as well have been in Russia, had been a torment in itself. For him to leave so soon? Every masochistic bone in my body had mourned his loss.

So, while seeing him here was an unexpected delight, for him to be evidently waiting on me came as a surprise.

"Hey, Etta."

My heart went thunk in my chest at the name only he called me.

My royal name was Princess Alexandra, but my family called me Alice. When I registered for classes, I always registered under Alice in the vain hope for anonymity, which lasted only long enough for them to catch a glimpse of me. But to Tin? I was my second name—Lisette.

Which he shortened to Etta, because he said I had a voice that could rival Etta James.

The yearning to go to him was strong. Every part of me wanted to be nearer to him, needed to be close. Even though another part of me pondered over playing it cool, it had been so damn long since he'd called me that, since he'd come looking for me, that I just walked toward him. And when his arms opened?

I started to cry.

I didn't hear it at first.

The soft popping sound.

My ears were rushing with blood as the urge to be close to the man I'd loved since I knew there was more than familial and friendly love had overwhelmed me. But his face?

It morphed from sheepish and welcoming and, wonders would never cease, *warmth* to horrified and...

No. It couldn't be.

Scared?

Why?

"Etta!" he screamed, like I wasn't a few feet away. "Duck!"

He ran toward me, his body tense as he hustled closer, and I twisted around to see if what was freaking him out was freaking Andrea out too. She was always calm under pressure, so I took her as my measure of whether to freak out or not.

Only, when I turned around, I didn't see her.

After a second of scanning, I found her—on the ground.

A bullet between her eyes.

And I screamed until my lungs burned and I had no choice but to allow Tin to tackle me and drag me wherever he saw fit.

ELEVEN

TIN

I'D KNOWN there might be an active threat against her, but knowing of a potential issue and seeing it were two different entities entirely.

I heard the pop, knew what it was, and saw that she hadn't recognized it at all.

Even as my heart soared at the happiness on her face, a happiness that was founded in my presence, everything inside me froze as I saw Andrea, the guard who'd been at Alice's side for years, murdered before our very eyes. I had to wonder why they'd taken out Alice's security when they'd had such a clear shot at her, but even as strategic thoughts flooded my mind, my body reacted to my years of training first.

After screaming, "Duck!" I surged forward, forced her into my arms. The threat came from behind me, so I tucked her into my embrace even as I anticipated the next shot—one I thought would pierce my chest from behind. I accepted my death, welcomed it if it would save her, but fuck, I didn't want to die. Not when she was in my arms. Not when the love of my fucking life had just looked at me like she'd forgive me for all the years I'd left us out in the cold.

Determined that today wasn't going to be our last day, I pushed her toward the hall she'd just left. I felt her freeze as we came to the same level as Andrea's body, but I forced her to move, snarling, "Move, Etta, dammit. We need to get inside."

This wasn't her first brush with violence or death, and I knew that was why she'd frozen up on me, but if we weren't going to be sitting ducks then I needed to move us into the building.

In the end, I hauled her inside because moving a brick wall would have been easier. The second I shoved us into Casterby, a few rapid-fire shots blasted and screams burst from around the campus as people recognized the sound of gunfire and reacted to the active threat that Veronia was known for.

With the chorus of terror and violence, I managed to get us a few feet away from the glass doors, and the second I did, I felt the damp stickiness against my stomach...

Fuck.

Adrenaline could mask pain so, for a second, I wondered if I'd been shot, but after a quick check, I realized some of my stitches had burst. Because that didn't matter right now. I pulled Alice away from me and, cupping her cheeks, snapped, "Etta, I need you to focus. Did you get hit?"

Her bright green eyes were hazy, the pupils tiny pinpricks as she stared into mine without really seeing anything.

I shook her, needing her to get back online. "Etta! Dammit, concentrate."

After a second, she whispered, "Andrea's dead."

"Yes, baby, she is." I ran my hands across her cheeks and smoothed over her jaw until I was cupping the back of her head. "But can you tell me if you were hurt?" I didn't think she was, but until I knew whether she was injured or not, I wouldn't be able to focus on anything else.

"N-No," she stuttered before she pushed forward, not stopping until she was resting against me. This was a side of Etta she didn't really let anyone see. She was the Ice Queen to the media, the princess who had zero fucks to give, and while Veronia loved her because she was their future queen, liking her? I didn't think so. But she was dutiful, loyal, *and* she was beautiful. It was irritating how the latter helped sway public opinion, yet it was true.

This side of her? The side that gave a shit about her people, her staff, who knew their names and as much of their family as they'd share? No one knew Princess Alexandra cared so much. Hell, not even Mum knew how deeply Etta felt. Me? I knew. I knew because the love she had for me was endless. Eternal. How could someone with that capacity for love be cold and unfeeling?

As she butted her forehead into my chest, she whispered, "Someone else died for me today."

I swallowed, well aware she was thinking of that time, in the Veronian embassy in Marrakech, when rebels had infiltrated the compound. Fourteen of the family's security detail had died to spare the lives of the royal family...Etta had been twelve at the time and, that summer, I'd heard our mothers talking about the nightmares she'd suffered in the aftermath.

Even then, I'd had feelings for her. Feelings that went beyond friendship. I hadn't known what to do with them, so I'd just stuck to her like glue, not leaving her to her own devices so she couldn't let her sorrow overwhelm her.

I hugged her to me and whispered, "You didn't ask to be shot at, Etta. You didn't ask to be a target. This isn't your fault. The blame lies with whoever wanted to harm you."

She swallowed, and a shudder washed through her as she huddled in my embrace. Having her so close was bittersweet. It felt so damn good to hold her, to have her here in my arms, but this morning, when I'd landed in Madela, I'd never expected this would be how my afternoon would end.

"Tin? I smell something." She flinched when, outside, there was a rapid flurry of shots, followed by screams that sounded far too close to home.

"They'll have the situation under control soon. You know Andrea wasn't working on her own."

She nodded, then her hands, flat against my chest, began to move. For a second, I thought she was feeling me up, then I winced when she brushed the bandages that were sticky with my blood.

"My God, you were hit!" she shrieked, pulling back to look over me. Her eyes were filled with a terror so thick that I wanted to fucking cry for her, but instead I grabbed her hands, and, holding them firmly in my own, told her, "The wounds are a few days old."

She frowned, but I saw the fear disappearing, fading away as she demanded, "What happened?"

My nose wrinkled. "You know you're married when your wife starts to nag you."

She tensed again and her fear was replaced with wariness. "That's the first time you've called me that."

I shrugged as I reached up and placed my hands on her shoulders. "It's the first time I've wanted to call you that," I admitted.

No man liked to be manipulated, and I knew Etta had led me to the altar. Maybe not kicking and screaming, but she'd planned it. I knew why too. Not just because we'd always had feelings for one another, but because she knew what her fathers were like.

I was surprised the topic of her being married hadn't been raised by Parliament by now, if I was being honest. But she'd used me.

By using the feelings we had for one another, she'd made it so something that would probably have happened in time, instead, became a commodity. She'd cheapened it, and me? I'd had to get away. I'd needed space to come to terms with what she'd done. Not only in regard to our relationship, but for my future too.

Sure, I could have petitioned for a divorce but...

There was always a but, wasn't there?

I hadn't *wanted* a divorce. I knew, just as she did, that her fathers would force her to make a political alliance, and now, after years of sulking, I had to admit I wanted her tied to me.

Tied but suffering from what she'd done.

The choices she'd made.

Fuck, I was a bastard for what I'd put her through. But, in my defense, she'd hurt me. God, she'd hurt me worse than that prick of a rebel had in Turkey.

"I have so many questions," she whispered. "So, s-so many, but I need to know if you're okay first."

Because we both worked the same way, I understood.

But now wasn't the time.

With her more responsive, I needed to get her somewhere safe.

"Little incident in Cizre."

Her eyes widened, and though Etta was shit at most things school related, she'd had a thing about geography since we were little. "Turkey? What were you doing there?"

Now definitely wasn't the time for this conversation so, ignoring her question, I gruffly informed her, "I'm okay. Just got sliced," before I started hustling her along. "We need to move, Etta."

She nodded even as she whispered, "Been a long time since you called me that."

It had been a long time since I'd *wanted* to call her that, since she'd been that to me. I didn't say that as I pulled her toward the nearest door though. Didn't answer at all, just focused on moving her because I needed to get us out of the main thoroughfare.

I had no doubt that her security detail was handling the shooter, and that the gunfire we'd just heard had been from her guards and not the active threat, but that didn't mean we were safe.

The classroom ahead of me was distressingly free of shelter. There was a desk on a dais and the seats were in a hive shape. That was it. The desk was the obvious place to hide, and the obvious place for someone to find us, but I was packing, and I knew Etta would be able to fire one of the two guns I had holstered. The blood on my stomach was starting to darken my shirt—a quick glance told me that—but we didn't have time for me to bleed out.

"The desk. We need to get under it," I told her, even as I winced at the prospect of having to bend down—just getting out of the damn car had been a nightmare.

At my prompt and a gentle push, she ran down the stairs. I followed at a slower pace, grunting with each jarring step.

As I dropped to my knees with a thud, unable to use core control to kneel, she peered out from under the desk and with concern in her voice, questioned, "Are you okay?"

My smile was tight. "I've been better, and I'll be better when your guards have things under control." My brow puckered with pain as I slipped underneath, joining her in the relatively unsafe cocoon.

It galled me to hide instead of heading outside to help her detail contain the threat, but the wound was fully open now—I could feel it. Anything I did would only compromise her safety. It would also have been the height of hubris and ego to think I could help in a situation I wasn't trained for.

My place was best served with Etta. Keeping her contained, protecting her by staying close.

There were no legs to the desk, only solid walls beneath the tabletop, which was more of a curse since I couldn't peer between the gaps between it and the floor.

"What are you doing here, Tin?" she queried after watching me grunt as I tried to get myself situated. Even crouched beneath a desk, fear etched on her face, she looked regal. Like grace personified. Whereas me?

I was bleeding out onto the navy polyester carpet.

I wasn't the right man for her, I knew that, but I was the only man she'd ever have.

"The truth is complicated," I hedged.

She pulled a face even as she drew her knees up to her chest. I was surprised when the seams of her pencil skirt didn't split with the move, but seeing her look so vulnerable didn't sit well with me, and I reached over and rested my hand on her left ankle where a little glimmer of gold twinkled in the faint light.

"You still wear it," I stated, touching the ankle bracelet I'd given her for her eighteenth birthday.

"Of course," she said, surprised at the direction I'd taken.

"I wasn't sure it would survive." The chain was delicate, but it had a small cluster of charms that bobbed at the midpoint—a tiny crown, a quaver, and a small Yorkie terrier to commemorate Hank, the pup she'd had as a little girl—we'd both gotten puppies at the same time, and though I didn't remember why because I was too young, I knew Devon had been behind that scheme. Only he'd bring four dogs home from the shelter without Mum braining him for it.

"It breaks, but I get it repaired." She swallowed then reached for my hand. "Tin, please, explain." Her gaze drifted to my stomach, and the pain that flashed across her face looked worse than the suffering I was actually feeling.

That was how love worked though, wasn't it? I'd seen it time and time again with my parents and Etta's.

I gnawed on my bottom lip for a second then, after a few more, muttered, "You won't like it."

"I don't expect to."

I grimaced. "There was a mission breach last week. I'm only a desk jockey. I'm not supposed to get hurt, but somehow, the group we were targeting found our base and this happened." I waved a hand at my stomach then regretted it. She eyed it again, then me, and started slipping out of her coat. When she'd made a tight bundle, she moved forward and her hands went to my torso, where she pressed down with the coat, stemming the flow of blood.

The pressure was excruciating and holding back the cry of agony took more guts than were already spilling out of me. A choked cry escaped me against my will, and I shoved my fist into my mouth to stanch it.

"A few cuts, my ass," she muttered under her breath.

"Husbands lie to their wives," I choked out, wondering when the black spots would stop dancing around the edges of my vision. "Makes them feel better."

With the pain, and an unhealthy dose of nausea too, there was no way in hell I could go Jack Reacher on anyone's ass. Even if I'd have preferred that to baring all to my wife.

And not in the way I'd expected today to end either.

"Best way to be unmarried is to think you can lie to your wife," she groused, the bridge of her nose pinching as she complained at me but, also, I knew from concern. Not unsurprisingly, she wasn't that great with blood. And my blood? This was undoubtedly her idea of hell on a stick.

That, and that alone, was the only reason I didn't snap at her. My bitterness had no place here at the moment, but it wasn't always easy to let go of a powerful emotion and where Etta was concerned, I'd always gone from zero to one hundred and eighty MPH in the blink of an eye. She just did that to me. Always had.

Always would.

There was no point in snapping, 'You wouldn't divorce me even if I was the biggest bastard in Veronia.' I'd admit to thinking it, because letting go of years' worth of bitterness wasn't easy. But when you almost died, you realized that letting go of negative emotions, relinquishing a hold on things that didn't serve you, was the only way to live.

For years, I'd lived without the woman I loved. I'd cut ties with her. Denying us both of not only that love, but of a friendship that had been forged over decades...

But the truth was, she'd hurt me. She'd used me. And getting over that level of betrayal wasn't easy. Hell, it was pretty fucking impossible.

Her shriek made me realize that I'd closed my eyes, and when I opened them, those black dots were doing more than just sparkling at the edges of my vision, they'd taken over.

"Sorry." My smile was as weak as my voice. A gasp escaped her, and I realized she was silently sobbing.

If that didn't break my fucking heart, I didn't know what could.

"It will be okay," I reassured her, but when her face crumpled, I figured it didn't work.

"Tin?" she whispered.

Blinking at her, I muttered, "Yeah?"

"You know I love you, don't you?"

I sighed. "Sometimes, that's all that got me through the days—"

The sound of the door opening had me tensing. I sat up, jerking myself into a straighter position so I could reach for my weapon. But the agony that speared through me made my stomach rebel. The wave of pain overtook everything else, drowning my senses to the point where I couldn't rely on them to help us.

Frozen, I cast Etta a beseeching look, saw she'd clapped a hand over her mouth to stem any noise she might make, but the terror in her eyes would stay with me until the day I died.

I just really fucking hoped that today wasn't that day.

I sagged back, my body acting of its own volition, and muttered, "Get my guns. They're holstered. Shoulder," I slurred, "and my left ankle."

I tried to stay conscious, I tried so hard to focus on the pain to the point where it would make me aware. But it was like a blanket. It encompassed everything. Drowning my world in nothingness.

I needed to protect her. But my body wasn't going to let me.

Not sure of what would happen next, and feeling like my tongue was as thick as a slug, I managed to whisper, "Love you, Etta," before everything went blank.

TWELVE

ETTA

THE SECOND TIN PASSED OUT, the tension in his body disappearing like it had never existed, I felt certain he'd died.

I stared at him with unseeing eyes because his stillness was terrifying, and then I heard the faint whisper of someone's footsteps and I knew, just like Tin had, that if it had been one of my detail, they'd have announced themselves. Which meant, God help us, that the person approaching us was an enemy.

Someone who'd killed Andrea.

Who was here either to kill me or to take me captive.

With my lungs burning, and wondering where the fuck my security was because we trained for this way too often, and it was all going wrong, I dug my hand into my mouth to stem the sobs that longed to break free. But even as I sobbed, I knew I needed to get to the guns Tin was armed with and use the damn things.

Slipping my top lip between my teeth, I bit down, not stopping until the pain was so acute, my brain focused on that rather than Tin and his limp form.

Knowing I had to protect him when I heard those footsteps move ever closer, I forced myself to touch his stillness. Blood seeped through my coat, drenching it even as I found his holster. The need to press down on his wound was unabating, but I had to keep us safe. When I found his other gun, I acquainted myself with the Glock and the Beretta.

I'd been familiarized with weapons since I was a girl, but it had been a long time since I'd practiced mostly because I hated the damn things. Blowing out a breath, I unclipped the safety on both and situated myself in front of Tin. His prone body, hidden by my coat, made it difficult to see if he was breathing, and only the faint whistle between his lips every now and then gave me the reassurance I so desperately needed.

Armed, I braced myself for the recoil, and I forced myself to remain alert.

My entire being was focused on Tin, but he needed me to keep us both safe now. That was what he needed from me. Not panic. Not for me to break down and be useless.

He needed me to protect him.

When a floorboard creaked about a foot away from me, I tensed and forced my eyes wide open. Refusing to blink, I waited until a pair of feet approached from the side.

I recognized them as the Jack boots some of my uniformed guards wore. A sob tried to escape me as relief filled me, but when he lowered down, slowly, I didn't recognize him. Our eyes caught and held, his wide and filled with something I didn't understand, but it made me scan him further, the need for reassurance as to his affiliation making me cautious.

I saw his gun next, saw it wasn't pointed down at the dais now that he knew it was me, and I didn't think twice. I fired both weapons and eliminated the threat against Tin and me.

No guilt filled me. No shame would either. This wasn't adrenaline talking—this was cold hard fact, because I lived with this threat on a daily basis.

Kill or be killed.

And there was no shame in self-defense.

I didn't care whether that made me fucked up or not. I knew, point blank, that if I hadn't acted, Tin and I wouldn't be living to see another day.

When the sound of sirens pierced the air, I wanted to shout hosannas to the sky, but we weren't out of danger yet. I knew every single guard in my detail. Just because I refused to have them close didn't mean I was unaware of them.

Having strangers near me at all times made me feel isolated, so I made it a point of learning who my guards were. We didn't always become friends, but I knew them. Knew most of the Guard Elect too. This man? I didn't know. I'd never, ever seen his face, and as I crawled out from under the desk to approach him, I wondered if he was a soldier or if, somehow, he'd stolen the uniform.

Still armed, I placed one gun on the floor, then reached over. When I pressed my fingers to his throat, I found no pulse, and while I could breathe easy for a moment, I knew he could be just the first wave of the offensive against us. After scanning the area for other attacks, I sighed in relief when I saw we were alone.

Reaching for my cell, I sent out a text to the line my family used in an emergency.

Me: *In Art History classroom. Need EMTs. Valentin Dubois is bleeding out.*

And just in case that didn't light a fire under their asses...

Me: *I've been hit too. Hurry.*

The next few minutes were the worst of my life. I put pressure on Tin's wound, hoping that would do something, but I knew if the EMTs didn't arrive soon I'd be a widow before I could become a wife.

As the doors slammed open and a voice called out, "Princess Alexandra, where are you?" The sobs I'd been choking down escaped and, scrambling out from under the desk, I screamed, "Hurry, he's dying." Seeing Yann and Mika made me feel safe, but the only thing that stopped me from breaking down entirely were the team of four EMTs.

"Fix him," I commanded, using a tone of voice I'd never heard myself use before—one I recognized as being my father's. The king.

When Mika tried to drag me away, I slapped at his hands and hissed, "Don't touch me. I'm not injured. I lied to make you hurry!" After he let me go when I wouldn't stop slapping him, I focused on the care the EMTs gave my husband, not giving a damn about explanations or justifications.

Just needing to know he was stable.

A nod was the only reassurance I was given as the team spread out and worked on getting Tin onto the gurney.

His beautiful features were drawn, his skin pale and pasty, and if I looked at his stomach, where the blood was no longer red but close to black? I knew I'd just burst into tears. Mika pressed a hand to my arm. "Your Highness, they need to take him to the hospital."

I knew that, dammit. Where were they going to take him? The vet?

I started to shrug off his hold when he stated firmly, "*Without* you. We'll follow, but give them room to work on him. They don't need you in the way."

I resented that he was correct, but I stopped pushing against his hold on me and, instead, sagged. I felt him nod and the EMTs, in barely the blink of an eye, were dragging Tin's gurney down the disabled access ramp. For a second, I wanted nothing more than to crumble, to break down and disintegrate into a thousand pieces, but I couldn't do that. I was Princess Alexandra, and I had a role to live up to.

So, I sucked in a breath, and demanded, "UnReals?"

"Yes." Mika's stern retort had me nodding shakily. "The threat is contained for the moment."

And those were the key words.

'For the moment.'

Another breath flowed into my lungs as, in my head, white noise took over everything else.

The UnReal threat had plagued my family for centuries, and no matter how hard I wished it, or other DeSauviers did the same, it got us nowhere.

They were a deadly scourge on my family's reign, and while the DeSauviers might have begun their familial dynasty amid blood and war, back in those days, blood and war was the goddamn gold standard.

Nowadays? It was not how things worked, but the UnReals hadn't received that notification.

I'd lost my grandmother to their threat, and we'd lost good men and women to their evilness, and now there was even more blood spilled thanks to whatever plot of theirs had just been foiled.

Even though I wanted to do something, I didn't have a cure-all. No magical remedy could heal these wounds, but also things had to stop.

Forever.

My father hadn't achieved that in his reign, but I vowed to myself, and to Andrea, and to all the royal protective personnel who'd lost their lives in the fight to keep us safe from the terrorists, that I'd figure something out. That I'd do what no other DeSauvier had.

And while that might have been beyond bigheaded of me when I wasn't exactly queen material, I would, dammit, have Valentin DuBois at my side as consort. Together, we were capable of whatever we put our minds to.

"Your Highness? Don't you want to follow the ambulance?"

I did.

God, how I did, but I was a princess. Not just any member of the royal family either. I was the crown princess, the heir to the throne, and while the only duty that really mattered to me was Tin, I knew there was nothing I could do for him. Nothing other than fretting in a hospital waiting room as I awaited news from a frazzled surgeon on his status.

Here, I could do something. Not much. But *something*. And I would.

But first things first, I grated out, "Mika, make it known that Valentin DuBois is my husband, and, as such, is due the respect and treatment granted to the station of a member of the royal household."

My statement had him tensing, and his eyes widened even as his skin paled. Not much scared Mika, but I figured I'd just scared the ever-loving shit out of him.

"Your Highness, you can't be serious. How is he your—"

I raised a hand. "Now is not the time to argue. Make it known, Mika."

His tension was evident, as was his desire to avoid making such a declaration over the radio. He knew, as well as I did, that news of the shooting and subsequent updates would trickle down to my parents.

It wasn't particularly kind of me to make him reveal the truth to them, but this went beyond my family's feelings. I wanted it known that Tin was my husband and, in time, my consort. That meant something in this world, and I wanted him to have the best care imaginable.

It was elitist of me, but I'd pull every string in the known universe to make sure that Tin made it out okay. I couldn't even think of the word A-L-I-V-E. He had to survive. He just had to.

I could live in a world where he wasn't talking to me. But one where he wasn't in it? No. Just, no.

"Do it," I commanded grimly, mouth firming when he made no move to pick up his radio. There was a little staring contest, one I won because I refused to concede on this matter.

Tin was a DeSauvier. Whether he liked it or not. And that came with duties and protocols and perks. There was no way you couldn't take one without the other, and in this instance, I wanted him awash with the perks because I knew the doctors would stop at nothing once they knew who was in their surgery.

An explosive breath burst from Mika before his hand snapped out and he reached for the radio, then he did as bid. Finally.

Taking a step away from my guard, I moved toward the staircase I'd ascended such a short while ago. My only concern had been the upcoming dinners I'd be having with my parents and family over the festive season, but now, in the space of an hour, God, maybe even less than that, my world had totally changed.

I didn't wait for Mika to approach me. Instead, I returned to where I'd first met Tin on the top step, just outside the doors to Casterby College.

When Yann didn't appear from out of nowhere to stop me, I figured the threat was as clear as it could be, and I gave a silent 'fuck you' to the UnReals because there was no way in hell I wasn't going to Andrea.

She lay where she'd fallen, a pool of blood spilling around her upper body, seeping into the folds of the blanket that had been used to cover her.

The sight of her, so still, when she'd always been the exact opposite, set me on edge. I half expected her to leap up and chivvy me inside where I'd be safe.

For years, every day, without fail because, in my memory, she'd taken criminally few vacation days for herself, she'd protected me. And today? She'd shielded me with her life.

It wasn't enough that she'd be honored with medals. Wasn't enough that our family would attend her funeral and that hers would receive compensation for her loss.

There was no way to say 'thank you' for this kind of sacrifice, but I knew of one small way I could honor her further.

All around me, security personnel worked to contain the area. The screams of before, the gun shots, and sounds of violence had been replaced with brisk military commands being barked out as the troops worked with the police to put things back under control. In the distance, I could hear traffic, as well as the chopper that was either going to take me away from here or contained one of my parents who wanted to fly in to make sure, with their own eyes, that I was alive and well.

The tree lined square beyond the gates to Casterby would forever feel the taint of this moment, and I cast a weary glance around, depressed and hurting, when I saw the blazing lights of several ambulances nearby, which meant civilians had been caught in a crossfire that was intended for me alone.

Every DeSauvier child was gifted a ring upon their baptism, and I dropped to my knees beside Andrea's lifeless form, amid the chaos of the moment, and I worked my ring off my index finger and, reaching for hers, I carefully worked the cylinder over her knuckle and curled her hand around it just so it wouldn't slip free.

Bowing my head, I paid her my respects before I got to my feet once more and waded into the madness that was the aftermath of a shooting.

Which was where Xavier found me, ten minutes later. The second he saw me, parts of me drenched in Tin's blood and dotted with other's, my hands clutching at a girl I recognized from my class who'd hung back to watch the professor ream me a new one, and who'd been shot in the shoulder, I knew he'd forgotten last week's recurring argument. I saw his irritation with me, an irritation that was forged in my inability to do anything right—including marrying someone without anyone's permission, the groom included—disappear.

As the EMTs began to wheel the girl away, I was left alone with my papa who instantly hauled me into his arms and held me close, which allowed me to relinquish some hold on my control.

He was my papa, after all. How couldn't I find solace in his arms?

"Your mother is worried sick," he rasped in my ear, even as his arms tightened about me to the point of pain, telling me he was just as worried, and he was standing here with me. Safe and well.

I understood the tight clasp of his embrace, and I didn't complain even though it was starting to hurt. If anything, the pain was surprisingly grounding, and it helped keep me connected to the moment. The last thing anyone needed was for me to go off the rails. I needed to maintain my composure because royalty never had any alternative but to be in command of the situation. Whatever that situation might be.

"I told you college was a bad idea," I joked. My tone was warm, not bitter at all. If anything, it was as jovial as I could be right now.

He huffed out a short laugh that sounded like it was squeezed out of him. "No change. You've always got to be right, haven't you, sweetheart?" he countered, even as he hugged me tighter.

My lips twitched because I knew he was teasing me back. "I try."

"Are you okay?" he murmured.

"Been better." I pulled back to look at him. "How mad is everyone?"

A twinkle appeared in his eye, and it surprised me. Xavier could be surprisingly stern when he chose to be. "As mad as you can imagine. But we'll talk about that later. We need to get you home. Your mother won't believe you're okay until she sets her eyes on you."

And because the army was out, and the police were here in full force, our Guard Elect would have put her under what was essentially house arrest. That meant she couldn't come to me.

But... "No. I need to be at the hospital with Tin."

Xavier's mouth tightened but he nodded. "Of course."

I peered up at him. "I love him, Papa." I whispered that last word, and his gaze softened on me.

"You always did."

He was right.

I had always loved Tin and I always would.

And for him and for that love? I'd fight until I drew my last breath, even if it had me brushing up against the scum that was the UnReals.

THIRTEEN

TIN

BEFORE I'D PASSED OUT, if I'd imagined waking up like this, I might have passed out sooner. Okay, that was pretty much a lie...especially when Etta had been in so much danger. But to wake up with her at my side, tucked into me?

I knew it was royal privilege that enabled her to splay out the way she was. Anyone else would have been made to wait out in the waiting room, but she wasn't your average visitor, was she?

A sigh escaped me as I took her in, absorbing the sight of her, and recognizing just how fucking much I'd missed her in the long and lonely years that had passed with us not speaking to one another.

Before I'd loved her like a man loved his woman, I'd loved her as a friend. As family. Doing without her had been hard, but I'd been punishing her while being intent on being a martyr. I could see that now. Could see how much time I'd wasted, time where we could have been happy together...but I couldn't think of that. I was already loaded down with regrets, and when I looked at her, I was just relieved. Content. Because she was there. At my side.

Where she should have always been.

I loved that her hair cascaded out in a wave, the bronze-striated, chestnut-hued locks liberated and drifting over the white sheets that covered me. At some point, she'd changed into loose, comfortable clothing which wasn't dotted with blood and wasn't, most definitely, a part of her 'princess wardrobe.'

As I stared at her, glad to see she was resting and at my side, something inside me settled. I was in pain, even though I didn't doubt I'd been doped up. My body was stiff, my back fucking caned, but she was here, and while things weren't right with my world, not when she was still under threat, I felt a damn sight better than I had the last time I'd woken up in a clinic alone—which had been barely a week ago.

Fuck, this had not been the best seven days of my life.

A throat cleared, snatching my attention from my wife, and when I saw Edward, the King of Veronia himself, slouched in an armchair in the corner of my room, my brows lifted.

"Uncle Edward?"

His lips pursed at the title, but I didn't understand why. "Hardly 'uncle,' Valentin."

My family, the people who knew me, never called me Valentin. Except when they were mad at me. As far as I knew, Edward had no reason to be pissed. After all, I'd gone a long way to making Etta safe this afternoon...yesterday afternoon...whenever the goddamn shooting had taken place. So his failure to use my nickname had me wondering what the fuck I'd done.

Wasn't like you could cause offense when you were lying in a hospital bed, snoring your head off, was it?

Warily, I queried, "What do you mean?"

Edward's eyes narrowed. "Look around you. Tell me what you see."

Brow puckering further, I glanced around the hospital room. It looked like a standard clinic, and I'd been in enough over the years to know what a standard clinic was in pretty much most of the major countries in the world.

Those odd plugs and adapters that connected to equipment. IV lines and clusters of beeping monitors which, I knew, once the cadence made it into your head, were impossible to ignore. The bed appeared to be standard...except—

Eyes narrowing, I saw a tiny impression on the sheet. It was faint, but a quick squint had me freezing in place as, putting two and two together, I realized where I was.

This was no standard clinic, and the DeSauvier crest on the sheets revealed that truth to me. When King Incumbent Philippe, Etta's grandfather, had been diagnosed with cancer a year before he succumbed to the illness, the family had added an extension to the palace. Before, there'd been a medical unit, but this was pretty much a hospital in and of itself, and thus, they'd created a freestanding medical center that catered only to the royal family.

Which I wasn't...not officially anyway.

"Alice insisted we transfer you here," Edward continued tightly. "Maybe you'd care to explain why?" When my mouth worked for a few seconds as I tried to figure out what in the hell I could say to that, he swept on, "Why Alice would insist on installing you into a clinic that exclusively serves our family?"

Gulping, because I'd never seen him so pissed off, I muttered, "Did she tell you?"

"No. She didn't. She told her guard to inform the hospital staff that they were treating a DeSauvier."

Well, there wasn't much I could say to that except, "Fuck."

His face, as a whole, puckered like he'd started sucking lemons. "Exactly." Nostrils flaring, he muttered, "With the fallout from the shooting, this is the first time I've been able to visit you and, because she's been by your side for the past three days, without fail, it's the first time I've been able to see my daughter." He leaned forward, and I only just realized he was wearing the crumpled remnants of an expensive suit. His shirt was creased, his sleeves were up by his elbows, and his trousers no longer had the central crease down them.

For Edward, this was about as messy as it came. "I'm tired of waiting for an answer, Valentin. Explain."

"The shooting happened three days ago?" was all I could think to say.

"Yes," came the taut response. "We almost lost you three times. Your mother is frantic, your fathers are close to a meltdown...so it's about time you woke up."

I cringed. "I mean I'd have woken up sooner if I could've."

"Good to know. Now, why are you my son-in-law and how did I only find out about it yesterday?" He grunted. "For God's sake, you two have barely spoken to each other for the past few years..." Edward blinked at me as his words faded. Then, grimly, he snapped, "What did she do?"

It might have been logical for him to blame Etta, but I'd always thought her folks never cut her any slack. Well, save for Auntie Perry. But she was chill.

As chill as a queen could be, at any rate.

"Nothing," I denied, irritated on Etta's behalf.

He squinted at me. "You're a rational child, Tin. Always have been. Your influence on her has always been appreciated as a result. Like your fathers, you're steadfast and loyal. Like your mother, you're loving and kind...Nowhere in that assessment into your character does it make sense for you to essentially abandon a friend you've loved since childhood.

"On top of that, I've followed the rise of your star for King William's government. It has not gone unnoticed by my staff either. For some time, the Guard Elect have been monitoring you with a view to bringing you into the ranks because of your success in recent campaigns..."

While he took a breath, he leveled a look at me that, along with his other statements about the Guard Elect—a body of guards that had been introduced in his reign to counter the threat from an organization of rebels who refused to accept that most of Veronia was not only happy with their country under the House of DeSauvier, but that Edward was a beloved king, even more so than his popular father had been—had me tensing up.

While all his remarks percolated in my head, making me aware that he *knew* about my job, Edward's mouth flatlined in grim disapproval before he grated out, "So, Tin, I repeat, what did Alice do?"

I cast a look at Etta, who tipped her head to the side in her sleep. She was tired...and I sensed an unhappiness about her that I knew stemmed from our discord. Her face was turned from her father, but it soothed me to study the woman I'd loved since my heart knew what it was to love in this way, and I whispered, "Nothing, Uncle Edward. We just had a falling out." Her eyes flashed open at that, and I saw the gratitude in them, and its presence rankled me on her behalf.

Etta's family was close knit, but it couldn't be denied that her fathers were harder on her than they were her sisters.

Of course, Etta would be queen one day. That changed things.

Hadn't it changed things with me too? Hadn't the thought of being her consort terrified me? I'd always felt sure we'd be getting married at some point. She was the love of my fucking life. What was I supposed to do without her? But the illusion of choice was a powerful thing. She'd taken my illusion away.

Entirely.

Edward sighed even as he reached up and pinched the bridge of his nose. "Always loyal to the last."

I cut him a look. "I love her, sir."

"That much is clear." He frowned, and before he could start with the inquisition again, I turned it around.

"Sir, how the hell did they get to her? Why weren't her team on her faster?"

His eyes flashed. "Don't think you can change the subject on me," Edward grated out. "Her team has been dealt with. Heads are rolling with the Guard Elect. Mistakes were made, mistakes that people will pay for with their careers..." He sucked in a sharp breath, like he was trying not to get agitated, probably because—the last time I'd been with them—Auntie Perry had been worrying about his blood pressure, and grated out, "To get things back on track... You should have asked for her hand."

Well, that diversion hadn't worked as well as I'd have liked. Grimly, I told him, "You had to know she was mine, Uncle Edward. As much as I'm hers—"

"I'm not refuting that. Just saying there is a way of doing things, and the way you chose for yourselves is not the right one. Where did you even get married?"

"It wasn't in ideal circumstances," was all I'd admit to.

"We might as well tell him, Tin." Etta's voice was hazed with sleep.

Edward sighed, even as he pinned her with a focus that could only be considered laser hewn as he demanded, "Tell me what, Alice?"

It amused me when she yawned, stretching her arms to ease the kinks that had to have formed while sleeping against the bed the way she had.

It touched me to think of her staying so close at hand. After all, we were in the palace—her family home. She could have gone to her bedroom, could have had the staff inform her when I woke up...but no. Not Etta.

Edward's mouth firmed. Again. Spotting it, and as aware as I was that it was his signal he'd reached the end of his temper, she muttered, "We married in Vegas. Elvis officiated."

Though her face was expressionless, I happened to see the slightest glint in her eye...she was amused.

The minx.

"Elvis?" Edward intoned, every inch of him rejecting what she said as he stared at her, evidently unable to compute what she'd just told him.

Hell, I don't think he'd have been more horrified if she'd told him Martians had officiated our ceremony.

Alice, shooting her father a disinterested look when he just sat there, sputtering, yawned again—like she didn't care about Edward's opinion, which was outright bullshit because she'd always been a people pleaser even if, more often than not, it never worked out. "I need to get your mom, Tin. We've been taking turns to sit with you."

My lips curved. "Uncle Edward said you didn't leave my side. Once." I made sure to enunciate every letter of the word, 'once,' and grinned when she pulled a face.

"Father!" she whined. "What did you tell him that for?"

But *Father* was still aghast at his daughter, the Crown Princess of Veronia, heiress to the throne, getting married with Elvis as the registrar behind the ceremony.

She, quite wisely, didn't wait for an answer, just huffed and said, "I didn't want you to wake up alone."

Her admission had me sighing then. Unable to bear any space between us, not after what had gone down the first time we properly met in years, I reached for her hand, wincing as the move necessitated me leaning forward slightly. "God, I missed you."

Her lips curved in the faintest of smiles. "I missed you, too." Her heart was in her eyes, and I knew if her father wasn't there, she'd have said something else. I wasn't sure what. Maybe she'd have told me what I needed to hear—that she loved me, even if I'd been a jackass. Maybe it would just have been her clambering into the bed to give me an awkward hug—I wasn't averse to cajoling that out of her. But Edward *was* here, and he was already astounded. Considering Edward was the most unflappable man I'd ever met, that was a list I could include my fathers in, and that he was still gaping said it all.

No one could stun him like Etta.

Hell, I was almost proud about that.

When, heart still in her eyes, she patted her side, I cocked a brow, wondering what she was doing. Then, she pulled out her phone which she promptly passed over to me. "Here, call her. It'll make her feel better to hear from you. Everyone's been worried sick." There was, as there had been with Uncle Edward, the faint note of accusation to her tone.

Exasperated, I muttered, "I didn't do it on purpose."

"Uncle Devon told us you've been working for British security."

I arched a brow—he had, had he? Damn turncoat. "You make it sound like a bad thing."

Her eyelashes fluttered. "Isn't it? You could have been in danger."

"I wasn't. For the most part." Wafting a hand at my belly, I stated, "This was a one-off."

Edward's raised brows told me two things. One, he knew more about my record than I might have liked, and two, that my BS was enough to drag him from the stupor our marriage with a king who wasn't him had sunk him into.

Still, he was a wise man, and he knew better than to give Etta ammunition, so his brows were the only indication he gave me that he knew I wasn't telling the whole truth. With the bit between her teeth, Etta could be a real pain in the ass. That side of her didn't come out often, but with things she cared about, it sure did.

Eying her cell, I placed the call to 'Auntie Sascha,' and waited for my mother to pick up.

"Alice?" She sounded tired and drawn, but there was a note of hope in her voice that made my heart twinge.

"Mum, it's me," I said a shade awkwardly. Knowing you'd made your mother worry wasn't the best feeling in the world.

"Oh, Tin. Thank God," she whispered fervently. Then, even though I *knew*, knowing and hearing were different things entirely, I suddenly became aware she wasn't alone as she rasped, "Andrei, Kurt, Tin's awake." In the near distance, which told me Devon was somewhere in her bedroom too, I heard my father rumble, "Is he okay?"

"We'll find out," she told him. To me, she stated, "We'll be there in five minutes."

"There's no need to wake everyone up," I chided, because I'd seen from Etta's screen it was four in the morning.

"There's every need," Kurt muttered, keying me in on the fact she'd put us on speaker.

"You almost died, Tin," Andrei rumbled in Russian. "She's, *we've*, been frantic."

"You know I hate it when you speak Russian," Mum grumbled, making my lips twitch. "Coming, baby," she added, and I had the feeling she was going to run here from wherever Auntie Perry had put them up in the palace.

We didn't normally stay here. Usually, we'd just lodge in the vacation house the family had on Xavier's estate, a short car journey away. That the family had been invited into the royal residence was a big deal. It usually only happened with dignitaries, and while we were many things—loaded, and my mom was technically a lady—we definitely weren't dignitaries.

Wondering how they'd managed to wrangle it, wondering some more if they'd pulled out the good work my fathers had done to shore up the Veronian kingdom, I *stopped* wondering when Edward ground out, "They were aware of your marriage." Edward's irritation was clear. And, to be fair, I didn't exactly blame him.

"I told them. The day of the shooting," I admitted. "They were surprised by my visit here, so I had to explain. You know what Mum's like." A bit too much like Etta for my liking. Mum was a pain in the ass, too, when she was fixed on something.

"I'll bet, considering your stays here have been far and few between." His eyes were narrowed on me, and I knew he wasn't going to let this lie. He wanted to know, wanted to understand what had gone wrong between the pair of us. I couldn't blame him. Not entirely. He was Etta's father, after all. More than that, he was my father-in-law, and a king who was concerned about his kingdom.

Still, I shrugged, not willing to incriminate Etta. "Things don't always work out according to plan."

"You don't say," he retorted gruffly, his sarcasm clear.

I blew out a breath, then winced when the move had my body protesting. Spotting it, Etta whispered, "I'll get the doctor."

"No, it's okay—"

"We should have gone for him the second you awoke." She glared at Edward. "Daddy, you should—"

"I wanted a word with my new son-in-law," was his unrepentant answer.

She licked her lips. "Hardly new. And it's not like you don't know him, is it?"

Edward tensed more at that, and I muttered, "That probably wasn't the best comeback, Etta."

Her nostrils flared as she surged to her feet. "Just because you wanted to marry me off to some asshole that would shore up the country's defenses doesn't mean you can give me the third degree. Lots of royals marry for love now. Hell, you did it yourself! So, to my mind, this is totally unnecessary and a bit like the pot calling the kettle black."

"I care for my daughter's wellbeing," Edward snarled. "I never had any intention of marrying you off. Jesus, Alice, is that what you thought?"

"You paraded enough eligible bachelors in front of me to start up our own reality TV show," she growled back, making my brows rise in the process. She'd always been a gutsy wee thing, but it seemed like she'd grown more spine in the years we'd been distant.

The notion didn't upset me. I wanted her to have more spunk—I really did. She'd always been so torn between her duties to the crown, to her family, and to herself that, along the way, I knew she got lost. As her friend, it had always felt like my obligation to forget everything other than Etta the girl, the teenager, and finally, the woman. Ignoring all the other bullshit which was all just window dressing.

Maybe not to the Veronian people, but to me? Yeah. She was just Etta.

"I want to see you settled," was all Edward had to say to her claim.

"Settled? Like you were in your early twenties, you mean?"

"It's different for you—"

Her hands fisted at her sides. "Is it? Really? Why is it? Because I'm a woman? You were allowed to lead a regular life until you got married the first time."

"Jesus, Alice. That marriage was all duty. Nothing more, nothing less."

"Yeah, and look how that turned out," she snapped. "The best thing you did was the opposite of duty. Mama wasn't the best choice for queen, but look how perfect she is now! Just because something's odd on paper doesn't mean it isn't right.

"I know exactly what your problem is. It's his family. Your friends. Which makes you a hypocrite."

"That's bullshit."

Despite myself, my lips curved. "Is it though?" I wasn't particularly offended.

How could I be?

Edward had a lot of his own secrets to keep buried, and I couldn't be offended, not when his own situation was precarious. It was a testament to his love for his wife that he allowed the friendship between our families at all.

I was used to being one of two things.

A pariah.

Or, alternatively, an oddity that merited goggle eyes and creepy questions.

To be honest, I wasn't even sure which one I preferred. Both were irritating, but after a lifetime of dealing with both responses to my parents' relationships, I couldn't be mad at Edward. Not when this was a cementing of ties between our two families that could bring us all under suspicion.

Yeah, suspicion. Like we were doing something wrong.

It really beggared belief. We might be approaching the middle of the fucking century, but hell, that didn't seem to matter. The same stiff-necked asshole bigots still existed, and I figured they always would.

Edward rubbed his brow like he was getting a headache, and I didn't blame him. This was the start of something big, something that none of us really knew how to handle, but handle it we would because we were family now.

One big, weird family, and as much as I'd resented our marriage, now? In the face of what she was dealing with, and what the royal family had to cope with? I was glad that the Ts were crossed and the Is were dotted.

Etta was my wife, and I'd strangle any fucker who thought they could take her from me—kings and prime ministers included.

FOURTEEN

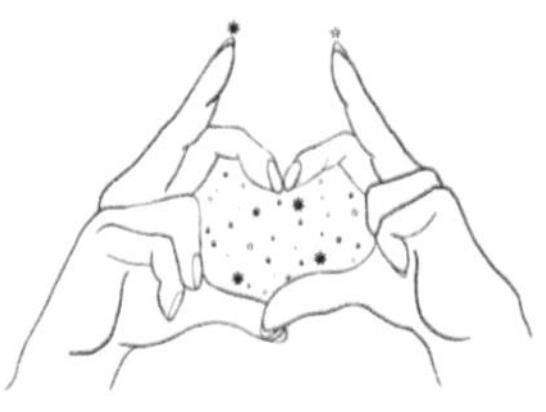

ETTA

"I CAN'T BELIEVE you didn't tell me."

I hated disappointing Mom. It was...ugh. I just hated it. She wasn't the stickler my fathers were, and she actually gave me some freedom. Hell, the trip to Vegas was something she'd had to twist my fathers' arms over. They'd said I'd get into trouble and she'd vouched for me...Yeah, she probably shouldn't have done that.

But Tin and our wedding was my one rebellion, and though the aftermath had been a nightmare, years of no contact between us had cemented my foolishness into place, now I was glad for it.

Now, it was done, and even though my fathers were pissed and were going to be the ones facing the Parliament and, in particular, the privy council's wrath, I was happy. They couldn't take him away from me.

They couldn't. And wouldn't.

My hand was tucked in his as he slept, still tired out from the massive blood loss as well as the surgery he'd had. That I'd almost lost him, again, was enough to make my heart pound.

It could so easily have been Tin who'd died the day of the shooting. I grieved Andrea, truly, I did, but I'd be desolate without Tin. Just knowing he was in the world made me get up on a damn morning. Just praying that, someday, he'd come for me—exactly as he had—made me focus on the future rather than wallow in the past or present.

Tin was my future.

I loved him.

Had always loved him.

And I knew he felt the same about me.

We'd always been tight. From childhood, our mothers' friendship had pushed us together, so I wasn't entirely sure why it came as such a surprise, and I said as much. "Mom, we were together all the time. As much as we could be. And when we weren't, we were always texting and we spoke every day. I don't get why this comes as a shock."

Sascha snorted from her position on the other side of Tin's bed. She was a beautiful woman, her spirit gracious, and I was grateful that she was my mother-in-law even if, I knew, she didn't always approve of me and my antics.

I thought everyone knew the wedding had been my idea, even if Tin had refused to say a word against me—which made me love him that teeny-weeny bit more.

I was used to always being held accountable for my actions. That wasn't necessarily a bad thing but...It meant, small or large, I was held to a different standard than everyone else I knew. A small mistake for me was akin to an international disaster in some other households. It wasn't fair, but I wasn't going to complain—I was just grateful for Tin's defense. He knew I'd get crap from my dads, and he was taking the wind out of their sails by not admitting to anything nor explaining shit.

Sascha, who was my mom's best friend, knew most of the stuff I'd gotten up to over the years. Small fry shit, granted, but Mom was always the one who got upset when I was in trouble. I was glad Sascha had her back, just wished that she liked me more.

I figured I had a lifetime to prove I was going to be a brilliant wife to her son. That was the least I could do, right?

At her snort, I shot her a sheepish glance to which Sascha murmured, "I can't believe we weren't there for it."

"How could you be?" I countered with a shrug. "Father would never have allowed us to wed." And I'd known that. Had known it since I realized the choices that women took for granted, like their husbands and who'd be the father of their kids, weren't going to be simple for me.

No, I'd never be forced into marriage, but as had been the case, my family had picked men they approved of.

Only, I hadn't.

Tin was the man for me.

Always.

She pulled a face, then shared a look with my mom. That look said it all—things they couldn't, *wouldn't* say out loud.

It was weird how close our families were, especially when it all went without being spoken that they were a bit of an albatross around our neck.

I knew that, whichever prime minister was in power, they usually advised my father against the summer holidays we all had together. I knew that Parliament wouldn't approve of my choice, thanks to Tin's family, and so did Sascha and Mom.

That look said it all.

And that look, and what it represented, sucked.

"I think it makes sense."

I cut Devon a look. As usual, he wasn't far from Sascha's side, her shadow even, but he was tucked away in the corner of the hospital room with a notepad on his lap and two tablets on the floor with chamomile tea and water in tumblers around him.

The sight made me smile. Devon had insomnia, severe insomnia, so Sascha had taken to making him drink chamomile tea, even at eight AM to encourage him to relax and maybe sleep.

It was weird logic, but I got it.

You'd do crazy shit for the people you loved.

Tin had told me once that Sawyer drank the grossest shakes in the world every morning just for her. Sascha made them, loaded them down with all kinds of stuff that was supposed to keep him healthy. Ever since his cancer diagnosis back when Tin and I had been babies, then another when we'd been ten, he'd been in remission ever since—Sascha intended on it staying that way.

Which was also why Kurt was pretty much vegan now, because Sascha was working on his cholesterol, thanks to two heart attack scares.

All the stories and gossip my mom had told me about the family who were our best friends had been stored away in my head, along with the craving I had—a craving for them to know who I was to them. For them to recognize me for what I was too.

Their daughter-in-law.

Not just friends, but kin.

I bit my lip at the thought as Sascha muttered, "Your sense and the rest of the world's sense don't often go hand in hand, love."

Devon sniffed. "That's hardly a fair surmise."

"I don't have to be fair." She twisted around in the armchair she'd been sprawled in for the past two hours and shot him a look. "I just have to know you."

He rolled his eyes, which had her sticking out her tongue. Their playful side made my heart warm. My parents weren't always playful. They had too many responsibilities for that, and it made me hurt for them. As well as for myself.

I refused for Tin and me to be like that...

That is, he had to be back here for good, didn't he? He was here to make a go of our marriage, right?

"What are ye two arguing about now?"

"Not arguing," Devon countered, not even glancing at Sawyer as he swaggered in. The second he was behind Sascha's chair, he bent over and pressed a kiss to her head.

"Ye two are always arguing." Sawyer huffed, then winked at me, making me grin at him.

"Hi, Uncle Sawyer."

"Hi, lassie." His eyes twinkled. "Guess you're a part of the clan now, aren't ye?"

"I am." My cheeks pinkened. "Thank you for being so nice."

He snorted. "Dinnae see what the problem is."

"Ha!" Devon exclaimed. "Sawyer agrees with me."

Another snort escaped Sascha.

"Aye, I do. God help us all. But you'll find most of this side of yer family get it, even if yer side don't."

At that, Mom winced. "Sawyer, don't say that."

"Why not? It's the truth." He shrugged. "And I get it. The government here, the people, they've all got sticks up their arses." He sniffed. "Lovely folk, warm-hearted, but old-fashioned." He whistled between his teeth. "Christ, they make me feel like I'm back in the nineties."

Mom winced again. "I know." Her hand shot out and she grabbed mine. "It'll be okay."

I knew it would be. We didn't have a choice.

Thank God.

Sawyer dragged out another armchair from the side wall.

Overnight, since Tin had awoken yesterday, more chairs had made an appearance. Enough for an entire conference of the now extended family.

Which meant, I knew, what was going to go down—a congress.

Great.

"Where are Jack, Rosie, and Bethan?" I queried.

"Bethan's still stuck in Boston, Rosie can't leave because one of her horses is going into breech birth and might die without her," Sascha groaned. "Jack is on his way. He insisted on driving here when he learned Tin was stable. Little shit."

Sawyer grunted. "The boy likes his cars."

His defense had Sascha scowling. "He should be here with his family."

"If I had to fly down and we couldn't take the train, I don't see why Jack couldn't have flown too," Devon muttered, earning himself a scowl from Sawyer and a triumphant grin from Sascha—both, of course, went unnoticed as he was concentrating on his work.

"He'll be here soon enough!"

Jack was only sixteen, but he'd been racing since he was a boy. They'd taken him all over the country, all over the world for competitions. He was aiming for Formula One, and with his backing and skill? It was clear he'd achieve his goals. The twins, Rosie and Bethan, were a bit more sensible. Rosie was on the path to being an equine vet, and Bethan wanted to be a human rights lawyer. Both were studying for those roles, but Rosie, with a stable of her own horses at the family estate, had more hands-on experience.

Before they could argue, Mom butted in, "We're going to have to arrange the wedding, Sascha. There'll have to be a vow renewal. You know that, don't you?"

My heart plummeted, even though I'd anticipated this back when I'd had my first wedding.

Sascha's nose crinkled. "Jeez. Really?"

"Yeah. I think Edward is going to sell it as a, 'whirlwind romance' kind of thing." That statement went with air quotes. "Forged on a friendship that's been blossoming since they were children."

"Well, it's not a lie," Sascha pointed out.

Just like Tin often said, Sawyer, sounding annoyed, retorted, "The best lies have a snippet of truth tae them."

His irritation had me staring at him, and his smile made me realize I had an ally.

He liked me. He always had. Most of Tin's fathers did, actually. It was Sascha who had a problem with me. Well, sometimes. I didn't think she *dis*liked me, it was more like I thought she didn't believe I was good enough for Tin.

Considering I was a future queen, I wasn't sure who *would* be good enough for him, but I got it.

I did.

She was protective of her family, and I loved her for that.

"A vow renewal or a wedding ceremony?" I asked Mom, who was as much of a tigress defending her cubs as Sascha, just in a different way.

Sascha was more of a 'if I don't like something, I'll bust balls to change it' kind of woman.

Mom? She was a maneuverer. She used common sense and logic as well as my fathers' love for her to get her own way. It worked too. She was a brilliant role model, and I probably let her down every damn day by being the fuck up I was.

I couldn't do anything right.

Mom was smart, beautiful, and capable of so much—she hadn't been born to this life like I had, but somehow, she navigated it like she had.

Me?

I struggled. Constantly.

It sucked.

My sisters were the perfect princesses, and they never fucked up. It just seemed so unfair that I was the one who'd take the throne, but...Shit. There wasn't time for a pity party.

Seemed like I was getting married again.

And the arrangements, again, were going down while my husband/future spouse was out of it. The first time, thanks to vodka. A lot of it. The second time, thanks to morphine.

Sigh.

At least he'd be more *compus mentus* than the last time.

Guilt speared me, as it often did, when I thought of our wedding—

the shitty chapel, a gin-sozzled Elvis with a gut as large as Nevada in a white catsuit with more rhinestones on it than a showgirl's—but I pushed it and the memories aside.

What was done was done.

And I didn't regret it.

Not really.

How could I?

I wanted him. Loved him. And he'd have petitioned for divorce if he didn't want or love me—that was the cold comfort I'd clung to all those lonely days and nights without a word from him.

"Lass?"

I blinked, suddenly realizing I'd zoned out and, evidently, Sawyer had asked me a question.

"Sorry, Sawyer. What is it?"

"Your ma was just talking about the wedding and the funeral."

My brow crumpled. "Yeah. The funeral." I blew out a breath. "When is it? I want to be there."

Mom's hand reached out and grabbed mine. Her fingers entwined with my own and she murmured, "I knew you would."

"Of course! She died protecting me," I muttered, a little annoyed that there'd been a question over my attendance.

She rubbed her thumb over my pointer finger which was signet ring free. "That was kind of you," she pointed out, obviously aware I'd given the ring to Andrea.

"Not kind enough. I'd give Andrea her life back if I could."

Her smile was sad. "Your father wanted to keep you here, but I knew you'd want to be there."

"Why? I thought he'd be all for me doing my duty."

If there was resentment to the words, then so be it. I loved my father, I truly did, and most of the time I even liked him. It was the king I had a problem with.

I actually thought it worked the same for him.

He loved and liked me as a daughter, just not as his heir.

"Your safety, darling. The threat is still active."

I shrugged. "When isn't it? Which DeSauvier hasn't had to deal with the UnReals?"

A sigh gusted from the door. "Unfortunately, she's right."

Mom's eyes lit up and her hand shot out. "George!"

The most chilled of all my fathers swaggered in, a grin on his face in response to the joy Mom had imbued in his name.

Sometimes, just seeing my folks together gave me hope. It was sad that they weren't allowed to be out and proud, as it were. People would be happier for knowing just how in love they all were. But haters always hated—damn their hides.

He gripped her hand before he ducked down and pressed a kiss to her temple, then he cocked a brow at me and, resting a hand on my shoulder, squeezed.

The squeeze, I knew, was reassuring.

Daddy had always been the most easygoing of my fathers. I knew he'd been a bit of a rebel in his day, and that was how he'd met Mom. By his refusing to stick to Veronia, by wanting to attend college and eventually work in the U.S.

That was the real joke about all this. Their relationship was so much weirder than mine with Tin, but there was all this hullabaloo over it!

Damn cheek.

Not that I said that. I wasn't a fool.

"Xavier isn't happy about you wanting to attend the funeral either," Daddy warned. "Just keep your tongue skills sharp."

I snorted. "I'm not that acerbic."

"Aren't you?" he retorted. "I saw you cut down Prime Minister DeWitt the other day."

I narrowed my eyes at him. "The idiot deserved it. His foreign policies make Hitler look forward thinking."

Daddy laughed. "That's what you said to him?"

"I did."

Mom groaned. "Baby, you can't say stuff like that to Parliament—"

"Why not? I'm the future queen, aren't I? Why can't I say things like that to the men and women *my* people voted in?" I shrugged. "Mom, seriously, you should have been there for the session." Father made me sit in on Parliament—I felt certain it was because it bored him senseless, but he could pass it off to me as though it were homework. "He was going on and on about how we needed to shore up our nuclear weapons because of our proximity to the Middle East." My eyes bugged out. "Our *proximity*. I mean, for God's sake, we're nowhere near Turkey, so how can we be in the Middle East when we're in Europe? The man has no concept of geography."

Mom's lips twitched. "I know, but he's who the people wanted in."

"Democracy is stupid. In fact, it's democrazy. Father would have picked a much better politician to lead the government."

"He would, but then he'd get more shit for being an autocrat," Daddy reminded me. "Then, when you eventually took over, you'd have three times as much responsibility as you do now." He arched a brow at me. "I don't think you want that, do you?"

I winced. "No."

It was weird thinking of my future job, because that future job involved my father's death. I hated that.

I was essentially preparing for a time when my father was no more, and no matter how often we argued, I didn't want to think about that.

It was a shame, though, that the UnReals, bastards that they were, never seemed to stop bringing death to our door.

"What did they want this time?"

Daddy didn't seem surprised at my change of subject, if anything, he just muttered, "What do they usually want?"

"To abolish the monarchy." I narrowed my eyes, and guilt speared me because it was the first time I thought of my sisters and their safety. "Are Christel and Victoria safe?"

"Of course." Daddy smiled at me. "Don't worry. They were on lockdown the second the shooting happened. They'll be flying in once things are a bit more secure."

I released a relieved breath. Christel was studying in London at their school of economics. Victoria was in Sydney at the moment on a conference. Unlike me, they were both smart, had inherited all our parents' genes, and actually knew what they were doing with their lives.

Me?

I was just a queen-in-waiting. Learning all the crap I needed to know for a job I didn't want, and hoped I wouldn't have for decades.

"I'm surprised you haven't spoken to them."

I shrugged at Mom, not really having an answer. I hadn't wanted to talk to anyone once I'd seen Tin wheeled out of surgery.

Only when he'd awoken last night had I felt a bit chattier. Even then, I was conserving it for him and the family in the vicinity.

I was close to my sisters, and they knew what I was like. When I was under pressure or stress, they knew I turned into a turtle, so I figured they wouldn't be offended.

If they were, it was tough.

There had to be some perks to being the eldest sister.

A rustling in the sheets had me twisting to Tin, and I saw he was stirring. His face was puckered with pain as he awoke, and when his eyes opened, the lashes fluttered like tiny butterflies against his strong cheekbones—they were the most feminine thing about him—I knew the second he was aware.

He saw me.

Me.

It was like he pierced me straight through to my soul.

He didn't see the hospital room or the monitors. Didn't notice our families or what was happening.

He just saw me.

Someone cleared their throat, and I wasn't altogether surprised it was Daddy when he muttered, amusement lacing his tone, "Nice to see you awake, Tin."

Tin didn't break eye contact with me. "It's nice to be awake, Uncle George."

I reached for his hand, relieved when he entwined his fingers with mine. My grip was stronger than his, but that made sense. He looked weak. Everything about him was unlike the Tin I knew.

The Tin who was beyond active. Who'd go snowboarding every day if the snow didn't melt come summer. Who'd swim and cycle and generally be so crazy active that it was like being around a Duracell bunny.

I was used to him being a big bundle of health. He was never down for long, and I found comfort in that because I knew he'd be up on his feet, testing the doctor's patience the second he could.

I looked forward to the arguments.

"God, Tin, you gave us such a fright."

His nose wrinkled as he turned to look at his mother. "Sorry, Mum."

She heaved a sigh. "It's not like you did anything wrong."

"No. But I scared you. I didn't mean to."

"I'm curious what you were doing there in the first place."

Devon's words penetrated the room like nothing else could. Tin flashed his father a look, then his gaze shuttered. "It was time."

"I don't doubt it, but why?" Devon countered, his focus on his notepad.

I used to think he had an issue with eye contact, either that or just looking at people's faces was hard for him. Then Tin had told me his dad could multi-task. Split his attention in ways he'd never heard of before.

And I hadn't either.

Devon amazed me, and I knew Tin felt the same way. As a kid, his parents had called him Devon's mini me, and I could actually remember him following Devon around, traipsing after him, usually wearing the same clothes as he did. It hadn't been a phase either. It had gone on for years and years until Tin hadn't exactly grown out of it, he'd just grown up.

Still, he looked at Devon like he had all the answers to the world in his head. That level of respect always made my heart thud. Devon was a genius, and it was easy to forget that or to underestimate him when you looked at him.

Sitting there in a ratty pair of jeans, some Converse sneakers that he should have tossed out a few years back, and a tee shirt that I swore had holes in it—and not the designer kind—it was difficult to believe the man had millions in the bank.

That was nothing to the billions Sascha had in her bank account either.

In fact, if anyone was marrying down, it was Tin.

His family was *loaded.*

Mine was just rich.

Yeah, there was a difference.

They were royalty of a different kind, but they led their lives pretty much like average folk. Well, save for the fact they had a helicopter in their front yard, of course.

"I'm tired," Tin muttered, and my brows rose at that.

He'd just lied.

He'd just lied to *Devon.*

Now I was curious.

He shuffled in bed, like he was trying to get comfortable but physically couldn't because he'd just lied. *To Devon.*

"I knew you were coming here, but the timing was too strange, son," Devon murmured pleasantly, like he was discussing the weather. "I think you shouldn't start married life on a lie."

Tin's eyes flared wide, and I saw his temper stir. But, again, this was Devon who was chiding him. Had it been Andrei or Sean, I had no doubt that they'd have argued.

But Devon, and usually Kurt and Sawyer too, he was pretty calm around.

His free hand moved to rub at his forehead, and he swept his hair off his face before he cast me a glance.

"There was some news I wasn't supposed to hear."

"What kind of news?" Mom queried, enunciating each word.

"It was just a trickle of information. It concerned me."

"You knew the UnReals were going to attack?" George demanded. "Why the hell didn't you say something?"

"What could I say?" he retorted, his eyes flashing hotter now. "Dammit, I shouldn't have seen the report I read. It was only because I can read shit upside down that I happened to see it on my superior's desk. I could have been wrong. It might have been a falsehood. You know how intelligence works, dammit. Sometimes there's more bullshit to wade through than in a cow field."

"You believed it enough to come here," Sascha snapped, her shoulders bunching as she glared at Tin. "You believed it enough to tell us the truth about your marriage—"

"Of course I did. I wasn't going to risk Etta. I came as soon as I could. They didn't let me out of the clinic until the morning before I arrived, and even then, they bitched at me for discharging myself—"

"I wonder why," Sascha sniped, eying the many bandages that had been wrapped around Tin's torso.

"I got the first flight I could out of there. Made it to Etta's school and did a check of the vicinity. I thought the information was wrong, so I went to meet with Etta."

"But the information *wasn't* wrong," Devon pointed out. "There was a sniper."

Tin winced. "Yeah. There was."

I shook my head. "Why didn't you tell my parents?"

"I couldn't." He blew out a breath, and there was guilt in his eyes. "It was just chance that I saw it. Even more of a chance that I could read it —it was in Russian of all things." His hand slipped to the back of his neck and he rubbed it. I tried to ignore the way his biceps bulged, and managed to when he muttered, "It would have been treason to share that kind of news, and I wasn't about to get strung up when I'd just decided to start living."

Daddy argued, "What do you mean?"

"I mean I'd decided that I was coming home anyway."

"Home? You didn't come to the estate," Sascha retorted.

"No, not that home. *My* home," Tin muttered, then he peeked at me through white gold lashes. "Etta's my home. She always has been."

I damned myself for a fool because my heart started to pound like crazy.

Those were words I needed to hear. All those years of his rejection couldn't be wiped away with just that one remark, but it went a small way to making me realize that he loved me just as much as I loved him.

He'd just been punishing me.

And while it sucked, I'd done a shitty thing.

Choices...if anyone knew how important it was to have choices, it was me. I had so few of them really. I was forced down one path every day, guided down another every other day. I pretty much had to stay in Veronia all the time, unlike my sisters who could travel the world. I had to go to college. I had to, I had to, I had to...

Okay, it sounded like I was whining. But I wasn't. I was just saying that I knew what it felt like to be denied my will and I'd forced that on Tin.

But that he'd forgiven me was etched on his features. Written into his eyes.

Because his words touched me, I inquired, "You came here for me?"

"Of course I did, Etta," he rasped. "Do you know how much bumfluff I've sifted through over the years? Intelligence isn't always intelligent. Sometimes there are false leads and BS. I figured you were safe, but I wasn't going to risk it anyway. I wanted to be there, just in case, but I wanted to be with you period." He wafted a hand at his stomach. "This stirred me into action. I did almost die, so I was handing in my resignation—which they weren't happy about, Dad—"

"I'll deal with them," Devon mumbled, his focus still on his notepad where he was now sketching something with a pencil.

"Thanks. I handed in my notice, and just happened to read something I shouldn't have. Veronia was never where I was based. Central Europe wasn't my scene."

And I knew why. His glance at me confirmed it.

"I tended to stick to either North Africa or the Eastern border of Turkey. So it was only chance that I saw it—"

"You could have given us a heads-up."

"In hindsight, I know I should have. I genuinely just thought it was chatter," he replied, and I knew he meant it.

Tin, even at his most furious with me, would never want me to be hurt.

Or, worse, dead.

But Andrea had died because I shouldn't have gone into school that day. I should have stayed at the palace, safe in my pretty prison.

Wincing at the thought, I muttered, "Poor Andrea."

He flinched. "I'm so sorry, love."

I shot him a weary smile. "Me, too." How was I going to face Andrea's parents? The rest of her family?

I guess I'd just have to.

"Is there any other chatter you could have told us?" Daddy snapped, and I got it—I did. He was going to be mad at Tin for a good long while, and Father and Papa probably would be too. Tin deserved it, even if he'd done what he believed to be the right thing.

"No," Tin replied earnestly. Then, his brow puckered. "Maybe watch your allies in Russia."

Daddy jerked back at that. "What the hell does that mean?"

Tin's mouth just firmed. "You know what I'm talking about. I worked for my government. I worked for my king. You can't ask me to break my oath—"

"And he won't," Mom intoned darkly, shooting Daddy a warning look. "Tin is right. We'd string him up by his balls if he gave away state secrets too."

"This is different—"

"No, it isn't," she snarled. "Don't you dare push him on this, George."

He ground his teeth. "Edward won't be happy about this."

Mom sniffed. "That stick has been up his ass for quite a while. I'm sure it gets uncomfortable from time to time—now is one of those occasions for him to have to grin and bear it."

My lips curved and I squeezed the hand I was still holding. Tin squeezed back.

He'd compromised, and I was grateful for that. I just wished...

God, I just wished Andrea hadn't paid the price of Tin's honor.

FIFTEEN

TIN

IT WAS A GRIM DAY, and I guessed that fit. Everything about this was wrong, and the guilt, I'd admit, was cutting me to the quick.

But when you worked for your government, even if it was just as a glorified pen pusher, in the U.K., you signed the Official Secrets Act. That was hardcore. You didn't piss around with it. But you made damn sure you were with your woman as soon as you could be. You made damn certain that you were ready to take a fucking bullet for her—just in case.

And, in this instance, the 'just in case' had come to fruition. Except I hadn't been the one to take the bullet.

Andrea had.

I knew Andrea. She'd been on Etta's detail for a long time, long enough for me to get used to the miserable bitch. The thought had me wincing, even if it was true. She'd been beautiful, but had a face like a smacked arse, as Sawyer called it. I don't think I'd ever seen her crack a smile.

Ever.

And I wondered at that as I stood beside her grave with Etta's hand in mine.

I felt like one big bruise, one big broken bone, but there was no way in hell I wasn't going to be here, no way I was going to let Etta do this on her own.

Andrea was in the grave because I'd let duty run over everything else. Duty to a country over my woman.

It hurt.

It hurt because my loyalties should always lay with Etta, but the stuff I'd done, the stuff I'd seen and heard in my years with MI6? It was heavy shit. Even though I'd done mostly admin, hadn't been a younger Daniel Craig roaming around the world with a gun constantly half-cocked, my position, my own security had rested in the ability of other people like me being able to keep their goddamn mouth shut.

There was a unit assigned to the UnReals, a British unit, and if I'd said something, I'd have been potentially bringing them into the light.

I knew what that felt like.

Knew how the shit could hit the fan when your cover was blown—that was what had happened to me. It was why my stomach was shredded like I'd been through a blender because someone had dropped the ball. But, even though I'd been trying to save *many* people's lives by being there for Etta, by hoping to be the one who could keep her safe, Andrea had died as a result, and there was nothing I could do to take that back.

The graveyard was filled with people all outfitted in their dress blues. Or, in this instance, their blacks and reds. The Guard Elect wore a different uniform than the regular armed forces, and they were proud of that uniform—I understood.

To become a Guard Elect required the training of a SEAL crossed with the steadfastness of a British Beefeater. They were Veronia's elite force, dedicated to serving their crown, and today, they'd lost one of their own.

In honor of Andrea, with the royal family in attendance, the queen and Etta—Edward couldn't be here, not out in the public, not while Etta was here too as it messed with the line of succession—hadn't been saluted.

Andrea earned that right today.

The forty-strong unit saluted the coffin that was covered in the Veronian national flag, then topped with the DeSauvier family crest.

They stood to attention as the minister gave his final words, and then, as a team of eight moved to lower the coffin, Etta cleared her throat. It was part of the schedule, and probably as much of an honor as she could give Andrea, but Etta started to sing.

Fuck, her voice.

She sang the Veronian national anthem, hitting all the highs and rumbling through all the lows. As the soldiers lowered the coffin into the ground, her teammates—a few I recognized, Yann and Mika and some others—helped take her to her final resting place as Etta serenaded them all.

There wasn't a dry eye in the cemetery as Etta sang. Her voice pierced me, and I knew everyone felt the somber notes in the anthem. They were usually rousing, inspiring patriotism, but there'd been a lot of bloodshed in Veronia's history, and that was evident in the words—

For my country, I will bleed. For my country, I will perish. For my country, my family, I'll stand. Veronia, the land I call my own.

Her voice stayed true, filling the area with more emotion than I could stand as I stayed by my woman's side, watching the guard I'd sacrificed in honor of my patriotic duty.

The last few notes warbled as Etta started to cry, and a few flashes of cameras recorded the moment forever, as the anthem echoed around the graveyard where too many men and women had died to keep the DeSauviers safe from other Veronians.

I stood there, feeling helpless and useless and guilty.

Etta's hand tightened about mine, and the strength in that hold gave me some strength too. It was like she knew I was faltering, but then she'd always known how to read me.

Seemed all these years apart hadn't changed that.

It was oddly reassuring even if, at times, it could be disconcerting. To have someone know you so intimately that they knew how to read you without having to do much more than cast you a glance from the corner of their eye? It was intimidating.

But, equally, I needed that.

Maybe it was too much time spent with Devon, or maybe it had something to do with my ADHD, but feelings and I didn't go hand in hand. Never had. I preferred to act on how I was feeling rather than analyze them and wonder how I could make myself *be* better, not *feel* better.

Etta, on the other hand, was a thinker. An analyzer. She was also a people watcher. Not just me. And I knew that came from her training. There was a lot of work that went into making a man or a woman become king or queen material. Nobody really knew how intense it was, not unless they were going through it.

Or if they were the best friend of someone who had to go through it.

I hadn't been by her side as she did it, but I knew the toll it took on her.

Knew how it affected her relationship with her parents. How, sometimes, Edward was king first and father second. Knew that she couldn't travel much, knew that she was stuck in Veronia a lot while her sisters could see the world, knew that life for her wasn't the barrel of roses some might think it was.

Hell, today was proof of that.

And this wasn't the first time her life had been in danger.

No, being a future queen sucked, and I'd probably made it suck harder.

More guilt on my soul.

"If you keep on huffing, people will notice."

The words were whispered to me, but I had no doubt she hadn't moved her lips and she hadn't cut me a look.

Did they teach royals how to be ventriloquists?

Fuck.

I was the exact opposite of someone who'd be good in public service, in the spotlight, but my woman? That was her place.

And I had to suck it up, because my place? It was at her side.

Forever.

"Sorry," I mumbled.

"What's wrong?"

"I feel bad."

"She died for me, Tin."

"Because I didn't pass on—"

"Because you couldn't." She gave my hand a squeeze. "I understand."

Did she?

Because I wasn't sure if I did anymore.

It had made sense back at HQ in London. Now? With the consequence of that decision right in front of me, it was making less and less sense.

All around me, the Madelan cemetery was bright, like it was in full technicolor, winter be damned. There was frost on the ground, but somehow, it amplified the green of the grass and it made the uniform rows of black marble headstones gleam all the harder. The sky overhead was a dull gray, and the sun wasn't that bright, hidden behind thick clouds that brought rain to the city. But, for all that it was miserable, it was sunny enough to make me wish I was wearing sunglasses.

If I was, maybe I'd be able to hide behind them.

I sure as hell felt like hiding behind something.

The service took forty minutes, and I stood throughout it even though my doctor had insisted I leave the private surgery in a wheelchair. The least I could do was honor Andrea properly, but as Perry and Etta shook the hands of the Guard Elect—an honor bestowed only on occasions such as these—my entire body ached like I'd been whipped.

But I gritted my teeth, and stood behind Etta as she shook hands and murmured condolences to Andrea's family, and made small talk with each guard.

It didn't surprise me that she knew them all by name.

Didn't surprise me that she knew something about them too. Either she asked after their kids or their wives or, in one instance, their Labradoodle, Thor.

Proud of her, even if it was weird, because I was proud that she wasn't an asshat who gave a damn about the people who laid down their lives to keep her safe, I gritted my teeth as the pain worsened throughout the gathering. I'd admit to being relieved that the royals didn't attend the wake in the aftermath of the official service. That was only for the Guard Elect, and was paid, as set down in the constitution of the Guard Elect, by the DeSauviers in thanks and in honor of a fallen member of their team.

Sometimes, it was weird to think they were a newer body of guards, only twenty or so years old, but even though they were, there'd been too many losses along the way. Too many times, the Veronian royal family had been targeted by civilians who caused so much unrest in an otherwise peaceful country.

I was quiet on the ride back to the palace. I let Perry and Etta chat among themselves as I kept my head tilted to the window.

As we passed the cemetery, we moved onto the road that was pure coastline. In summer, it was majestic, with unrelieved and unsurpassable views of the Mediterranean Ocean. This road was in every guidebook known to man on the bucket list of things to do before you died. Up there with driving down Route 66 or going to the top of the Eiffel Tower.

Even on a miserable day like today, it was magnificent. A reminder of how timeless nature was and how *we* weren't.

"You're in pain, aren't you?"

The words were more of a statement than a question, and I recognized that Etta had stopped talking with her mom because Perry had received a call.

I blinked, surprised I hadn't heard it ring, and murmured, "I guess."

She sniffed. "Lies."

"I'm ready for bed," was all I'd admit to.

She cleared her throat. "The doctors say you should stay in the ward."

"I don't want to," I replied, and it wasn't just because I was like Sawyer—hated doctors and hospitals and clinics. It was because ever since I'd awoken after the initial coma I'd been induced into, Etta refused to leave my side to sleep.

The bed was large enough for me, but not for her, not with all the wires on there, so she often slept at my side, making a pretzel look like it was bent straight. She was getting shadows under her eyes, and I knew she had to be exhausted.

I reached for her hand. "I don't want to be in there."

She sighed. "It's for your sake. What if there's a complication?"

"Then you can put me in the damn wheelchair and guide me to the ward, can't you?"

She snickered. "You'd let me push you, would you?"

My lips curved. "Who else?"

"I dunno, I thought you'd be a prick and insist on wheeling yourself."

My nose crinkled at that. "Okay. Maybe. But I'd imagine I'd have to be in crippling pain to want to go to the ward."

She huffed. "It isn't even like a hospital. It's pretty."

"I don't care. All the monitors give me the creeps." I shrugged. "Plus, I need space. Your bed will do nicely."

Her chin dropped, almost butting her chest. "I don't know if—"

Because I knew exactly where she was going with that sentence, I cut her off. "Etta?"

"Yes?"

"Are you over the age of twenty-one?"

"Yes."

"Am I?"

"Yes."

"Are we married?"

"Yes, but only the family knows that—"

"Do you really think they're going to keep us apart?"

She bit her lip. "Father won't like it."

"I don't care," I rumbled. "I really don't. Lie about my presence in there, hide me, I don't give a shit. I know things can't be official until we get married in front of your father, but until then, I refuse to be without you any longer than I already have."

"It's about time you fought for her."

Aunty Perry's grumble had my eyes widening, and I shot her a surprised look. "Pardon?"

"I was mad at you before, Valentin. Dumping my daughter like a hot potato. But she never complained, so I didn't think I had a right to meddle. Your friendship was between the pair of you.

"But to think you let her wallow for years—"

My left eye twitched, and the desire to tell her the truth of exactly how our wedding had come about tasted good on my tongue, but, and it was a big but, I *had* let Etta down.

Because I didn't want to say a word, and because Etta's cheeks had turned pale as if she expected me to set Auntie Perry straight, I turned away from her and, staring ahead, murmured, "Behind closed doors, we never know what's happening."

Perry sniffed. "You can use that with someone else, but not your *wife's* mom. Now, I know something funky went down between you two. I know you refuse to tell Edward what that is, and to be frank, I don't particularly blame you. He can be a stuffed shirt sometimes, for all that I adore him. I wouldn't want him to know either, and I'm not asking you to tell him, but I will say this—if you let Alice down again, I will make your life hell, Valentin DuBois, do you understand me?"

I nodded stiffly. "It happened for a reason. I wasn't being cruel or mean—"

"He wasn't, Mama," Etta whispered, and the tremor in her voice had me reaching for her hand.

Etta was such an odd duck sometimes. She craved her parents' approval, to the point where it made her do the most stupid of things.

I sighed. "It's in the past. I won't let her down again."

"I won't let *him* down again," Etta murmured. "I let *him* down, Mom. I deserved—"

"You *didn't*, Alice." Perry shook her head. "Decades of friendship can't be swept away by a single act. Unless she cheated on you—which I know my daughter wouldn't—that's the only reason I could use to justify what you did to her.

"Tin, you and Alice have been friends since you were babies. Dammit, you used to have baths together! I never suspected that something would develop between the pair of you. I thought you were more like brother and sister. But now that I know things are serious, I want you to understand that you've not only let her down, you've let me down.

"I understand about the issue with MI6. I really do. I'm not happy about it, but I get it. It's this other stuff I can't get behind."

"You don't have to," I retorted, uncaring that I was being an ass. "Things happened the way they did for a reason. I was young, Etta was young, and I couldn't cope with what went down." I sucked in a breath, trying to seek patience, because Perry's only crime was giving a shit about her kid. That was something I could support, especially when Etta was in the crosshairs of her momma bear mode. "We're still young. I made mistakes, she did too. I had always intended on coming back here, even before I was injured. That's why I saw the files in the first place," I retorted. "All you need to know is that I love your daughter, and while we've had a shakier start than most, I will do my damnedest to make sure she's happy."

Perry narrowed her eyes at me. "You promise that?"

"I promise to do my best." I shrugged. "I'm stubborn, she's stubborn too. We're going to butt heads."

"I don't mind you butting heads. I just mind you getting into an argument and thinking you can run back to the U.K. every time something doesn't go your way—"

My eyes flared wide at that. "When have I ever given you the impression that I was flighty, Auntie Perry? Jesus. I'm not a kid anymore. Neither is Etta. I have no doubt that we'll argue, and if I'm mad enough to need some space, I can go into another room. Far as I'm aware, the palace has a ton of them.

"I'm done with distance, all right? I'm also done with this conversation. I'm in pain, I'm tired, and your daughter is exhausted from sleeping beside me. I want to get back to the palace and sleep. With her. Because she's my wife. Maybe not in the eyes of the Veronian king, but in the eyes of the law, she's mine and I'm hers." I narrowed my eyes at her, not giving a damn that I was talking smack to a queen. "You won't take her away from me, not when we're just finding each other again."

"You're only finding each other—"

"Mom!" Etta butted in, midway through Perry's snipe. "Thank you, thank you so much for caring about this but..." She blew out a breath. "Please, don't give Tin a hard time. It was my fault. I deserved this...I broke his trust."

Perry shook her head. "You're not like that, love. Never think you deserve to be treated badly."

"I don't think I do," she whispered, her voice a low rasp. Then she ducked her head and whispered, "I got him drunk when we were in Vegas, Mom. He didn't know what he was doing. The chapel didn't care, not when I gave them a couple hundred extra to look the other way."

Perry's mouth dropped open. "You mean you got him drunk so he'd marry you?"

She licked her lips. "I-I'd heard you and Father talking about Lawrence Fortsythe."

Perry's cheeks blanched, but as stark as her reaction was, it was nothing to how the wind fell from her sails and she murmured, "Oh."

At Etta's confession, Perry's umbrage had switched from me to her, but at her dropping that name, something changed.

"Who's Lawrence Fortsythe?" I demanded, needing to know what the hell he had to do with Etta getting the crazy notion into her head that she needed to get me drunk so we could marry. I'd always wanted to know what the trigger had been, but she'd never said, and to be fair, I'd never given her a chance to explain. I'd just woken up, remembered Elvis, asked her if it was true, then I'd gotten the fuck out of the hotel room and hadn't seen her again for months, much less spoken to her.

"He offered for Alice's hand," Perry whispered, her eyes on her lap. "Edward accepted."

My eyes flared wide. "On her behalf?"

Perry reached up and rubbed her brow. "Your father is set in his ways, Alice. You know that. H-He wouldn't have made you marry him. I wouldn't have let him."

"Edward's an asshole. I swear to fuck," I growled under my breath. "I love him like he's my uncle, and as an uncle and as a dad, he rocks, but when he's in king mode? He sucks. He sucks fucking hard."

"And that's treason," Perry snapped, color flooding into her cheeks. "I convinced him that this wasn't nineteen fifteen," she continued, glaring at me all the while. "All he's ever wanted is what's best for her! And Alice never helped him do that." She cut Etta a look. "And you didn't, love, you know you didn't. You were never like Christel or Victoria. You never wanted to study, never showed an interest in anything really." She sucked in a breath. "I think he thought you wanted to be a homemaker, and Lawrence was as good a candidate as any."

Etta's voice was flat. "Not for me. Never for me. So I made sure that couldn't happen. I always wanted Tin, and I knew, a few years down the line, he'd want me that way too. But I couldn't...I knew I needed to make sure that he couldn't force a marriage between us."

"He wouldn't have done that! I would never have let him. He gave the Fortsythe boy permission to ask you to marry him—you misunderstood. It was just an idea he got stuck in his head. Nothing more, nothing less. He will always do what's in your best interest, love. Always."

"It doesn't feel that way."

"No. It doesn't," I retorted. "More like it's in Veronia's best interests, not Etta's."

Perry bit her lip, and that alone told me that, at least partially, she agreed. "Edward has more responsibility than you'll ever know. And when you do know, he won't be around to guide you anymore, Alice. I dread the day you take his place, not because you aren't worthy of the throne, because you are. You'll rule in your own way, a way that's different than your father's, but that's a day when he won't be around.

"Yes, he's intractable and stubborn. Yes, he's set in his ways, but he's the finest man. He loves you. Hell, he adores you. He wants only what's best for you, and if he could, I know he'd live forever to spare you the duties you have when he passes." Perry paused, seemed to seek patience, then in a calmer voice, asked, "How many hours do you spend serving the crown, Alice?"

She frowned. "I-I don't know. Maybe twenty hours a week."

"When he was crown prince, he worked eighty. Eighty hours. He worked the equivalent of two full time jobs just keeping things afloat. Of those sixty hours that he used to work, that *you* don't work, who do you think picks up the slack for you?"

Etta frowned for a second, but I saw her cheek turn concave as she nipped it. "Father?"

"Yes. Father. He works every hour to give you more freedom than he had. It might not be the freedom you want, but you're as tied to this nation as he is. He makes mistakes, I know he does. He doesn't always make the right decisions, and I'm there to guide him the right way. Do you think I'd have allowed him to force you to marry the Fortsythe boy? Of course not. He gets the bit between his teeth sometimes. Decides you need to settle down, decides that he knows how to make you happy, but it's all from a good place.

"He's king second, always father first. Whether you believe that or not, it's down to you. But there's many an hour where I sit with him in his damn office when he's doing work that should be on your shoulders—"

Etta gulped, then reached for Perry's hand. "I'm sorry, Mama."

Sun beamed in through the window, revealing a glint in Perry's eyes that couldn't be denied.

"Don't be. Just don't judge him too hard."

"I don't," she whispered. "Tin was my ultimate rebellion. He's all I've ever wanted, Mama."

It was weird, listening her talk about me, saying those words to her mother and not to me, but they touched me nonetheless.

They weren't throwaway words. Weren't something she was saying only to justify her actions. She meant them.

I knew she did.

Hell, the morning after our wedding, I'd known then. I just hadn't been able to forgive her.

Being her husband meant being her consort. It was that, as much as the prospect of being a husband, that had terrified me.

I'd been a kid. Wet behind the ears and just finding my feet in the world. I'd always been out of place. Being home schooled hadn't helped, but two years in a regular school had proven how normal education just wouldn't work for me. I'd been ready for university a couple of years before I'd attended, and when I was eighteen, I was so out of it, so uncomfortable with people my own age that what she'd done to me, that the one person I trusted had betrayed me...I just hadn't been able to deal with it.

It had all gone so wrong so fast.

And I'd done a Devon.

Found solace in my work. Escaped into a world where nothing was expected of me save for my service and duty. But I was tired of that life. I wanted Etta. All of her. The fuck up, the Calamity Jane...the future queen.

The tension in the limo was palpable, and I was grateful for the privacy screen that was shielding us from the driver's ears. No one needed to hear this conversation. No one.

I murmured, "Now that I'm here, once things are official, I can help. We can take some of Edward's workload. He doesn't need to do it all."

Perry eyed me, wary to the last. "You mean that?" she questioned after a few moments.

"I do."

And I did.

God help me, I really did.

She bit her lip. "Thank you for that."

"You're welcome." I sucked in a breath. "Perry?" Another nod, I inquired, "Please, don't tell her fathers. I don't want them to know."

At that moment, I saw the respect for me in her eyes increase tenfold. She dipped her chin. "I won't tell them. I don't want them to know either. They'll be disappointed in Alice, and I can't say that I blame them. Even if…" She rubbed her eyes. "I understand, Alice. I do. But you must stop making these rash decisions."

"I know, Mama," she whispered, sounding utterly unlike my Etta at that moment. I had no choice but to reach for her hand and tuck it around my arm.

"We'll deal with the future together, Etta, won't we?"

Her eyes were bright with hope, but guilt shadowed that too.

"Won't we?" I repeated.

"We will," she murmured.

I squeezed her hand. Things weren't set in stone, but after this shitstorm of a conversation, some things were resolved. For the time being.

This was a secret between us, and at least if I had Perry on my side, that was one step nearer to winning over her fathers.

Because, even though Edward suspected that Etta was the reason for my breaking off our friendship, he didn't know for certain. What he did know was that I'd ignored her for years, had cut her off like she meant nothing to me…

Hardly husband material, was it?

So, no, I had a long way to go in repairing my past mistakes, but I was okay with that.

First, I needed my body to repair itself, and that involved a big bed with my wife in it.

SIXTEEN

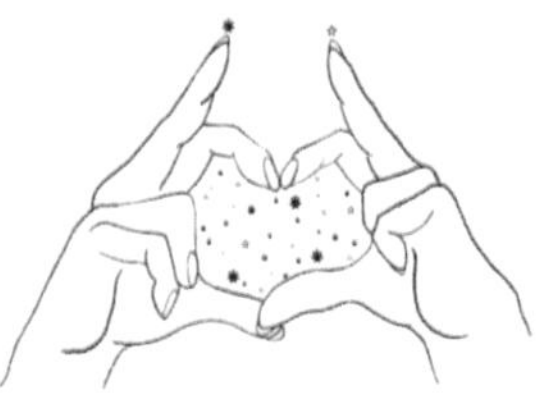

ETTA

WAKING up with Tin was both a dream and a nightmare. A dream because I hadn't been sure he'd ever let us have this. And a nightmare because I wanted, so badly, to touch him.

For years, I'd waited for this moment. But I couldn't have what I wanted most.

Tin had taken my virginity when I was seventeen and he was sixteen. It had been fumbling and awkward, and I had the best memories of it. It was before everything had started to go wrong. Where we'd known that we were in love with each other, had known that we were always going to be in each other's futures. Then, things had started to derail.

We'd had that one night together.

That was it.

One stolen night.

The rest had just been a mishmash of days filled with longing for him. For more of what we had together. Even if it hadn't been all that great, I'd felt the promise of more, and that promise made it hard to be in the same bed with him, to share the same mattress, and not be able to touch him. To have to keep a wide distance between us because he needed space, he needed time to heal.

I could do it, but it was temptation and I'd never been all that good with temptation.

"I can feel you looking at me."

Though my cheeks burned, I murmured, "Then you shouldn't have come to bed without a shirt on."

He snorted. "So it's my fault?"

"Of course."

"Bandages are your weakness, huh?" He rolled his head to the side and looked at me. His eyes were sleepy, and there was a hint of pain in the lines about his mouth, but I knew, probably better than he did, that he wasn't allowed any more meds for at least another hour.

I hated seeing him in pain, so I figured the best thing to do was to distract him.

"I'm pretty sure you could wear a sack and I'd think you were hot."

A laugh escaped him. "You haven't seen me in a sack. I might not look hot in it."

"It's what's underneath it I'm interested in."

Even as a kid, he'd been toned and strong. I supposed that was what happened when you had Sawyer for a father. Post-cancer, he hadn't let his diagnosis get him down. He'd forged full steam ahead back into being a health nut. Tin, in the same house, probably couldn't help being swept along for the ride.

"I guess I understand," he murmured.

"Big head," I teased, even though he totally deserved to have a bigger head than he did.

The trouble with Tin was that he compared himself to his fathers. Always had, always would, and I knew he'd always think he was lacking. In their house, it wasn't looks that mattered, but smarts, and by comparison to his fathers, Tin was only super-duper smart, not super-duper pooper scooper smart.

Yeah, there was a difference.

Knowing Tin, he'd prefer to have a bigger IQ than, like most men, a bigger cock. Although his eight inches were more than ample for me.

"What's that smile about?" he demanded.

"Nothing." I grinned. "What were you going to say? Why do you understand?"

"Because you look as hot in a bedsheet as you do in a Prada dress."

Underneath the bedsheet, and behind the silky nightdress I wore which was all lace and sin, my body reacted to his statement.

I blew out a breath. "Those are fighting words, and you aren't ready to fight."

"True," he conceded with a grimace. "Even my cock agrees. You've been in that lace all night, and normally, I'd have it off and on the floor before you could slip between the sheets, but I'm just too fucking tired right now."

I winced, and my arousal disappeared with his words. "I'm sorry—"

"Don't be." He sighed. "I didn't mean it that way, love. I just meant that even if I wanted to, and trust me, I do, I couldn't do anything right now." He scowled. "Which sucks."

"It does," I rasped.

"Yeah, so to make up for torturing me, you can tell me what that naughty grin was about."

Lips twitching, making my grin widen all the more, I admitted, "Remember when we measured your dick?"

He groaned, raised a hand to cover his eyes, and muttered, "Don't make me laugh."

I couldn't stop myself from snorting. "Every time I touched it to hold it against the ruler, it would twitch, then I'd drop it in surprise and—"

"Yeah, I blew my wad in the shortest time imaginable." Another groan escaped him. "I was mortified." He peeped at me from under his hand. "Trust you not to have forgotten that. Memory of an elephant," he groused.

I couldn't stop myself from rolling onto my side to look at him in all his morning glory—and yeah, he was right. There was no morning wood.

Okay, so that sucked, but equally there were plenty of other things to be looking at and drooling over.

Still, I contained my snicker, so I didn't shake the bed because he looked so disgusted at my long memory that I had no choice but to lock down my amusement.

"You were only..." My eyes widened as I tried to think back to that day. I whistled. "What? Fourteen?"

His nose crinkled. "If we have kids, then we're locking them down from thirteen."

"Our parents were too trusting," I agreed, my lips twitching. "But..."

I shrugged. "We were, I guess, childhood sweethearts, and we waited until we were old enough that first time!"

"We did," he admitted. "And waiting was fucking hard." He groaned as he raised a hand and scraped it over his jaw. "I can still remember how you looked when I came on your face." He snickered. "Oh fuck, now I want to laugh so badly."

I chuckled. "I didn't expect it to explode!"

"Yeah, well, you got what you were asking for even if you didn't expect it." He pinched the bridge of his nose. "I can still remember your wide eyes, and then, you scooped some cum up on your finger and sucked it off—fuck."

"At least I got a chance to measure it again," I rasped, amused and turned on by the memory of his second hard-on. Which had lasted about as long as his first one. Only this time he hadn't come on my face.

Just my chest.

I snorted at the memory.

Knowing what I was laughing at, he grumbled, "You deserved the double blast. It was your suggestion to measure it!" He huffed. "What's a guy to do when he gets that kind of challenge from his best girl?"

I stuck out my tongue. "You were curious too. I don't know why you hadn't measured it yourself. You're all about the math. I thought you'd have it all mapped out and everything."

"Know the angle of the curve of it?" He rolled his eyes. "Yeah, I'm not that interested in my junk."

"Said no man ever," I retorted, deadpan. But inside me, something was wriggling around like a happy puppy.

Fuck, I'd missed *this*. I'd missed it so much. Just shooting the shit with him, giggling over our shared pasts, bitching at each other and sniping. He never let me get away with shit, and I was just as hard on him.

To him, I was Etta. Not Alice. Certainly not Princess Alice. I was just me. And because I was just me, before shit had gone wrong, I'd been just *his*.

I wanted to be that again so badly. I knew it would take time. Weeks, maybe months, but I could deal with that. I could. I just needed to feel that link with him once more.

"What are you thinking?"

His question was soft, and I focused on him, then murmured, "Just thinking how much I missed this."

"Me, too." His lips twisted. "Punished myself as much as I punished you." He blew out a breath. "But, Etta, I need you to know this—I'm here because I missed you. Not because there's shit going down in Veronia. I got hurt, and I needed to come home. Do you get that?"

I wasn't going to bullshit—I did. I did get it. I'd been a bit taken aback by his admission to our families when he'd revealed all, but equally, Tin wasn't like that. There were years separating us, a chasm that I'd created, but I knew him. Knew the man. Tin didn't do anything unless he wanted to.

And he wanted me.

I'd always hoped it would be a matter of time, even if, on my down days, I thought that might never come. I'd just never imagined it would be triggered by a grievous injury.

Tucking my hands under the side of my face, I rolled my legs toward my belly to get more comfortable.

There was way too much distance between us on the bed, and for the first time in my life, I resented how big it was.

In sleep, I was like a monkey, always moving across the mattress. It wasn't unheard of for me to wake up at the foot of the bed, laying horizontally...so yeah, I liked my space.

But now?

I wished I slept on a double bed because he'd be within touching distance. And I wanted to touch him. Even if I knew it wasn't wise.

He was so yummy. All pale, creamy skin that was golden on his forearms, throat, and face. His pecs were defined, his belly rippled with muscle, and his biceps were way more delineated than they'd been before.

The last time I'd seen him like this, he'd been skinnier, younger. He'd been a kid, just like me. But now, we were adults. We were both grown up, and we had the bodies to prove it.

I'd had a bit of puppy fat on me that years of being glum had slimmed down, my boobs were bigger though, and my hips were rounder. I had a butt that wasn't going anywhere, and I hated how I resembled a ruler because I had zero waist, just went up and down, but for all that, I knew he liked what he saw.

There was no way he didn't.

It was there, in the fiery heat in his eyes that was only banked because of pain. It was there, in the interest he showed me as he touched me with his gaze.

I knew, just as much as I wanted to touch him, as much as I wanted to pull the sheets down and throw myself at him, he wanted to hurl himself at me too.

And fuck, what a ride it would be.

I nibbled my bottom lip as my heart began to pound. This wasn't a girl's nervous need but a woman's. It was like the difference between a full-bodied glass of red wine and a spritzer that had been left out to sit in the sun.

I was full of need and none of it was G-rated.

"Stop looking at me like that," he rumbled, his voice low and deep, sending shivers into my core.

"Not doing anything wrong by looking."

He grunted and turned to stare up at the ceiling. "You totally are." Another grunt. "I can't believe you're still in this room."

I shrugged. "It's where the crown princess sleeps."

His nose crinkled. "It's like a museum."

I glanced around the room that *was* like a museum. "I quite like it."

"You hated it when you were fourteen."

I huffed. "Of course I did. I was fourteen. I hated everything but you."

His lips twitched. "True."

He sounded smug, so I rolled my eyes. "I couldn't put posters up, couldn't get speakers put in here. I had to preserve everything. It sucked. Now I'm used to it. I guess, more than anything, I just like the space. Plus, because it's a suite, I don't have to leave it if I don't want to see anyone."

He rolled his head on the pillow again, no longer looking at the gilt moldings and the frescos that decorated the ceiling—Aphrodite in her bath as cherubs washed her. Yeah, it was weird going to sleep looking at a Michelangelo, but that was how the cards fell sometimes—and pinned me with his focus. "How do you feel about yesterday?"

"About what Mom said?" I shrugged. "I feel bad."

"Why?"

"I guess, in my head, I always give Father a hard time—"

"Understandable. They've always been hard on you."

"Yeah." A breath whistled out of me. "Thank you for thinking that."

He frowned. "Why? Why are you thanking me?"

"Because, sometimes, I feel like it's only me who thinks that way."

"You should have told me about Fortsythe," he grumbled.

"I was scared, Tin. Terrified. I could see my life changing all around me. I could—" I reached up and rubbed my eyes. "I made stupid decisions, but they were out of fear and panic, not malice. I didn't do what I did to trap you, I did it to trap *me*. To make *me* inaccessible."

"I can see that." He sighed. "I just wish you'd told me."

"I do, too. It might have saved us a lot of misery, but, also, it might not have. Back then, I wasn't as strong as I am now."

"Weren't you?" He smiled a little. "Far as I know, you've always had a mouth on you."

"Yeah," I agreed, not even bothering to get sniffy about his less than charming compliment, "but there's being all mouth and then not having the balls to stand up for yourself. You gave me that, Tin. Knowing, even though it was a secret, that he couldn't do anything when the privy council made suggestions and murmurs about me getting married, it gave me strength. It changed me and liberated me in ways that you don't get because, to you, it just tied you down. It didn't free you."

My tone was sad, and it hurt me that he didn't, *couldn't*, understand, even while I was glad he'd never been put in the position I had.

My father might come across as a hard ass, and in some things, he was. But I knew that was partly down to my position, but also me. Mom was right. I'd never been like Christel and Victoria. If I had, maybe it would have been different. But I'd never had a clear path. Never really had an interest in something like they had.

I guessed that was down to the fact that I believed I didn't really have a say in it anyway. Whatever I wanted to do, I'd never be able to do it. Once upon a time, fashion design had fascinated me. But who'd heard of a future queen doing something like that?

Unheard of, no?

Whatever I *did* enjoy, it wasn't something I could ever make into a career anyway. My duties always rested with the House of DeSauvier. Which wasn't exactly the House of Chanel.

"What are you thinking?" he rasped, neither agreeing nor disagreeing with what I'd just said.

"I was thinking that I wish I knew what direction I'd like to take my life in, because then Father might not have been so hard on me if I'd had more sticking power."

He shook his head. "Whatever you wanted to do, you know the privy council would never have let you do it."

The privy council were my father's advisors. They were appointed by the cabinet of the ruling government, and they had a direct effect on what we could and couldn't do as a family.

We were autonomous to a certain degree, but the council could make things difficult for us.

If I wanted to go study something, the subject as well as the university location would have to be approved by them.

"I think, more than anything, when I've been mad at him for restricting me, I think he was probably sparing me from the council."

Tin sighed. "I think I agree with that. Your mom loves him too much for him to be that big of an arsehole."

My lips widened. "Treason."

He shrugged, but his eyes twinkled. "True, all the same. Plus this *is* a democracy." He winked, making me snicker. "Anyway, things are going to change now. I'm ready."

"Ready for what?"

"To do shit with you." He blew out a breath. "Not going to lie, Etta, never wanted any of this. Part of my anger was that I'd never wanted to be your consort, but to have you, I had no alternative, so it was just a knee-jerk decision that I let go on for far too long. And you know what I'm like. My past, my education—I'm not great with people. I'm better behind the scenes. All the years of social anxiety just overwhelmed everything, until that was all I could see. I didn't even see you. Just that. Just my fear. Just my anger."

I hitched my shoulder. "You were angry. You needed to burn it off."

"I needed to get stabbed," he retorted grimly. "I needed to be betrayed. I needed to realize exactly what I tossed away when I walked away from you."

"You were betrayed?" My eyes flared as I jerked into a seated position. "Who by?"

He wafted a hand. "Don't worry about it. They're in jail now. But...you'd never betrayed me. It felt like you had, but when I shoved the two instances up against each other, I realized that you'd just pushed things ahead quicker than I'd anticipated." He winced. "I missed you, Etta. I missed you so fucking much, but I was too much of a stubborn dick to admit it.

"Not a goddamn day passed where I didn't want to call you. Where I didn't want to tell you about some wanker I was dealing with, or laugh about some shit one of my dads pulled." A breath whistled from him. "In future, if I'm ever that stubborn, feel free to kick me in the balls."

Though I snickered, I countered, "That wouldn't be much fun for me though. We have a lot of time to make up for."

His nose wrinkled as he stared back up at the ceiling and grumbled, "This is my punishment. Not being able to have all the sex I've been missing out on—"

"What?" I shrieked, leaning toward him slightly.

He blew out a breath but didn't look at me. Just carried on staring at the ceiling.

Fucking Aphrodite. I was going to get jealous if he didn't stop studying her conical tits.

Softly, hope loading the words, I whispered, "You haven't—"

He finally cut me a look. "I tried. Fuck, I tried." When I winced, he shrugged, utterly unapologetic. The asshole. "But I could never do it. You're mine and I'm yours. And I knew, no matter what, no matter how long it took, you'd never betray me that way, so I couldn't do the same to you because I knew, deep down, you'd never forgive me. You'd forgive me of many things, but never that."

I'd always imagined he'd have a girlfriend or some kind of fuck buddy, and I'd tortured myself over it. Had died a little inside when I thought of him with someone else.

Now?

I knew the truth, and I didn't know what to say. I just sat there, gaping at him. My nightdress was rucked up, the strap half slipping down my arm revealing God knew what, but I didn't care.

All I could see was him.

All that mattered was him.

"Thank you," I whispered shakily. It was too small a reply, too unworthy of the sacrifice he'd made. And yeah, it was a sacrifice. He'd been faithful to me, even in the aftermath of what I'd done to him.

He'd stayed true to us even though he was a young man. A *hot* young man who traveled all over the world, had a face like an angel, the body of a sinner, and was a nice guy to boot.

My mind was frazzled. More so than it had been yesterday when Mom had told me how much work Father shouldered on my behalf. The concept of Tin not sleeping around was enough to have my elbows blowing out from under me and I sank back onto the bed, uncaring if I plopped down ungracefully, and just stared at Aphrodite's tits.

"Etta?"

"Yes?" My voice was low, quiet.

Unlike me.

"I thought you'd be pleased."

I closed my eyes. *Pleased*? Everything inside me was ablaze with need and want and love and desire.

I didn't know how to show him how he'd made me feel by telling me that, by sharing something I knew most men would find weird.

But Tin and me?

We were made for each other.

And he'd just confirmed that.

He could have used other women to get back at me. He could have done whatever he'd wanted and I'd never have been able to say something, even if the knowledge *would* hurt, because I'd been the one to start our life together atop a bed of lies.

I released a shaky breath and whispered, "I love you."

"Ah." He hummed. "I love you, too."

And I knew he understood. I knew he *got* why I was speechless. Knew he wasn't worried about my reaction anymore because, deep inside me, there was a war going on. A war of feelings and emotions and...God, too many things. I wanted to kiss him, to fuck him, to make love to him, to caress him and hold him. I wanted to be in his arms, to have him touch me, caress *me*, I needed that. So many damn things, and we couldn't do any of them.

Not a single one.

"If I promise to lay still, can I come closer?"

He grunted. "Of course, Etta," he rumbled, so I carefully twisted onto my side and half crawled across the wide mattress, only stopping when I was about a foot from him. I wasn't touching him, but I could feel his heat, and that heat warmed me right through.

"I missed you."

"I missed you."

I tilted my head to the side and pressed it, carefully, to his shoulder.

"I won't break," he rasped.

"Not going to risk it. Not now."

He sighed. "I know." He reached for my hand, tucked it in his, and murmured, "The first night we were in bed together, I never imagined it would be with you on the other side of the mattress."

"Our blue balls are mutual."

"You've grown a pair since the last time we did it, huh?"

Chortling, I told him, "I've grown something."

"I'll bet." He snorted, then I felt his lips brush my temple. "All in good time, yeah?"

I hummed. "Definitely."

We stayed there like that for hours, only moving when one of us needed to use the bathroom, but we returned to the bed after, and didn't bother to get up and go about the start of the day. Surprisingly enough, or maybe not considering my mom knew about us, we weren't disturbed, and I was grateful for that.

A nurse came in to change his bandages and to give him the shots I couldn't give him, but I didn't consider that a disturbance. That was important. What wasn't, not right now, was the council or government or self-serving pricks who called themselves politicians.

When the nurse retreated, we moved from the bed to the sitting room. As with most rooms in the palace, there was always something we weren't allowed to change. Be it a mural or a fresco, or some kind of fancy architecture that was living, breathing history. In the bedroom, it was the fresco over the bed and the bed itself—over eight feet of Veronian carved pine with more detailing on it than mantilla lace. It stood tall and proud, and was draped with reproduction silks that mimicked what had been hanging there for centuries.

Sometimes, it was easy to get lost in all the history. To forget that it was actually the twenty-first century. But in the living room of my suite, things were a bit simpler.

There was only a fireplace to protect, and I'd been allowed to move out and replace the furniture with things that were comfortable.

I'd left my bedroom alone—the four-poster matched the other cabinets in there, and anything else would have looked silly. The cabinet, the armoire, and the dresser were all crafted by the same carpenter and carver, so I left it well enough alone even though it made the large, cavernous space seem clustered—that was how big each piece was.

In here, I let my own taste reign supreme.

There was a huge sofa with more pillows on it than I knew what to do with. It was high backed with a long body so I could slump against the cushions and kick my legs up, free to be unlike a princess by actually slouching and not having to sit just *so*.

It was dark blue in color, so I didn't have to worry about stains—which I tended to have issues with. Princesses spilled shit too, okay?—and it was comfortable as heck, especially when it was cold out and I could stare directly into the fireplace that was roaring merrily away.

In front of the fireplace, which had a massive DeSauvier crest at its peak, there were two matching armchairs, but they were a light cream. Two guesses which chairs I never used, but they were functional and neat, and meant my sisters or Mom had somewhere to sit if they came and visited me here, but they didn't. Not usually. We had family rooms and then we had our personal suites. The suites were private, and we tended to give each other space because, in our daily lives, privacy wasn't a commodity that came cheap.

Between the sofa and armchairs, there was a modern rug which was a light, dusky pink with bands of gold and black, interspersed with navy and cream that matched the furniture. There was a glass coffee table—again, to avoid stains from mugs—and on either side of the armchairs, I had two nestle tables with lovely lamps that let me read by their light all the way over in my nest on the sofa.

Above the fire there was one of my favorites from the family collection—a Monet watercolor, and around the walls, between heavy navy drapes, there were pictures of my family when we were on vacation or during parties that mattered to me—like my ascension to the role of crown princess when I was fourteen. Everyone had been there, Tin included, but he'd been there as a surprise, and I'd managed to dance with him.

Another two guesses for which picture was up on the wall.

Me in a ballgown wearing the official surcoat of my new station, my hair loose about my shoulders, and Tin in a tuxedo, looking skinny and young.

When we'd come into this room earlier, he'd seen the picture and shaken his head at the sight of it. "You have it on the wall."

"Where else would I have it?"

His lips twisted and I'd watched him glance around, getting the measure of the place. "This is more you."

I shrugged. "You know how it works. We can only change so much. This room had fewer period features in it."

"Will we have to live here?"

My heart started pounding at that casual question. The way he'd said it made things sound so real. And I knew that was crazy because why would he be here otherwise? But it cemented things home in a way I wasn't used to, in a way I needed.

On the brink of having a heart attack from the mere suggestion, I just watched as he blinked at me, then, with a shake of his head, smirked before strutting over to the sofa like he owned the place.

Watching him climb onto it had my eyes widening. But I understood. Normally, you'd just sit down. But his muscles were all torn up.

Ouch.

He pretty much crawled onto it face forward, and when he had to twist around, then plunked himself back on the cushions with a heavy grunt after a dozen panting breaths, I murmured, "Well, that was elegant."

He didn't bother raising his head, just lifted his hand and gave me the finger.

I smiled, an hour on, from the memory.

To be treated like that was bizarrely romantic. Yeah, I knew that sounded crazy, but I wasn't going insane or anything. I didn't have tendencies that meant I liked to be treated like shit. It was just so normal. And I was never treated with normalcy.

Normal and my life did *not* go hand in hand.

"What are you laughing about?"

"I'm not laughing," I instantly denied.

"Liar."

I huffed. "Charmer."

"I try. It's the English gent in me."

"Oh yeah, they should call you Byron."

"I'm not mad, bad, or dangerous to know. I don't think that would suit me."

I snorted. "Didn't he have all the ladies flittering at his feet?"

"Wasn't that Beau Brummell?"

"Maybe."

"Maybe? Thought you were the historical romance buff?"

I whacked his arm. "Shut up," I whined.

He laughed. "That means yes."

"No, it doesn't."

"Yes, it does." He rolled his head so he could look at me. "Georgette Heyer still your fave?"

I glared at him before I raised my hand and covered my face. "If you dare tell Christel, I'll kill you myself."

"So bloodthirsty," he chided.

"Of course. With Christel, she's savage. You know I'll never hear the end of it. How romance books perpetuate non-feminist ideas—" I yawned. "I can't deal with that BS. I just like what I like."

"Yes, you do." His teasing had me smiling at him, and as our gazes connected, the flames from the fireplace flickering in each of our eyes, I had to admit that it didn't feel like it had been months and years since we'd sat this close. It was like time had never stopped rolling on without us being this way.

"How are you feeling?" I inquired softly.

"Better for being in here and not in that clinic. Better for being with you." He sighed. "Don't think we'll be as lucky in the morning."

"No." I pursed my lips. "I don't think so either. I think this was a stay of grace that we were lucky to get."

"Me, too." He hummed. "Shame, though, I'd have liked it."

"I would as well, but you'll be allowed to rest. It's me the parents will drag out." I cleared my throat. "You know there'll be a ceremony, don't you?"

I asked that hesitantly because I was concerned that it would irritate him. That was a new development and one I'd have to work on. I couldn't spend the rest of my life being 'careful' around him just because

I was scared he'd go off in a huff and leave for another two years. What kind of relationship was that?

No, I'd have to grow a pair, but for the moment, and on this matter, I wasn't comfortable in being so frank with him over it.

This was, without a doubt, a tetchy subject, and I couldn't blame him. Not in all honesty.

"Of course. I knew that before I even made the decision to come back here."

I arched a brow. "You did?"

"I did," he confirmed. "Our marriage is legal and binding—but not enough for Veronia."

My cheeks blanched at the memory of how exactly I'd made sure of the legal and binding part of the ceremony. "I'm sorry, Tin. What I did was terrible."

He grunted. "Hardly."

I winced. "You wanted it?"

"I did. I always wanted you. Still do." He blew out his cheeks. "I mean, I guess I wasn't complaining at the time about you consummating our marriage on my behalf, so I can't complain about it now either, can I?"

"If you say so," I rasped.

"Well, I do. I'm not going to cry over spilled milk anymore, Etta. You made a lot of mistakes. So did I. I think we need to work together as a unit to make sure that neither of us does anything that can irreparably damage our relationship again."

Though it wasn't a question, more of a statement, I whispered, "I'll never do anything that heinous—"

"Let's stop referring to the ceremony that almost made Edward have a fit as heinous, hmm? At least you're mine now. Otherwise, there'd be issues. I know my family is a problem, and this way, it's a fait accompli. I prefer it that way."

Me, too.

But I didn't say that.

"You'll rest tomorrow, won't you?"

"I don't have a choice," he groaned. "It still hurts like a bitch."

"There'll be things I have to do, but we're going to start arranging the ceremony."

"Like you're going to have much to do," he said with a laugh. "Mum and Auntie Perry will take that over and no mistake."

"True." I shrugged. "I'm not that interested anyway."

He arched a brow at me. "Should I be offended that my bride isn't blushing and eager?"

"Oh, I'm eager, and I'll blush, just not about having to go through the whole ceremony shit." I rolled my eyes. "It's going to be a lot of pomp and no glory. Plus, you'll have to be crowned, Tin, you know that, don't you?"

"I do."

I peeped at him from the corner of my eye. "Are you okay with that?"

"If it means you're my wife for real, then I have to be, don't I?"

"I'm sorry," I whispered. "I wish things were simpler."

"I know you do, and I thank you for that, but you don't have to feel guilty for being who you are. I wouldn't love you so fucking much if I didn't think you were awesome, would I?"

"No, I guess not." But marrying me wasn't like marrying a regular woman, and I knew he was brushing over it, which, in turn, made me thankful.

I didn't want to keep ramming home how different things would be for us, how much ceremony there'd be to the event—more so than with a regular wedding—but I just needed him to know, I needed him to be aware so that the next morning, when he realized what had happened and what he'd done, he didn't rail at me and tell me I'd destroyed his life before storming off and refusing to talk to me again for years.

God, these were issues I was going to have to work on. Already.

Wanting to facepalm myself for being a dick, I just muttered, "I hope they do take over to be honest. It's never been my thing."

"I'm not even sure how that's possible considering you love the books you do."

"Yeah, in books. And they never go on about the weddings, do they? I've never liked romances like that. I have too many ceremonies in my life to be happy about that.

"If it was down to me, I'd be happy going back to Elvis," I admitted. "I can't go to the bathroom without there being some formality I have to complete sometimes."

He snorted. "I'm sure your bathroom habits are of interest to no one."

"Ha!" I exclaimed. "Just you wait until it's official. I bet we have problems with people trying to figure out if I'm pregnant."

He twisted his head to gape at me. "You can't be serious."

"Bet your non-royal-soon-to-be-royal ass I'm being serious." I grazed my bottom lip with my teeth then mumbled, "You don't want kids right away, do you?"

He cut me a look. "Do you?"

"I mean, there'll be pressure from the council. But there always is." I hitched my shoulder. "You know me. I hate kids."

"Do you want a family?"

"I want a family with you. I assume I won't hate our kid or kids."

He laughed. "No, I'd hope not. But I don't want you to want a kid just because of the line of succession, babe. There's more to having a child than that."

"Yeah, I know," I murmured drolly. "Honestly, I do. But it's different with you. Anyone else, and I probably wouldn't. I dunno, I'd pretend I was sterile or something. Which would be really awkward because I bet they'd make me go and get tested." I heaved a sigh, not seeing his horrified glance. "But I want your child. Just, like, not for another six or so years."

"They'd make you get tested?"

"The council? Hell, yeah. They're all about the line of succession."

"The UnReals should just be a fly on the wall for this conversation and then they'd realize it sucks to be you."

I snorted. "Thanks."

He shook his head. "I can't believe they'd make you get tested."

"The line has to stand true, even if my sisters and their kids would ascend if anything happened to me."

His hand snapped out and grabbed mine. He clenched his fingers around me, then growled, "Nothing's going to happen to you."

"I know. But nothing had better happen to you either."

He squeezed my hand again. "It won't. I don't intend on us finding each other again only for things to end with me taking a bullet."

"Good."

"Anyway, I'm down for six years. There's no need for us to have a family so young."

"It's weird that we're talking about this. I'm sorry," I said earnestly. Most men were just thinking about boning their woman, and here we were talking about stuff that wasn't pertinent to our lives at the moment.

"Don't be sorry. In fact, stop saying sorry. You fucked up, Etta. I'm not going to say you didn't. You fucked up, now it's over, and now we move on. I'm well aware of the clusterfuck I'm diving headfirst into, even if some of the details are going to boggle my brain because you never told me the council was so invasive, but, even so, it doesn't matter.

"I know I need to prove this to you, but believe me when I say this, that I meant it from the bottom of my heart—it's you and me until the end, babe."

I felt like such a sap when my eyes started leaking at that, and I wanted to hide, wanted to shield my stupid tears from his gaze, but I couldn't because when I made to twist my head to the side, to avoid his penetrating look, he reached for my chin—evidently forgetting about his injuries—and forced me to look at him—while he was wincing in pain from the exertion. "No. Don't stop looking at me. This is important.

"When I got these wounds in the first place, I remember laying there, wondering if I was going to die, and all I could think about was the shit I'd missed out on doing with you.

"I wasted years, Etta. Years. We could have done so much together in all that time, and instead, I was throwing a tantrum. So, love, I have to say this to you—I'm sorry, too. You messed up, I messed up. But we have to make sure that neither of us messes up again."

"You're right," I rasped. "I don't want anything to come between us, Tin."

"And it won't. Not your father or the council or the government or whatever. And I mean this as well, if you decide in a few years' time that you don't want kids, I will fuck up any goddamn council in the land who thinks they can send us to a fertility specialist to figure out if there's something wrong with us, do you hear me?"

My lips twisted. "Rebel."

"Damn straight. At least, on this score." He laughed. "I've been anything but a rebel in the last few years. Being told to jump and I've asked how high...but no more."

I clenched my fingers around his. "We can't always ignore them. Sometimes, they won't allow it."

"Screw them. Rules were made to be broken, and laws were made to protect everyone, including the future queen. If someone dares question you, then I don't care how long it takes, I *will* analyze the shit out of the situation and find a way to make the council pay."

Despite myself, I had to laugh. "I'd pay to see that."

"For you, I'd offer my services free of charge."

When he winked, I beamed a smile at him, one he returned. My heart, beating fast from the conversation, began to slow down as we stared at one another, and everything just fell into place.

Like it always would, because this was meant to be.

SEVENTEEN

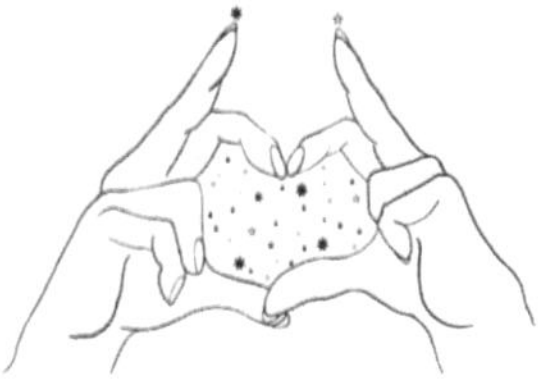

TIN

"HOPE YOU'RE PROUD OF HER," I muttered, my gaze on Xavier as he watched Etta on his screen.

The country's main news channel had decided to cover Etta, and her comportment over the past few weeks. Someone had managed to grab a picture of her bowing over Andrea's body at Casterby, then there were more of her with some of the victims who'd been caught in the crossfire. There was even footage of her singing at Andrea's funeral, and I knew, for damn sure, that there wouldn't have been a dry eye in any household who'd seen that on the nine o'clock news.

"Yes," Xavier rumbled simply, and I left him to it, because he was looking a bit teary himself.

Deciding to cut him some slack, I groaned as the tailor tugged on the shirt covering me. When he started messing around with my pants and the jacket he was trying to fit to my form, I bit off, "You do know I have injuries, don't you?"

The guy, a little mouse with a bald pate that gleamed more than a mirror and had an honest to God toothbrush moustache that made him look like a rotund Hitler, glared at me. "The suit must be tailored to you to perfection."

I cocked a brow at him. "I'm not going to be walking down the aisle any time soon if you're tugging and pulling at my stitches."

Sawyer, standing at my back, snorted, but Xavier, who was still watching Etta on his phone a few feet away, muttered without looking up, "He has a point, Jean Luc. Try not to cause too many injuries with your poking and prodding."

Sawyer wandered over to a stand that was like a wooden kitchen island. It had dozens of drawers on either side with tiny handles. I'd seen Jean Luc pull out all kinds of shit from within, but atop it were fabric swatches, and my dad started to flip through them with an idleness that didn't suit him.

None of my fathers were idle. Mum wasn't either, not really. I mean, she could slob around the house in her PJs all day, but she was usually yelling at someone on her phone to do some shit or other so she didn't have to go out.

My fathers, on the other hand, were workaholics. Though Sean had retired from his original position with Scotland Yard and the Met back when I was a baby, he'd never really stopped working. Kurt was constantly writing, or if he wasn't writing, he was editing or working on a screenplay or something. Mum usually helped him with his projects too, which added to her workload, but I figured she enjoyed it, otherwise why would she do it?

Sawyer and Devon were always busy, a project or a puzzle that had their brains constantly ticking, and Andrei never stopped. Whether he was floating an IPO in the States, or trying to manage the family's hedge fund, sitting still wasn't something he did for long.

So, to see Sawyer dawdling was definitely an unusual sight.

I cocked a brow at him. "What's up with you?"

His lips twitched, but Andrei, in the other corner, opposite George, muttered, "Insolent boy," in Russian.

I just grinned. "I try." I'd have bowed, but I didn't. It wouldn't have been worth being stuck in the balls with a pin by Jean Luc.

Andrei sniffed, but Sawyer muttered, "Just cannae believe it. That's all."

"Yeah, I know." My brow puckered as I stared around the tailor's shop that had been dressing men of the DeSauvier line for over two hundred years. There were the ceremonial robes of two kings in here, encased in glass, and there were countless other memorabilia that would have boggled my mind on an ordinary day.

Today?

I was just over it already.

My body was aching, my stomach felt like a tiger had been gnawing on it as a treat, and I really just wanted to sit down.

But this, crazy as it seemed, was my world.

My. Fucking. World.

Incredible. *Insane.*

I was going to sit on a throne and help rule a country someday, but boy, was I grateful that Edward was in rude health. Just like Etta, there was no way I was ready to rule this place. Shit. I couldn't keep myself contained, never mind deal with the fuck ups Edward handled on the regular.

I was willing, and more than able, to take on more work, to take on a role in society and to support Etta. Mostly because what Perry had told me hit home.

I had always thought Edward was a hard ass to Etta. I'd always faintly disapproved of him. But hearing Perry's staunch defense? It'd made me cut the guy some slack, and if anyone deserved a bit of a break, it was him.

"I knew it would happen."

Sawyer rolled his eyes at the voice that chimed in from a corner of the tailor's. Devon was sitting somewhere out of my line of sight, but I knew he was on the floor somewhere because, otherwise, I'd have been able to see him.

"You're a regular feckin' psychic, ain't ye?" Sawyer grumbled.

"No, I just know my son." Devon sniffed.

The irony was, Devon *did* know me. Even though he was vacant in some ways, he was also the most aware of me.

I knew, whenever I was in the room, Devon always knew where I was.

Okay, that sounded weird, and I guessed it was, but it was true nonetheless. He usually knew more about how I was doing than I did, which for a man who couldn't understand his own emotions was pretty powerful shit.

Another reason to be terrified of fatherhood.

I knew I could never compete with *any* of my fathers.

And, I mean, I'd had five. Five guys to cut the slack. If one was busy, there'd always been another one to play with or to talk to—how was I supposed to cope when I was just one person?

Slightly terrified by the prospect, I muttered, "You guys can't die for like eighty years."

"That would make us older than the records indicate as being possible, Tin," Devon intoned, sounding like he was reading the *Guinness World Records* book there and then.

Etta said she might not want kids, but if she did...Fuck. "I don't care. Break records. If I have to have kids, you guys need to be around to help me."

Sawyer laughed, so did Andrei. "Aye, ye were lucky."

Jean Luc tutted under his breath, which had me narrowing my eyes at him.

"You have a problem with my family, Jean Luc?"

Silence fell at my declaration, and the tailor froze. The smile he pasted on his face was wholly professional, though, when he tipped his head back to look at me. "No, of course not, sir."

"Well, I heard you tut."

"You moved."

"I didn't," I countered, glaring at him. "If you have a problem with me, then I don't think I want you measuring my inseam."

His nostrils flared, his eyes flashing with outrage. "My family has fitted the coronation robes for—"

"I don't care. Traditions were meant to be broken," I retorted, uncaring that Xavier and George had both tensed at my statement.

But I *didn't* care.

I knew things were precarious with my family. I knew the number of fathers I had raised eyebrows, but I wasn't about to deal with that bullshit, and my fathers-in-law needed to know that right from the start.

I *wasn't* ashamed of my past. I loved my fathers. They'd given me an epic childhood, had made me into the man I was today, and I'd never be without them if I didn't have to be.

No way in fuck was some pompous jackass going to tut at them because they dared to love one woman.

Jean Luc cut panicked looks at George and Xavier, flashing between them like they were going to back him and not me, and to be fair, I almost expected they would. Veronians were built on tradition. Just look at Etta. Her bedroom was like something from a Victorian movie, creepy as fuck, but she dealt with it because it was tradition.

Well, I wouldn't be dealing with that.

She might be willing, but I wasn't a Veronian. Hell, I was a Brit and we were used to the whole stiff upper lip shit, but this went beyond the pale.

"I think you should apologize, Jean Luc," Xavier rasped, his focus off his phone and firmly on the tailor.

"But I didn't say—"

"You didn't have to," Xavier rumbled. "I could feel your disapproval from over here."

His jaw clenched at the dressing down, but I didn't care.

Stiffly, he muttered, "I apologize."

It wasn't the most gracious of deliveries, but I'd take it. It wasn't like I gave a shit about the man's opinion, but I wasn't about to let that slide either.

The rest of the fitting took place in relative silence. It was uncomfortable, but I had zero fucks to give.

All the guys in my family save for Sean and Edward were here, because they were with their wives, sorting out some wedding crap with *mine*.

Mine.

I liked the sound of that.

The others suffered through their fittings, and while ordinarily I'd have been bored as hell watching men getting measured up for penguin suits, I was actually relieved. It was wonderful to sit down, wonderful to be with my fathers, and wonderful not to be fucking dead.

Plus, if I wasn't here, I'd have to be with Etta, and she was tasting cakes today. Or so she'd grumbled at me earlier.

Etta had to be the only person I knew who didn't like cake. Give her cheese, a cake made of literal cheese, and she'd be happy. But cake? Nope.

Me, on the other hand, I'd have been happy with the tasting, but it was all the other BS I didn't care about.

Neither of us were really that into the ceremony, but I got a kick out of how psyched Mum was. Last night, she'd barged into our quarters with a binder, and a few minutes later Perry had appeared with a large bottle of wine, some chocolates, and a bag of chips for Etta because, again, Etta didn't like sweets.

They'd camped out in front of the fire where we'd been chilling, and had started discussing things like table settings and venues and how many chairs they'd need.

Apparently, Etta and I were going to have to hand sign over two thousand invitations—three hundred for the wedding ceremony itself, which would be televised—God help me—and then the remainder were for two parties we'd be having in the aftermath. A further four hundred would be invited to the meal, and then the others would be invited to a night party.

As I thought about having to sign my name two thousand times, Dad gripped my shoulder and muttered, "Ye cannae let these pricks get to ye, lad."

I blinked at him, not really online, then I glared at Jean Luc when I figured out what Sawyer was talking about.

"Yeah, not going to happen."

Sawyer tutted. "Think we care about what people think of us?"

"No, but I do. You're the best fathers a man could ever hope for, and I'm bloody lucky that you're mine. If you think I'm going to let some dickhead start talking shit about you—"

"He tutted, lad. Don't ye think yer being a wee bit melodramatic?"

"Maybe." I shrugged. "But I don't care. I'm going to start as I mean to go on. I refuse to be ashamed, Dad."

"You dinnae need to be ashamed, just don't be getting on your high horse over things that have nae importance in the grand scheme of things."

I grunted under my breath as he hauled me onto my feet. When his arm wrapped around my shoulder, he muttered, "Honestly, lad, it'll only get yer heart rate pumping."

"Isn't that a good thing?"

He snorted. "When it's fer sex and work outs, aye. Stress, no."

Every couple of years, Dad had a bit of a health scare, and everyone in the family was aware that he was prone to illnesses more than most. Every year we had with him was a blessing, and that was why I was so staunch in my defense.

I loved this man, just like I loved all my fathers. Even if they never failed to try to teach me something along life's way.

"I try not to get stressed," I mumbled.

"I dinnae think you try hard enough."

"Please don't make me meditate," I half complained.

"I won't, but only because yer a whiner when it boils down to stuff like that."

I pulled a face at him, but I didn't argue as he hauled me closer to him and together, we strode out of the backroom of the tailors.

"I'm used to wealth, lad," Sawyer admitted as we strode into the storefront, "but this is a whole other ball of wax."

I knew what he meant. We were rich. Richer than the DeSauviers, but royalty always did things a little differently.

I'd been to the tailors before, I had a regular tailor who made my suits on Savile Row, for God's sake, but this place was something else.

There were pictures lining the walls of old kings and coronation wear Jean Luc's family had made for centuries, and then there were oil portraits, too, of the royals who'd been tended to within these walls.

"Can ye believe that little prick only works for the family? How many suits do they need cut for them each year?"

"You'd be surprised." Sawyer and me both jerked in shock at George's insertion, and I yelped as I twisted around because my entire body ached like a bitch the second I moved.

George winced. "Sorry. Didn't mean to make you jump. I thought you heard me."

"No worries," I panted, holding my side even though that didn't do shit.

"What would we be surprised about?" Sawyer asked after he glanced at me, then took the spotlight off me—thankfully.

"How many suits we need. Don't forget, there are a league of cousins who need outfitting too."

"Seems excessive," I grumbled.

"Jean Luc also maintains a lot of the outfits we have that are hundreds of years old and that go into museums around the country."

"He preserves them?"

"Yes. He's an annoying asshat, but he's damn good at what he does."

As we strolled past a bank of seats that looked mighty fine to me, I was relieved to note that, on the outside step, there was a car waiting on us. Well, several cars.

I almost staggered over to the vehicle and was relieved when the driver was there with the door open for me.

As I began to duck down into the limo, it was only the odd way I had to climb into the car that let me see it. I couldn't get in, ass first, like usual. My body wouldn't let me. So I had to put one knee on the seat then kind of climb in. But because of that unusual, and undeniably graceless, positioning, I saw it.

A weird glint in the window opposite me.

I frowned at the sight, unsure why I found it odd. The sun wasn't shining, again, and it was bitterly cold out. I was freezing since I was only wearing a light cotton jumper, because anything else on my body made me feel like I was wearing chainmail that constricted every breath I took, so the fact I noticed anything untoward at all had me tensing in place.

I'd never had any covert training. I wasn't bullshitting about not being a spy. But I *was* an analyst, and sometimes I was sent overseas to help the James Bonds of my government with sticky situations.

I'd been given the basic defense course—which was anything but basic, but not as intense as what the covert ops agents went through—and I figured it was those instincts that had been drummed into me that had me hollering, "On the ground! Shooter!"

The second I screamed that, I heard it.

That fucking whistle.

That goddamn, motherfucking whistle that was going to plague me until the day I died.

Even as I hurled myself backward, trying to cover my father and Etta's, my body screaming with the movement, I heard someone grunt, heard others fall to the ground at my command, but I knew from the scent of blood in the air that someone had been hit.

Four of my fathers, and two of Etta's, had been walking out behind me...

If any of them were dead, the UnReals were going to wish they'd never been born.

That was more than a fucking promise, it was a goddamn vow.

EIGHTEEN

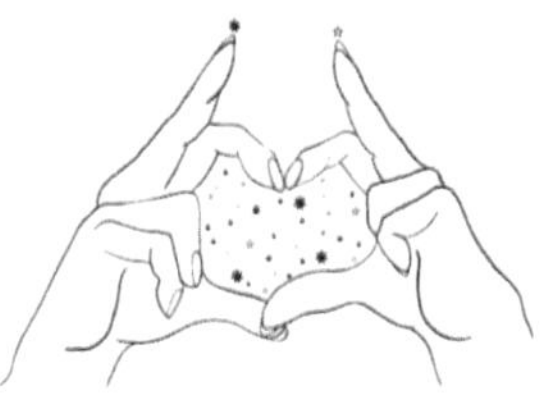

ETTA

MOM SCREAMED when she saw Daddy being rushed into the private ward. She ran after him on flip-flop covered feet as the doctors pounded their way down the hall toward the medical unit, and I watched her, my heart shrieking like I'd been running as I stared at the line of blood on the ground.

My Daddy's blood.

He couldn't die.

He couldn't.

My mouth trembled as I raised a hand and touched my mouth. A scream was building inside me, a scream that made my very brain rattle.

How was this happening?

How did this threat still exist?

For a second, that white noise reappeared again, and I felt sure I was losing my mind. It overtook everything, all five of my senses, coating each of them until it invaded every part of me.

Then I heard it, a howl of grief. A howl of pain and rage and fury and hurt.

Hurt.

My body shuddered, and then he was there. A hand slipped around my waist as he hurled me into his side. He smelled like mine and home, like warmth and love, and I missed him even as I was grateful to have him again.

His other hand moved to the back of my head, and he cupped it before he pushed me toward him, not stopping until my face was burrowed in his throat.

Another howl.

Like an animal in pain. Raging grief.

No.

No.

No.

It couldn't be.

He couldn't be dead. My daddy couldn't be gone.

My entire body was one big tremor. I felt like I was in the middle of an earthquake, every part of me being torn apart as different emotions tugged at me.

I'd known hurt and I'd known loss—hadn't we all? But I felt like I'd lost more people than most. More death surrounded me as people gave their lives, sacrificed everything to keep me safe.

But here I was, sobbing against the love of my life's chest.

Rage unfurled through me, and I knew I couldn't stay here, listening to my mom's grief. If I did, I'd hurl myself into that abyss too.

I needed to act.

I needed to do something.

The saltwater of tears burned my eyes, but I blinked them back as I tilted my head so I could look into Tin's face. His expression was grim, and there were spots of blood on his face, splashed on his throat.

My daddy's blood.

My throat tightened. "Help me," I rasped.

"What do you need?"

The reply was instant.

"I need you to forget your honor," I whispered. "I need you to think of *this* country and not yours."

His eyes flashed. "I acted in both country's best interests."

"With the scales tipped in the favor of the U.K. I got that. I did. You were just coming out of active service. It's hard to break ties, hard to sever ties. But you have to act. They're not going to stop."

His mouth worked. "They wanted me."

My jaw tensed. "What makes you say that?"

"The angle of the shot. I only noticed it because of the way I'm climbing into cars at the moment."

"It could have been my fathers—"

"Maybe it was. Call it gut instinct."

"Do you know *anything*, anything at all that might help us?"

His eyes shuttered. "I do."

I grabbed his hand and dragged him down the corridor, out of the private healthcare unit that tended to my family and my family alone, and drew us into the garden.

"What do you know?"

"There's a British team stationed here."

"That's not unusual," I retorted. "I bet they have someone everywhere, even if it's not authorized." I grunted. "Especially if they're not authorized."

Tin shook his head. "They're here for a reason."

I swallowed. "What reason?"

"It's in Britain's best interests that Veronia's royals stay on the throne."

My brow puckered—but I got that. In a world where royal families were considered a drain on the economy, we were a dying breed. We only remained on our thrones, continued to rule with power in our hands by the will of the people.

"So, why's that a bad thing?" I queried.

"It isn't. But their presence here indicates something else."

I reached up and rubbed my temple. "Speak clearly, Tin."

"I only know they're here by accident. I heard some chatter, and I knew a couple of sharpshooters who were redirected suddenly—"

"Wait, you can't think they're the ones who did this today?"

His head slashed to the side. "No, of course not. I'm saying that, like on a chessboard, pieces have been mobilized."

"And if they haven't come out to play, then what? They're waiting for something bigger?"

"Maybe." Tin's mouth firmed, his top lip flatlining and, behind his eyes, I could see the cogs working. Could see his brain flushing through strategies as he did what he did best. He was smart, not as smart as his daddies, but in his own way, just as intelligent. Capable of so much that I knew I had to stay quiet, let him piece things together.

We were far enough away from the ward not to hear anything, but my mother's grief ricocheted in my ears like it was on a constant echo.

I still refused to believe.

I wouldn't.

Not until I saw him with my own eyes. Not until I held his hand and felt his lifelessness.

So I had to stay away. I couldn't deal with that yet.

We needed to act.

"Why now?" Tin muttered, raking a hand through his hair.

"Why do they ever decide to do anything?" I demanded bitterly. "The UnReals just strike whenever they feel like it."

"No, we may believe that, but they act for a reason." He gripped the back of his neck and pushed back from me. When he started to pace, I noticed his gait was wooden, wondered at it, wanted to tell him to sit down, but didn't. Couldn't. I needed him to think this through, to figure out what the fuck was going on.

"There's a reason for everything. Why they targeted the economy the way they did, why they drained it dry for a good solid few years—let's face it, they gained enough to fund themselves for a lifetime."

"That's not good news," I ground out.

"They were quiet for a while, weren't they? Maybe five years?"

I nodded. "We had a few threats, but nothing enacted. A bomb in a shopping mall we were opening, but it turned out to be a hoax."

His pace quickened, like he needed to expend the effort to form the answers.

Then he stopped.

Then he turned to me.

"Two groups."

My brow puckered. "What do you mean?"

"I mean, there are two opposing forces here. One was cerebral. Smart. It takes brains to be able to create sieves in the economy like what they made back in the day. It took someone of Devon's capacity to find it, for fuck's sake. You plugged in the leaks, and figured out ways to regenerate, but even so, that takes brains.

"This is brawn. This is thoughtless. This is action but with no gain.

All they're doing is pissing people off, shooting in public areas, making the general population unsafe in their own homes."

"Since when have they cared about the ordinary folk they hurt to get to us—"

He ignored my snarl. "They always act to get public gain. It's the only real way they can topple royalty. Nothing happens without stirring the masses, and this is doing the opposite."

My head was starting to ache. "Tin, then—"

His mouth firmed. "These shootings, they're making people hate the UnReals."

"It can't be a coincidence," I rasped. "It can't be that sharpshooters have been brought here—"

He raised a hand. "No. It can't be." He rubbed his head. "I must be wrong."

"You don't sound like you think you're wrong," I whispered. "You sound like you *hope* you are."

"Of course I do. I don't want to think my country is capable of this."

"All countries are capable of this. Even Veronia. Who the fuck knows what the Guard Elect really does? We have security services of our own. You think they don't do stuff that most people would disapprove of?" I released a shaky breath. "You know how dark and grimy politics are."

"Conspiracies don't exist—"

"Now you really are clutching at straws." He'd been a conspiracy buff back as a kid. Looking for answers where there were none to be found, asking questions where he shouldn't.

"I can't believe that—" He shook his head. "I just can't."

He looked at me with entreaty in his eyes, like a little boy who had just been told Santa Claus wasn't real.

The trouble with Tin was he was all man, and his brain was worth two men, but he was naive. He was a hoper. He might not think he was, in fact, he'd probably say that I was the dreamer, but they were two different things, weren't they?

Maybe I dreamed. Dreamed about freedom and choices and things that most people thought they had but couldn't afford.

Hope, on the other hand, was far more expensive. Far more costly.

Tin wanted to believe the best of people. What had he told me?

That it took being betrayed, in earnest, to realize that what I'd done to him was a walk in the park.

That didn't make me feel better about myself, about what I'd done, but I figured that summed up Tin right there.

He was good people. The best. He wanted to wish others well. He didn't want to think the opposite was true. That it was happening.

I blew out a breath, and because I loved him and didn't want him to hurt, I murmured, "Maybe you're wrong. Maybe you should call up some people you know and see what's happening?"

He shook his head. "No one will talk to me now. Not only because I quit, but because it's hit the news about us. Why would they give me information—they have to know it will bounce back to the DeSauviers."

My shoulders slumped. "True."

"This is all speculation," he rasped.

"More than we had to begin with."

He winced. "Yeah." Tin turned to me and murmured, "All I know is that there are two different methods here. Maybe my people are behind the economy drain?"

I snorted at that and his hopeful tone. "Will that make you feel better?"

"What? Than thinking my government is willing to kill members of the Veronian royal family, or at least put them in serious danger, just to shore up public opinion? Damn straight."

His words had me frowning. "It doesn't make sense."

"Doesn't it?" he snapped. "Seems like it does to me."

"No, look, why would they do things on our soil to protect us when the family is popular? We have no need for help in gaining public support. For over a century, we've been popular! Even in dark times, people look to us for strength and support, and we always give it.

"Since Mama became queen, people love us even more. You know what she's like. She's always doing something to help the country, more so than my grandmother did."

Tin rubbed the back of his neck again. "Follow the money."

I blinked. "Huh? Didn't Devon already do that?"

Tin shook his head. "No. He didn't. He had a breakdown—I didn't even know about it until—"

I frowned. "Until when?"

"It was when I was a kid. He'd just figured out the money was being systematically drained out of the economy, then Sawyer collapsed." He blew out a breath. "Devon had a complete meltdown. Didn't talk to anyone for two months."

I'd sat through enough boring history lessons on this subject to know the facts. "But pretty soon after, we had issues with the UnReals because the truth came out. Mom took me and we stayed with you, didn't we?" I blinked, but trying to remember was hard going. I'd been, what? Two, maybe, at the time? I'd seen the pictures though. Me and Tin in the bath. With his puppies. No pictures of my dads around because they'd been here, while we'd been safely tucked away in Sascha's paternal estate.

"I know for a fact that Devon was working on other stuff when he was in the middle of that meltdown. The Hodge Conjecture, to be precise. He'd pretty much done eighty percent of his theoretical work on it by the time Mum got him to break out of it."

"So, he was working on other stuff in the aftermath?"

"Yeah. I have to guess that someone, probably Andrei, gave Veronia Devon's findings."

"Then they dealt with the leak, plugged it up, and...what? Never looked for the culprits?"

"Maybe they didn't." He shrugged. "Seems stupid to me, too, but maybe it isn't. I know you guys had a lot of issues back then, and it looked like you were on the brink of civil war—"

"We're popular with the majority. You know we have issues in the North," was all I could think to say. It was to our nation's great shame that we'd almost had a civil war, and so close to the new Millennium.

"Doesn't matter. What I'm trying to say is that priorities have a way of pushing things to the background."

I pondered what he was saying, then blurted out, "So, what? You think if we find who was behind the original embezzling scheme, we'll figure out what's happening today? But you said you see two motives."

"I do," he rumbled. "Just thinking it was the UnReals—"

"Surely the security services looked into it," I ground out. "They're not incompetent."

"They had bigger fish to fry."

"Why are you two arguing?"

Was it fate or chance that it was Devon who wandered out into the garden?

He stared at us like we'd just landed in the yard from a trip to Venus, his head tilted to the side as he took me in in a glance, then studied Tin with a laser-like stare.

Tin, quite used to that, didn't flinch. Devon seemed to take everything in. The blood spatters, the slight fleck of blood on his belly where I knew he'd started to bleed through his bandages—fuck, he'd split his stitches again and hadn't realized it. Then, he took in the lines of strain, the tension in Tin's body—it was weird knowing what Devon was assessing, but it didn't take a rocket scientist. Devon knew everything about Tin. Whatever there was to know.

I doubted Tin had many secrets from him.

I was probably the biggest one, and even then, Devon claimed he'd known how Tin felt about me.

"You're bleeding," Devon said flatly.

"It's nothing. It's from—"

"Yes. George. He's asking for you, Alice."

My heart stopped. "He isn't dead?"

Devon blinked. "Would he have asked for you if he was?"

Hope filled me. "I-I thought—"

"You thought wrong." His mouth firmed. "I believe he'd like to see you before they operate. You have approximately two minutes. They're setting up the surgery as we speak."

I didn't wait, didn't think to hang around. My daddy wasn't dead, and I needed to see him more than I needed my next breath.

NINETEEN

TIN

"YOU'RE BLEEDING."

I sighed at his repeated comment. "I know, Dad."

"If you know then why aren't you trying to stop it?" Devon tipped his head to the other side. "Mum won't be happy if you go into a coma again."

"No, I think she'd be the opposite of happy," I groused, peering down at my stomach. "It's nothing. Only small. I just pulled some stitches."

"That was insane what you did today." Devon's tone was flatter still. "I saw it."

I shrugged. "What was I going to do? Let them get hit?"

He narrowed his eyes on me. "Since when did you carry a gun?"

"You don't know everything about me, Dad," I rasped, but I twisted away and stared out at the garden.

The palace was famed for a fountain that, even though they'd had issues with water conservation—issues that stemmed from another round with the UnReals—they hadn't shut down. It worked, if memory served, thanks to high water pressure. It had a geyser spouting dozens of feet into the air and had been a feat of engineering back in the day—hell, it was pretty impressive now. Especially when you realized that not an ounce of electricity powered it.

"There were guards there. You should have let them do it."

"He was in my line of sight. The second the glass shattered from the shot, I knew where he was. I was faster than him."

"You killed a man, Valentin."

I shrugged. "Some man. A traitor." Then, jaw working, I twisted around, ignoring the ache in my side and demanded, "You know who was behind the embezzling, don't you?"

Devon's eyes shuttered. "Not personally, no."

My nostrils flared—but once again, I was reminded of the importance of patience with my father.

He'd never hurt the Veronians. Would never hurt anyone. Especially not people Mum or I cared about.

"Don't be pedantic," I rasped. "I don't care if you know them personally. I want to know if you know their identities."

"Of course I do." He eyed my belly. "You're bleeding more."

"I'll get stitches when you answer my questions."

"I'm not under trial, Valentin," he rumbled, folding his arms across his chest.

"No, I don't think you are, but I want answers, and I'm not going to stop until you give them to me. What happened?"

"You know what happened. I told you when you asked how I solved the Hodge Conjecture."

"Yes, you told me that, but I didn't find out about your meltdown until Mum told me."

He sighed. "Why would I tell you about that? I was ashamed."

My heart softened at that. "You had nothing to be ashamed of," I countered. "We all have moments where we can't cope."

"Do we?" Devon's lips formed a thin line. "Even you?"

"Of course. Why do you think I ignored the love of my life for a few years? I didn't want this." I lifted my hand and waved it, encompassing the palace and all it represented. "I wanted a quiet life, like you have with Mum and the dads."

"You think we have a quiet life?" Devon's smile was small. "It's anything but."

"You know what I mean." I sighed, then ran a hand over my head where a headache was blossoming.

I felt no guilt for what I'd done today. I'd probably saved my fathers from being shot... "Is George okay?"

"He died. Twice." Devon shrugged. "They brought him back."

That was why Perry had been howling like she had.

I knew how that felt. My grandmother, Jacinta, had passed like that. Two heart attacks, she'd been dead twice, then they'd brought her back only for her to be brain dead.

The memory of her was still strong enough to make me weep.

Such fire and sass in one so frail, but she'd have been happy, I knew, to be back with her Hamish.

My lip quivered at the memory, and I whispered, "What's going on, Dad?"

"I don't know."

And Devon would have told me if he *did* know. Unless I hadn't asked the right question.

"Do you know why Etta was targeted? Why someone was targeted today?"

"No." He hesitated for a second. "I can postulate."

"Postulate away," I rasped.

"Someone knows that Etta is Edward's daughter."

I frowned. "Of course someone knows that—everyone does."

He shook his head. "You're my son, but your blood is Andrei's."

My heart thudded in my chest, and I thought about Etta and Christel and Victoria. Victoria with her auburn hair, Christel with her blonde, and Etta with her dark chestnut locks.

Like her father.

"Someone knows," I whispered.

"I'd hazard a guess, and you know I don't like to guess," Devon said with a sniff.

"No, you prefer to *postulate*," I ground out, trying to think of the implications. "Why target me today?"

"They were targeting George." Devon tutted. "Use your common sense, son."

"He's the third in line if someone can reveal the paternity—"

Devon raised a hand to his lips. "Hush. Loose lips sink ships."

I blinked at him. "So, the Brits aren't involved?"

"Of course not," he scoffed. "They're helping."

"How?"

"I told Edward a long time ago that if someone had the capacity to infiltrate as many of Veronia's ministries as they did back when you were a baby, then they had the power to find out other things...things he'd never want people to know." Devon shrugged. "I didn't think he took me seriously, so I set my own traps."

"What kind of traps?"

"I have people who are useful in these situations."

"MI6."

Devon smiled. "Yes. Very handy."

"Handy?" I echoed. I knew my father was powerful, even if he didn't appear to be so, but thinking that he might have the run of MI6 when he forgot to tie his shoelaces some days was pretty fucking terrifying. "You're the reason there's a team here?"

"Of course." He tapped his nose. "Russia."

"The big bad wolf of Europe," I rumbled.

"Indeed," Devon replied with a smile. "Although Putin was very friendly when I met him once."

"You met him?"

"Just once. When Vasily was alive."

I hadn't thought of Jacinta, Hamish, or Vasily in too long, but today, I'd thought or heard their names in the space of five minutes.

God, I missed my grandparents something fierce.

"He was very shrewd," was all Devon said. "Russia gave the hackers who infiltrated the ministries a home."

"They back a lot of people," I muttered.

He hummed. "These were Veronian."

"UnReals."

"Definitely."

"What about this situation?"

"More UnReals. There's no conspiracy," he surmised. "Just someone in possession of a secret they shouldn't be."

"Who told the UnReals?"

"I have no idea. Loose lips sink ships," he repeated. "There's a reason that's been floating around since time began, and they have a lot of staff here. Someone could have mentioned how the king's brother has a tendency to drift into the queen's private rooms..." Devon shrugged. "It's probably a badly kept secret."

"I don't like this. I'd prefer to think there was one clear enemy."

Devon snorted. "Don't be so facile, son. Life is never cut and dry like that." His eyes were alight with excitement. "Did you know Andrei and I managed to get every single Euro back?"

"From the embezzlement scheme?" That had my brows rising. "Wow, Dad. No, I didn't know that."

"Well, to be fair, you weren't supposed to." Devon raised a hand to his lips in the universal sign of silence, to which I just nodded. "And we had the Russians toss them out."

"You mean Andrei did."

His eyes gleamed. "Handy to have the Bratva on your side, isn't it?"

"That means they have no resources now."

"Nope."

"I don't understand these UnReals," I whispered. "It's not like the DeSauviers are bad for the country."

"There's money to be made from civil unrest, Tin."

"You just said there was no conspiracy."

"There isn't. Just a nice, old-fashioned plot." He rubbed his hands together. "What do you reckon an arms dealer is behind these shootings?"

Stunned, I gaped at him. "You can't be serious." Devon stared at me, and I stared at him. "Stupid question," I muttered.

TWENTY

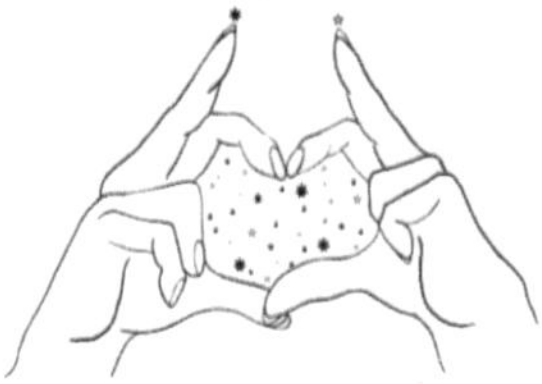

ETTA

SEEING Mom cuddled up to Daddy was enough to make me want to start crying again. She hadn't left his side in days unless it was to use the bathroom, and even then, Christel and I had to force her to get clean and take a shower.

She wasn't budging from his side, and because I knew how it felt to be her after what Tin had gone through, I didn't pester her, just watched, and kind of marveled in the love my parents had for each other.

Papa was on an armchair that had been brought in for him, and just off this room, with the door wide open, was my father's new makeshift office. Daddy was *okay*. But that wasn't the best word for it. The wound had suppurated because, for a while, they'd been scrambling to treat it with effective antibiotics, and now he was going through a bad fever. Once it broke, things would be better.

A hand slid around my waist, pulling me back against someone hard.

Someone tall.

Someone who was mine.

My lips curved a little, and I caught Christel's eye who rolled hers at me when she saw how I snuggled up against Tin.

"Time for you to get some rest," he rumbled in my ear, and because I wasn't about to disagree when I felt like I was living on my nerves, I just nodded.

Then, as I stepped away, I caught my sister's gaze and mouthed, "You going to be okay?"

She cast a look at Daddy, then shrugged.

I got that.

If he was fine, she was.

Same with me.

Tin's fingers slipped through mine as he tugged me out of the sick-room and deeper into the private wing of the palace.

Mom had insisted that he not stay in the medical ward, that he be brought home even if it was only a wing away, and Daddy had been in there ever since. In the bed that, officially, the king and queen slept in.

Raised eyebrows were nothing compared to what was happening in the Madelan palace right now.

I figured most of the staff had known, and that was why, to work here, it involved jumping through so many hoops that you were pretty much Michael Jordan—and the NDAs that were a part of the contract? Nothing to be sniffed at.

You blabbed about *anything* you saw in the palace and you weren't only fined more than the average person earned in a lifetime, you were sent to jail. And, dependent on what you shared, be it official or family secrets, you could be tried for espionage, which came with the tag of execution at the end of it.

So, yeah, people kept their mouths shut.

Until they didn't.

When Tin tugged me into our suite, I sighed when he deposited me in the armchair beside the fire, and rather than taking a seat in the one opposite, he moved behind me and began to rub my shoulders.

"You're tense."

"I am." No point in denying it.

"He'll be fine."

"Almost lost him, almost lost you. I'm tired of losing people—"

"You're tired of 'almost' losing people," he corrected. "No one has gone anywhere. You're fortunate. Even if it *is* stressful."

I pulled a face at the back wall even as I shuddered, deep inside, when he hit a good spot that made my body want to purr.

"That feel good?"

I could hear the amusement in his voice and didn't even care. "Yeah, that feels good."

He leaned over me, pressing his forehead to my crown, and murmured, "Want more?"

I bit my lip. "Depends."

"On what?"

"If you're ready for what it will bring."

It had been three weeks since Daddy had been shot, Christmas and New Year had rolled on by without any of us thinking of celebrating, and complication followed complication with him. He'd had three surgeries all to correct something or other, and every time he came out from under the knife, something else went wrong.

Heads had rolled, and safe to say, we now had a new lead surgeon, even if I wasn't sure that was entirely fair.

Maybe Mom had sacked him, and Father had just shuffled him along on vacation and told him not to come back until the prince was better and the queen wasn't likely to make rash decisions.

Wasn't the surgeon's fault, was it, that we'd learned Daddy was allergic to penicillin?

All these years, and they'd never known it.

"I can deal with the repercussions of a massage," Tin rasped. "Just not sure if you're ready for it."

I'd just left my father's sickbed, so, technically, the last thing I wanted was sex, but the connection? With Tin? I needed that more than I needed my next breath.

Reaching up, I let my hand sift through his hair and ruffled through the short waves. It was spiky thanks to his shade cut, but the top part was long enough to slip through my fingers.

He shivered, and my heart skipped a beat as I contemplated how much power I had over him, and how much I loved it. Because he had that much power over me.

"Are you sure?" he murmured, making me fall for him even more.

"I'm positive."

And I was. I needed to feel him, to be one with him, and God, I needed that so badly my skin ached with the demand to have his on me.

He pulled back, then with our fingers still connected, rounded the armchair so he could tug me onto my feet.

He was beautiful, even if his face was drawn. I wasn't sure what he was doing with his days, just knew that at night he was here with me, but whatever it was he was doing, he was with my parents, Devon, Sean, Sawyer, and Andrei. Kurt was with Sascha mostly, and their kids who'd just arrived too.

That they were all doing something for the state put me on edge as much as it filled me with relief to know that things were moving, some*thing* was happening.

The Guard Elect, as good as they were, could never beat what happened when five men as clever as Tin and his fathers put their cerebral might together, as well as their experience and connections.

I knew we were going to be safe.

Call me naive, but I did.

My father, when I'd been a baby, had thought the UnReal threat was no more. He'd felt certain it had died out, and I'd seen his speeches, had been made to study them because, as an orator, my father was one of the best. But I'd never be *that* naive. I thought, like usual, they'd scurry into the cesspools of society and stay there, laying low, until the next time they rallied together. For now, I just wanted heads to roll for what they'd done to Andrea and Daddy, and I knew my father felt the exact same way.

When Tin tugged me to my feet, I pressed my hand to where I knew only a small gauze rested on his belly.

"Are you sure?"

"Doctor approved me for exercise." His eyes gleamed.

"Exercise?" I hummed. "Interesting."

He grinned. "Best way to burn off calories, I think."

"I agree." Snorting, I reached down and cupped him. He was hardening, like he was excited by the prospect but wasn't expecting much—I figured he thought I was going to cut and run on him at the last moment because of the situation.

He tensed when I cupped him though, and his dick went rock-hard the second I shaped him further. Letting my hand fall from his, I reached for his zipper and tugged him free.

A shaky breath escaped him as his dick pierced the slit in his briefs, then his fly, and was out in the open.

It boggled my mind to think that he'd stayed true to me, and I could only think of how grateful I was, and how I needed to show him my gratitude.

So I slipped to my knees.

I'd seen this in enough porn movies to know what I was doing. Kind of. Although maybe not. It was thicker at the tip than I remembered, so I ran my tongue down the underside like I'd seen a porn star do, fluttered it here and there, slickening him from root to tip with my spit.

Every time I touched him, he shuddered where he was standing, but he let me do what I wanted. He let me kiss him and suck him and nip him and nuzzle him and I was astonished by his patience.

I could feel his cum leaking onto my cheek every time it bobbed and tapped me there, but he let me play.

Until he didn't. And his hand was in my hair and he rocked my head back so I could see the blue fire in his eyes.

"Suck it," he growled, and his voice sent that fire in him surging through me.

I opened my mouth even as I let my head fall back, and groaned as, with his free hand, he grabbed his cock and aimed it at my parted lips.

He was strong and forceful and everything I needed.

He was mine, and I loved him, and wanted him so badly that I was close to crying and laughing all at the same time.

He was also salty. A little bitter. And a lot to handle. I gulped when he pushed the tip onto my tongue and thrust in an inch. He pulled back, his gaze trained on my face, looking for my discomfort, and he murmured, "Clean the tip."

I shuddered at the order, but did as bid, letting my tongue smooth over the little hole, slurping him down even as I cleaned him up as requested.

His hand tightened around my hair to the point of pain, but I didn't complain.

"Gather spit in your mouth," he demanded next, making my heart soar.

I nodded, then nearly melted when he rasped, "Show me."

It was strange to open my mouth, to reveal the saliva I'd collected in there—I was a princess. I didn't even sit with my legs crossed, for God's sake, and this...it made butterflies settle in my stomach.

But I did it.

I showed him, and he hummed his approval.

"Open your mouth wider," he commanded, and I did, then his cock was there, inside the haven of my mouth. Not all of it, maybe not even half, but he rocked his head back on his shoulders like I'd driven him to the edge—like I'd deepthroated him or something.

"Fuck," he growled, his hips pulsing like he was helpless, rocking his cock back and forth, fucking me slightly, even if I got the feeling he wanted to push in deeper.

If I was being honest, I wanted that too, even if I didn't know if I'd gag.

Could you spew around a dick if they thrust too far in?

That was not something I wanted in my memory banks.

Or Tin's.

Every time I gave him a blowjob in the future, he'd tease me, and then I'd have to kill him.

But I couldn't stop myself from giving him what he needed. When I thought of all the women he could have had, I wanted to thank him. And sure, I could have had a hundred different men too—equal rights, sista—but my life was different.

I couldn't date, and getting any man near my bedroom, or near *a* bedroom, was harder than planning a war.

Tin had freedom, he'd had opportunities, and he hadn't taken them.

Not a single one.

So I reached up and cupped his hips even as, carefully, I pushed myself onto him, taking more of him, accepting what I could, breathing through what I couldn't.

I closed my eyes so he couldn't see me panic, and I forced myself to focus on breathing first, even as I moved my head, letting him into me, letting him claim what belonged to him, what he could have always had, had he not been so angry with me.

I shuddered when I opened my eyes next. I looked straight at his pants, and suddenly realized that the reason I couldn't breathe so well through my nose was because I'd pushed into his pants-covered belly.

I swallowed, which had Tin groaning like I'd done tongue acrobatics, then I pulled back some so I could breathe again.

It was uncomfortable and big and awkward, but I kind of liked it.

Kind of, because it was Tin.

But I *did* like how he was shaking, his body trembling, and I knew why—he didn't want to come yet. Sure, the poor guy hadn't exploded in anything other than his fist for years, so I was proud of him for not having busted his wad the second I licked him, but also, I knew he liked what I was doing and didn't want it to end.

I wore an A-line skirt and a simple strappy tee, and I'd never been more grateful for the comfortable clothes I'd put on this morning. As I reveled in the feel of him against my tongue, I dropped my hands, reached behind me, and unsnapped my bra. Slipping out of it, I pushed the neckline down so that my breasts were supported by the fabric hammock I'd created. Then I shucked my skirt up my thighs, so he could see my panties if he looked.

When I pulled back, I surged up onto my knees, and as I grabbed my tits, I cupped him with them, wriggling the flesh around him, wanting him to feel all my curves.

I needed him to come now, needed it because otherwise, he was going to get inside me and burst, and I really thought I deserved an orgasm after all these years of waiting.

So, and it was awkward and definitely wouldn't win a pornstar Academy Award, but I sucked the tip of him into my mouth every time I could, and I sucked hard, urging him to explode inside me.

When a gargled groan escaped him as I did this for the fourth time, his knees buckled before he righted himself and then he came.

My mouth was full of the stuff, and for a second, I didn't know what to do with it. Spit it out? It was bitter and salty and really not something I felt like eating, but they always did in porn, didn't they?

So, I looked up at him, saw he was watching me through lash sheltered eyes, and I gulped.

He shuddered.

And I smiled.

He shuddered again.

I pulled back, and moved onto the floor so I could let my legs out in front of me. Within seconds, I had my hands on my hips and was wriggling out of my panties. The second I was bare, I fell back against the rug, shoving the skirt I still wore out of the way, and I could no more stop myself from slipping my hands between my legs than I could stop myself from looking straight at him as I did so.

Tin stood there, panting like he'd been running, his body one big tremor from his first blowjob, but his face, his eyes, they were alight once more.

He stared at my pussy, stared at my fingers, then he rasped, "Did I say you could do that?"

Whatever I'd expected him to tell me, it wasn't that.

My fingers stilled.

"N-No," I whispered, wondering where that timid voice had come from.

He stood there, so self-assured, his cock hanging through his pants, but otherwise fully dressed.

He could have headed out the door the second he'd zipped up.

Me?

I was a mess.

My mascara had run whenever my eyes had smarted from taking Tin a little too deeply—I could feel the dampness on my cheeks—and my tits were out, my pussy on display, and I was wet, so wet. Achingly so.

I felt dirty and filthy and needy.

I felt like he was the prince and I was a nothing, a nobody. Then he whispered, "Clean your fingers."

And I moaned.

I wiped the tips on my leg, but he shook his head.

"Suck them clean."

Shivering, I reached up and slipped one in, then another, then another, until the three I'd used to touch my clit were, relatively speaking, clean.

He crouched down in front of me, one knee coming to the ground as he moved between my legs, and he gazed at me. His eyes everywhere.

I wasn't sure why he didn't touch me when I needed his touch so badly. But he just looked. Studied.

Stared.

Then, he reached up, and with the tip of his pointer finger, rimmed the areolae of my left breast.

Instantly, the nipple puckered and my belly rolled. I could smell how wet I was, which was kind of embarrassing, but from the way he was looking at me, also kind of hot.

I hadn't expected this. I'd thought we'd roll around on the bed, playful and laughing, giggling as we made love for the first time.

But Tin was a man now.

And it seemed like I was a woman, because my needs weren't playful. I didn't feel like laughing.

I felt like howling. I felt like begging.

I shivered when that finger moved to the hem of the top I was wearing. It was pulled taut the way I had it supporting my tits. He tapped it, then he dug around in his pocket with his other hand and revealed a pen knife.

My eyes widened as he flicked out the blade and pressed it to my skin, just below the hem, letting me feel the cold chill of the steel, before he plucked the top and cut it straight through without stopping.

The remnants of the—very expensive—shirt fluttered to my sides. And my skirt was next. He let the penknife sit on my belly as he plucked the waistband up, then he collected the blade once more and set it to destroying another expensive item of clothing.

But did I care?

Nope.

I wasn't sure I could breathe, but I didn't give a fuck. He could destroy my entire wardrobe if it meant making me feel like this.

I'd never anticipated this, had never expected this level of intensity. But Tin was a man of depth, many, many depths. I should have known that he'd have changed.

Hell, that I'd change, too.

I was trimmed neatly down there, and when he properly looked at me, he turned the blade over to the dull edge and he tutted as he scraped it over me. "I want to see you bare."

I shuddered. "O-Okay."

He hummed, clicked the knife back into its slot, then tossed it on the floor beside him.

"Spread your legs. Wide."

I did as he ordered, aware that his gaze was trained on my pussy, and I bit my lip as I stared up at the ceiling, wondering why I felt so anxious, wondering why—

"Ahhh!" The high cry escaped me as he slipped a finger into me.

"So wet," he rasped. "So fucking wet."

And then he was there.

No longer distant. So close I wanted him to crawl into my skin. His mouth was on my clit, then his tongue in my pussy, and he fucked me and sucked me and in seconds, I was screaming, my legs clamping down on his head as I rocked from side to side, crying and sobbing and shrieking as he carried on, not stopping, not stopping until—

I squealed.

Fuck, I squealed like a pig. His hand came up to cover my mouth and I bit him, dug deep into his palm to shut me the hell up, even as I locked down elsewhere, my body juddering with the power of the orgasm he gave me.

When he finally pulled back, I felt like I'd been given a drug. I stared at him, my body limp and lax, my eyes sleepy and tired, but he was the opposite.

He was incandescent.

So alive with energy that everything inside me craved to be nearer to him, to feel that power too.

His mouth was wet with the taste of me, and his face was stern with the need I saw down below—his cock was hard again.

"I want to come home," he rasped, melting my fucking heart even as he set me on fire with need.

I lifted my arms, beckoned him close, and didn't stop until he was on top of me. I curved my arms and legs around him, wrapped him tight in my embrace as he moved between us, grabbed his dick, and slipped it into my gate.

I knew, in time, we'd get better at this. That had been out of sync. It would be much easier for him to slip inside me before I wrapped around him like a pretzel, but it was perfect all the same.

Even if it hurt.

He was big, I was still small, and I closed my eyes because even though I couldn't be wetter, it had still been a long time since this had happened, and even then, it had only been twice.

With every inch he took, I moaned in pain and he groaned in sweet agony. But I clung to him, pushed my face into the side of his throat, and refused to let go, to let him stop. I dug my heels into his hips, pushed him on, urged him inside me even if I was the one in pain, and then, he was there.

And it was, as he'd said, like he was home.

At long last.

I shivered, Tin groaned. Then he pulled back, and he showed me how, together, we could reach for the stars.

TWENTY-ONE

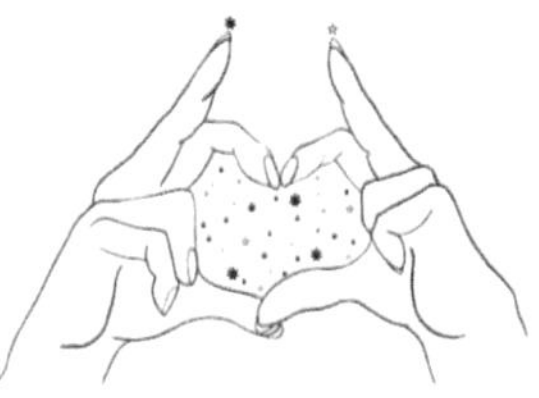

TIN

"YOU LOOK BETTER."

I cleared my throat. "Thanks, Dad."

Devon tipped his head to the side. "You do." His brow puckered. "A lot more relaxed."

Kurt snorted, and I damned my pale coloring because I blushed.

Fucking blushed.

"Fuck's sake," I muttered under my breath, grateful only Kurt and Devon were here with me after breakfast, otherwise it would be a thousand times worse.

Devon had no boundaries, while Kurt had all the boundaries. It was as worse and as good as it could be.

Kurt clapped me on the back, squeezing a little, before he murmured, "Always best when you're with the woman you're meant to be with."

Devon frowned. "Of course it is." He huffed. "Tin's lucky. You didn't waste nearly thirty years waiting for yours."

"No, just two." I winced.

"Still doesn't explain why you looked so relaxed. Are you well?"

"I'm sure he's never been better," Kurt retorted, but it sounded like it was a warning.

Which I was grateful for, even if I knew Devon wouldn't understand it.

So, even though I felt like I was five, I muttered, "Etta and I are together. Together. You know?"

Devon tipped his head to the side, studying me as was his usual way. I sometimes felt like he was an X-ray machine. Like, if I was ill, he'd somehow be able to see it.

Where I was concerned, he had this kind of attention span that none of his other kids had been graced with.

I still wasn't sure whether to pity them or to be jealous.

To be sure, he loved them. The twins were the apple of his eye, and he had countless hours for them even if he didn't understand what the hell they were talking about. He'd bought Rosie her first horse, and she'd told him first about getting into university. Bethan argued with him on the phone over human rights just so that she could be prepared for class —I'd been there for that. It was amusing watching her blow her top over Skype because Devon could talk about the worst things and still remain calm.

War, famine, plague, he was untouchable. Not because he was cruel, but because it was how he was.

Mum cut her finger while she was cooking? It was like WWIII had been declared.

Rosie fell off a horse and bruised her arse? She had a hard time stopping him from calling an ambulance.

The world, while large, was somehow tiny for Devon. We were his everything, and I knew that.

Jack probably had the easiest of it. Devon hated driving, but that hadn't stopped him from teaching Jack when, at six, Jack had wanted to know how cars worked.

Of course, Mum had seen them in the drive and had pitched a fit, but Devon had just said, "He wanted to know."

And in our house, knowledge was power.

Knowledge was never ignored or shied away from. It was embraced.

If I'd wanted to know how to make a bomb, I was sure Devon would find out and teach me. Life was a lesson, a constant one, and Devon was the best teacher imaginable.

"Why are you looking at me like that?"

My lips twitched. "How am I looking at you?"

"Like I'm looking at you," he stated simply, making me laugh outright.

"That's probably because I am." I sighed and decided there was no use in being embarrassed around him. "We had sex."

"I should hope so," Devon blustered. "You mean," he paused, "that's the first time since you've been back here?"

"The boy was bleeding out for the first half of his stay here, Devon," Kurt groused, sitting back in his seat, even as his eyes were bright—like he was taking in a show.

"But..." Devon shook his head. "A man has needs."

"I couldn't get into bed without help, Dad, never mind do anything the second I was in it."

He winced. "Do we need to have *the* conversation?"

"No!" I barked the same time Kurt did. "I already know way too much about your sex lives." My ears turned pink. "Fuck's sake," I repeated.

"Well, you're a young man." He frowned. "Maybe I should talk with Alice."

"No!" Kurt and I barked in unison again.

"You're a young man," he repeated, like that explained it all.

"So? I haven't had sex for years," I rumbled, dipping my chin so I didn't look at either of them. "Not since the first, well, second time we did it." Not that I remembered much about the second time.

Well, I remembered Etta's hair and her smile, I remembered how she'd gleamed in the gold lights of her suite in a Vegas mega hotel, the name of which escaped me. I remembered her skin turning to cream against the black marble in the bathroom as I took her—

Huh. Maybe I did remember more than I thought I did.

Tugging on my bottom lip, I didn't realize my fathers still hadn't spoken.

"You've never been with another?" Kurt asked carefully.

I blinked. "No."

"You waited all those years for her?" Devon's question had me staring at him.

"Yes. If you'd known Mum—"

He raised a hand to stop me. "Fair point."

I smiled, as always, appreciating his devotion. "I think I'm like you," I rasped. "I-I just need her."

Devon frowned at me, then muttered, "Does she feel the same way?"

Kurt clucked his tongue. "Of course she does. She looks at him like he made the world just for her. Stupid question, Devon."

"It was a fair question." Then he smiled. "I knew I always liked her."

"Why doesn't Mum?"

Devon shrugged, but Kurt answered, "I think she always knew Alice would take you away to Veronia."

That had me frowning. "That makes no sense when you all spend a couple of months here a year anyway."

"You're her baby." Kurt laughed a little. "Nothing has to be rational where you're concerned."

I gnawed on my bottom lip. "Can you talk to her? Etta has enough crap to deal with without Mum giving her a hard time."

"Your mother's hard time is hardly—"

"Hardly, what?" I interrupted. "Etta gets enough crap from her parents about always being perfect, then there's the government, and did you know that if we don't get pregnant right away, the privy council might make us go see a fertility specialist?"

Kurt's brows rose. "I doubt it."

"Etta doesn't," I stated grimly.

Kurt frowned, and he shared a look with Devon, but he was quick enough in saying, "I'll talk to her."

"Thank you." My mind flittered onto more pressing matters than whether or not Mum liked the love of my life. I released a worried breath, because I was exactly that. My wife and her family were in danger, and I felt like there was nothing I could do to help. My contacts were useless. I'd burned them by quitting. "I'm scared for them."

"You don't have to be."

"I do."

Devon reached over and scrubbed a hand over my head. "It'll be okay, Tin. You know that, don't you?"

"You can't promise that, Dad."

His eyes turned hard. "Yes, I can."

When he got up, leaving the dining table where we were sitting without another word, I eyed Kurt blankly. "What was that about?"

"Your father just turned into Robocop."

My lips twitched before I let out a chuckle. "Not funny."

"Was funny."

The twinkle in my dad's eyes made me grin wider. "What do you think he's doing?"

"Being Devon?" Kurt shrugged. "You know he and Sawyer have friends in high places. I think he pulled a few favors and was hoping things would be sorted by now."

"Things being the unseen threat against the Veronian royal family?"

"Yep, those kinds of things."

Kurt tilted his head to the side. "Will you be happy, son?"

"As long as Etta's by my side, yes."

The simplicity of my answer seemed to settle him, and he rocked back and murmured, "You're a lucky man."

"I know."

"I wish I'd met your mother at your age. Of course, we might not have lived the lifestyle we do if that had happened, but like Devon said, she would be worth waiting for."

"Etta's..." I blew out a breath. "She's always been a part of me."

"But the life put you off?"

"Can you blame me?"

Even now, we were sitting in an informal breakfast room, and it was like being in a museum. There was a carriage clock the size of my torso that was decorated with flowers and metal and all kinds of crap and a little bird flew out and didn't just cuckoo, it danced around the clock itself on some kind of special mechanism.

The chairs were ornately carved, the wallpaper made of silk, and until a half hour ago, there'd been two footmen lining the back wall waiting to see if we required anything else after our meal.

This kind of life?

No. I didn't want it.

"You'll get used to it. You'll be good for her, and she'll be good for you, and together, you'll be good for the country."

"I don't care if I'm good for the country," I stated firmly. "Don't mean to sound selfish, but I don't. I'll look after her, and that's it. Whatever she needs from me, I'll be there. I'll work with her, do what she needs, but she comes first."

Kurt's eyes gleamed. "We raised you well."

My brows lifted at that. "I thought you'd lecture me."

"Why? Because you don't care for a country that isn't even your own?" He snorted. "You are British, American, German, and Russian, Tin. You, by marriage, are now Veronian too. I think that's enough countries to worry about, don't you? Your duty is to be honorable, to respect your mother countries, but never kowtow to them." He shrugged. "Easy for me to say that, but it's not that difficult. Be impartial, care for the people, not for the land, and you'll do well."

"Thanks, Dad," I said, but my voice was low.

"No need. It's the truth. You're a good boy, Valentin. You always were. We were fortunate that you came first and not Jack, because he'd have been a hellion as a consort to Etta."

My nose crinkled, but I just inquired, "Do you think Devon will be able to fix things?"

"I'd be surprised if he doesn't. To be honest, I think he expected results before now. He's been in a mood—couldn't you tell?"

I shook my head. "He's been more talkative than usual. That's all."

Kurt dipped his chin. "That's his way. Has been ever since you were a baby."

"What do you mean?"

"There was a time when he shut us all out. Locked down."

"Mum told me. After Sawyer's initial diagnosis."

Kurt nodded. "*Ja.* Well, he melted down, and he wouldn't talk or, well, anything. He barely lived. He made your mother a promise, so now, if he talks more than usual, that's his way of keeping that promise."

Despite myself, I had to grin. "He's so literal sometimes. It always amuses me."

"Yes," Kurt agreed, reaching for his dainty cup of coffee and taking a sip. "I don't think Sascha anticipated she'd be getting a chatterbox instead of someone who made a ghost look silent, but that's how the cards fall, I suppose."

"I suppose." But we shared a grin as we both finished off our coffees.

Etta

WHEN I LOOKED up from the paper I was reading my daddy, who was snoring now and fast asleep, I saw Sascha standing in the doorway, eying me like I was a rattlesnake on the brink of attack.

"Is everything okay?" I asked, surprised she was here.

With Daddy finally out of the woods, finally able to get up and go to the bathroom and do things on his own, Mama had decided she could go and get some sleep, but only if someone stayed with him.

Papa and Father, seeing that Daddy was well, had also decided to get some rest, which I knew meant they were going to make sure Mom slept.

I really didn't want to know how that was going to go down, but I was adult enough to figure it out, and still their kid, so kind of icked out by it too.

Alone with Daddy, reading to him, I'd felt something settle inside me, something I'd never really felt before. Tin was somewhere in the building with his fathers, but he was here.

He'd slept with me last night, I'd woken up with him this morning, and tonight, we'd be getting into bed together again.

This was going to be my life. No more yearning, just being. Just having it all.

I'd never expected that I could be happy when my country was undergoing a crisis like this, when Daddy was recovering from gunshot wounds and allergic reactions, but that I could, at my base self, be content? Just because Tin was here? It blew my mind.

I'd known he was my soul mate, and I'd known I'd been grieving him as though he were lost to me, but I hadn't really known how depressed I was until now.

So, to see my mother-in-law studying me like I was crap on her shoe didn't dampen my mood much.

I wished Sascha liked me, but I got it. I did. And I'd deal with it, and hope, in time, she'd forgive me for whatever I'd done to irritate her so much.

"Daddy's asleep," I muttered, waving a hand at the obvious snoring figure.

She nodded, and requested, "Walk with me?"

"Of course." It didn't occur to me that I was the princess here, just that I was this woman's daughter-in-law and if she wanted to boss me about, she could pretty much tell me to jump and I'd ask how high.

When I got to the door, I hesitated, remembering something. "I promised Mom I wouldn't leave Daddy."

Something softened in her eyes. "Okay." She leaned against the door, deepening her stance as she relaxed, and murmured, "You love my Tinny, don't you?"

"Of course I do," I whispered, knowing full well that my heart was in my eyes.

She sucked her top lip into her mouth as she stared at me, then muttered, "You're a good girl, Alice. I can see why he loves you."

Whatever I'd expected her to say, it wasn't that.

"You're not what I'd have wanted for him," she admitted, "but maybe that's why you're perfect. Please, whatever you do, try to keep him safe. It's quite clear that he can't keep himself safe, getting into knife fights and throwing himself at would-be assassins—"

My eyes widened at that. "What?"

She studied me, then a smile curved her lips. "He didn't tell you. Interesting."

"What's interesting?" I snapped.

"He took down the shooter." She huffed. "I didn't even know he could fire a gun. Since when do desk jockeys carry weapons?"

My nostrils flared as outrage filled me. "They don't."

"Exactly." Her eyes gleamed with amusement, and she reached up, patted my shoulder, and murmured, "I'll leave that news with you. He's too old for me to spank, but wives have ways and means of punishing their men, and I think he deserves it."

Before I could say another word, she drifted off, and I was left sputtering at the doorway.

"Ignore Sascha, *carilla*," my daddy rasped from the bed, making me spin around to face him.

He looked pale and gaunt, and I was so tired of sickbeds that I wanted to scream.

"Daddy!" I exclaimed, relief filling me.

George was the father I related to most, the one I could be most at ease with. Though he was smart—very, very smart—he was the most playful. The least scholarly of all my family. It made me feel like I could fit in with him, because academia and me definitely didn't get on well together.

I rushed over to the bed and grabbed his hand the second I was sitting down.

"I thought you were going to sleep all day," I chided, but I was smiling, because I would have been happy for him to sleep. A least, then, he'd be getting the rest he needed.

"I'm uncomfortable," he divulged. "I drift in and out of sleep, but I heard Sascha. Don't punish him for his past, Alice. Be grateful for it. It means he's even better suited as your husband than he was before."

My eyes narrowed on him. "I'm not okay with him being James Bond."

"He wasn't." At my raised brow, he smiled. "We've all seen his file. He truly was a desk jockey, a fine analyst but still an analyst. He was trained well because they used to put him into the field where they wouldn't usually, but he was adept at fitting in. With all the Middle Eastern languages he speaks, it would be ridiculous *not* to put him out in the field."

I didn't want to admit that I was totally in the dark about what he was saying. And it hurt that Tin could speak Arabic, never mind however many dialects he apparently spoke, and I didn't even fucking know.

Blowing out a breath, I muttered, "Sascha said he took out your shooter."

"He did. I was on the brink of consciousness, but I remember that much. He screamed at us to duck then pushed Sawyer back and down, but it was too late for me. Before I knew it, he had a gun in his hand and was taking a shot. I didn't know, until now, that he'd hit the target."

Death and I weren't old friends, but I was comfortable enough with it not to wince at the fact Tin had taken a life. Every day, in my world, there was a warzone at play. Just because no one else saw it didn't mean it wasn't there. But I resented that Tin hadn't told me.

I told my dad as much.

"Did you tell him you shot the man who came for you in Casterby?"

My nose crinkled. "No. He never asked."

"Well, you never asked him either, did you? Maybe he thought you'd view him differently. And wouldn't he be right? Tin can do many things. It would be silly to punish him for his skills."

I pulled a face. "True."

His lips curved in a smile. "So feisty. I like to think you get that from me."

I grinned at him. "I do." I reached for his hand and pressed it to my cheek. "I'm glad you're getting better, Daddy."

"Me, too. I've got far too much to do still. Bugging your mother is a full-time job."

"I think she's quite happy at the idea of you bugging her until she's old and gray."

He laughed. "Nice to know."

I closed my eyes. "Everything is changing."

"Yes, but that's not a bad thing. You'll get married to Tin, and you'll settle down. You'll be happy again—I've missed that, love. I've missed seeing you be happy."

My smile wobbled. "I've missed feeling that way."

"He might be an asshat for what he put you through, but, and it's a big but, he came through in the end."

I gnawed on my bottom lip for a second before I asked, "Did you know?"

My father wasn't stupid. "About the wedding?" When I nodded, he smiled. "What do you think?"

I released a shaky breath. "Why didn't you say anything?"

"Because it was your secret to tell." He shrugged. "I'm the one who reads the security reports. Though you evaded your guards for a few hours, they dragged in CCTV and spotted you at the chapel. It didn't take much to find out more."

"I'm surprised you kept it from Father," I whispered, ducking my head so I didn't have to hold his stare.

"Your father forgets we all have our little rebellions. Tin was made for you, and vice versa. He was shortsighted if he didn't expect you and him to end up together.

"Although, in his defense, he knew you were so unhappy and wanted to fix it too."

"By marrying me off?" I spluttered.

George shrugged. "For a smart man, he can be an idiot sometimes."

"Pot calling kettle springs to mind."

We twisted around to see Mom standing in the doorway looking brighter, but her eyes were narrowed as she stalked in. "You knew? You knew our baby got married?"

Well, it was clear Mom definitely hadn't been lying about being in the dark.

"Of course. I helped keep it a secret though, and I'd do it again."

Mom squinted at him. "If you weren't a bag of bones, I'd rattle you."

"If I weren't a bag of bones, I'd let you," he retorted, and I groaned.

"Please, I'm too young for that talk."

He laughed, his eyes glinting with a fire that made him look much more like my daddy. "You're a wife now, Etta. You're as grown up as it gets."

Mom grunted. "She'll always be my baby."

Despite myself, I had to grin. I got to my feet, rounded the bed, and slipped my arm around her waist. "I love you too, Mama."

She pressed a kiss to the crown of my head and mumbled, "Love you, baby. But don't think you can keep anything else major from me, or I'll lose my shit."

I snorted. "Don't you know? I'm the boring daughter."

She snorted back. "If you believe that bullshit, then you're as crazy as your daddy."

I shot him a wink, was glad to see I got one in return, then Mom mumbled, "Oh, go on with you. I'm sure you've got your own husband to scold."

Brows lifting, I demanded, "You knew, too?"

"Just spoke with Sascha. Don't be too hard on the boy, love. He did save your daddy."

I nodded, but I was definitely going to give Tin something to think about.

And no mistake.

Tin

"FUCK," I rasped. "Fuck." If I could just keep on repeating the litany, I would have, but Etta stole my breath as she dropped her head and kissed me.

I liked bossing her around in bed, but fuck, the feel of her, what she was doing to me? I was quite happy to be ensnared in her net.

And ensnared in other things.

Shuddering, I let her tongue play with mine even as she toyed with me. She'd climbed on top of me with promises of riding me, but then the second I was inside, the second I was home, she just stayed there and tormented me by twitching muscles I had known about scientifically, but not physically.

She slipped her fingers through mine and pinned our hands on either side of my head as she finally moved, taking an age to release me then to drop back down.

After four more thrusts like that, I was about ready to beg when she pulled her mouth from mine, dropped her lips to my ear, and whispered, "Tin?"

"Y-Yes," I stuttered.

Could a man go blind from this torment? I was pretty sure I was cross-eyed.

"If you ever—" She nipped my ear lobe. "Ever keep something like —" Another nip, followed by her sucking on it with enough force my goddamn eyelashes fluttered. "Shooting an assassin from me—" Suck, suck. "I will make you pay."

If this was the price, then I'd pay it.

Fuck.

"Who told you?" I grated out.

"Never you mind." She squeezed me, hard enough to make me throw my head back and for the veins to pop out on my throat.

"Fuck," I whispered.

"That's right. You own me in here," she whispered back, filling me with lust at her statement, "but I own you, too."

I shuddered, and though I'd let her have her own way, I was a lot stronger than her. I reared up, making her shriek, grabbed her hands, and didn't stop rolling until she was under me and I was on top of her.

Then I fucked her.

And I fucked her.

I went so deep I knew she'd taste me in the back of her throat. I went so fast that the bed shook and rocked. She screamed as she exploded into orgasm, her sobs filled my ears, filled me with a white noise that had me seeing stars when, finally, I burst into a thousand of them as I reached my climax.

But still, I carried on, thrusting into her until I was soft and she was moaning, her head rocking from side to side like she couldn't take anymore. Then I pushed down, even though I was soft, ground my pubis into her clit, and her eyes popped open and she let out a groan so guttural, I felt it in my fucking balls.

As she cosseted my cock in another orgasm, I let myself fall against her. Limp as spaghetti, I just flopped, and she let me. Though she was the same, it didn't stop her from propping her arms and legs on me in a way that made me feel like she was hugging me, even though her muscles evidently had no strength to hold me.

After a few minutes, when I felt certain I was probably squashing her, I did the gentlemanly thing and heaved off her. Only she tightened up on me, so when I flopped down on my back, she came with me.

My cum and her juices started to trickle out, until I felt the slickness slide onto my skin. I wasn't sure I'd felt anything as fucking sexy in my life, and I muttered that into her throat.

Muffled laughter escaped her, at my expense, but she nipped my chin and wiggled into me like she agreed but didn't have the words to say it.

I sighed as I stared up at a Michelangelo, wondering how this had become my life. How this was now a part of my day.

With one hand sliding up and down her back, I began to relax and she did too.

Maybe I should have expected it, but I didn't. We were all pretty good with privacy, knowing full well that Mum and the dads could get it on in any room they chose so long as the door was shut.

But I never expected Dad to come bursting into the bedroom like the mad genius he was.

Because it was Devon, even though we both jerked up, and Etta shrieked in surprise, he didn't even notice.

I quickly wrapped her up in the sheet, and she huddled into me as he began pacing, talking about Russia and the U.K. and some North Koreans, until, finally, I roared, "Dad! What the fuck?"

He blinked at my outrage, then turned, looked at me, and did the damnedest thing.

He grinned.

"Good lad," he praised.

"Sawyer says 'lad,'" Etta muttered, "not you."

"You stick around someone long enough, you pick things up here and there."

"How about you pick up on the fact that I'm with my wife, Dad," I growled, my eyes flashing with anger.

He huffed. "Just thought you'd like to know...the organization behind the shootings—we've taken them down. They'll be in custody within the hour."

I jerked upright at that, but just when I had questions in need of answering, he stormed off and made a distinct show of closing the door and not slamming it.

We both stared at the wide set of doors for a long time, then I muttered, "Did that really just happen?"

"Did your dad really see me naked?" Etta rasped, burying her face in my throat.

"I doubt it. I don't think he even knew we'd been having sex until I shouted at him."

"Thank God it was Devon—"

"If it had been anyone else, they'd have knocked," I pointed out.

She sighed, pushing her forehead into my chest. "Never going to be able to look him in the eye ever again."

I rubbed her back. "Don't worry. He's on Mum more than butter's on toast. We can get them back."

Her nose wrinkled. "I don't really want to."

"It's the only way to teach him anything," I reasoned. "And you and I both know, now that I'm here, they'll be visiting. A lot."

She sighed. "I'm not too upset about that."

"Me neither," I admitted. "So we'll teach him a lesson that Mum will ram home."

Etta snickered. "Okay, I'm down for that." Then, she whispered, "What was he talking about?"

"You know he always says exactly what he means. His contacts found the organization and they're dismantling it."

"Organization? He didn't say UnReals, did he?"

"No. That means there's a story." I kissed her cheek, then let my tongue trail over to her mouth, not stopping until I was tracing her lips with it. "Want to hear it?"

She peered into my eyes. "If Devon says it's sorted, then, I mean, it's sorted, right?"

I grinned at her. "You know it."

"I mean, I'm supposed to be taking on more responsibility—" She let her words taper off.

"It can wait another day, can't it?"

She laughed. "Yeah. It can."

Eyes flashing, I twisted us both over so that my body was on top of hers once more, then I kissed her, and thoughts of assassins and organizations and espionage disappeared because when I was with her, nothing else in the world mattered.

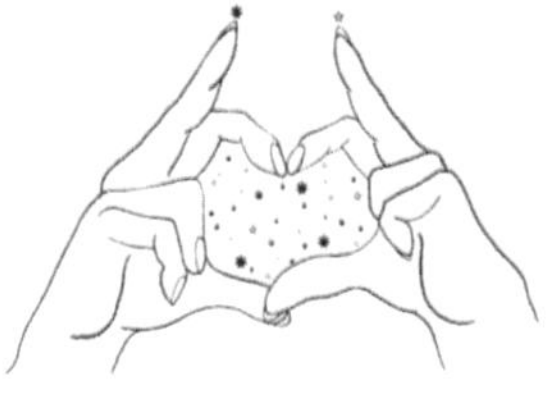

EPILOGUE

ETTA

"YOU LOOK BEAUTIFUL, BABY," Mom rasped, and I had to hide a smile when I heard her tears, literally heard them in her voice.

If I looked beautiful, so did she in a champagne dress that showed off all her curves, draping down to the floor in a frothy cascade, while discreetly revealing a slither of her décolletage. I knew Sascha's dress was a little less formal, as would all the other women attending today, but Perry was Queen. She'd be draping on the ceremonial surcoat the second she made it to the cathedral and had to take her place on the throne at my father's side for the wedding service.

"She's right. You do."

Not having expected my father to make an appearance just before I was about to head to the cathedral, my eyes flared wide when I twisted around and saw him, complete in ceremonial dress, staring at me in the mirror.

My dress was everything I wanted it to be. Not fancy and finicky, not like anything a royal really should wear. It wasn't demure and tidy. I didn't look asexual or like a doll.

I looked like me.

The skirt was bouncy, but not too bouncy. It drifted around my legs, delineating my hips and butt, while surging upward into a bodice that was rounded with a sweetheart neckline that wasn't afraid to show off my tits to the only man I wanted looking at them—Tin. Parts of my dress were covered in the lace Veronia was famed for, I even had some silk from a tiny fabricator in the East, but the design was nothing like my Mom's dress. It wasn't formal and strict, didn't make me look virginal.

I looked like a woman.

A woman who was ready to be married.

And I knew I glowed, positively glowed, because I was so ready for this. So ready to be Tin's in the eyes of the world.

Mom reached up and rubbed her handkerchief to the corner of her eye so she wouldn't spoil her make-up, and Father lifted an arm and squeezed her, muttering, "Can I have a minute with her, love?"

As he pressed his lips to her temple, she gave him a tear-soaked smile before she disappeared, and with a wave of her hand, all the staff and the maids and the ladies-in-waiting dispersed too, leaving me alone with my dad.

His smile was rueful as he murmured, "This is nothing like your first wedding."

"Complete opposite." I jerked my chin up. "I wouldn't change it."

"Even though it was a disaster?"

I winced. "No. Not even then. He's mine. Always has been."

Father sighed, and raised his hands. "I didn't come here to fight."

"No?" I tipped my chin to the side. "I hope you came to give me a kiss."

He laughed, strode forward, his fur and velvet surcoat draping behind him as he moved toward me. His arms opened and I settled into them with a sigh.

"I needed this," I muttered against his chest, careful not to scrape my make-up onto the suit jacket he wore. He sported a Veronian iris in his buttonhole, and it scented fresh and reminded me of our summer vacations in Laurela where there was a field of irises nearby.

"You nervous?"

I sighed again, even as I squeezed his waist. "Nope. But I am for Tin."

"He'll be fine," Father retorted.

"I know he will, for the wedding." My nose crinkled. "It's the coronation bit I'm nervous about."

"It's easy. You know that."

"For us," I grumbled. "But he must be nervous. I wish I could see him."

"You've broken all other customs," he said dryly. "I'm surprised you didn't sneak out to see him—" He broke off, shaking his head. "Let me guess, you did?"

I grinned up at him. "Do you really want to know?"

"No!" he retorted forcefully, making me chuckle.

And I didn't blame him. Tin had stayed in the other side of the palace, far away from my quarters last night, but that hadn't stopped him coming to me and waking me up with a smile.

"He'll be fine," Dad continued, rolling over that little awkwardness with the ease of a consummate diplomat. "I don't want you to think about that, I just want you to think about today. About enjoying it. It's your day."

I pulled a face. "If it was down to me, I'd have Elvis marrying us again."

He sighed, then reaching down, touched my chin with his thumb. "You never did like any of the ceremony, did you?"

"Nope, never."

Shaking his head, he pressed his mouth to my forehead. "Never think, my darling, that I don't love you for who you are—"

"Even if it means I'm awkward and difficult?"

"Even then," he said with a laugh. "I'd prefer you to be you, to knock heads with you than for you to be who you're not." A sigh escaped him. "I'm sorry if I made you conform—"

"You were doing what's best for me. I know that." I squeezed him. "You don't have to apologize, Dad. I mean it."

"You're too kind." He blew out a breath that made the baby hairs around my hairline bob and dance. "But then, you always were the best of us, even if we were too stubborn to see it, trying to push you, a round peg, into a square hole."

My nose crinkled. "Thanks, Dad. I really want to be likened to a round peg on today of all days."

He snorted. "You look beautiful. And you know it."

Eyes twinkling, I shrugged because he wasn't wrong. I looked epic, even if I did say so myself. "Why are you being all maudlin anyway? That's not like you."

"If a man can't take stock of his life on his daughter's wedding day, when can he?"

I sighed. "Does that mean Christel and Victoria are going to get visits like this just before they're ready to drive to the cathedral?"

His smile was dry. "Maybe not. Maybe I'll be kind and just speak to them after the ceremony, but you?" He shook his head and squeezed my chin again. "You changed my life, baby girl, and I wanted to thank you for that."

Eyes wide, because I hadn't expected him to say that, I whispered, "You really mean that?"

"I do. I was older than you when I met your mother, and I never expected to love her the way I still do. It was a gift, and I think I forgot that where you were concerned. I'm glad Tin is that for you. I'm glad he—"

"He does," I whispered. "He's the love of my life."

"I'm glad, baby." A knock tapped at the door, and he grimaced. "That means I need to be on my way." He sighed, kissed my temple again, then called out, "Two minutes." Pulling away, he strode toward the door, where I saw there was a large box. Clad in a velvet that looked antique, my brows rose when he opened it and brought it to me.

Inside was a majestic crown. Hundreds of different gemstones inset into a headdress that would offset the virginal white of my dress. It was about four inches thick all the way around in a perfect circle, and I knew, without even touching it, it would be heavy and by the end of the day, my neck and shoulders would ache like a bitch.

"Great-grandma's crown?" I whispered.

He smiled. "I thought you might like to wear it today."

My mouth rounded. "I'd love to." It was a more modern style and it suited me down to the ground, but I'd expected to wear one of the more commonly known crowns, one of the big ones that we tended to wear for matters of state like today.

"Hold it for me," he said, and I did, gently lifting it from the cushioned bed and placing it there for him, accepting the gold pins he placed on my palm next.

He reached for it, and with an ease that few men would ever display where it came to hair pins, he raised it and rested it on my head. Then he secured it, and all the while, my eyes were closed because I hadn't expected him to do this for me.

It was more than an honor—I felt his love. When it was secure atop my head, he murmured, "You look even more spectacular than you did before." Resting his hands on my shoulders, he said, "It's my wedding gift to you, darling."

Eyes flaring wide, I whispered, "Seriously."

He dipped his chin. "Seriously. And, as for Daddy and Papa, we've all decided to let you have the Laurela Palace."

This time, I gaped at him. "The Summer palace?"

"It's your favorite, and... you're newlyweds. I think you need some freedom before we draw you into the fold."

I gulped, never having expected that. "I-I... are you sure?"

"I'm deadly sure." His lips twitched and he shucked my chin. "But, less of the death, hmm? We've all got lives to lead, and today's the first day of your new one. I just wanted you to know..." Another kiss to my temple. "I couldn't be prouder of you."

In a flash, he'd swirled around and was heading to the door before I could even process everything he'd said. Still, I couldn't stop myself from calling out, "Dad?"

He peered at me over his shoulder. "I love you. Thank you."

His eyes twinkled. "I love you, too."

And with that, he left me, and for a few seconds, I had no choice but to look at myself in the mirror and see that, for the first time in my life, in my father's eyes, I was a woman. No longer his recalcitrant daughter, the naughty girl... a woman. And he'd given me a gift to match.

Not just the crown and the palace, but acceptance. Somehow, that meant more to me than anything else. I didn't doubt that, in the future, we'd butt heads, but maybe we were always supposed to do that. Maybe that was just how we were supposed to show each other we loved one another.

Hey, it didn't have to make sense. It worked for us!

Another knock sounded at the door, and I called out, "Come in!"

Mom's head peered through the crack, and she beamed at me when she saw my crown. "It looks amazing—it suits you. I always looked like a tit when I tried to wear it."

A laugh escaped me, maybe as she'd intended, and I grinned at her. "Thanks, Mom."

She winked. "Are you ready?"

Ready to marry Tin? For everyone to know he was mine? That I was his?

"Hell, yeah."

Tin

I STARED at the stained-glass windows at the head of a cathedral that had seen God only knew how many DeSauviers getting hitched, and smiled at the sun gleaming through the elaborate panes. It was still only early spring, but God, as the minister had told me earlier, was smiling down on Etta and me.

I figured we deserved more than a smile—more like a laugh—but I'd take it.

Today was the day.

Etta was about to become my wife—officially recognized by the king himself—and I was about to be crowned as her consort.

Was I nervous?

Yes.

But, equally, I was ready for it. Maybe I'd been born ready for it, born ready for her, but I was still a little on edge, still ready for today to be over with when we'd be on our way to our honeymoon in Mauritius.

I felt like we'd spent the last three months with everyone up in our business, and while I was okay with that, I was ready for the three weeks of freedom before life really, truly hit us.

Of course, it could be said that life had already done that.

What with my stabbing, Andrea's death, George's injuries, and everything else, it wasn't like things had been quiet.

Because Devon was Devon, he'd solved things by creating havoc, and Edward still wasn't talking to him over what he'd done.

See, when I'd thought he was going to MI6 or some other U.K. body for help, he hadn't.

He'd gone to the Bratva.

He'd called in Andrei's ties, *again,* had used the links my father shouldn't have but did, and he'd done so to protect us.

They'd done what officials couldn't.

They'd taken out the trash.

Eight Véronians who'd moved to Russia because they were anti-royalist, had decided to make things shit for the DeSauviers while getting rich off their country's misery.

And, with their skills, when they'd learned the truth about Etta being the true sole heir to the crown, they'd decided to create mayhem once and for all by teaming up with an arms dealer who was locked and loaded to ship a couple of crates of semi-automatics to my new home.

The Bratva had dealt with them, and they would continue to keep an eye on things on their side of the world because Andrei had asked them to.

Unofficially, of course.

And they now had a couple of crates of guns as their payment.

Yeah, none of us were happy about that.

I still wasn't sure why a group of people gave enough of a shit to wreck so many lives, but trolls did that stuff for fun, didn't they? And in this instance, they had more power than anyone could imagine.

I wasn't sure what Edward would pay to keep his family's secret, but I knew it was a lot. I also knew that this probably wouldn't be the last time we had shit over the DeSauviers' secrets, but with our connections, mine too, I was hoping we'd be able to stem the flood.

And if we didn't, then they might just have to go public with it, which would mean Edward might have to abdicate and Etta would be queen sooner than anticipated.

But that was a nightmare waiting to happen, and I didn't borrow trouble unless I could help it.

A hand grabbed my arm, and I knew it was Jack. I'd wanted one of my fathers standing up here, maybe Sean because he was always the voice of reason, but it wasn't politic to remind the country that I had five dads, so my brother was my best man.

I twisted around, aware that the doors to the cathedral had opened, and took a quick glance at the first few pews on either side of the aisle.

The cathedral was massive, to the point where I couldn't see Etta anyway, not without squinting, so I checked in with those I could see.

I saw Mum crying into her hanky, her hat a little askew from where Devon kept shoving his face to kiss her cheek to make her feel better. Sawyer held her hand, and she was surrounded by Sean on one side, and Andrei and Kurt on the other, and they were all muttering among themselves. They were doing me proud in that ass Jean Luc's suits, but I had to admit to being a little bit prouder of Sawyer. He might not have wed Mum in a kilt, but today, for *my* wedding? He was rocking the tartan all the way to the bank, and he looked damn good in it too. No knobbly knees in sight—mostly because Mum's hand kept fondling them.

Didn't need to see that—did. Not. Need. To. See. That. But the sight was impossible to delete now it was in my memory banks.

Etta's family was seated to the left. Well, most of them. Her Uncle Xavier and George were there, along with her sisters, but Edward and Perry were at the side of the altar, seated on their thrones.

I was dreading the moment I'd have to approach them, where Perry would place a small crown on my head and Edward would decree me Etta's consort, but I'd do it.

I had to.

Etta was worth putting up with that crap.

I sucked in a breath when I finally saw her. Resplendent in a white gown that was loose about her legs, not full-on like a princess dress, no meringue in sight, but swaying with each step that had her sparkling and glittering. The bodice pulled taut at her waist, and her tits were pushed up with just enough force that I resented gravity for torturing me—I wanted to get her out of that dress.

Or, maybe, I wanted to fuck her in it.

Then, I winced, because I was in church.

But hell, God gave me her, so why should he complain if I wanted to make her mine?

Again and again and again.

And again.

I sucked in a breath as I took in the glimpses I could spot of her face through the heavy lace veil, and only when she approached me, with the prime minister at her side because the jackass had the right to take her down the aisle—Etta was right, this was *democrazy*—did my heart start to slow down to the point where I realized it had actually been racing.

As I looked at her, I could breathe deeper.

This was nuts, everything was insane, but she wasn't. She was my world, and this was just a formality.

Dotting an I.

Crossing a T.

I sucked in a breath when her hand slipped into mine, and as her matron of honor, a cousin, stepped forward to help her lift the veil, DeWitt, the prime minister, disappeared, and I was left looking into her eyes.

She was beautiful.

Everything about her was perfect. A jewel that outmatched the crown she wore on her head.

And she was mine.

I smiled at her, grinning because, at last, I was fucking happy, and when she grinned back?

I had no choice but to lean forward and to press a kiss to her lips.

I heard laughter, tutting, and a few claps, but I ignored them. Even ignored the minister who told me that kissing was for after the service, and instead, I whispered in her ear, "I can't wait to fuck you with this dress on."

Her breath caught, and her eyes glinted with excitement.

And that's how we got married.

Not with nerves, not with worry about being a shitty consort or saying something wrong, or worse, *doing* something wrong and fucking up live on film that was being shown around the world.

Just with thoughts of later.

Thoughts of when we were behind closed doors, and the world was suddenly filled with only two people.

Her and me.

Forever.

THERE'S A TINY BONUS SCENE… if you'd like to read it… click here. It takes you to the end of the book. <3

THEIRS

And, if you'd like to read more about Perry, Alice's mother and her men, then be sure to check out the 'THEIRS' collection.
It's available on KU!
THEIRS: www.books2read.com/TheirsVeronia

AFTERWORD

Want more from the Quintessence family?

COMING DECEMBER 12th 2021!

A Christmas Second Gen - Quintessence Story :O

www.books2read.com/QuintessenceTinAndAlice

How are you feeling?

Happy?

Sad?

Teary?

Please, talk to me. Let me know what you thought.

Join me in my Diva reader group: www.facebook.com/groups/SerenaAkeroydsDivas

Email me: Serena@serenaakeroyd.com

Or follow me on FB and message me there: www.facebook.com/SerenaAkeroyd

I want to hear from you!

PLEASSSEEE.

Love you all, hope to hear from you, and, if you're feeling in a generous mood, could you leave a review? <3 They mean everything to authors, and they can make or break whether or not someone buys a book. Just a few words, that's all it takes. <3

Thank you for reading this, thank you for loving Quintessence, and thank you for being YOU!

Love

Serena

xoxo

FREE BOOK!

Don't forget to grab your free e-Book!
Secrets & Lies is now free!

Meg's love life was missing a spark until she discovered her need to be dominated. When her fiancé shared the same kink, she thought all her birthdays had come at once, and then she came to learn their relationship was one big fat lie.

Gabe has loved Meg for years, watching her from afar, and always wishing he'd been the one to date her first and not his brother. When he has the chance to have Meg in his bed—even better, tied to it—it's an opportunity he can't refuse.

With disastrous consequences.

Can Gabe make Meg realize she's the one woman he's always wanted? But once secrets and lies have wormed their way into a relationship, is it impossible to establish the firm base of trust needed between lovers, and more importantly, between sub and Sir...?

This story features orgasm control in a BDSM setting.
Secrets & Lies is now free!

CONNECT WITH SERENA

For the latest updates, be sure to check out my website!
But if you'd like to hang out with me and get to know me better, then I'd love to see you in my Diva reader's group where you can find out all the gossip on new releases as and when they happen. You can join here: www.facebook.com/groups/SerenaAkeroydsDivas. Or you can always PM or email me. I love to hear from you guys: serenaakeroyd@gmail.com.

ABOUT THE AUTHOR

I'm a romance novelaholic and I won't touch a book unless I know there's a happy ending. This addiction is what made me craft stories that suit my voracious need for raunchy romance. I love twists and unexpected turns, and my novels all contain sexy guys, dark humor, and hot AF love scenes.

I write MF, menage, and reverse harem (also known as why choose romance,) in both contemporary and paranormal. Some of my stories are darker than others, but I can promise you one thing, you will always get the happy ending your heart needs!

www.ingramcontent.com/pod-product-compliance
Lightning Source LLC
Chambersburg PA
CBHW030623310726
48979CB00003B/860

* 9 7 8 1 9 1 5 0 6 2 9 0 1 *